The

Kingdom

Treasure

GREG TRESEDER

DEDICATION

To my wife Debbie, who inspires me in so many ways. To Jack and Alex, for giving me such a bright view of the future. To my family and friends for all the things you do every day to help our world grow together in humanity. You all make me smile.

Dad, you always loved sailing ships and tales of the Pacific. Here's one for you.

Mom, enjoy the tales from Idaho. I always loved that place.

TABLE OF CONTENTS

ACKNOWLEDGMENTS

Thanks to Debbie for editing my manuscript. Among many observations, your diligence helped me to realize how often I used the word 'and' when I write! Less is more. Thanks to Alex, Bill, Jack, Lisa, and Paul for your valuable feedback. You each had different insights, and your suggestions and comments were much appreciated! They helped me to improve my story in countless ways.

November 20, 1511. The Strait of Malacca, between the Indian Ocean and the China Sea.

The *Flor de la Mar* was in peril. She was a sturdy ship, well-built by skilled Portuguese shipwrights, and had survived many trials in her nine years at sea. But this voyage would be a back breaker. Her captain and crew were pushing her to the point of failure, running from a host of pursuers that bore a righteous anger. This alone was enough to wear her down, but now a raging storm was pummeling her as she tried to make her way through a treacherous strait full of jagged, unforgiving reefs. The furious wind whipped her rigging and the salt spray scoured her decks. She slammed into the trough of each ocean swell with a gut-punching wallop then gasped for air at each crest. She wouldn't last much longer. Even worse, night was coming on.

The troubled seas and the wild wind punished the ship repeatedly. She began to unravel as her rigging snapped and her hull planks popped loose. She was taking on water faster than the crew could pump it out. Her heavy cargo quickly became a burden that the crew would happily jettison…if only they could. Despite the dire situation, her captain Afonso De Albuquerque of Portugal wasn't the type to entertain thoughts of failure. To the chagrin of many and the joy of many more, his optimism on this night would be the greatest failing of his long career.

Albuquerque was an esteemed member of the Portuguese seafaring hierarchy. He had spent the vast majority of his travels in the Pacific Ocean; most recently in the China Sea. One could summarize his resume in several ways, across a wide spectrum of firsthand experience. He could be labeled a world conquest military genius, a decisive and effective leader, a skilled sea captain and military officer, a deeply misinformed envoy, a boorish irritant, a bloodthirsty pirate, or a war criminal. He could occasionally be all of these things on the same day, much to the dismay of the Malaccans, the Chinese, the Indians, the Dutch, the Sumatrans, the Egyptians, the Turks, the Muslims, the Hindus, his peers, his king, his crew, his slaves, and even the local wildlife. As a result he had several nicknames, your use of which depended on which end of his sword you were standing on. He was known as *The Terrible, The Great, The Lion of the Seas, The Portuguese Mars,* and several names that aren't readily translated into civilized tongue. To be fair, he was a product of his age. There had been many like him. There would be many more, on both sides of the ageless conflicts of man.

In February of 1511, Albuquerque and his forces attacked the wealthy city of Malacca, in what is now modern day Malaysia. Malacca was the largest commercial center in a vast region of Asian-Indian commerce. Albuquerque's reasons for engaging with the Malaccans were varied and complex, but included a demand that he be allowed to build a fortified trading post in Malacca. Malacca was an important crossroads of Asian and Indian trade, as the Strait of Malacca was the strategic passage between the Indian Ocean and the China Sea. Merchants from many nations sailed its waters trading a wide variety of goods, including valuable spices. Albuquerque intended to secure this trading route for Portugal, rather than allow the peaceful and profitable (but not to Portugal) commerce to continue on its own.

Predictably, the Sultan of Malacca refused Albuquerque's demands.

Albuquerque responded by burning and looting the mostly wooden city. He then built a fortress to protect against counterattack, using stones from the mosque and the cemetery. He appointed a new Portuguese administration to rule the city. His actions effectively destabilized the rich commerce of Asia and India, as he perturbed the free trade that had existed for so long. The resulting outcry, from many countries, was loud and full of expletives. China, for example, arrested the Portuguese envoys stationed in their country, then imprisoned, tortured, and executed them. All before dinnertime.

Over a period of months, Albuquerque's forces looted a vast sum of riches from the Malaccan kingdom. In November of that year, they loaded them onto the *Flor de la Mar*. The ship had proven difficult to sail, but it was large and could carry an impressive cargo. Portuguese sailors kept careful records of this treasure. It included *sixty tons* of gold and an impressive array of jewels including diamonds, rubies, sapphires, and pearls. Albuquerque wrote that his bounty was *"the richest treasure the world had seen"*. He may have been right. Based upon the detailed manifest, the cargo's worth in today's currency is estimated to be between $1 billion and $3 billion. Not content with treasure alone, Albuquerque also kidnapped several dozen Malaccan women and children as slaves, imprisoning them on the vessel. He then set sail for home, looking forward to the gratitude of king and country.

The Strait of Malacca, which is still one of the most important shipping lanes in the world, is long and narrow. It lies between the Malaysian Peninsula and the Indonesian island of Sumatra. In Albuquerque's time it was difficult to navigate, but he set sail in an overloaded ship, through a reef-laden narrow passage, undoubtedly pursued and harassed by the Sultan's surviving forces and by merchants and representatives from many nations. His unauthorized withdrawal from Malacca irritated the sensibilities of many.

On the afternoon of November 20th, as Albuquerque was trying to outrun his troublesome pursuers, a storm arose. The seas grew heavy. The wind increased to a gale force. Even on a good day the currents in the strait were a challenge to predict, especially for the wallowing *Flor de la Mar*. She may have been named the *Flower of the Sea*, but *Pumpkin of the Sea* would have been more descriptive. The storm added a new dimension to Albuquerque's challenges, but he had no choice but to sail ahead. He hoped that nightfall would bring a respite from his pursuers. He may have been right. But fate knows no clock, and the storm raged on.

The first impact with the reef knocked Albuquerque off his feet. The sailors felt the ship's grinding against the reef as an odd, low-in-the-gut sort of rumble. It was quite different from the vibrating, whistling rigging above the deck, which the driving wind was playing like a discordant harp. The ship's sheer mass (blame the gold) made it almost unstoppable. Like a speeding freight train, she rammed everything in her path. In this case, 'everything' was a sharp, unyielding reef that had formed over the centuries with one apparent purpose - sink the *Flor de la Mar* and put Albuquerque in his place.

It worked. The four hundred ton, nine-year old ship was already exhausted from its many voyages. She had been repaired again and again as the result of previous misfortunes in various locales of similar conquest. She could give no more. The reef opened a wide gash in her side and liberated the ship of her rudder. The combination of punishing seas, bruising reef, and whipping wind did what the Sultan couldn't do. It halted Albuquerque's departure from his Malaccan treasure trove. The *Flor de la Mar* fell into the strait, exhausted and finally retired from service. Albuquerque barely survived the wreck. He and a portion of his men made it to safety. They abandoned the women and children, leaving the survivors to die upon a low-lying rock in the middle of the storm. According to Albuquerque's writings, *"Nothing was saved except the crown and sword of gold and the ruby ring sent by the king of Thailand to king D. Manuel."* The remaining treasure, the wealth of an entire kingdom, sank with the ship.

As fate would have it, a mother and her son survived the wreck. The sea was kind to them as they made their way to shore. They were taken in by a local tribe who were wise beyond their collective years. And patient beyond their collective lifetimes. The pair told their story of imprisonment and of miraculous escape. They shared the location of the wreck. Their tale would be passed on from generation to generation. The treasure would be passed over, lying in exile in the waters of the Strait of Malacca, for four hundred years. The storm would move on to a new locale, but would never stop until all was made right. Paradise takes a long time.

The voyage of the *Flor de la Mar* - and its rich cargo - had ended. In all the years since, nobody has ever claimed to have found the wreck or the treasure. *Don't believe everything you haven't heard.*

PART ONE. A WING AND A PRAYER

Chapter One

It was May of 1940. We were getting knocked around something awful. It seemed the wind was gusting from every direction. Just as I got the wings level from one gust, we'd get rolled by another. It was all I could do to try to keep us flying straight and level. It was wearing me out. We were surrounded by dark, roiling clouds and I could see ice crystals rushing past the windshield. Despite my inexperience, I had the presence of mind to turn on the wing anti-ice heaters, but they sucked power from the engines and the high, thin air was already challenging the heavy plane. I didn't have the luxury of some newfangled airplane to make my journey safe and pleasant.

I was piloting a C-47 cargo plane; a twin-engine hulk of a workhorse that was flying as if it was made of bricks and mortar. I guess that's both good and bad. Good in that these planes were solid. Bad in that this thing was heavy as an overdue heifer and at the altitude we were flying there wasn't much air to lift our wings. I was fairly sure the wings weren't going to snap, but I also knew that if the mountains ahead were higher than we were, it would be a short, sad trip. So I had to sacrifice the cabin heat to save power and keep us in the air. It began to get darn cold. My teeth were chattering something fierce and I wished I had a chaw of tobacco. I would have chewed a piece of my boot leather if I could have reached it, but I couldn't take my hands from the wheel, nor raise my feet from the rudder pedals. I was trying my best to maintain course in this muck and gloom, and it was really taxing me.

Through all of this, the Tibetan just sat there in the

copilot's seat, bouncing and swaying with the turbulence, smiling with a sort of subtle calmness. He was one cool customer. If I didn't know better, I'd think he was an old retired fighter pilot. He was singing the same simple chant repeatedly. It began to merge with the drone of the engines and calm me a bit.

He was wearing a woolen tunic and pants. He had no jacket, nor a hat to cover his shiny bald head. As I surveyed his attire, I realized if I was cold in my thick leather and sheepskin jacket, he must be just about blue. I motioned to him to take hold of the controls. After a bit of hesitation he grabbed them with conviction. This allowed me to remove my jacket, and I offered it to him. He shook his head with a smile, but I insisted and placed it around his shoulders. He didn't protest. Despite his small frame, he was doing a fine job of handling the heavy controls, so I let him fight the weather a bit while I rested my arms. After a blessed few minutes, however, the inaction started to cool me off. Now I was really chattering. I took back the controls, although I could see in his expression that he would have been happy to continue flying us to wherever it was he had to go.

I started thinking about what the world I was doing here. Well, I'd been thinking about it for months, but now I was *really* thinking about it. If I was going to die, I at least wanted to understand why. I was a twenty-year old cowboy from Idaho, and here I was flying a rattling C-47 over "The Hump" in Southeast Asia - Burma - in the middle of a winter storm. All so this tiny Tibetan could get to some all-fire important meeting in the city of Kunming in western China. I was feeling lonely and homesick. I began to dream of the smells of springtime in Idaho. You probably know them yourself whether you're from Idaho or not. The way you can suddenly smell the earth as it thaws out after a long winter. The sweet smells of wet grass and hay. The feel of the warm wind as it flows down the slopes of the ranges. Then I was remembering that first day at the end of winter when the snow begins to melt. You can suddenly hear water trickling all around, and then you realize you haven't heard that joyous sound for months. I recalled the soft hush of the warm spring breeze as it brushes across your winter weary face…

Then the blaring alarm plum scared the hell out of me, jolting me out of my daydreams. I looked at the instrument panel. The *ENGINE FIRE* light for the starboard engine was flashing, and the related alarm was rattling my teeth. I looked past the Tibetan out the right window and sure enough, the engine was lit up like a bonfire on the Fourth of July. The fact that one of the two engines on my plane was burning to a crisp just mesmerized me into a state of blissful inaction. I think I must have stared at it for a long while, for the Tibetan glanced at me then jumped into motion. He shut off the alarm, yanked the engine shutdown lever, and pulled the engine fire extinguisher handle. He did it all as if he'd done it a hundred times before. I watched as the fire retardant smothered the fire from within the engine cowling, but the vicious flames reappeared within seconds. The Tibetan reset the handle and pulled it again. I recalled Jack Campbell, my informal flying instructor, telling me that the extinguisher only carried two charges. We had just used the second charge, but nothing was happening. *Come on, come on*, I thought, as I watched the fire. *Work, please work!* I was overcome with the bittersweet notion that I was about to be killed by a blazing fire instead of a snow covered mountain.

The problem was, if the fire kept burning, it would hit the wing fuel tanks within seconds and that would be *all she wrote* for yours truly, in the form of a big explosion over the

Himalayan mountains - a brief, final flare to a short life hopefully well-lived - followed by nothing but silence and snow. *"He bought the farm,"* I could picture my family saying of my demise, *"only his patch was somewhere in the snow covered mountains of Burma."* They could be funny in the face of loss. A family trait that wasn't reassuring at this particular point in time.

Finally, after what seemed like hours, the fire slowly waned and then was gone. It simply blew itself out. I sucked in a breath of air to restart my heart. The propeller on the dead engine had stopped spinning, and before I could think, the plane swung violently to the right as the dead prop dragged through the air. The jolt snapped me back to reality and I quickly feathered the prop to minimize the drag, pressing hard on the left rudder pedal to straighten our flight. Despite the feathered prop, it took a lot of pressure on the pedal to counteract the dead engine, and I knew I couldn't keep it up for long. My bronco-busted leg just wasn't that strong. Although we could fly on one engine, we carried a heavy cargo. We were now losing altitude and there was nothing I could do to change that. Worse, the right engine provided power for the anti-ice system, so it was only a matter of time before the wing iced up and dropped us like a dead mallard. Remember when I said I was cold? Now I was sweating like a grizzly bear on a hot summer day. Sweat was running down my face and stinging my eyes. Damn I was scared. I had Jack Campbell to blame for this entire mess.

"You've got to get Lhasa," referring to my calm Tibetan passenger and now co-pilot, "to Kunming in China," Jack had said. "From there he's heading on to Malacca in Malaysia. Help him get a good start. And Hank," Jack emphasized, "It's the most important thing you have ever done, and maybe the most important that you will ever do. Lhasa carries the hopes of thousands on his shoulders, and you've got to make sure he gets there. Promise me you will!" I promised, and with that Jack passed out from the effects of Yellow Fever.

That was only yesterday, and whatever it was that prompted Lhasa's journey meant that we couldn't wait even a few days for the weather to clear before beginning the trip. Jack's unusual desperation wasn't lost on me, and I had to trust him. I had no choice but to honor my commitment and take off in an airplane I hardly knew, and had only flown a few times under Jack's supervision. I considered the possibility that Jack's request was borne of delirium, but one look at the expression on Lhasa's face convinced me otherwise. This guy had to get to Kunming. That was clear enough to me. Problem was, I wasn't going to be a very good chauffeur if we both died in a big puff of snow, and Jack hadn't taught me anything about how to fly this plane in a bad storm at high altitude with one good engine. I cursed him as I recalled the October evening when I first met him on the Salmon River in Idaho. It seemed like so long ago. But worse, home seemed so far away that it just made my heart ache!

Chapter Two

Present Day. Oh what a night that was! The stars were so bright and sharp that even now they're burned into the fabric of my mind like a thousand tiny pinholes. When I close my eyes I can see them plain as day. Then the scent of an autumn evening in Idaho floods my memory and it makes me smile, as I always do when I remember that time of my life. It's all so vivid in my mind that some days it seems like I could reach out and touch it if I could just stretch a bit more from this comfortable old chair. Other times it seems so distant - especially on these cold winter nights when the wind howls down the mountain slopes to rattle my windows. A distant memory like a lonely old coyote crying in the night.

Don't get me wrong. I'm not tired and I'm not worn out. I could still give a strong salmon a good fight with my reel and pole. I've got a lot to be happy about, and I wake up every morning with two spry feet hitting the floor. But I'm reaching the end of my days and that's fair enough. I'm not one to sit around and look with nostalgia at happier times.

Lately I've felt as if I have a bunch of things to get done. Urgent things – as important as anything you can possibly imagine. The type of things that you know you have to complete to bring the proper closure to your life. You might be too young to understand, and I'm happy for you in that regard. Enjoy your youth and make the most of life.

Of all those things that nag me in a bittersweet way, there's one in particular that keeps me awake at night. Every night lately. You see, I've got this story to tell and it's been bangin' on my insides trying to get out something fierce. So on these winter nights – the ones where the cold air seeps through my windows and makes the fire jitter and pop – I start to think again about those days, just trying to make sense of it all. I'm just about there. It's like when you're trying to think of the perfect word to say, and you know you know it, but you just can't quite get it to your mouth. I disassemble the events like a Marine cleaning his rifle, only when I reassemble all the parts, I'm missing a spring or something and the dang thing doesn't quite work right. I've got to get this story together before I lose that spring. I've got to sit here tonight in front of my fire and think it all through. My winter days are getting shorter. That's why you're here – you've got to listen to this story to help me remember. I'll admit that I'm a little anxious, because I have this nagging fear that you're not gonna believe that all this really happened.

It all began on a autumns' eve over seventy years ago. I sat that night on the crest of the hill, unable to sleep and just marveling at the sky and the ground and the whole big scheme of things. It's that same hill you can see right outside my window. The full moon lit the landscape in a soft, cool glow. I looked out across the whole Salmon River Valley, from the Galena Summit on one end to the Sawtooth Mountains on the other. I swear this part of Idaho has something magic about it – when you take up a handful of dirt it feels solid and alive, no matter the time of year. The moonlight shone on the Salmon River winding the length of the valley, and I could see the ripples on the water glinting in the night air. The big dome of the sky was so massive I felt it was going to just plain crush me, and as I sat there and thought about it, the sheer size of the universe started pressing down. I felt as small as a grain of sand in the Sahara Desert, blown here and there by the wind with no choice in where I settled. Don't let me mislead you - I'd never been to the Sahara Desert. Still haven't. Maybe I saw a picture of it once. But I could imagine clear enough how it would be to swirl around in a huge ocean of sand, just rolling along under a hot blue sky. You don't need to have been somewhere to imagine what it's like. *I can see that in your eyes already.*

My name is Hank Evans. To be precise, it's William Evans, but my Grandmother, being a good Christian soul, liked the name *Hank Evans* because it sounds like *Thank Heavens*, a saying that she repeated liberally. The name *Hank* fit better than a pair of worn-in gloves; it stuck from the time I was three years old. I was born in 1920, and grew up right here in the Salmon River Valley of Idaho. I love every square inch of this place. I'm sure of this, for I can probably say that I *know* every square inch of the valley and the surrounding countryside.

In 1940 I was tall, thin, tanned, and strong. I kept my dark brown hair cut short, my blue eyes focused, and my grin uncovered. My family came from a long line of ranchers, and I joined the family business on day one. I was a cowboy. Contrary to most folks' notion of what a cowboy does day to day, it's much more than just *ridin'* and *ropin'*. In fact, a true cowboy is a master of so many skills and disciplines, that it's not easy to explain without just describing what it's like.

Basically, a cowboy lives to serve. He serves the livestock, the land, the ranch owner, his fellow workers, the community, the wildlife, and himself, in that order. A cowboy's day is so long, that there's usually about five minutes left at the end of day to think of oneself. Which means that a good cowboy can't even spell *selfish*. A cowboy works hard every day, and if he's lucky he gets a few lazy hours on a Sunday afternoon to wash some clothes and mend a shirt or two.

The thing is, nature never takes any time off, and someone always has to look after the livestock. Plus, things break all the time and stuff gets used up. So even if all the livestock is healthy and happy, which never happens, there's still equipment to fix, and fence line to repair, and ditches to clear, and tools and sharpen, and hay to harvest, and supplies to gather. You get the idea. Although the work is shared, there's more than enough to go around. It's a seven-day a week job, and a cowboy goes to work most every day whether springtime or winter, sunny or blizzard. And whether he's healthy or not.

It may sound like a cowboy would jump at the chance to take a different job – one that was predictable and comfortable and left more time for leisure. In fact, good cowboys would just about work on a ranch for free. They almost did in my day – being paid mostly in the form of a bunk to sleep in and some good grub to keep their bellies full. Add a bit of change to pay for boots, clothes, and a few luxuries, like some chewing tobacco or an occasional cold beer, and a cowboy felt like the richest man alive. Hasn't changed much even now. Money doesn't buy happiness, and hard work is its own reward, a fact that I've always found liberating. There's just something about using your muscles almost to the point of failure, then surveying what you've accomplished as you catch your breath. Add to this the opportunity to participate in the amazing cycle of life that nature continuously provides, and you can begin to see the attraction. The birth of a new calf can put even the most weathered cowboy in a state of awe, and the simple pleasure of seeing a deer bound through a field can put a smile on your face on the bleakest day. It's no wonder there seems to always be an endless supply of hearty folk willing to work a ranch and to take on so much hardship.

My grandfather, then my father, worked hard enough to have their own small outfit – no comparison to the big ranches you would find in Montana or Texas, but big enough to keep a few hands busy and tired. I and my sister Angela Jean – we called her AJ - helped on the ranch from the time we were toddlers, and we celebrated every minute of it. I rode my first horse solo before I was three, and helped with the birth of a calf shortly thereafter. AJ rode her first cattle roundup when she was seven. On her own horse. With no supervision. And she got stuff done. That just about sums it up right there. In ranch country we started early, both in terms of years and time of day, and we *got stuff done*.

During the summers of our youth AJ and I mended fences and tended horses, and explored every corner of the Salmon River Valley. On lazy afternoons after our numerous chores were complete, we fished the Salmon River for dinner, always savoring the taste of fresh steelhead or salmon grilled over an open fire. Follow that with a warm piece of cornbread and a good story or a few songs, and we were in heaven. We never thought our life was difficult; it was just how things were, and everyone we knew lived the same way.

We took care of ourselves so others didn't have to. But when the unexpected happened, as it always did, our family helped our neighbors and they helped us. I also remember great events during particular times of year when everyone from surrounding outfits would gather at a certain ranch to help with a big seasonal job – branding new calves or harvesting a windfall of hay or alfalfa. Looking back I wouldn't have traded our hard work for anything – the ranch and surrounding community instilled in me a sense of value, purpose, honesty, and pride. The older I get, the more I value those simple traits, and the more I appreciate the people that taught them to me.

So now you know me a little better. I need to get back to the story before my mind begins to wander – I could talk about Idaho and the ranch all night long and keep a grin on my face 'til sunup.

Say, it may be dark outside that window now. But if there's one thing I've learned it's this: in the darkest night, the smallest of candles can light the way. And the most unlikely person might have the match.

Chapter Three

The day I met Jack Campbell back in October of 1939, I had worn myself out clearing irrigation ditches. It was a long, hard day, no different than most. The sun played tag with a flock of clouds all afternoon, and the mid-October breezes stayed crisp and cool throughout the day. My back and shoulders ached from dragging the summer quagmires out of a thousand miles of mucky ditches. Being as tired as I was, I planned on falling into my bunk shortly after my fine supper of beans and cornbread, and after savoring my last cup of coffee that evening I had grand visions of flopping down like a rag doll for a solid night of good sleep. I planned on working hard at that, too.

Then the wind came.

Here in Idaho, as in most places along the foothills and ranges of the Rockies, the weather can be extremely unpredictable. I've seen it snow in the morning and warm up to shirtsleeve weather in the afternoon, and vice versa. The *vice versa* isn't as fun as the former, but both happen all the time. A big factor in all of this is a thing we call a *Chinook Wind*. Around here folks just call it a Chinook. A Chinook is a strong wind that blows out of the west, climbing over the ranges and descending into the valleys like an avalanche. When it descends it compresses and warms itself. When a Chinook comes to visit, the temperature can climb faster than a bobcat with a bee sting.

It was the end of a long day, and I was tired. But I love a Chinook wind on a mid-October evening. It feels fresh and alive, and at that time of year its warmth postpones the notion of winter for a spell. It just makes you want to be outside. So I finished my supper, grabbed a small canteen of coffee, and hiked to the top of my favorite hill to enjoy the countryside and the wind. A full moon was rising over the ridge, and I found myself a good seat for the show. I sat there for a while, letting the Chinook push me to and fro, enjoying the sounds and beauty of nature. The rising moon was over my back shoulder and it cast my shadow on the ground ahead. The sky above was dark and filled with stars. I sat there for a long time just drinking it all in.

Then I heard the drone of an airplane. It wasn't unusual to hear an airplane these days - ranchers had begun to use them to get a better survey of their land. To hear one twice in the same week or so would be unusual, but not unheard of. But it *was* unusual to hear an airplane this late in the evening. It was dark, and I wasn't aware of pilots that flew at night. So I figured this guy was either desperate or lost. Turns out I was wrong on both counts.

I tried to get a bearing on the plane. Its drone echoed off the slopes of the mountains and bounced around the valley. I eventually figured it out, and caught site of a small plane as it descended into the valley. The moon was higher now, and it lit the valley in a soft glow. Any rancher will tell you that a full moon provides plenty of light once your eyes adjust. I often work outside at night during a full moon, especially after a hot summer day. The moonlight glinted off the wings of the plane as it was buffeted by the wind, and as it neared I could see that it was a float plane, made to land on the water. I looked immediately to the Salmon River, which wound through the center of the valley below. It looked like molten silver in the moonlight, and I figured the pilot could see it clear enough. I was right. He banked toward the river and landed in a long, straight run of water that was nice and calm. I knew that place well - AJ and I had floated there during many summer days. It was between two bends in the river, and since it broadened out at that spot the current was nice and slow.

My curiosity got the best of me, and I decided to take a quick ride down to the river to greet our visitor. I descended the hill to the stable and grabbed my horse Denim, leading him toward the barn where we kept our tack. I roped him to a post and entered the barn, returning with a saddle, bridle, and blanket. I had him saddled and ready to go in five minutes. He was fresh - he hadn't had much work today as it was all me in the ditches. The fact that he didn't have thumbs was a blessing to him on many a day.

I refilled my canteen with coffee from the bunkhouse and wrapped some leftover cornbread in a cloth, putting both into my saddle bag. Then Denim and I headed out toward the river, to see what was so dang important down there, during a full moon in the month of October.

Chapter Four

We were losing altitude, and the clouds below were as thick as a new Grandma Evans quilt. I had a fairly good idea of where we were - we had crested the peak of the Himalayas over Burma and were on the downhill run toward China. But even if there happened to be a ten-thousand foot runway directly below us, which there wasn't, I would have no way of knowing. I couldn't see a darn thing. So I kept us moving straight ahead despite the pain in my left knee, and maintained a gradual descent toward the cloud deck. It was a lost cause to try to maintain our altitude anyway. We were flying on a wing and a prayer, and I knew there was no way we would make it to Kunming.

I thought about dumping some of the cargo we had in the back in order to lighten us up. But it was a bunch of crates of food for the hungry folks in China, who were suffering mightily under the burden of a nasty Japanese occupation. Besides, Lhasa would need to dump the food while I flew the plane, and it was hard to imagine him muscling the crates out of an open cargo door in the face of a withering slipstream of cold mountain air. I decided to keep the food, but I would learn later to never underestimate Lhasa's strength of will. Lhasa was an unusual sort of guy. If you were standing in the desert with no visual reference to size or scale, and saw Lhasa walking toward you, you would assume he was a giant of a man. A giant with a shiny bald head, piercing brown eyes, a smoothly shaved face, and a subtle smile. The kind of smile that's not a smirk, but that says "I know something you don't know, but I'm willing to share it with you." You would think he was a giant of a man

23

because of his stature - because of the way he carried himself, and walked, and from the deliberate motions of his limbs. Then as he got closer, you would realize that he wasn't a giant after all. That he was just a regular sized guy. A regular sized guy that just *seemed* large. Then as he drew closer still, you would suddenly understand that Lhasa was, in fact, small. But you would be unsure of yourself, because he seemed larger than he was. Larger than his sub-five-foot height. So you would find yourself wanting to actually measure his height. Maybe convince him to step on a scale to see if he was made of flesh and blood, or of a ton of solid granite. Your eyes would say "small", but your mind would say "giant". Lhasa was an enigma that way.

Perhaps Lhasa could push the cargo out the airplane door. But I decided to keep it. So we flew ahead, descending into the clouds and keeping our eyes peeled for a glory hole – an opening in the clouds that would let us catch a glimpse of the ground. The clouds were cold, gray, and cheerless, with no hint of sunlight. It was mid afternoon but it seemed like late evening. You know that time of day - when the sky above a mountain valley is a deep gray and about to turn black. I lost track of the time and just focused on the clouds and the instrument panel, continuously reassuring myself that our one engine was still alive and healthy. From time to time I glanced at Lhasa. He had finished his chant or prayer or whatever it was and focused on the clouds with deep concentration. I appreciated the extra pair of eyeballs.

We droned along for a while in this manner, slogging through the soup and dreaming of the blessed dirt somewhere below. My leg was killing me and from time to time I crossed my feet and used my right leg to press the left rudder pedal. Each time I did this, we momentarily swung to the right and Lhasa would fall over on my shoulder. It didn't faze him at all.

Just when I thought I couldn't stand it any longer, Lhasa yelled and pointed ahead and to the right. I leaned forward for a better view and saw a break in the clouds, with a nice patch of brown turf below. I didn't waste a second. I banked us hard to the right in a diving turn, and dropped us straight into the hole in the clouds. My desperate action inadvertently put us into a diving spin, which was unhealthy for both airplane and crew. But in this case the tight corkscrew served us well, keeping the spinning ground within site as we screamed down the pipe. When I say "screamed" I do mean it. The airplane was howling like a banshee due to the rapidly accelerating airspeed, and I was screaming like a stuck pig, the result of a strange mix of joy and complete terror.

Jack had drummed a few things about flying into my thick skull, and I remembered one now. When looking for a place to land in an emergency, the right thing to do was to pick a flat spot quickly, then focus on it like it was the only thing in the entire universe. Indecision at this point usually resulted in a big bad thud.

So I focused. I stomped hard on the left rudder with all the strength that remained in my leg. This stopped our right-hand spin and brought us into a steep, straight dive. The view of the ground now made sense to me. I could see hills. More hills. Rocks. Bigger rocks. But I also saw a river, and with my eyes I followed it along until it made a broad turn. At that turn the river had wandered a bit and carved out a flat little half circle, depositing a nice layer of sand over the rocks. Just like so many bends in the good old Salmon River back home. That sandy spot became my entire world.

I pulled back on the wheel to level us, but the diving heifer fought against me. "Lhasa!" I yelled. Lhasa didn't need explanation. He grabbed his wheel and pulled with me, and with our combined strength we raised the nose bit by bit. The banshee calmed down and I had control again.

I tried to find some indication of the wind direction, but there just weren't enough trees or even grass below to get a good read. Oh to hell with it. I didn't care what direction we came in from. We were going to hit that spot of sand and hold on for dear life. So I put us into a gradual left bank, pulled back on the throttle, and dropped the wing flaps to slow us. Lhasa wisely activated the landing gear lever to lower our wheels, and I maintained a slow left turn and focused on the field.

I crossed below one thousand feet and straightened us out for our approach. I misjudged the distance and we were coming in hot and high. So I put us into a side slip, banking to the right while turning the rudder to the left. Normally a great way to lose altitude and airspeed quickly, for this configuration forced the airplane to crab into the wind and created a bunch of drag. But I forgot that we only had one engine, and that really messed us up. Our attitude stalled the airflow over the right wing stall and it fell toward the ground. Now instead of focusing on landing I was suddenly focused on keeping us airborne. I corrected the controls and said a quick prayer. The sack of bricks responded, but as I brought us back on course toward the field we were now low and wobbly. I added a bit of engine power and prepared to hit pay dirt. Then I saw it. Unbelievably, there was a dirt landing strip about a quarter mile to the west, on my left side. *Don't that beat all.* There was no way I was going to get us there now, so I focused on the dark gray sand at the near edge of the half circle and planted the wheels smack into it. We bounced as high as a bird's nest in a lodge pole pine. I pushed us back down and we hit a bit lighter the second time. I pressed hard on the brake petals, pulling back on the wheel to keep us from nosing forward.

We rumbled along like a jeep speeding down a washboard road. For a long time. We finally came to a stop with a bit of room to spare, and the sturdy plane settled into the sand at the edge of the river. I shut down the remaining engine, and the prop slowed to a stop in a soft whirr. Then all was quiet except for my pounding heart. We just sat there for a while, looking out the windshield at nothing in particular. Then we caught our breath and looked at each other. I could see my relief mirrored in Lhasa's face.

Now that we were down and safe, I had time to consider the situation. We survived. No complaints there. The cargo was safe. But it wouldn't feed anyone if we couldn't get it to them, and I wasn't quite sure where we were. That was our first concern. The Japanese Army occupied large swaths of China, and their severely abusive nature was well known. At this point, America wasn't technically at war with Japan, but we were actively trying to help the Chinese (and Burmese) by training them and by flying funds, supplies and evacuees to and fro. The Japanese didn't like it, but they weren't sure how to handle America's involvement. It was an uneasy tolerance for the time being. They merely took their frustrations out on the helpless Chinese and Burmese populace. Later, once they had attacked Pearl Harbor and declared war on the US, they attacked the multinational cargo planes whenever convenient. In response, the American Volunteer Group, led by Clair Chennault, a retired officer of the US Army Air Corps, would soon arrive to even up the fight. The AVG were mostly pilots from the States, and they flew a wide variety of cargo planes and fighter aircraft. The most famous of their aircraft were the P-40 fighters, with their distinctive paint scheme - a gaping shark's face on the front of the plane. The pilots, nicknamed the Flying Tigers, were heroes to the oppressed, were despised by the Japanese, and would kick some butt. But they were still a year away. We were on our own for now.

I was able to catch a quick glimpse of the airstrip to our left as we were landing, but I didn't recall seeing any aircraft, whether friend or foe. The strip was barren, but that didn't mean it was unused. I was in a strange situation - potentially in danger, but not technically in enemy territory. If we were found by Japanese soldiers, would they care that I was *not* a declared enemy? Or would I feel their wrath for being an American pilot? Surely they saw us as the enemy. How would they treat me and Lhasa? I assumed the worst. I'll be honest. I feared it. I was no soldier. I had no idea how to fight a Japanese platoon. I figured Lhasa didn't either. I would learn later that he was partner who could handle a fight just about anywhere.

I unfolded some maps and flight charts to try to make sense of our location. Lhasa unbuckled himself and moved aft to check the cargo. I glanced out the window and saw snowflakes beginning to fall. It was early evening, and the sky was darkening quickly. The storm had now caught up with us, and it would get cold. So be it. I was from Idaho, where the winter chill could freeze a hot cup of coffee before it left the pot. How cold could it get?

I found out soon enough. We had to go outside and tie down the plane. I wasn't sure how strong the wind would be, and a strong gust could easily move an airplane. We gathered some rope and stepped outside. It was below freezing, but bearable. We were now outfitted with warm clothing courtesy of our cargo, and the fresh air felt good.

We worked together to tie down the tail and each wing, piling boulders as weights to hold the ropes.

"Lhasa," I said. "I have to ask. Why do we need to get to Kunming? Why is this journey so important?"

"Hank, it's not the journey that's important. It's the people."

I looked around. There weren't any.

Lhasa waited patiently for the next question. He didn't waste words if none were needed.

"What people?" I finally asked.

"Well for one, we must find Marco. He's from the Philippines. He's a pearl diver."

I was speechless for a couple of minutes. It took my brain that long to formulate a response to Lhasa's last three sentences. "I see. Can I ask *why* we're meeting a Filipino pearl diver named Marco in China? In a snow storm?"

"Because *China* is where he is. We need him for our task. The snow storm is just unfortunate. I doubt it will be snowing in Kunming. Warmer there." Lhasa brushed the fresh snow off his shoulders and stared into the distance. Looking for Marco, I figured. I had just completed the longest conversation so far with Lhasa. But I knew less than when I started. Lhasa had a funny way of doing that to me.

"What was our task again?" I asked hopefully. Until now, I didn't know we had one.

"To right a wrong. If we succeed, to right many more."

"What wrongs?" I asked.

"The first happened four hundred years ago. Long story."

"I see. What about the other wrongs. Did *they* happen four hundred years ago?"

Lhasa shook his head. "Haven't happened yet."

"Are you pulling my leg?" I slapped my thigh like my

granddad did whenever he figured someone was pulling his leg. It was just a reflex. No disrespect intended.

Lhasa looked straight at me. His eyes locked with mine. They were intense. He had a fire in his belly about something. But his eyes also held humor, and warmth, and compassion. I could see that whatever was burning him, he was on the right side of it. "I'm not yanking your leg, Hank. We have important work to do. We'll need more than just you and Marco. We'll find them along the way. The less you know right now, the better. But each person has a skill we need. I can also tell you that this is going to be a long and difficult journey. Dangerous too." He paused for a moment. "Hank, it's also going to take a lot of faith."

"I'm a cowboy, not a pearl diver".

Lhasa snickered in a funny little way. "I know. You'll be a cow*man* before we're done."

I couldn't figure out how roping and riding was going to help in a place where a Filipino pearl diver would be needed. Up until now, I'd been blissfully ignorant of all the turmoil going on in China. I'd followed Jack here because it seemed exciting and exotic, and because there was a genuine need for pilots to help the Chinese. So I flew back and forth between Dinjan and China, over the "Hump" of the Himalayas. I was doing something useful and valuable, and helping a bunch of folks at the same time. But most of all, I was just having fun. I wasn't Chinese. I could leave at any time. It wasn't my country that was suffering. I couldn't do anything wrong. It was all just useful, exciting, and fun. Until I got sucked into this little emergency with Lhasa. Now things were getting serious. I was involved. I'll be honest. It was inconvenient for me, as I now had a stake in something that I hadn't asked to be a part of. I was afraid of where this whole cattle drive was going. Afraid of where

Lhasa was leading me. Afraid to say 'no.' Then I realized that, more than anything, I was afraid of disappointing Lhasa.

I told him so.

He reached up and put his hand on my shoulder. "Hank," he said warmly, "I said this journey would take a lot of faith. You may not have any special skills on this quest. But you bring *the faith*." He studied the uncertainty in my face. "Don't be afraid. Just believe."

Now I was as confused as ever. I didn't feel that *the faith* was one of my skills. In fact I just felt small. Like that little grain of sand in the great Sahara desert. Where it was now snowing quite hard.

Chapter Five

By the time I arrived at the moonlit Salmon River on that October night in Idaho, the float plane was tied to a bunch of willows on the bank. The pilot was standing on one of the floats retrieving his gear from the back of the plane. "Howdy," I yelled, as Denim and I approached. The fellow turned and smiled. I reigned in Denim a few yards from the bank.

"Well hello, friend. Mighty fine evening, isn't it?"

"You can say that again," I replied. "A bit warm for October in these parts. Can't complain about that."

"You'll never catch me complaining about an evening like this." He walked towards me and extended his hand. "Name's Jack Campbell."

I dismounted and shook his hand. "Hank Evans." He had a firm handshake, like so many people I knew. But he also looked me straight in the eye as he spoke. He had an easy going manner that made me feel as if I had known him all my life. As if he had nothing to hide. As if he wanted me to ask him a question, which he would gladly answer. He was about four or five inches shorter than my six foot height, had broad shoulders, trim waist, darkly tanned skin, and not an ounce of fat. This guy worked for a living. His brown hair was closely cropped and he had a few days of stubble on his face. His brown eyes were playful and bright. He wore a pair of olive dungarees, a tan shirt, and a pair of well worn brown boots. By the lines in his face, I guessed he was ten years older than me. "So what brings you to the Salmon River Valley tonight?" I asked.

"A steady tailwind, a bright moon, and a true compass,"

he replied.

"Well good for you. Care for some coffee and cornbread? It's the best you'll find in these parts."

"The coffee or the cornbread?"

"Well I'll be honest. The hands never finish the pot of coffee. We use the leftovers the next day to clean the rust from the tractor. But the cornbread recipe was handed down across the generations on my mother's side. It's as perfect as a summer day is long."

"Well then I'll take both. Much appreciated."

I tied Denim to a willow branch. He happily began nibbling on a clump of fragrant spring grass. I grabbed my saddle bags and we sat ourselves down on a pair of boulders at the edge of the river. Jack unpacked the cornbread while I poured some coffee in a couple of tins from my bag. We ate and drank in quiet for a few moments. Around these parts, we don't feel the need to hurry into conversation. Good company is good enough. I appreciated the fact that Jack understood this. He put me at ease.

After a while, my curiosity finally got the best of me. "Where you from, Jack?"

He took a sip of coffee and didn't grimace. He was tough. And polite. Nice combination. "Montana, just outside Libby. Grew up on a ranch there. I expect it's about the same as the ranches around here. I'm on my way there now. Been away for a couple years. I plan to stop at home in Montana for a month, visit with my kin, then head back out for another year or so."

"Back out?" He had my interest. Wherever "back out" was, it sounded exotic and far away.

"Hawaii. I'm a cattle boss at the Parker Ranch on the Big Island of Hawaii. Long story, but they were looking for a pilot to help them survey their spread. They also appreciate cowboys. I was both."

Well don't that beat all. "I didn't know there were cowboys in Hawaii."

"Hank, there are cowboys everywhere. You just gotta watch for the ones that are all hat and no cattle."

I chuckled. I knew the type sure enough.

"Parker Ranch is a huge outfit. Been raising cattle since the 1840's. 250,000 acres. More cattle than any of the ranches around here. More than a big Texas ranch too. Beautiful place. Nestled on the slopes of an old volcano, between the mountains and the sea."

It was hard to picture a cattle ranch in Hawaii. But it sounded nice enough. We sat in silence for a bit. The fish were biting now. Every now and again they'd splash in the river as they caught themselves a fly.

We sat there for a while and chatted about everything and nothing, until the cornbread was gone and our coffee tins were empty.

"Say Hank, we're looking for a good ranch hand to help train horses. We have a lot of cattle and need more horses for the cowboys - the *paniolos* as we call them in Hawaii. Got plenty of broncos. Need someone to tame 'em. That's half the reason for this trip. I planned to find a good bronco buster in Montana. You interested? I think you'd be a good man for the job."

"What tells you that?" I asked, a bit perplexed.

"Couple a things. First, you're a cowboy. You handle that horse well. Second, you walk with a slight limp. The kind you likely got in a hard fall from a bucking bronco. So I figure you've got some experience in that respect. Third, you're out on a night like this to welcome a stranger with some cornbread and coffee. I'll forgive you the coffee," he chuckled, "but the cornbread was State Fair blue ribbon. So you're skilled, kind, and curious. I can tell you firsthand, that's a powerful combination."

I watched the river flow along in the moonlight for a long time, thinking about the wanderlust I often felt. It came and went like the snow in March. I knew that one day I would settle down here in Idaho, with my own family and my own house, and live a great life. But I'd ridden every square inch of this valley. I'd always wondered what was over the mountains. Or across the sea. If there was a time to find out, this was it. I was young and single. The ranch would do just fine without me. My family would likely agree. I picked up a pebble and absentmindedly flicked it into the gravel between the boulders. It bounced several times before finally coming to rest in a little pocket of grass.

"Well Jack," I said, "it all sounds great. But it's a lot to chew on. How long you planning to stick around these parts?"

"Two, maybe three days. Then I'll be flying to Montana. I'll be back this way in a month. Think on it and let me know."

"Deal. In the mean time, we've got an open bunk for you at the ranch. I'll take you there tonight, if you don't mind the walk."

"Much appreciated, Hank. I'll take you up on it. I'll work for my breakfast. You just tell me what and where."

"I got a few ideas on that. Sunup is at six o'clock."

"Then I'll see you at five thirty."

I liked this guy.

The next morning Jack the Hawaiian cowboy pilot was awake and ready for work at five thirty, as promised. By the time I found him he already had our two horses saddled and ready to go. I had known him less than twelve hours. I was already impressed. His word was good so far. But I tempered my enthusiasm. It was still early, and many a potential ranch hand got winded by noon. We had a full day of character-building work ahead of us. It was one of my favorite ways to get acquainted to folks. We ate a hearty breakfast, carefully packed some coils of wire and tools on our horses, then rode off to the fence line for a day of repairs. October in Idaho doesn't quite mean winter yet. But there was snow in the shadows from an earlier dusting, and a heavy morning frost sat everywhere else. A layer of fog hugged the lowlands along the river. We could see our breath as we rode the trail. I turned up my coat collar to ward off the chill, thinking about the oncoming winter. It would be cold, no doubt. But winter was also the slow season on a ranch. There was plenty of day to day work to do, but the long nights meant a bit more time to relax. More time to sit by the fire and let your mind wander. We rode side by side for a good thirty minutes. We had plenty of time to talk. Jack told me more about Hawaii and the job we had discussed. It was a good story. The job was familiar to me. I was convinced I could do it well. Then there was the added bonus of being in Hawaii. It was mighty compelling.

On this particular morning, there were a couple of things on my mind. First, it was cold. Not winter cold, yet. But fog cold. They're both about the same in these parts. Hawaii sounded warm and inviting. Second, in a year or two it would be time for me and AJ to take the lead running the ranch. I was nineteen now. My father had taught me everything I needed to know. It would soon be time for him to wind down and just do the fun stuff. AJ had an intermittent interest in the ranch. She loved the country, the horses, and the outdoors. But she also dreamed of a family of her own. Her attachment to the ranch wasn't as deep as mine. That was fair enough and no issue for me at all. I had my own attachment to a fine cowgirl named Sara Hudson. But Sara was about to leave for Denver for a spell to attend nursing school, and there was no set future for us.

Soon enough it would be time for me to settle down on the ranch, for many years. I looked forward to it. But once I did, going off to Hawaii for a year or so wouldn't be possible. So if I was going to take a journey, now was the time. I had previously considered the military. Thought the Navy might be a good little rodeo for a couple of years. I've always had a hankering for the sea. But the doc in town told me I didn't qualify. Despite my youth and my strength, I couldn't pass the physical. I had taken a bad fall from a wild horse when I was seventeen. My busted leg was in a cast for two months. It hadn't healed correctly and gave me a slight but noticeable limp. On most days it was just an inconvenience. But on some days it was a real pain, and didn't have the strength that it should. Apparently in the peacetime of 1939 the Navy didn't need that many sailors, and could find better candidates. So I had a wanderlust that I was looking to quench. The window of opportunity was closing a bit more every month.

Jack and I worked together all day, replacing fence wire and fixing fence posts, mile after mile. The fence line is a never ending job. It never stays put for long. The weather, the wildlife, and the livestock are hard on fences. So no matter what, there's always a section somewhere that needs repair. My father always called the fence line an opportunity for guaranteed lifetime employment. But it gave Jack and me a chance to work together. To get to know each other. He was a solid guy. He worked hard and well. He came from a ranch family in Montana. His trip to Hawaii was his own answer to the same wanderlust I had.

His uncle had a stake in the Parker Ranch, and convinced Jack to get his butt over there and check things out. Apparently their Montana ranch is well manned by an extended family of siblings. It gave Jack the opportunity to ship out. It all made sense to me.

That evening I talked it over with my parents and AJ. They agreed I should finish things up and hit the road. They didn't know if Jack was the guy to travel with, but they left that to me. I'd see Jack in the morning and planned to give him an answer then. I was leaning toward accepting his invitation to work on the Parker Ranch. I went to sleep dreaming of palm trees under a blue, sunny sky.

At the time, I had no idea how much that decision would change my life.

But neither did Jack.

A month later I was on the Big Island of Hawaii. I could hardly believe it. After I accepted Jack's offer, he made a trip to Montana for three weeks, then flew back to Idaho to pick me up. He had a nice twin-engine Beechcraft Model 18A float plane. I loved flying in that thing. It was built in 1938 as a conventional land-based tail dragger, but could also be fitted with skis or with floats. Its original owner racked the landing gear trying to set it down on a dirt ranch strip in Montana during a fierce crosswind. Jack bought it from him for a song. The landing gear was a loss, but Jack loved to fish, and he preferred floats to enable him to reach his favorite fishing holes. He added small wheels to the sides of the floats, so technically the plane was an amphibian, able to land either on water or on hard surface. Very useful when one wasn't quite sure where one would be landing.

It took a few hops to get to the West Coast. Jack was more than happy to teach me to fly along the way. I picked it up pretty quick, and eventually learned how to takeoff and land, and to fly on one engine. He taught me to land on the water, but only in certain situations when the wind was light and the water smooth. A water landing usually takes more skill than I had.

We stopped in San Francisco for a few days to provision Jack's plane for the 2,400 mile transpacific flight to Hawaii. We added extra fuel tanks inside the cabin. Then we made a detailed inspection of every aspect of the plane. We fixed a few things ourselves, hiring a mechanic to fix the rest. We based ourselves at Treasure Island just to the east of San Francisco. It was connected by a tiny spit of land to Yerba Buena Island in the middle of San Francisco Bay, midway between San Francisco and Oakland. It was a manmade island, completed just in time to host the 1939-1940 World's Fair, which was just getting started. Perfect timing. Even better, Treasure Island served as the brand new home base for the Pan American Airlines fleet of flying boats. The big China Clippers. Beautiful, exotic airplanes. I had never seen anything like them. I immediately sent a pile of postcards home.

What could be better? I suddenly found myself in the middle of a World's Fair, surrounded by an exotic fleet of PanAm seaplanes. They had flown to every corner of the world. It was an ideal place to prepare for a cross ocean flight. It was easy to find aircraft mechanics for hire, as they often had spare time between flying boat arrivals, and always wanted some extra cash. So we got a top notch mechanic for a couple of days. During that time I had the opportunity to listen to great stories from PanAm pilots as they filled my head with visions of the South Pacific and beyond. The World's Fair had the same impact. It was all a sudden introduction to the vast horizons beyond Idaho. I'll admit, after a few stories from the PanAm crews, I began to think of Hawaii as a stopping off point on a longer journey. I had the travel bug. I was itching to get underway.

We departed for Hawaii two days later, and were soon over the vast Pacific Ocean. I do mean vast. The windshield was filled with nothing but water and sky. Even the demarcation seemed a million miles away. I could see whitecaps in the water below. They gave me a sense of the scale of the ocean. It was difficult for me to fathom. My adventure had begun, sure enough.

Fourteen long hours later, we reached the Big Island of Hawaii, the nearest island to the US mainland. We had originally planned to land in Honolulu on the island of Oahu, but it was another 220 miles to the west. We battled a fierce headwind throughout the second half of our flight and even with our extended tanks we were running on fumes. So to be safe we set down in Hilo on the eastern shore of the Big Island. Hilo was lush, green, and wet. It was raining. But when we stepped out of the plane onto the tarmac, the rain was warm, the air humid. I grew up in the western US. I had never experienced humidity. It was the first thing I noticed, and a sure sign that I was far from home.

We buttoned up the plane, grabbed our gear, and walked into the small terminal building at the airfield. It felt wonderful to stretch my long legs. Especially my busted left leg, which always grew stiff when I sat still for a long while.

The air smelled like flowers. *Don't that beat all.*

Chapter Six

We were safe on the ground inside our wounded C-47, somewhere in western China. We had plenty of food and supplies, and the plane provided decent shelter. We huddled inside for the night. I listened to the howling wind, imagining that I was back in the bunkhouse at home. I thought about my family and the ranch, and drifted off to sleep with a melancholy feeling of displacement. And misplacement. I felt out of place, far from home, detached from all that I knew, and generally about as low as a bug in a post hole.

I awoke at dawn, sensing the morning light. It was lighter than it should have been during a snow storm. I leaned forward to brush the frost from the side cockpit window and saw a beautiful sight. The storm had cleared, leaving a fresh layer of bright white snow across the landscape. The sun was just rising above the mountains, and the sky was deep blue. There was a layer of fog settled down along the river to our right. The sun played through it in a magical way. Had I not been so unsettled, I would have thoroughly enjoyed the view from my windshield. As it was, I was nervous and anxious. I felt the urgent need to start moving. But where to? In what direction? I revisited my maps and tried to make sense of them.

We were originally headed east for Kunming, a city in Free China just to the east of the Burmese border, before our starboard engine barbecued itself. I'd maintained our original heading despite the calamity, so I knew we were now somewhere along a generally straight line on my map, between Dinjan to the west and over the border in India, and

Kunming. We'd crossed the "hump" over the mountains on the northern side of Burma and were on the downhill run, so that helped me to narrow it a bit. We were definitely in China, along a fairly large river. I just wasn't sure exactly where, nor did I know how far it was to Kunming. If we could repair the starboard engine, and offload the cargo, we could possibly take off again from this riverbank. The ground was frozen hard, which actually made for a nice makeshift runway. But the chances of fixing a fire-damaged engine were almost zero. I didn't have any tools to speak of. Besides, I was no aircraft mechanic. There was no way this heifer could take off from this beach on one engine. I had never even heard of a C-47 taking off from a *paved* runway on one engine. So we were in for a hike. Question was, how far? Even more important, what to do with the cargo? The Japanese would certainly take it if they found it, but that would be a sad waste. What about the plane? I now owed somebody a C-47 cargo plane, because this one wasn't going anywhere. The parts alone would greatly help the Free Chinese, but I had to find them first.

Turns out they found *us*. I was a novice here in this part of the world. I didn't realize what war can do to a population's resourcefulness. Due to the Japanese invasion of China, the Free Chinese had built a remarkable air raid warning network. It wasn't complex. It depended on the ears of a thousand Chinese, in hundreds of villages and hidden on hilltops and caves across Free China. Each station had a simple radio, often powered by a hand-cranked generator. The operators could relay messages from station to station in seconds, for hundreds of miles. A duck couldn't quack without someone knowing about it. This network eventually enabled the Flying Tigers to lay waste to the Japanese fighter planes whenever they got the notion to torment the Chinese. The Chinese were listening for Japanese attacks, but any plane got their attention, including ours. A thousand Chinese knew about our crash landing about ten seconds after it happened. That was the easy part. The challenge was to get to us before the Japanese did. The Japanese weren't the dullest tools in the shed. They were undoubtedly interested in our little excursion.

Unfortunately the Japanese reached us first. As I alternately glanced from our maps to the cockpit window, half a dozen Japanese soldiers suddenly appeared ahead and to the left. It was easy to see their uniforms against the fresh new snow. They were a couple hundred yards away, having just crested a small rise to the west. "Lhasa!" I whispered. "We have a problem."

Lhasa moved quickly to the cockpit and surveyed the situation. The soldiers were rapidly approaching, spreading out as they neared our plane.

"Stay here, in the cockpit," Lhasa said. Then he slipped back to the side door and stepped outside. I was beside myself. We had a couple of pistols for protection and I was a good shot. But we were no match for seasoned soldiers. They were going to use us for target practice, and Lhasa would be the first tin can. I couldn't let that happen. He was my passenger, and was under my care. Besides, I had promised Jack that I would get Lhasa to Kunming. I never broke a promise. So I grabbed my pistol from the bag behind my seat, checked its ammo, and devised a plan as I watched the scene outside the window. When the timing was right, I would fire on the soldiers to allow Lhasa to get back to the plane. That was the sum total of my plan so far. I was awaiting some inspiration for the more challenging parts.

Lhasa walked forcefully along the left side of the plane,

directly toward the soldiers. He meant business. As I've said, he was small of stature but when he wanted to look big, he seemed as tall as a full grown grizzly bear standing on its hind legs. It was all in his attitude. The soldiers saw him immediately and slowed their advance. They looked to each other, obviously not knowing what to make of Lhasa. Their victims usually cowered at their presence. Lhasa was an aberration.

Lhasa yelled at them. If I could speak "Primal Lhasa", I would have guessed that he said "Go away, you're bothering me and I have more important things to do, like right a four hundred year old wrong. Don't piss me off!" As it was, the entire sentence was one syllable long. One. Loud. Word. It had the desired effect. The soldiers froze, apparently amazed at Lhasa's disrespect. His command hung in the air and it took several seconds for its echo to die out. Lhasa was wearing a leather flight jacket, but he removed it and nonchalantly dropped it with an outstretched arm. It fell into the snow in a crumpled heap. He was still wearing his Tibetan robe underneath. He yelled again, motioning with his right arm for the Japanese to go back the way they came. Then he just stood there with outstretched arms and stared them down. They seemed confused, both by his actions and by his maroon robe. I'd never seen anything like it in my life.

Where I come from in Idaho, we often encounter wildlife. The predators are dangerous even to humans. A grizzly, a mountain lion, even a bobcat can be deadly. Not to mention the occasional wolf. I had been taught, from an early age, that the best way to save your hide was to back away slowly, and never, ever, look the predator in the eyes. That was the most blatant form of threat, and a sure way to get yourself invited to dinner with the predator. *As the dinner*. I was transfixed as I watched Lhasa intentionally break this rule. He had himself in a standoff, and neither side moved. Then he yelled again, a crisp, low in the gut kind of howl that was forceful and primal. I'm not convinced that it was even a real word. Two of the soldiers actually jumped. Two others took a step backward. That was all it took. Lhasa had the upper hand. The soldiers engaged in heated conversation. They pointed in different directions and kept pointing back to Lhasa and our plane. They were clearly unsure of what to do. Then they yelled an apparent command at Lhasa. I didn't understand it. If he did, he didn't care. He didn't move an inch.

Then a rifle shot cracked out of the blue sky, somewhere to my right. I guessed it came from the top of the ridge just on the other side of the river. The Japanese soldiers reached the same conclusion. They instinctively dropped to the ground and raised their guns. Then all hell broke loose. The snow around them looked like popcorn in a hot skillet, as bullets from several guns on the ridge peppered the ground. The shooters were too far away to be accurate, but that didn't matter a bit. The Japanese soldiers were outnumbered and exposed. They executed a hasty retreat, backing over the hill to my left. The echoes of gunfire faded away and all was quiet again. Lhasa had dropped to the ground when the onslaught began, and now he stood up and retrieved his jacket. He turned to me with a reassuring look, motioning to the crest of the ridge to my right. I looked out the right cockpit window and saw dozens of Chinese coming down the hill. They weren't soldiers. They didn't wear uniforms. But they had rifles and packs, and they meant business. I guessed they were a collection of Free Chinese fighters. They crossed the knee-deep river to join us. A small team split off to keep a watch on the retreating Japanese.

I stepped outside the plane to join Lhasa. "How long were you planning to stand there facing down those guys?"

"The rest of my life."

He wasn't kidding. It had worked though. He bought us some time. The standoff lasted a good twenty minutes. Enough for the cavalry to arrive.

"Hank," he said, "I knew that they would be confused by me. If they saw an American, they would have been surer of themselves. They would have taken us prisoner to figure out why we're here. I couldn't let that happen. You did well. You had faith in me. I appreciate that."

The leader approached us, and he and Lhasa conferred in Chinese for several minutes. Then Lhasa translated for me. "This is Wai-sun. He doesn't speak English. He and his team were told of our landing last night. They have good radio communication with many lookouts across the countryside and the mountains. The Japanese soldiers that we just met were an advance team. They're far from their base, but they'll be back with more. He suggests that we depart as soon as possible."

"To where?" I asked.

"To Kunming. In our plane." Lhasa glanced over my shoulder at our giant wounded duck.

"Can Wai-sun help us fix the engine?" I asked.

"No. But we have a plan. We need to offload the cargo. Then we need to move the plane to the airstrip," Lhasa motioned over his shoulder to the airstrip I had seen earlier. The one that was a quarter mile away. "Then you and I take off for Kunming. Do we have enough fuel?"

I postponed my obvious questions. "I need to know where we are. I'll get the maps from the cockpit."

I returned with the maps. Wai-sun studied them briefly then confidently pointed to a location on the map. It was one of two different possible locations that I had worked out myself, so it made sense. We had landed at the Mekong River. The Yangtze River was about 50 miles to our north. The Burma Road, which ran east-west between Yashio in Burma and Kunming in China, was about 125 miles to the south. The Mekong ran south all the way to the Burma Road, then to Thailand. I pictured a nice leisurely float trip down the river to the Road, then a comfortable drive to Kunming. I could see by all the frantic activity that it wasn't in the cards, so I didn't even bother to suggest it.

We were 220 miles as the crow flies from Kunming, which was almost directly to the east. This was easily within range considering our remaining fuel. With one engine it would be a couple of hours in the air. Not too daunting. This didn't solve the most fundamental problem though. Our plane was a quarter mile from the airstrip. The ground between it and the strip was bumpy, rocky, and covered in clumps of willows. The plane weighed 20,000 pounds empty. Were we going to carry it on our backs? Even if we got it to the airstrip, could we take off with one engine? I'd never heard of anyone doing that. I figured I was going to find out soon enough. Felt I really had no choice in the matter. It was simply time for decisive action.

"Lhasa," I said. "If we can offload this plane, and get it to the airstrip, I can get us in the air. Kunming is two hours away by plane."

"I knew you could," Lhasa responded. "Wai-sun and his men have a plan. They'll offload the cargo here, distributing it as quickly as they can. Help is on the way to get it out of here. Then they'll help us get the plane to the strip."

"Who will?"

"Wai-sun and his friends. There are more on the way. They've been journeying since last night. They're bringing some muscle with them."

That they did. Within an hour, they began to arrive from every direction. Chinese farmers, laborers, and peasants with powerful oxen, carts, baskets, poles, ropes, and many other implements. I'm not afraid to say that it brought me to tears. They were tattered, they were obviously hungry, and they came to work. To help us, to help each other, to help their countrymen. They worked hard, urgently but joyfully. We offloaded three tons of cargo in less than an hour. By hand. Simultaneously, a contingent of men used machetes to clear a path through the willows to the airstrip. We fashioned a series of bridals, ropes, and harnesses to connect to the tail of the plane. The C-47 was a tail dragger, so once you lifted the fairly light tail, you could swing the plane around easily. We pulled the plane by its tail using the oxen and our own manpower. It was slow going but we made progress. How could we not? The sheer muscle power, multiplied by the determination of the men, was staggering. From time to time the landing gear would sink into the mud or the sand. We used strips of wood from the cargo pallets as levers to raise the stuck wheel out of the muck, and then ran the wheels on the wood across the soft spots. It was early spring and the ground was still frozen. In another few weeks, after the spring thaw, the ground would have been much too soft. It all just worked out. It took the rest of the day. But we got the plane to the strip. I was amazed and inspired. These people had done this for me and Lhasa, with the meager resources they had. Sure they would benefit from our cargo, but they put their lives at risk to help two complete strangers. I was touched beyond words.

The sun was low in the sky as we finally settled the plane at the end of the runway. She was ready to go. We would take off in the morning.

Wai-sun warned us against lighting a fire. No need to clue in the Japanese to our plans or our numbers. The night was cold in temperature, but warm in humanity. We prepared a small feast for all the Chinese that had worked so hard all day. The cargo provided plenty of resources for our celebration; we hardly made a dent in it. Wai-sun told me quietly that it was the largest meal that the peasants had eaten in months. We loaded the remaining cargo into their carts, onto their oxen, and onto their backs. They left at the first light of dawn, in as many directions as they had come. Their backs were full but their burdens were light. Their families would eat this month.

The Japanese Army got nothing.

Chapter Seven

Jack and I made our way to the Parker Ranch on the Big Island of Hawaii. It was a beautiful place. It covered a fair bit of the lush valley between the island's two volcanoes – Mauna Loa and Mauna Kea, surrounding the little town of Waimea. The two volcanoes were still active from time to time, and I hoped to see a little example while I was there. Turns out one could feel the volcanoes almost every day. Especially in the quiet bunkhouse. From time to time the ground would shake or rumble for a few seconds in a miniature earthquake. It was a bit unsettling at first, but after a few days I simply didn't notice anymore.

The *paniolos* at the ranch were a skilled bunch of cowboys. Some were Hawaiian, some were American. All were talented. They didn't accept me right away. I had to earn their respect. But once they saw me ride a few wild broncos, they treated me like one of their own. The ranch boss was tough but fair, and I got along just fine. I had a little time every week to do some sightseeing, and I often took a newly tamed horse on a ride through the surrounding countryside. I covered a good bit of the huge Big Island on those rides, and realized that it had distinct climates. The western side was arid and severe, the eastern side lush green. The northern side had a constant wind, and in Hilo, on the southeast edge of the island, it rained almost constantly. There were rugged lava flows at various parts of the island. I dared not take a horse through them for fear of injuring or breaking a leg.

I traded letters with the folks back home. It was now wintertime in Idaho, and the ranch was covered in the snow and ice that I knew so well. But I spent my Christmas in the tropical warmth of Hawaii. It was an odd feeling that was difficult to get used to. But I couldn't complain. I could imagine the winter chill in Idaho easy enough. I had now been at the Parker Ranch for a full month, and I was feeling at home.

When Jack wasn't doing aerial surveys in his plane, he managed a team of cowpokes, who rode the ranch keeping watch on the cattle. We often crossed paths in our daily work, and saw each other at the chow hall a few nights a week. He worked hard but enjoyed himself. He took me on a survey flight as often as he could. I loved those flights. They gave me the opportunity to see the island from the air, to hone my flying skills, and to watch for wild horses in the backcountry. He eventually had me do all the flying, while he did his mapping and observing. It suited me just fine. I was becoming quite good at handling the plane. I kept a logbook where I recorded every flight, with its origin, destination, flight time, weather, and any particular skills or maneuvers that I had practiced. My flight hours began to add quickly, and before long I had one hundred, then two hundred hours in the twin engine plane. I was acquiring a valuable skill, and having a great time while doing it.

The weeks went by, and I settled in to my job and grew comfortable at the Parker Ranch. But I still had my mind on my earlier conversations with the PanAm crews back on Treasure Island in San Francisco. Their stories of Southeast Asia rattled around in my head like gravel in an empty tin can.

In mid January, Jack invited me to join him on one of his survey flights. The ranch was so big that the flights were the only real way to keep tabs on the livestock, the fence lines, the condition of the feed, the creeks, et cetera. So we always had a bunch of work to do, and many things to watch for. I flew as he studied a creek that ran from the volcano slopes down to the ranchland.

"So Hank," he said. "Sounds like you're doing a great job here. Do you like it?"

"Sure enough. I'm enjoying myself."

"I'm glad to hear that. You planning on staying on for a while?"

"I committed to four months, which takes me to mid March. Then we'll see how things look," I responded.

"I'm glad to hear that." He paused. "I've met my commitment, and I've pretty well finished up my survey work. No sense in the ranch keeping me on the payroll as a pilot much longer. So I'm thinking on taking a trip to China."

My ears almost jumped right off my head. "China?"

"A friend of mine, a Tibetan fella named Lhasa, asked me to join him in China to help some folks. I met Lhasa a few months ago when he passed through here. He's an amazing guy. He recently sent me a letter and told me about an urgent need for pilots in China. The Japanese invaded China a couple years ago. But the western part of the country is fightin' mightily to stay free. Seems they badly need food and supplies, and the British and a few others are trying to help. So they're beginning an airlift from India and Burma into western China. They need pilots."

"You don't say. You planning to take him up on it?"

"Yep. Hard to explain. I don't know a wick about China or India or Burma. But in the short time Lhasa was here, I got to know him pretty well. It's a strange thing but I feel strongly about helping him. He has that effect on people. I'm going to trust him, and take a trip out there and see what I can do."

"Sounds to me like you're placing a lot of trust in this Lhasa fella. Who is he? What's he do?"

"Lhasa's a Tibetan missionary. He travels around Asia and the Pacific, searching for folks in need and figuring ways to help them. He told me that since he's Tibetan, no one sees him as a threat, and he can travel freely. He seems to make friends anywhere. He certainly did with me. Then he contacts them when he thinks they can help with one of his projects. I suspect he came to Hawaii because he needed to add some Americans to his list. I was one of them. I didn't realize he was recruiting me until, well, he did. So now he's in Burma trying to find folks to help fly supplies. I just can't say no to Lhasa."

"Well Jack, it sounds like a good plan, if you trust this guy. When you figure you'll head out?"

"Next week. I'll take this plane with me. Can't part with her now. Looks like she's going to get a taste of the skies over Asia."

"Well I'll tell you what," I said. "I'm sorry to see you go but I wish you the best of luck. It's been a real privilege ridin' this far with you. Keep in touch, and let me know if they need another pilot. Like I said, in mid March I have an option to either sign on for the summer, or hit the trail."

"I will Hank. I already know they need another pilot. Think on it while I pave the way."

Think on it? I already had.

By the end of March I was in China. I finished my obligation to the Parker Ranch and left them with a good number of well-trained new ponies. We parted ways with a hearty handshake and they invited me to come back whenever I wanted. Can't complain about that. I used some of the money I'd earned and jumped on a PanAm China

Clipper flying boat. Damn that was a fun trip. It was a four day flight, as we hopped from Pearl Harbor in Honolulu to Midway to Wake Island to Guam to Manila in the Philippines. I convinced the crew to let me sit in the copilot's seat on occasion when we were in midflight. It was a dream.

From Manila I made my way to Dinjan, India to meet up with Jack. He was flying a C-47 cargo plane between Dinjan and Kunming in China. He took me on the roundtrip flight to show me the lay of the land and to teach me the C-47. At first the plane felt massive to me. But after a couple of landings and takeoffs, I realized that it was just another airplane. I mastered it pretty quick, and started flying the route myself, paired with another pilot or copilot. It was challenging, exotic, rewarding, and impactful. I really got addicted to playing a small role in a big cause – the cause of Chinese freedom. I just jumped in with both feet and my busted leg and went to work.

Then Jack came down with Yellow Fever, and asked me to fill in for him and fly Lhasa to Kunming. We were short handed and I didn't have a copilot. Until then I hadn't spent any time with Lhasa, but he became my copilot for that flight. Jack thought the world of Lhasa, so I figured I could trust him. Besides, it was just another flight to Kunming. I'd done several of them so far. What could go wrong?

Chapter Eight

I had never taken off in a damaged twin engine plane on one engine but I was willing to try. Didn't really have a choice. I had to get the C-47, and Lhasa, out of here and on to Kunming. I turned it over and over in my head. I finally decided that I would just ram the one good engine to full power and hold on. I could counteract the lopsided thrust with the rudder, and keep us in a slight bank to counter the offset rudder. It made sense to me, but I was a novice with twin engine aircraft, so at dawn I rummaged around the cockpit until I found what I was looking for - the Flight Operations Manual for the C-47. It was remarkably simple for such a large, complex plane. I found what I needed in Section 4.6 - "Engine Failure On Takeoff". I discovered the answer to a key question that had been bothering me.

We said goodbye to Wai-sun and his men, who had diligently guarded us during the night. It was difficult to leave them. I knew they were in for a world of hurt when the Japanese returned, and I felt guilty leaving them there. But it was their choice and more importantly it was their land. They intended to keep it. They moved off to the side of the runway to watch us. Lhasa and I buckled ourselves in. I started the left engine to let it warm up for a few minutes. It purred like Grandma's tabby cat on a warm hearth. No worries there. I showed Lhasa how to activate the main-gear brakes, using the push tabs on top of the rudder pedals. It wasn't easy for him to reach them with his feet, even with his seat fully forward. We padded his seat back with an eight-inch thick parachute pack, which allowed him to push on the brake pedals and still reach his seat back.

It was time to go. I nodded to Lhasa. He pushed hard on both brake pedals to keep us from moving. I revved the engine to fifty-percent power, gave us some left rudder, and said a quick prayer. I nodded to Lhasa. He released the brakes and we lurched forward. We accelerated slowly, though I was tempted to push the throttle to full power, as I had originally intended. Turns out that would've killed us. One engine at full power was too much for the rudder to counteract. I would have stalled the rudder and put us into a deadly spin just above the ground. I had discovered this in the flight manual. I thanked God for Section 4.6.

We reached our rotation speed, at which I was able to push the wheel forward just enough to raise the tail gear from the ground. We were no longer pitched nose-up, and were now at the proper attitude for flight. More importantly I could now see the runway in front of us and the end looked alarmingly close. The old girl was testing the air, trying to lift herself. But our airspeed was just too low. Having only one engine was problem enough. The canted rudder also added a bunch of drag, and it was slowing our acceleration. I decided Section 4.6 didn't understand our particular predicament, so I pushed us to sixty-percent power and held on.

We bounced on the dirt airstrip, floating a bit higher each time. I finally pulled back on the wheel with a dozen yards to spare, and lifted us about ten feet off the ground. I held us level and slowed the engine back to fifty percent. We stayed at that altitude for a long while, clipping the tops of the willow bushes past the end of the runway. But we didn't have the speed to climb yet. I used our level flight to build airspeed, watching the ground closely. Lhasa wisely resisted the urge to raise the landing gear, in case we had to hit the dirt again.

As we built our airspeed, hours of worries and uncertainty begin to fall away as sure as the ground below. My lack of confidence in my flying ability kept trying to pull me back to the ground but its impact on my life was diminishing with every foot we traveled. Now I felt a part of something much greater. I had a sense of kinship with the folks here in Free China. I might never see most of them again, but I felt that we were walking the same path. Going the same direction. I was a part of something big. I remembered that old feeling when I surveyed the night sky from the top of the hill, feeling like an insignificant grain of sand. Now I felt like a mountain. That old night sky was much smaller. I was ready for whatever Lhasa had in mind for me. I had *the faith*.

Our airspeed was now over a hundred and twenty knots. I pulled back on the wheel and we climbed steadily into the cloud-dappled sky. The ground fell away quickly and the landing gear folded into the wings with a satisfying thump. I banked to the east, toward Kunming and the rising sun.

Chapter Nine

Once we left the ground, our lame-duck flight to Kunming was easy enough. It was a partly cloudy day with light winds, and it was easy to follow the landmarks below. Our single engine hummed along with a reassuring purr. I was now an old.hand at flying a wounded duck. Two hours later we approached the city of Kunming. They called it The City of Eternal Spring, for it was located in a wonderful climate that was never too hot and never too cold. Even from a thousand feet high I could see a multitude of flowers and a large variety of crops. The city was on the northern edge of Lake Dian, a huge body of water that was impossible to miss.

We landed uneventfully at the airfield just outside the old walled city. I grabbed my rucksack. Lhasa and I left the plane in good hands. I suddenly realized that all my belongings and responsibilities fit neatly on my back. Within the last twenty four hours I had been relieved of one airplane, three tons of cargo, a dozen Japanese soldiers, and fifteen years of my life. I had gained a load of faith, preserved my sense of humor, and had Lhasa at my side. All three of which were virtually weightless.

My burden was as light as a wallet at the end of the month.

Our plane would be fixed here and would be returning to service, flying back and forth between Kunming and Dinjan in India, over The Hump of Burma. It would ferry many more loads of much appreciated cargo, at the hands of a host of volunteer pilots. I would later learn that this particular aircraft would survive World War Two, and would eventually be pressed into service as a commercial airliner in Nepal, where she would fly for twenty more years. She was a tough bird. I was used to her now and I felt like I was parting with my best horse.

We stepped inside the mess hall at the airport to get some much needed food. As my eyes adjusted to the darkened interior, I realized that it contained a wide cross section of humanity. There were American, British, Chinese, and French military personnel, Chinese businessmen, Chinese workers, Filipinos, Vietnamese, Burmese, and a host of others that I couldn't place. The conversations were in as many languages, with an underlying foundation of English. I had never seen anything like this. I just stood there and gawked until Lhasa elbowed me and motioned to the food.

We grabbed some grub and sat on crude wooden benches, apparently made from well-aged shipping pallets, at tables made of scraps of wood and metal that had been artfully assembled with fifteen different types of fasteners, a bit of dried oatmeal, and some chewing gum. We ate heartily, joined by contingent of British and American pilots who were apparently taking a lunch break from a reenactment of the Revolutionary War. I could tell this because they had swollen knuckles and bruises on their faces to match. I assumed they'd had a hell of a bar fight between them. *All in good fun, cheerio mate.* They immediately marked me as *the new guy*, and hazed me with remarkable stories of the dangers of Kunming and the vicinity. Apparently there's a snake here that only bites one's eyelids. At night. When one is sleeping. And beautiful women who wear poisonous lipstick, which causes immediate blindness if you kiss them, all to avenge a past lover who jilted them. Whatever. I did the same thing to my new bunk mates back at the ranch, and I always enjoyed a good *watchoutfor* story.

Then the conversation turned serious, and we told them of our close call at the Mekong River. They were clearly impressed by Lhasa, but didn't quite know what to think of him. They complemented me on my piloting, and gave me a few helpful tips about flying the C-47. They had all been through similar flying challenges. More importantly, they knew the general situation in western Free China. They warned us that the Japanese were advancing quickly, that eastern China was entirely under Japanese control, and then they told us of Nanking. If you've never heard of the Rape of Nanking, it's a nasty story. The Japanese Army invaded Nanking on December 13, 1937. Nanking was then the capital of China. During a six week period, Japanese soldiers killed hundreds of thousands of civilians and Chinese soldiers who had surrendered or been captured. The official estimate was 300,000 killed. There was also widespread rape. The depravity of man never ceases to amaze me. At the same time, I'm never surprised when I hear of a new atrocity somewhere in the world. But back then, prior to our conversation in the mess hall in Kunming, I had been happily ignorant of the worst evils of man. I just wasn't raised to even imagine these kinds of atrocities. But they had happened clear enough, and I suddenly understood the work ethic of the Free Chinese on the Mekong River. They weren't just fighting for their land. They were fighting for the right to live.

I was no soldier - there was nothing I could do to fight the Japanese directly. But words from my Grandma Evans came to mind. "Just care for your neighbors," she always said, "and that will undo a world of hurt." Now I fully understood her advice. My neighbors were a bunch of Free Chinese, their friends and allies, who were trying to keep their lives together in the face of a growing storm. I studied

Lhasa as he spoke with the pilots at our table, and I fully understood the fire in his belly. Well deal me in. I already had *the faith*. Now I had *the fire*. Grandma always told me that good things came in three's. I wasn't yet sure what the third leg was, but the hot oatmeal on my plate came mighty close.

The pilots at our table asked about our plans. They knew we were now sans airplane. Lhasa spoke with his usual brevity. I'll admit it was amusing to watch the effect it had on people. "We're here to meet a friend," he said. "Then we'll be travelling south to Hai Phong."

That got their attention. "You're going to Hai Phong, huh?" an American asked. Hai Phong was a port city in Vietnam, which was called Indochina in those days, due to their occupation by the French. Apparently you weren't anybody if you weren't occupying, or being occupied by, another country.

"Yes," Lhasa responded. "Hai Phong, for some urgent business." In other words, it's urgent that you mind your own.

"Well," one of the Brits remarked, "Will you be taking the railway?" He was referring to the 500-mile long Yunnan-Vietnam railway, which had been built by the French in 1910. It connected Kunming with Vietnam, all the way to Hai Phong on the Gulf of Tonkin and the China Sea. Lhasa nodded. "Then I would be vigilant," the Brit said in a low but convincing voice. "The Japanese can't be happy about that railway. It's being used to bring relief supplies to Kunming. It may belong to the French, but it's an easy target for the Japanese." He gave me a look of caution and of warning. I got the message. I would discuss it with Lhasa later. On second thought, there was no point in bringing it up. It's pointless to try to stop a stampede. It just irritates the cattle.

We talked with our new friends for an hour or so, and they helped us to understand the general lay of the land. When it was time to part, one of the Americans asked "Who's your friend, by the way? The one that you said you were looking for?"

Lhasa answered. "A Filipino named Marco. He's here in Kunming somewhere."

"Marco the pearl diver?" the American responded.

"Yes," Lhasa answered, a look of surprise on his face. "Do you know him?"

The American laughed. "Everyone knows Marco. He's hard to miss. Try the lake." With that he and his buddies left us at a now empty table, surrounded by the vast humanity of Kunming.

Chapter Ten

We left the mess hall to walk into Kunming proper, where I was able to view the city up close for the first time. I was struck by the turmoil of the place. Everywhere I looked there was a flurry of activity - purposeful and urgent. It was immediately clear to me that Kunming was a city in peril.

Back home in Idaho, I'd experienced a few wildfires in my time. When there's a fire, all the animals naturally run in one direction: away. If you're close by, you can see the fear and desperation in their eyes. They're running for their lives. They generally survive, because they're so mobile. But if it's an animal that has a home, that's built something for itself and its family, then it's not mobile and the situation is entirely different. In that case the approaching fire is a much more serious threat. The best examples, other than humans, are ants. If you watch an anthill that's in peril from a fire, or from a predator, or even from an unknown threat, you can see deliberate, desperate, rapid action. By all the members of the society. Because the ants can't leave. They've invested their lives in their home, and they have offspring to care for, and food to protect.

That's how Kunming felt to me. The residents knew about Nanking, and they knew the Japanese were moving toward the west, toward their homes. I didn't see people running for the hills. I could see the anxiety and focus in the eyes of every person I passed. Kunming was preparing for a wildfire.

The next day we traveled to Lake Dian in search of Marco, by bus then on foot. It took a couple of hours but it felt good to travel on the ground for a change.

"Lhasa," I said. "I have to ask. Why do you, me, and Marco need to get to Hai Phong? What's so important about it?"

Lhasa finally unveiled his plan. I think he decided two things - first, that he could trust me, and second, that he was taking me into danger and I deserved to know where we were going.

"Hank, it's not Hai Phong that's important. From there we'll find a boat or a ship, and go on to Malaysia."

"I see."

He patiently surveyed the shores of Lake Dian, looking for Marco no doubt.

"So," I said, "what's so important about Malaysia."

"Because Malaysia is where the *donation* is," he answered.

"Donation? For what?"

"Not for *what*," he replied. "For *them*." He gazed over my shoulder.

I turned around and saw a gang of monkeys, milling around waiting for a handout or something.

I must have stared at them for a long time.

"Hank!" Lhasa exclaimed, forcing me out of my self-induced stupor. "Not for the monkeys! For the people!"

"What people?"

"The people that are suffering". He gazed to the west, back toward Free China and Burma.

"Oh," I said. "For the refugees from the Japanese?"

"For them," he nodded. "And for all the others."

"How many others?"

He paused and his gaze fell downward. "A great many." His eyes softened. He paused for several moments and I waited. I'd learned that haste in these moments just irritated

Lhasa. An irritated Lhasa tended not to talk much, and right now I needed much talk. "You see," he finally continued, "we're going to Malaysia to retrieve the treasure of the Kingdom of Malacca. It was stolen, and then lost, four centuries ago. It's a kingdom's treasure. It's more than you can imagine. More than we could possibly need or want. But it's not for us. We're going to get it to people who need it, who can be trusted with it, and who will put it to good use. But we don't have much time. This Imperial Japanese plague is spreading fast, throughout Asia and beyond. It's a swarm of locusts. They're consuming everything. We must reach the treasure before the locusts do, before they can use it for their own means. It would fund acts of unbearable evil. We can't let that happen."

Lhasa explained the wreck of the *Flor de la Mar*. He told me that he knew where the wreck was. He told me what it was worth. Then he told me that we were gathering a team that would retrieve the treasure, and that Marco was to join us. He warned me that the Japanese would reach Malaysia soon, and that we were running out of time.

We were racing the wildfire ourselves.

The American was correct. Marco was hard to miss. He was in a canoe just off shore in Lake Dian. It was a traditional dugout canoe, carved from a single tree. He wasn't standing *in* the canoe, but rather *on* it, his feet placed on the tops of each side so he was straddling the canoe. He was lithely balancing there as the canoe rolled with the waves. He was fishing with a delicate net, repeatedly throwing it out to the side then gathering it in, dumping one or two fish each time in the bottom of the canoe. Each time he threw the net, he skillfully spread it to its maximum size just before it hit the water. Then he rapidly gathered it in, all while balancing on the sides of the rocking canoe. His appearance was striking. He was medium height, well tanned, and obviously strong. His legs, arms, and chest rippled with sinewy muscles. He moved with efficiency, not wasting any energy on his motions. But a couple things stood out about Marco. His tattoos. He had a massive tattoo across his chest. It was a manta ray with its wings spread wide, as if it was swimming straight out of his chest. His black hair was closely cropped and trimmed far back on his temples. In its place he had a tattoo on each side. It was some kind of warrior motif, tribal, complex and severe.

"Try the other side!" Lhasa yelled.

Marco reacted immediately by flashing a bright white smile. "The last time I tried that it cost me a year of my life," he yelled.

Lhasa chuckled. "I'm going to need to take another one. Come with us. We have something much bigger than those minnows to fish for!"

Marco took a deep breath, rolled his head from side to side, and glanced skyward, his eyes closed as if he was deep in thought. Then he sighed, pulled in his net, and stowed it in the canoe. He lowered himself into the canoe, raised a paddle, and moved toward us with smooth, practiced motion. Again, he didn't waste a bit of motion or energy. It wasn't so much his tattoos, or his obvious strength, that set him apart. It was the way he moved. He reminded me of a powerful salmon moving along a rushing stream. If you've ever watched a big fish, you know how they move. They're sleek, efficient, and quiet. That was Marco.

"Bring those goldfish ashore and let's eat some dinner!" Lhasa yelled, as he began to gather driftwood for a fire. I cleared a spot in the sand about 30 yards from the shore, found a few rocks to make a fire ring, and gathered some twigs for kindling. I finished as Marco reached the shore. I helped him to pull his canoe up onto the sand then introduced myself.

"Good to meet you Hank." Marco shook my hand with a strong grip. "What were *you* doing when Lhasa convinced you to join him, huh?"

"Just trying to keep him above the ground."

Marco flashed his bright white teeth. "Well you've done a good job so far. But I don't think Lhasa needs much help to stay on the correct side of the dirt. Where you from?"

"I'm just a dirt kicker from a cattle ranch in Idaho. A cowboy. And a pilot."

"Hmmm. I see that Lhasa's net is getting much larger, to reach all the way to your cattle ranch in America. So what brings you to Kunming?"

"Whew. Long story," I said, as I removed my hat and to dry my brow. "I traveled to Hawaii to help on a cattle ranch. Before I knew it I was over the Himalayas in a broken airplane with Lhasa and three tons of food. Trying to get here. Didn't make it. Not originally. But it all worked out in the end."

"With Lhasa, it usually does," he said. "I hope you make it back to Hawaii sometime."

Lhasa arrived with an armful of driftwood. We piled it into the pit and I lit it with my old Zippo lighter. I wasn't a smoker, never would be. But I always carried a lighter. One never knew when one would be having a beach barbecue with a Tibetan missionary and a Filipino pearl diver. In China.

The fish that Marco caught wasn't bad. Actually it was quite tasty. There was plenty to go around, and after a while my belly was full. We boiled water for tea, which Lhasa provided from the pouch he always carried. It wasn't coffee but it tasted great. As I enjoyed it, I realized how many things I *didn't* know at this point. What Vietnam - Indochina - looked like. What the treasure looked like. How we would get it and who we would give it to. How long it would take. What it would cost. Lastly, I realized I had no idea of the price of tea. In China.

Yep, that made me chuckle. Just like you.

Chapter Eleven

That night we slept on the beach. It was a calm, cool night and the air was fresh and clear. Then a few clouds ambled over and a soft spring rain fell for an hour or so. Nothing to soak us, just enough to make us appreciate being alive. I watched the raindrops in the starlight and thought about home.

Back home in Idaho, I was always busy. As I've said, there was plenty of work to do on the ranch, and a full day away was a rare thing. But even a self-sufficient ranch needs supplies, so every couple of weeks I had a reason to drive into town to get them. Those were glorious days. The town of Stanley was almost an hour's drive from the ranch, along a dirt road that paralleled the Salmon River. It was beautiful country and an inspiring drive. Still is. Stanley was a small town, but it had a decent general store, a hotel, a saloon, and about fifty residents. One in particular was named Sara Hudson.

Yes, I looked forward to Stanley because Sara was there. Yes, I had a hankerin' for her. We were the same age; I got to know Sara our last month of high school. Her family moved to Stanley that spring to start a river rafting business in town. During the summer, tourists would arrive from Boise and Sun Valley for rafting, fishing, and hunting. Sara's family would haul them upstream then drop them in the river close to our ranch. The tourists would raft down to Stanley with Sara and her brothers as their guides then they would stay in town or thereabouts for a couple of weeks to fish, hunt, or daydream. Sara was a talented guide for rafting, fishing, and hunting. I was talented at the daydreaming part.

Sara was a pistol. She had older brothers and she knew how to hold her own. I liked that about her, but I also liked her smile and her sense of humor. She could brighten an entire room with her presence. Her green eyes and long dark hair captivated me. She was also strong. I found that out when I offered to help stack some firewood for her one afternoon. She took it as a challenge and nearly kicked my butt in the ensuing competition. She had me on the run and one more cord of wood would have killed me. I learned to respect her rowing-hardened muscles, and her ability to find a challenge in almost anything. But mostly, just listening to her at school or watching her around town, I learned to respect her humanity. Sara had qualities of character that I aspired to match. It didn't hurt that she was easy on the eyes, if you know what I mean. Problem was, I always got tongue-tied around her. I never quite knew the right thing to say. I figured she thought me to be just another dopey cowpoke.

I must have been thinking about Sara at the dinner table when my Mom asked me why I was putting gravy on my green beans. Busted. I explained my predicament. Good ole' Mom gave me some great advice. "Just make her a gift," she suggested. "Something unusual that she would really appreciate. She'll love the thoughtfulness."

"Mom," I argued, "I'm good at making fences. But I don't think she needs one."

"Use your imagination!" she responded. "Make her a nice piece of jewelry. Remember Mr. Davis from school? He makes silver and turquoise jewelry when he's not teaching. Grab some change from that rusted coffee can of yours and ask him for a lesson. He'd be pleased to have a student ask for help."

I didn't see how Mr. Davis would make me into an artist, but Sara was worth the risk. I made an unplanned trip into town the next day. With hat in hand I asked Mr. Davis to teach me how to make a silver and turquoise necklace.

"What's her name?" he asked with a grin.

"Sara Hudson."

"I see. Yes, I can help. But you need to do the work. I'll ride shotgun."

"Deal."

After much patience from Mr. Davis, several deep cuts to my hands and a sizeable blister from Mr. Davis's welder, I had a nice little pendant of silver, with a smooth turquoise stone in the middle. The pendant was shaped like a raindrop. I'll say that I intended it that way. Truth was, I was trying to make it in the shape of a crescent moon, but my ham hands weren't that skilled at such small work. I liked the raindrop much better anyhow.

Now I needed a chain. Mr. Davis didn't have one. Next lesson: braid a fine rope out of soft calf's leather. Once I mastered the braiding technique, the work went fairly fast. After a solid afternoon under Mr. Davis's watchful eye, I had my gift. The leather necklace was a dark, shiny brown. It matched Sara's hair. The pendant reminded me of a springtime rain. That soft kind of rain that just kisses the ground and turns the landscape vibrant and fresh.

I digress.

I took my handiwork home and displayed it at dinner time. Mom loved it. AJ coveted it. Now I just had to get up the nerve to give it to Sara. But first I needed the opportunity. When might I see her again? I had expended my "go to town free" card for the next week or so and I had chores to catch up on. So I figured I'd have to catch her one day on the river by our ranch, when she put in with a new crew of tourists. So how would a cowboy casually run into a beautiful river guide at just the right time? I pondered that challenge all evening. No gravy on my green beans this time, but a teaspoon of salt in my coffee was a good giveaway to AJ. She quietly enjoyed my predicament.

I finally came up with a plan worthy of General Custer. As it turned out, I should've paid more attention to that lesson in history class. Sara probably wished I had too. By the time I was done with my grand plan, to create a casual but carefully planned meeting with Sara, we were both soaking wet. In addition, I now owed her a raft. Long story. But it all worked out that evening around a nice warm campfire.

Chapter Twelve

The sun rose fitfully over Lake Dian, peeking in and out of a heavy set of clouds on the horizon. The light rain of the night before had stopped. The sky above was streaked with high, thin cirrus clouds which resembled a delicate veil in the still and quiet morning air. We had some tea and leftover fish for breakfast. Marco sold his canoe and net to a fisherman at the lake, who got a fire sale deal. We didn't need much money. Jack and I had both saved a good amount of our pay from the Parker Ranch, and we brought it with us. A little went a long way in Southeast Asia, where everything was inexpensive. Our burdens were, once again, light. We collected our few belongings and made our way back to Kunming, where we would arrange travel to Hai Phong and gather supplies for the journey. Lhasa wanted to return to the airfield to acquire three parachutes, which he felt we would need in Malaysia. Why parachutes? He didn't explain and I didn't ask. If we were actually going to use them at some point in this adventure, I just didn't want to know. My day started in a nice way with thoughts of Sara. I didn't want to ruin the mood.

The airfield was in the midst of its usual frenetic activity. We weaved through the chaos to find our newfound pilot friends. After a few minutes of small talk, I told them, pilot-to-pilot, that we needed to borrow a few parachutes for an unspecified mission. That got their interest, but they'd learned from experience that secrets in wartime should be kept close to the vest. They didn't ask for specifics. My new buddy Lieutenant Woodleaf walked me to a large hangar and helped me pick out three parachute packs from a stack of odds and ends in a storage cabinet. I was mighty grateful.

"By the way, Hank," Woodleaf said, "the mail just arrived." He nodded over his shoulder. "Be sure to check with the master at the airfield office. You might have something there, if they knew you were flying back and forth over The Hump."

"Much appreciated," I answered. "And thanks for your help. Stay safe!"

"You too pal. Be careful in Indo."

With that I grabbed the parachute packs and headed to the master's office. The possibility of letters from home was the most exciting thing that had happened in the last few weeks. Our challenge at the Mekong River paled in comparison. I've learned that life puts things in perspective that way, both over time and over distance. Still, I didn't want to get my hopes up. At this point the supply line from Idaho to Kunming seemed unimaginably long and terribly complicated. At the master's office I learned, to my surprise, that mail makes its way *anywhere* when someone sets their mind to it. The system wasn't a Pony Express, but it worked well enough. I had a pack of letters that had been forwarded from Hawaii, addressed simply "To: Hank Evans, Hump Pilot, Burma/China, c/o Jack Campbell". *Well don't that beat all.* I was tempted to sit down right there and read them, but I decided to save them for the train ride. It gave me something certain to look forward to on a trip full of uncertainty, if that makes any sense.

We picked up a few more supplies from various merchants around town then settled into a small establishment for dinner. The menu was in Chinese. Neither Marco nor I could read it. By now I'd been back and forth between Dinjan in India and Kunming in China. I had a little bit of time to explore each city, but I almost always ate at our camps. The camp cooks, usually local residents, prepared simple stuff for us. Fish, chicken, eggs, and rice. With some fresh fruits and vegetables. I stuck to the simple stuff, not wanting to experiment with my food. Lhasa ordered for us. The food arrived five minutes later. Except for the rice it was all new to me. You see, I wasn't very adventurous in my cuisine. I ate hot and sour soup for the first time. I can't tell you how great it tasted. I would've walked barefoot over barbed wire for another bowl full. I had never tasted those flavors before. I suddenly realized that I needed to try some more Chinese food.

When our server returned, I pointed to an item on the menu and asked what it was. Our server hesitated for a bit, then bowed and motioned for me to wait. She returned with the cook, who apparently spoke a bit of English. "Yes?" he asked.

I pointed again to an item on the menu. "Can you tell me what this is?"

"Ah." He nodded, talked with the server in Chinese for a moment, then answered "that is pork."

Okay, that might be good. "How about this please?" I asked, pointing to another listing.

Once again the cook discussed my question with the server, then answered. "That is pork also."

Lhasa began to chuckle. Marco just smiled.

Okay I get it. "I guess I'll have the pork."

"You want diced or not diced?"

"Hmmm. Diced please. Big diced." I motioned a large amount with my hands. I figured it would be easier to eat larger pieces with chopsticks. I was still a novice. He shrugged and walked back to the kitchen.

Turns out he asked me "spiced or not spiced", not "diced

or not diced". I misunderstood him. Even worse, I asked for big spicy. Now, "barely spicy" would have been enough for my taste, being that I mostly ate beef, potatoes, and green beans back home. I asked for *Chinese* extra spicy, which was strong enough to power a locomotive from here to Hai Phong.

The first bite put me into a state of painful denial. The second bite plum blew my ears off. I couldn't drink water fast enough. Lhasa and Marco were laughing so hard they couldn't breathe. Unfortunately neither could I.

"The burning will go away in a bit," Marco explained. "You just have to tough it out."

"Try standing on your head," Lhasa suggested.

"How's that gonna help?" I asked, gasping for air.

"It's not gonna help *you*, but it's gonna be great for *us*!"

More laughter from Marco.

I wasn't sure it was ever going to stop. Both the pain, and the laughter. But sure enough, after fifteen minutes or so the pain faded away and I was myself again. Lhasa and Marco had had their laugh. I would even the score sooner or later. The more challenging life becomes, the more you need to laugh. There were challenges on the way, sure enough.

Chapter Thirteen

The new day dawned to a steady spring rain, the sky overcast and grey. We packed our gear, donned some light rain jackets, and headed out on foot. We grabbed some rice cakes and dried fish on the way, but I'll admit I was still craving last night's hot and sour soup. Without the spicy pork. The Kunming railway station was a mile to the east, just outside the old walled city in the more modern part of town. The city had long ago grown beyond its 14th century walls, but the old fortifications were suddenly valuable again. As the Japanese Army advanced, Kunming was being prepared as the national redoubt - the emergency capital of China if the government had to retreat this far to the west. The barriers would help to defend the government, and the nation's treasures, if the Japanese Army wasn't stopped. They were a grim reminder of the gravity of war.

We arrived at the station twenty minutes later. The Kunming - Hai Phong train was waiting at the tracks. Even then, in 1940, it looked old. It was a narrow gauge train - the rails were much closer together than the trains I knew back home. Lhasa explained that we would traverse several extreme mountain ranges and the narrow gauge made it easier for the train to maneuver. That knowledge got my morning heart beating a little faster. Turns out we were about to make the most challenging rail journey in the world. I assumed we'd have a nice sightseeing trip across a long expanse of rice paddies. But before we got to them, we would travel through 155 tunnels and across 107 bridges on the China side alone. Eight hundred Chinese workers died building one structure, the Wujiazhai Bridge over the Sicha River. Over 12,000 construction workers lost their lives by the time the railway was completed in 1910. The vast majority were Chinese laborers, working hard to earn a bit of sustenance for their families. Most were buried where they fell, often alongside the tracks.

We boarded the train and found ourselves an empty row of seats in one of the passenger cars. The train was eight cars long, an even mix of cargo and passenger. The cargo cars brought up the rear. The passenger cars were all the same - there was no notion of first class on this route. Each car had an aisle running lengthwise, with one seat on the left side and two seats on the right of each row. Lhasa, Marco and I found an empty row and sat ourselves down for the thirty hour trip to Hai Phong. I took the single seat; Marco and Lhasa sat together. The seats weren't comfortable, but at this point I didn't mind. The thrill of the trip, combined with the anticipation surrounding my satchel of letters from home, created a feeling that I rarely felt on the ranch. It was a level of excitement which was now a daily constant, and which seemed to surround Lhasa like a cloud of mosquitoes on a summer's evening. I suspected that this aura followed Lhasa wherever he went, regardless of the day's activities. I also hoped that I never grew immune to it. It was the raw feeling of being alive, mixed with the certain knowledge that you're doing the right thing, and doing it by the seat of your pants.

Dang I felt so alive it was almost killing me.

We started off soon enough, the locomotive belching black coal smoke as she built up speed. At first I was sure I could *walk* to Hai Phong faster. But we eventually hit a good pace. The rhythm of the rails and the swaying of the car put me into a nice little nap. Until the conductor blared his loud steam whistle, which I mistook for the *Engine Fire* alarm back on the wounded C-47. I snapped awake in confusion, immediately searched for the aircraft's instrument panel while grasping for the controls, then realized I had been dreaming. I exhaled a long breath then looked to Marco and Lhasa with a shrug. They were asleep, but I was now wide awake.

I gazed out the window for a long while. Then I surveyed my fellow passengers. Like the airfield in Kunming, the train held a broad cross section of humanity. At the station I noticed several Chinese Army soldiers. They appeared to have their own car. The civilian passengers in my car represented many nationalities and social classes, all trying to occupy themselves on a long journey. There were a number of families with children, most of which were young enough to sit on their parents' laps. One girl in particular caught my eye. She was roaming cautiously up and down the aisle, surveying the passengers as I was. She was Chinese, about five years old, with short-cropped hair, a plain pink dress, and a pensive expression. Her hands were clasped behind her back, as if she were an official apprising her passengers. She saw me, froze, and then broke into a subtle smile. Then she cautiously brought her hands forward and showed me a small wooden toy train engine. I nodded my approval. She grinned then ran back to her parents in the front of our car.

I needed to stretch my legs, so I took a walk to the back of the car. Each car had a narrow sliding door at both ends, which one could use to enter adjoining cars. I stepped out the rear door into the open air between cars, where there was a platform that was big enough for two adults. There was another passenger there already, an Anglo that I had seen at the station.

"Mind if I join you?" I asked.

"Please do." He had a British, or Irish, or Scottish, accent. I wasn't good at identifying them. I had learned in Kunming that it was best not to try. It usually started a long discussion about which was best. A discussion that persisted like the surf in Hawaii.

"How's the ride for you?" I inquired.

"Happily uneventful. Although I don't expect it to stay that way. How far are you traveling?"

"All the way to Hai Phong."

"Interesting. What's in Hai Phong?"

"Some urgent business," which I now knew was the special code for confidentiality.

"I understand," he nodded. "I'll tell you what. Since you haven't told me things that you know I shouldn't know, I'm going to tell you something that I think you should know for your own safety. Make sense?"

I figured the only proper answer to that question was a positive nod. Words escaped me.

"If you're going to Hai Phong, you're in for a world of hurt. Have you heard the latest from Guangxi?" He noticed my blank expression. "It's a Chinese city just this side of the border with Indochina. It's under attack by the Japanese Army. They're trying to cut the rail lines from Indo to China, and one of the routes goes through Guangxi. They've been quite successful so far. They're also moving to the west, to cut *this* rail line at Longzhou. It's the only other supply line from Indo to China. The Chinese Army blokes on this train are reinforcements to defend *this* rail line. They're headed to Longzhou. In case you didn't notice, there aren't near enough of them. You don't want to go that far unless you're a bullet collector. You follow?"

I exhaled a long breath. "Yes, I follow. Thanks for the advice." I extended my hand. "My name's Hank."

He shook my hand. "Keast. Paul Keast. Lieutenant in His Majesty's Service. Army, to be specific. Irish, to be boastful. On leave at the moment, at least as far as you know."

"Well," I said, "my friends and I need to get to the coast. Indo is between us and it."

"Well I'll tell you what. Just between friends, the war in Europe is a real mess. France isn't going to last three more weeks against Germany. When France falls, the war is over for them. When the war is over for them, they're going to give up defending Indochina from the Japanese Army. You Yanks aren't at war with Japan. But Indochina is going to be a dangerous obstacle course for you and your mates. You'd be better to find another way to the coast. It's about to get downright nasty around here."

"Well, Paul, I appreciate the update. You convinced me. How can I return the favor?"

"Tell your President to help us Brits. We're not going to last much longer. We need, as you say, a big stick."

"I hear you," I said. "Where I come from, we help a friend in need. If America's like Idaho, we'll be in this soon enough. I just don't know where."

"You from Idaho? I hear you've got potatoes there."

"They grow like weeds."

"Paradise."

I left Lieutenant Keast on the platform and returned to Marco and Lhasa. They were awake now, playing a game of cards. I explained, in a hushed tone, my conversation with Keast. The Japanese Army wildfire was rapidly closing around us. It was even clearer that we needed to get to

Malaysia quickly.

"Here's the plan," said Lhasa. "We're getting off this train at the next station. Then we're finding another way to the coast."

"I have two issues with that," I countered, in a moment of complete clarity. "First, let's forget about the coast of Indochina. Let's think bigger. Let's get ourselves closer to Malaysia. The Japanese are moving too fast. Second," I nodded toward the young girl with the toy train, "I have friends on this train. I'm not leaving them until I know they're safe."

Marco displayed his usual smile. The one that meant he was thinking as he was smiling. "I understand, my friend," he said. "I'll ride this train as long as you. Then, we need airplane."

"From where?" Lhasa asked.

"Easy," I realized. "From Jack Campbell. He owes me. Besides, it's time for him to join our party. We need his help."

"Okay," said Lhasa. "At the next station, during our stop, we'll get a message to Jack. Then we'll ride on until you say we're getting off."

"How do we reach Jack from here?" I asked.

"Remember the early warning radio network here in China?" Lhasa answered. "The one that noticed our landing at the Mekong River and alerted the countryside? We'll use it to relay a simple radio message to Dinjan *and* Kunming." He paused. "If Jack's still sick, he'll be in Dinjan. If he's well, he'll be flying again between Dinjan and Kunming. I just hope he's well."

"It doesn't matter if he's well or not. If we ask him, he'll come." I responded confidently. "Jack's as tough as a brick outhouse." Blank stares. "Jack's as tough as nails," I corrected. "And the message is simple. *Need airplane. Need Jack. Longzhou. Bring guns, bandages, and hot and sour soup.*"

I felt so *alive*.

At the next stop, Lhasa, Marco, and I jumped off the train and entered the modest station. We had a good hour to kill while they refueled and watered the engine. Lhasa talked at length to the station's radio operator, who then transmitted our message to Jack via the ad hoc early warning network. The message would hopscotch its way to Dinjan and Kunming.

Marco and I grabbed some food and water for the next stage of our train journey, all the while listening to news updates from the station's shortwave radio, which were being broadcast over a loudspeaker in the station. They were in Chinese, but Marco understood most of the updates. He had a grim look on his face as he translated the important points. "Your Irish friend was right. The Japanese Army has invaded Guangxi. They destroyed the rail line there. They're moving west to Longzhou to attack this rail line. The Chinese Army says they can stop them. But the citizens of Longzhou are in a panic. The radio says that many are running to the surrounding mountains."

A quick survey of the passengers in the station confirmed the grim news. Most were in worried conversation. Some were crying. There were several heated discussions, no doubt debating whether to stay on to Longzhou or disembark now. Many were deciding on the latter. The girl with the toy train was studying her parents. They were talking quietly, and then seemed to reach a conclusion. They boarded the train with their daughter. It was apparent that they were staying on, at least to Longzhou. We boarded as well.

Our car was only half full now, the missing passengers obviously deciding to end their journey here. I waited anxiously for the train to move. The minutes became twenty, then thirty. My impatience was increasing rapidly. Then two Chinese Army troop trucks suddenly appeared in a cloud of dust, speeding down the road to the station. They drove alongside the tracks and skidded to a halt beside the train. A dozen soldiers jumped from the back of each truck, grabbed their weapons and gear, and boarded the train. I figured they were reinforcements for the troops already on the train. The troop cars were apparently full. The new soldiers split themselves between two passenger cars, including ours. They looked grim, determined, and young. I *was* grim, determined and young. Birds of a feather are worth two in the bush. Is that how the saying goes? What the hell, I couldn't remember. I had bigger things on my mind, including a little girl and her family, who were very likely heading into harm's way.

We finally left the station for Longzhou and for all the uncertainty that surrounded it. It was late in the day now, the shadows growing long across the landscape, my worries growing long across my mind. If, and when, Jack received our message, it would take him three or four hours to fly to Longzhou, assuming he started in Kunming. Even if our message reached him quickly, he wouldn't fly at night. Best case, he would depart Kunming in the morning and reach Longzhou by midday. Barring any delays, we would arrive in the morning, a few hours before Jack. If Jack didn't get our message, or couldn't get to Longzhou, then we were on our own to get through Indochina to the coast, then on to Malaysia. Traveling through Indo on the ground seemed dangerous now. We were running out of time. We needed Jack. And an airplane. We had a train, some rice cakes, three parachutes, forty Chinese soldiers, and guns. Plenty of guns. Well, the soldiers had the guns. But I figured if the manure hit the fan, they'd share. I was a terrible shot with a pistol, but pretty good with a Winchester rifle. I could also rope, ride, tame broncos, make jewelry, and fly a plane. My life skills were mostly worthless now. But one out of five ain't bad. And don't forget, I had *the fire*, and *the faith*.

But faith in what? Lhasa? Marco? God's perfection? My imperfections? It was too much for me to figure out. It made me weary. I finally settled on a simple, profound faith in God, and left it at that. Even so, it was enough to lift a good sized burden from my shoulders. I sat back to ride the rails.

Chapter Fourteen

"Jack! Jack!"

Jack Campbell awoke from a troubled sleep, to the insistent pleas of his Chinese aircraft mechanic. Jack had arrived in Kunming the night before, on his first *over the hump* flight from Dinjan since falling ill with Yellow Fever. It was a difficult trip. He was still weak, often dizzy, and fought off vertigo three times during the flight. The weakness was one thing. The vertigo was the worst. He repeatedly felt as if the plane was rolling to the left or right, when in fact it was flying straight and level. He had to override his sense of balance and trust his instruments, lest he put the plane into a diving spin. This required intense concentration, resulting in nausea, which was mentally and physically exhausting. He landed hard, fell into his bunk at sunset, slept fitfully, only to be awakened at early dawn. He felt weak and shaky.

"What is it?" he asked, wiping the sleep from his eyes.

"Sorry to wake you boss," his mechanic Kam replied. He surveyed Jack. "Sheesh, you look like a flat tire." He passed a transcribed note from the base radio operator. "Message from your friend Hank. Says urgent."

Jack scanned it quickly. "Is this a joke?"

Kam shrugged.

"Have you read this?"

Kam hesitated then nodded sheepishly.

"Am I reading this right? Hank wants me, an airplane, guns, bandages, *and hot and sour soup?* In Longzhou? *Immediately?*"

"Yes boss."

"Am I dreaming?"

"No, boss."

"Then I must be delirious," he sighed. "This is an impossible request." He stared at Kam with bloodshot eyes. "Where am I going to get hot and sour soup at this hour?"

Kam studied Jack for a moment then replied with a sigh of resignation, "I'll gas up the Goose. You get some tea, boss. Strong."

Chapter Fifteen

March 12, 1940. Son I don't know exactly where you are right now. I'm sure it's exactly where you want to be. I'm proud of you for having the courage to take on this adventure. You've always been good at finishing whatever you put your mind to. Sounds like you did some good work in Hawaii. Now those pineapple punchers have a <u>real</u> cattle outfit to take care of! I'll confess I don't totally understand what's happening now in China and thereabouts. If you and Jack see a need there, I believe there's a need, and I believe you can fill it. I know you'll be careful. I know those folks are lucky to have you. You've grown into a fine man. You're filling some tough boots. Your Ma and I miss you fierce and even AJ admitted that she wishes you were here. Not much going on around here. Ranch is doing really well. Weather's been great. AJ took a liking to a young man from Stanley. Not a bad fella. Your Ma likes this new singer named Frank Sinatra. He's on the radio all the time now. Not bad if you're okay with that city singing. But that guy couldn't play a guitar to save himself. Flash in the pan if you ask me. There's a new show on the radio called Truth Or Consequences. Fun to listen to on the porch in the evenin. I hear tell that the war in Europe is getting mighty serious, and that it might spill over into Asia. You be careful out there. Hey the White Sox and Cubs are playing on the TV next month! Now they've even got baseball games on that thing. Might need to get one some year, but I can't figure how they get those big players to fit on that tiny screen. You take care now. Love Dad.

March 12. Hank I miss you so! I hope you're eating right and taking good care of yourself. You tell that Jack fella to keep you safe. There's some leftover cornbread sittin here since you're not home to finish it off. Seems strange. But I know you're doing what you want to do. I'm proud of you for being so brave. Hey Sara Hudson stopped by the other day to say hello. She's back from Denver now helping her family again with their rafting. Hank she sure is a pretty girl. She had a gleam in her eye for you. Do the right thing out there and come on home when you're ready. I can't wait to hear more about your travels. Write us as soon as you can. Stay safe. I love you. Mom

P.S. Hank get your cowboy butt back home. You have chores to do. The fence line ain't gonna fix itself. Love you. AJ

Dang. I forgot how much I missed simple things. Sittin' on the front porch in the evening listening to a baseball game on the radio. The smell of fresh cornbread. AJ's mischievous smile. A hug from my Mom. The smell of my Dad's jacket – that mixture of hay and alfalfa and old engine oil. And Sara Hudson's back home? *Don't that beat all.* I dropped the letters in my lap and just stared out the window for a long time. I lost track of the bridges and switchbacks and tunnels, drowning in the scent of alfalfa on a summer's day. How is it that our brain can remember smells like that so well? It all seemed so real, like I could just stretch out from this seat, stand up, and shake Dad's firm, calloused hand. And give Mom a proper hug. I was here in China, where I wanted to be, sure enough. But I'll tell you what. Home was in Idaho, plain as day.

Kam dutifully topped off the fuel tanks of Jack's Beechcraft Model 18A twin engine float plane, which he had nicknamed the "Goose". It was the only float plane Kam had ever worked on. Since it could fly *and* land on water, he felt the nickname was appropriate. The plane had been hammered in and out over the past two years, and had seen a lot of miles between Montana, Hawaii, and China. But it had two reliable and powerful 350 horsepower engines, could carry eight passengers comfortably, and could fly 1,200 miles at 200 knots. It was a *racegoose*. Jack loved to fly it.

Jack walked across the field toward Kam, carrying two cups of strong tea. He handed one to Kam. "How's she look?"

"Like she shouldn't fly. But she always looks that way. Most everything's okay. Compass still sticky. Haven't fixed. Radio works but don't forget - shut off every fifteen minutes, or it will overheat and blow breaker. Guns don't work though. You need them fixed."

"Kamshaft," Jack said sternly, "The Goose doesn't have guns. Never had guns. How could they be broken, unless you added broken guns to my plane, which will really piss me off!"

"That's what I'm saying."

"Saying what? You added broken guns to my plane?" Jack asked incredulously.

"No, no, boss. I just reminding you that the Goose doesn't have any."

"Doesn't have *any* guns, or doesn't have any *broken* guns?"

"Boss you're confusing me. It doesn't have any guns at all."

"I like it that way."

"But I think you might need guns in Longzhou," Kam suggested.

"I'm not bombing the Japanese Army. I don't plan to dogfight with Japanese fighters. I'll simply land, get the guys, and take off."

"Sounds very simple."

"I thought so too."

"Simple things go bad all the time. Think of apple. Simple thing. But goes bad fast once you take a bite."

Jack opened his mouth to respond, then closed it. It was often difficult to argue with Kam's wisdom. Jack paused and studied him for a moment, then took a deep breath and exhaled slowly to clear his mind. "I understand Kam. I'll be careful. I'm not planning on a fight. Just a *flight*. This isn't a military plane. It's not a target."

"A fat goose is big target in hunting season. Doesn't matter if it has symbol on wing or not. It's gonna be hunting season in Longzhou."

"I'm taking a couple rifles and some handguns. We'll be fine."

"You're a terrible shot. Well anyway I put firepower in copilot seat."

"What?" Jack walked to the plane, stood on the starboard float and looked in the cockpit window. "Firecrackers? You gave me a box of firecrackers?" Jack grinned. "Kam, I didn't get you anything."

"You'll appreciate it boss. Even *wolves* are afraid of firecrackers."

Chapter Sixteen

March 9, 1940. Hey there Cowboy! Just wanted to say a quick hello before your Dad drops this pack of letters at the Post Office. I'm back in town, hopefully to stay. Sure is nice to see your family again. They're kind people. Things went well in Denver, but it's great to be back. I'm running the river again when I have time, but I really want to use the nursing skills I learned. I'm hoping to help Doc Donner whenever I can. Pretty quiet in his office though. Not enough injured people around when you're not here. Hey that reminds me – you still owe me a raft. But Hank I really love the silver raindrop pendant. Reminds me of the water I poured out of my boots when you dunked me in the cold, cold river. Remember the campfire afterward? That was a nice way to warm up. Stay safe out there and come home when you're done. We'll make a fire. I've got a couple of matches left. I'll try to keep 'em dry. See you around, Cowboy. Warm Wishes, Sara

"What's her name?" Marco asked. He surprised me. I was glancing out the train window again, thinking about Sara Hudson and a campfire. Was it *that* obvious?

"Sara," I answered. "She's back home in Idaho."

"Hmm," he nodded. "Why did you leave her?"

"Well," I answered, "she left for Denver to go to school. Denver's a fair distance from my ranch. She planned to be gone for about a year. She left a few months before I met Jack, who talked me into joining him on what became *this* journey. I'm not sure I would've left if Sara was still there, but we had really just started dating. But she left, then I left, everything just worked out, and here I am." I paused. "And there she is."

"Well, I think it's pretty simple," Marco said. "We get to Longzhou, meet your friend Jack, fly to Malaysia, get the treasure, get it to safe hands, help a few folks, then you go home to Sara. She'll wait, right?"

"Well when you make it that simple, I'm sure she will."

Jack sped toward Longzhou in the Goose, pushing his maximum speed at an altitude of ten thousand feet. It would be a two and a half hour flight. It was nine in the morning. There had been a heavy fog at sunrise, and he had to wait nearly three hours for it to burn away. The delay gave him time to drink a few cups of tea and have a solid breakfast, which diminished his symptoms enough to put his mind at ease.

The fog's remnants made navigation more challenging than usual. Jack could see occasional glimpses of the ground, but not enough to help him reliably follow the railroad tracks from Kunming to Longzhou. He used a combination of his compass, which was a sticky and not completely reliable, and his radio direction finder. The direction finder was simple in concept – one tuned the receiver to a particular transmitter, then the finder indicated the direction of that station. In practice though, the signal was easily obstructed by mountains, storms, and other atmospheric phenomena, so at a long distance it tended to fade in and out. But within a hundred miles, at a decent altitude, in good conditions, the DF was quite accurate. Jack tuned it to the Longzhou transmitter. Predictably the signal was intermittent. He would get a better fix as he approached Longzhou. He could afford a bit of course slop, but at the same time, he wanted to take the most direct route. Hank's request seemed urgent, and every minute was important.

Jack scanned the instruments, made a quick adjustment to the engine fuel mixture to save a bit of fuel and keep the spark plugs clean, then reached over and opened the box of fireworks in the copilot's seat. It was a nice assortment of the big boomers that Jack loved. Not the puny poppers that made their way to the States. These blasters could strip the paint from a barn at fifty yards. He decided to light them as soon as possible, Japanese Army or not.

Longzhou was two hours away. The tension in our train car increased a notch with each clack of the undercarriage. The Chinese soldiers weren't affected. They merely dozed, or played games of dice or cards. They were resting while they could. Made sense to me. But the civilians were another story. There was much pacing, much window-glancing, and much watch-checking. We all imagined the Japanese Army speeding across the country to attack Longzhou, when it could take days or even weeks.

In fact, it only took hours. The Japanese Army was in a frenzy. They had been held at bay by the fierce Chinese resistance at Guangxi. But once Guangxi fell, the Japanese had some time to make up. Longzhou was a key part of their master plan. They weren't messing around. Over the next month they pushed through the countryside toward Longzhou like a hot knife through butter. The Chinese Army was spread too thin. With virtually no opposition, the Japanese were moving faster than the news could keep up. The update we received at the last station was already well out-of-date.

I walked to the front of the car and stepped outside to the platform between cars. The wind was brisk – colder than it was yesterday. I turned up my jacket collar and buried my hands in my pockets. I looked overhead to a patchy sky that was filling with dark clouds. The view ahead of the train looked more ominous. There was a storm building above the mountain range to our south. It stretched across the horizon to the east and west. The passing trees were bowing to a strong wind from the north. I hoped that this meant the storm was moving with the wind, toward the south, as well. I was wrong. The cold north wind was colliding with a moist warm front moving north from the Gulf of Tonkin. The unstable mix of cold dry air and warm moist air brewed a wild storm, full of rain, hail, and gusting winds. The two air masses were fighting above the range to the north of Longzhou. We would traverse that range using the last few bridges and tunnels of our trip. The weather didn't pose a problem for the train. But it would certainly pose a problem for Jack, if in fact he was on his way to Longzhou.

I stepped back inside the train, caught Marco's attention, and motioned for him and Lhasa to join me. They arose from their seats and walked back outside to the platform with me. It was a tight squeeze but Lhasa was small. "Storm over Longzhou," I said above the noise of the train. "Looks nasty. Not good flying weather. It seems to be building, but I'm hoping its heading south."

"How will we know?" Marco asked.

"If the wind shifts to the north, we'll know the storm is moving toward us. The wind shift usually happens just ahead of the storm front. We'll watch the trees – it's the best way to measure the wind from a moving train." Marco and Lhasa nodded. We stepped back inside, one more thing to think about.

The Japanese Army approached Longzhou in three columns of trucks and light armor. They didn't bother to disguise their movement. They didn't expect much resistance. They had air cover in the form of two fighter aircraft, in case the Chinese surprised them. Guangxi had been a pain in the behind for the Japanese Army. They had orders to make an example of Longzhou. They were ready.

Chapter Seventeen

Jack was reliving the vertigo he had experienced the day before, fighting the sensation that the Goose was rolling to the left and the right. Then he checked his attitude indicator and realized that the Goose *was* rolling to the left and the right. Until now he'd had a fair tailwind, but the wind direction had shifted and now he was fighting an unusual mix of turbulence. He immediately knew the cause, for the line of clouds ahead was a dead giveaway. It formed at the demarcation between two different masses of air, indicated by a stark wall of dark clouds. The clouds extended to the left and the right across the entire southern horizon. Anvil clouds, the hallmark of thunderstorms, towered high into the air behind the demarcation.

The Goose had two strong engines and a tough frame. It could handle a storm. But the gusts of a severe thunderstorm were more than its match. Plus, the storm was apparently masking the Longzhou radio beacon signal, as Jack's DF had lost its fix. From his last waypoint, he knew he was two hundred miles - about an hour - from Longzhou. He guessed the soup began about fifty miles - fifteen minutes - ahead. A prudent pilot would turn ninety degrees to the left or right, and land at the nearest airstrip. A foolish pilot would try to climb over the storm and weave the thunderheads, then pray for a break in the clouds before running low on fuel. A desperate pilot would descend below the cloud deck, push ahead into the storm, and muscle their way to a landing strip.

His decision made, Jack descended to five thousand feet, jammed the throttles to full power, tightened his harness, and pushed straight ahead.

Lieutenant-General Akito Humaki of the Imperial Japanese Army surveyed the terrain ahead. It was as he expected – the transition from mountains to foothills then a valley that held the city of Longzhou. No surprise there. But the weather ahead was decidedly *not* what he expected. He and his men were in for a cold, wet time. No worries in that respect. But it did mean that his fighter air cover couldn't stay with them for much longer. The storm would render them ineffective at some point. No matter. The Chinese were in for a world of hurt, air cover or not. Payback for the men he lost at Guangxi. Insurance against a demotion for delaying the completion of his mission. He would accomplish this one. Quickly.

The wind shifted. The rain started. Our train plowed ahead toward the lion's den. It was only midday but the dark clouds covered the countryside with a twilight cast. The train was climbing now, into the last range before Longzhou. A couple more bridges and one tunnel, then we would make a short downhill run into the city. Lhasa walked down the aisle and spoke with the apparent senior officer of the Chinese Army soldiers riding in our car. He wanted them to know that we were on their side, and would help if we could. We packed our gear. There was nothing to do now but wait. We were as ready as we could be.

The storm hit with full force over the mountain range to the north of Longzhou. The temperature dropped quickly and snow covered the range's upper elevations. The foothills were hit with a driving rain, pushed by a gusting, restless wind. The cloud ceiling descended to 2,000 feet, pressing in on the landscape. The mountain streams grew with the cold runoff, the excess washing down the mountainside in a thousand different gullies. Lightning danced within the clouds, the booming thunder echoing from hill to hill. The remaining residents of Longzhou sought shelter in their homes, shops, and schools. Those that had evacuated in advance of the Japanese Army's arrival wished they were back at home, out of the storm. They made the best of their situation there in the hills, squeezed between two calamities.

Jack was in the thick of the storm now. He descended to 1,500 feet to stay below the cloud ceiling. His DF was still intermittent, wandering across a broad swath of bearing. He couldn't rely on it. He used his compass instead to lead him on an easterly course, figuring he would soon intersect the Kunming railroad. At that point he would simply turn south and follow the tracks to Longzhou. He scanned the horizon continuously for the tracks, the rain pelting his windshield and the wind buffeting the Goose. He'd flown in worse wind. His main concerns were getting to Longzhou as quickly as possible, navigating the mountain range to the south, and avoiding the Japanese Army. If necessary he could land almost anywhere. A lake, a rice paddy, a road, a fallow field. Any would be suitable. Every few minutes he selected a new potential landing site just in case. Once he overflew it, he selected another somewhere ahead. Good practice but taxing. His eyes were strained and his arms tired from fighting the gusts. He could really use a copilot.

The box of firecrackers rode silently on, patiently awaiting a lit match.

Chapter Eighteen

March 7, 1940. Dear Hank, Thank you for the wonderful letters. I sure have enjoyed them! I love hearing so much about Hawaii. I still can't imagine flying over the Pacific Ocean. It makes my feet tingle just thinking about it. But it sounds so beautiful. By now you're probably in China. Hard to believe. Your Grandpa and I had always planned to travel somewhere exotic, but we never dreamed of going that far. It makes me smile just picturing you in such places. Remember them well so you can describe them to me when you get home! It sounds like you're on quite a mission. I'm not sure what it's all about, but I am sure you'll find success. Always remember that life is difficult, but God's wish for us is simple: just love your neighbor. You have a wonderful opportunity to meet a great number of new ones! Make the most of it. I wish your Grandpa were still here to share all of this with you, but I know I'll see him soon enough. We sure had a lot of good times. Remember how he wanted to rename our dairy ranch Dairy Air (laugh)...

...(groan). How many times had I heard the Dairy Air joke?

...I do miss your Grandpa. But I'm doing okay, just taking life a day at a time. Your parents are taking great care of me. AJ makes sure I have enough yarn for my knitting. The ranch is doing well in your Dad's capable hands. There are a bunch of new healthy calves running around. I just pray that this conflict in Europe comes to an end soon. It seems to be a sickness that's spreading with each day. I started reading a good new book called Gone with the Wind. It's about the Civil War, but it seems...

Suddenly an aircraft flew over the train, low and loud. It had the unmistakable sound of a twin engine bird, but I couldn't identify it by ear alone. Several passengers screamed. I shoved Grandma's letter into my pack and looked quickly out the right side window. Marco jumped to the window on the left. The Chinese soldiers were now wide awake. A pair moved swiftly to the doors on each end of the car and stepped outside, looking for the aircraft. They yelled chopped commands to each other, which I couldn't understand. I peered through the driving rain hoping for a glimpse of the plane, but it had passed us by. Would it circle back? It had to have been Jack.

There was a flash of lightning in the far clouds to the right. In its glare I caught sight of a twin engine float plane, flying low and fast toward the west. I knew it well. It was the Goose. I turned to tell Lhasa and Marco, when gunfire broke out on both ends of our car, almost simultaneously. I jumped up and ran to the front of the car, pushed through the door to the outside, and yelled to the soldiers "No! Friend! Friend!"

Then I realized they weren't shooting at Jack.

"Not friend!" one of the soldiers yelled, as he pointed to the left. His partner was shooting into the air. I looked where he was aiming, just as a Japanese Zero fighter plane screamed over the train, apparently in hot pursuit of the Goose. It was so low I involuntarily ducked. I turned to the right and watched Jack climb rapidly into the low clouds as the Zero closed on him. "Good idea," I thought. It was his only hope. The Zero had a huge 900 horsepower engine and could fly at a speed of almost 300 knots. It was fast, much faster than the Goose. It could out-climb, out-dive, and turn tighter than the Goose. It had guns designed to shred an enemy aircraft. Or a ship, or a train. A second Zero passed overhead just as quickly, a bit higher than his buddy but heading the same direction in a hurry. Jack had two of these guys to deal with. Damn! I felt totally useless. Then I snapped out of it and realized we had to do something. Jack had made us aware of the Zeros, before they surprised the train. Now he was taking them on a wild Goose chase. No pun intended. I'm sure they felt they could deal with Jack quickly, then circle back to the train at their leisure. I knew we didn't have much time.

The Chinese soldiers started yelling at each other. Whatever they were saying sounded like one word repeated. Lhasa finally yelled to me, "Tunnel!"

Yes! The two soldiers in the front entered the car ahead, undoubtedly making their way forward to the train engine to tell the engineer to put the spurs to her. I glanced around the car. The remaining soldiers were at work. They were ready for a fight. But if the Zeros returned, it would be a short one. The civilians showed a variety of emotions, ranging between stoic resistance and panic. The girl with the toy train and her family were somewhere in the middle. They were huddled together. The parents were both displaying a brave face for their kids. The girl looked over her mother's shoulder at me. Her eyes held fear and courage at the same time. I gave her a reassuring smile and mouthed "It's okay." I doubt she could read my words, but she blinked then gave me a weak smile of confidence. Then she buried her head in her mother's shoulder. What would I have done if I were her age?

Lieutenant Paul Keast entered our car from the one behind ours. "Hank," he said, "these chaps are planning to get us to the tunnel ahead then stop the train inside."

"That's what I thought," I responded. "When we get

there, I figure these guys will go to work." I motioned to the soldiers. "So why don't we get the civilians to a safe place."

"The tunnel *is* the safest place. Plus the train will provide shelter. Just keep everyone on the train."

Made sense.

"Then let's you and me take a look outside," he continued. "I've made this trip once before. If I remember, this is the last tunnel before Longzhou. We should be able to see the city from the far side of the tunnel. It's a good view of the entire valley. We'll see if the enemy has friends in the neighborhood. I suspect they do. Let's find ourselves some binoculars."

I could feel the train accelerating, slowly but surely. One of the soldiers from the engine returned to our car and held five fingers to his colleagues. Five minutes. Five minutes to the tunnel, and to safety. Five minutes for Jack to run. And to not be killed.

Chapter Nineteen

Jack was irritated with himself. Irritated that he hadn't allowed Kam to install broken guns on the Goose. Then fix them. Now he was being chased by two Japanese Zeros that would most definitely outrun him and shoot him down, and he had no defense.

A few minutes before, he had finally found the railroad tracks, turning south to follow them to Longzhou. Then he spied the train ahead. It was easy to find – it was belching a long trail of black smoke as it ran its engine hard to make the uphill grade. Jack leveled out and headed for the train. Then he saw the Zeros. They were coming in from the east - from the left – taking their time as they reconnoitered the area. They were looking first for enemy troops and planes, but Jack knew that once they established superiority they would focus on the easiest target – the train. He assumed Hank was on board, but it really didn't matter. He couldn't allow the Zeros to attack a civilian train. He had no armament. All he could do was distract them. But first he needed to warn the train of their presence. He pulled back the wheel to put the Goose into a steep climb, entered the clouds, then leveled off. He checked his compass heading and made a careful ninety degree turn to the left. He was now heading toward the Zeros and away from the train, and should be higher than the fighters as they were flying below the clouds. He counted off ten seconds, then rolled hard over to the left and dove toward the ground. As soon as he exited the clouds he leveled off toward the west, and was now heading again for the train. The Zeros weren't ahead of him; he hoped they were behind. He zigzagged so he could check to his rear. He saw them immediately. They were less than a minute behind him. They had to have seen him – he was a bright shiny object much more exciting than a lumbering train. Would they take the bait?

Jack descended to two hundred feet and lined up on the car in the middle of the train. He flew over it at full power, making enough noise to wake a grizzly in the dead of winter. He then flew straight on, away from the train as fast as he could go. He counted off forty seconds, zigzagged again, and saw the lead Zero chasing him. Perfect. He pulled back hard on the wheel and climbed again for the clouds. Once he was in the soup he leveled off, checked his compass, and made another careful turn, this time a full 180 degrees. Now he was heading back toward the train, but fully hidden in the clouds. The Zeros wouldn't know which way he had gone. He hoped they thought him a coward; thought that he would run hard to the west, away from Longzhou and the train.

Running was the farthest thing from his mind.

Thanks to Jack's timely diversion, we made it to the tunnel with the train stopped safely inside. During the five minute trip, we'd perfected a basic plan under the Chinese soldiers' guidance. The passengers disembarked and moved toward the last three cars. A handful of the soldiers deployed themselves on both ends of the tunnel to keep watch. The remainder split into two teams. One team exited the far end of the tunnel and spread across the hillside toward Longzhou, looking on foot for Japanese soldiers. The other team uncoupled the last three cars from the train, loaded their gear onto the forward cars, and directed the engineer to depart for Longzhou at full speed. They intended to reinforce their comrades before the Japanese

Army arrived. The presence of the Zeros was a sure sign that the Army was close behind.

The shortened train cranked its way out of the tunnel and accelerated toward Longzhou. Lhasa and Marco helped the civilians move themselves and their belongings into the remaining three stationary cars. Paul Keast and I exited the tunnel on the Longzhou side to get a sense of the situation. One of the soldiers gave us a beat up pair of binoculars. We studied the surroundings. The storm had settled into a steady rain but the wind was gusting stronger than before. The clouds were still low with good visibility beneath them, even through the rain. There was a dirt road just down the hill from us, which appeared to run all the way to Longzhou via a series of switchbacks. The railroad continued ahead and out of sight, making a more gradual descent to the city. We could see Longzhou from the hillside – it was at least five miles away but we didn't see any sign of attack. The valley to the right was full of rice paddies. The terrain to the left, toward the east, was more solid, crisscrossed by several roads and paths. It was there that we saw trouble. There were at least two columns of heavy vehicles moving toward Longzhou at a fast pace. The Japanese Army. It was clear that the Chinese soldiers wouldn't make it to Longzhou in time to prepare a defense. We somehow needed to delay the advancing Japanese.

I immediately thought of an airplane. Yes, it was becoming a habit, good or bad. When you're a pilot, you tend to want to apply your best tool, an airplane, to as many situations as you can. But we didn't have one. Jack had one. Jack was either in a mangled pile on the ground, or somewhere in the clouds overhead, perhaps on the other side of the hill. He had a radio. I didn't. We had to find one quickly. "Paul!" I said. "We need a radio!"

He returned a sheepish look. "I'm afraid I don't carry one with me, mate."

I looked helplessly across the landscape, with no apparent solution. Then I had a strange flash of inspiration. What would Sara Hudson do? Why she popped into my head at that moment, I had no idea. But I thought of the river back home...then a campfire...then...focus, Hank, focus!

This time, it wasn't *the faith* that helped me. It was *the fire*. My eyes found the answer. I had hope. For a moment. Until I realized what lay between me and it.

Chapter Twenty

The two air masses that spawned the storm fought above Longzhou; the cold air surging from the north and the warm from the south. Neither could prevail, so they pushed each other high into the air like two colliding ocean waves. The thunderheads were well over 30,000 feet high now, flattening out and spreading a dark shadow across the land below. The collision zone was almost 200 miles wide; its sheer size subjected it to the effects of the Earth's rotation. The storm began to circle in a slow deliberate manner, taking on the shape of a cyclone. It centered itself over Longzhou and settled in for a long fight. The wind became troubled and unpredictable – with sudden downdrafts racing from the thunderheads and rushing down the hillsides to the valley below. The rain was at the mercy of the wind, at times falling nearly sideways.

The storm's conflict simply echoed the never-ending struggles of an imperfect world, whether battles of countries, of cousins or of character. But in every conflict, in every instance of opposing forces, or ideas, or words, there is energy. Energy as fundamental as the power of an ocean wave. And that energy fuels *hope*. The hope of a blue sky, a warm handshake, a cool rain, a good harvest, a friendly smile, a laughing child. The hope of peace and love. In an infinite circle, hope smoothes the very conflicts that feed it. It's a cyclone in itself, a vast rotating jumble of ideas and words and actions that makes us human. Which makes us strive for so many things, and which makes us believe in perfection.

If one could possibly view the big picture across a storm

front of worldly proportions and across the generations, one would begin to see a slice of the perfection we seek. It's a perfection that we're always aware of – it lives in our conscience but it's always just beyond our grasp. Yet we never tire of reaching for it. It drives us to do and create remarkable things, as individuals, as countries, as multitudes. It's a drive that pushes Jack Campbell to circle in the clouds, fighting the weather to fight the Japanese Army. It's a drive that pushes Marco and Lhasa to calm the passengers on the train, who are themselves driven to return safely to their homes and their families. A drive that pushes Hank and Paul into the storm to find a radio. A drive that pushes each of us in countless ways every day. With that drive, with that desire for beauty and for harmony, with countless hands, we reach for the face of God. With grace and forgiveness, knowing that we live in an imperfect world, *He* reaches for *us*, imperfections and all.

As Hank knows, it's inspiring stuff to consider when you're relaxing in an easy chair by a warm fire. But when you're in the heat of the moment, in the thick of the storm, it's an entirely different challenge. One of reflex, guts, and faith. But in those moments, the desire for perfection in an imperfect world is one of the most powerful things there is.

Jack descended below the clouds and made a quick survey of his surroundings. The train was no longer in the open. The Zeros were nowhere in sight. Both issues out of his control, he turned his attention to Longzhou. He climbed to 10,000 feet and turned to the south, intending to cross the last mountain range before the city. He had almost no visibility, but merely needed to maintain course and altitude to cross the mountains. The turbulence was intense. He hit a downdraft and fell so fast the firecrackers jumped from the copilot's seat and hit the ceiling. He rode the downdraft for what seemed like minutes, then leveled out and climbed as quickly as he could back to 10,000 feet. Jack pushed on, but the floats on the Goose made it susceptible to wind gusts. It was a wild ride, full of energy. And faith.

Jack's radio, which until now had been silent, crackled with a broken transmission. He quickly dialed in the frequency and adjusted the receiver. *"Jack Campbell,"* he heard. *"Jack Campbell. Hank here, over."*

Jack grabbed his microphone. "Hank! Hank! Jack here. Where are you? Over."

He heard nothing but static in return, then got rolled by another gust. He fought to level the Goose, and pushed on, trying the radio every ten seconds.

Chapter Twenty-One

On the hillside below us, about 300 yards beneath the railway, there was a flat spot in the terrain. On that spot there was a shack. It was similar to thousands I had seen across China. Outside the shack there was a rusty fifty-five gallon steel drum, standing upright, with a rubbish fire burning in it. It was the fire that caught my eye. There was nothing special about the fire or the shack. But through my binoculars I could see two tall wooden poles, standing about ten yards apart and anchored to the walls of the shack. There was a thick wire, or cable, strung between them, one end running down to the roof of the shack. The cable was easy to see – it was wet and shiny, and it gleamed even in the storm-darkened afternoon light.

The wire was an antenna for a radio transmitter. Just like the one on my recent C-47, where it hung between the vertical fin and the fuselage just behind the cockpit. The occupant of this shack was a part of the nationwide early warning network. Which meant that he – or she – could contact the Goose. And Jack. I had found my radio.

The switch-backed dirt road that I noticed earlier seemed to wind its way to the shack, but in a long, roundabout path that disappeared around the hill before reappearing below. I couldn't be sure it was the same road, but how many could there be? Problem was, it would be a long walk, of unknown length. The hillside was steep. It was mostly dirt, gravel, and loose scree that had eroded from the hillside above. I couldn't hike down the hill in any reasonable period of time, and I had to contact Jack fast. I needed another way. I had no vehicle. Wait. I had seen one. But where? "Paul!" I yelled. "I found a radio. I need a way to get to it!"

Paul quickly joined me and surveyed the situation. "There's an old truck on the uphill side of the tracks on the far side of that outcropping." He pointed a thumb over his shoulder. "But it's been there for ages. It's just an old wreck. It's not going anywhere."

I ran toward it, with Paul close behind. When I saw it, I was instantly disappointed. The truck was old and decrepit. It looked like it had been immobile for at least a year or two. It was broken down and abandoned. It had four wheels. The tires were flat, but I wasn't going on a Sunday drive.

"It'll do," I said.

"It'll do *what*?"

"Get me down the hill to the shack."

"Hank, we'll never get that thing started. And it's not drivable."

"It only needs to be steerable. Help me push it to the edge. I'll just jump in and ride it straight down the hill. No engine necessary. Even if the brakes don't work, the hillside flattens out for a bit at the shack. I'll stop."

Paul studied me for a moment. Then he gave in. We pulled a door open on each side, the rusty hinges groaning in protest. I jumped into the driver's seat, which was made of thick canvas webbing and still intact. I tried the wheel. It took all the muscle I had, but I was able to crank it a bit each way. "Wheels steering?" I asked.

"Yes you're moving them. Try the brakes."

The brake pedal went straight to the floor. I pumped it a few times, but there was no improvement. I pulled the emergency brake handle to the left of the steering wheel. It still worked. It simply pulled a cable that attached to the rear brakes. It was still intact. "Brakes and steering work. That's all I need. Give me ten, fifteen minutes once I get to the shack. Stay close. I'll yell to you with an update. Help me push!"

I stepped out and pushed against the open door. Paul did the same on the passenger side. We muscled the truck over the tracks to the edge of the hill. I jumped into the driver's seat and slammed my door shut. Paul shut the passenger door, ran behind the truck, and pushed. It didn't take much. We were already on a downward slant and gravity was our friend. The truck moved slowly at first, but once the front end was over the lip of the hill, it started to roll on its own. All I had to do now was keep it pointed straight downhill. If I let the truck turn at an angle to the hill, it would roll over. And over. And over. And that would be the end of my trip, and my life. But the truck was front heavy due to its engine. I figured I was just along for the ride.

It was no ride. It was a pummeling. It started out safe enough. But I rapidly accelerated and as the truck lurched and bounced over the rough terrain, I felt like the steel ball inside a baby's rattle. I lost track of how many times I hit my head on the ceiling, or bashed my shoulder on the door frame. But I held tight to the wheel, pushed on the floor with my feet, and pulled myself toward the wheel with my arms. The combination kept me in place enough to keep a bit of control. Then the terrain got nasty. I had misjudged the size of the rocks and boulders – they looked smaller from above. They got big, and now I was fighting a violent up and down pitching as I hit, then cleared, various boulders. But there was also an extreme side-to-side rolling as the wheels negotiated the uneven ground.

When you're riding a bucking bronco, there are a few

things you learn pretty quickly. One is that you're going to fall off at some point, and it's gonna hurt. The second is that every horse has its own moves – its own unique way of bucking. For example, a horse might repeat a pattern of bucking to the right, followed by a spin to the left, followed by two bucks forward. The third, and most important lesson, is that if you want to stay on, you learn the horse's bucking pattern, and shift your weight in anticipation of its changes in direction. If you can do that, the horse eventually tires and realizes who's boss.

I realized after a couple of seconds that I was simply getting bucked. So I got my hopes up and naturally decided to treat the truck like a bronco that needed breaking. To bob and weave as the truck did. It didn't work. The truck was already broken. There was no pattern, and it was *me* that was experiencing *the breaking*. I was getting beaten like an old rug. The truck skipped off a slick boulder and caught at least two feet of air, before it hit hard and bottomed out. The impact rattled my brain and broke the side mirror off the truck. Another impact cracked the windshield. I gritted my teeth and rode it down, fighting all the way. I was nearing the shack, so I yanked the emergency brake lever and braced myself. My ride was almost done.

My Dad always said "You can do *anything* for thirty seconds." I started counting.

Chapter Twenty-Two

The hill flattened out near the shack. My descent came to a sudden stop when the nose of the truck planted itself hard on the ground. I had braced myself as best I could, but my forehead smacked the windshield. I was momentarily stunned, then came to my senses and pushed the door open. Well, I tried to push the door open. The entire truck was racked and the door was jammed. I pivoted in the seat, swung my legs up to the left, and kicked the door. Then I felt something warm and sticky running down my face. I wiped it from my eyes, and my hand came away covered with blood. I had a nice gash in my forehead. No matter. I had split my forehead a few times before and I knew it always looked worse than it was. The trick was to keep the blood out of your eyes, and find a bandage to close the wound long enough to stop the bleeding.

I kicked the door repeatedly, stronger each time, but made no progress. Then I realized I was leaning so far to the right that my head was outside the truck. The passenger door was gone, apparently the victim of one of the hard landings the truck had made on the way down the hill. In all the confusion I hadn't even noticed. I scrambled out the passenger side and hit the ground running. I moved quickly around the front of the truck and ran toward the shack, blood pouring from my face, rain pouring from the sky to wash it away.

The fire was still burning in the steel drum outside the shack. The owner couldn't be far. The rain was pounding on the shack's tin roof; I started pounding on the thin wooden door. I heard a yell from inside. It's amazing how well you can communicate with someone when you don't know their language. The yell I heard simply sounded like "I'm coming". Only it didn't sound anything like that, you know what I mean? I waited, wiping my shirtsleeve across my forehead to clear the blood.

The door finally opened and the occupant gasped. She was small – maybe a foot shorter than me - with grey hair tied in a bun. She wore a simple woolen smock and pants, the hallmark of a million Chinese laborers. She surveyed me quickly, looked past me to the left and right, studied the wrecked truck, then opened the door wide and beckoned for me to enter. I did gladly. She quickly shut the door. Apparently in these parts, people didn't hesitate to help a neighbor in need. Even if that neighbor was a tall white cowboy from Idaho, bleeding profusely from a head wound as a result of an accident in an abandoned truck.

The shack was tidy, simple, and dry. As my eyes adjusted to the dim light, I could see one rough wood table against the wall, covered with a few books, a candle, and a large radio transmitter. I had guessed correctly. The only other pieces of furniture in the shack were two wooden chairs and two bamboo cots. I figured two people lived here, perhaps she and her husband? But other than the two of us, the shack was empty. There was a stove in one corner of the shack with a small fire inside, providing enough warmth to make me realize how cold I was. The rain drummed on the tin roof and the wind howled through gaps in the two blanket-covered windows.

The woman motioned for me to sit on one of the chairs, which I did gladly. She opened a small cupboard and pulled out a cloth, which she helped me tie around my head to stop the bleeding. That done, it was time to communicate. I thanked her and she smiled in return, giving me a long list of instructions on how to prevent it from happening again. At least I think that's what she said. I pantomimed my journey in the truck, then pointed up the hill and tried to explain that I'd been on the train. She seemed to understand. I pointed to the radio urgently, and tried to explain that I needed to use it. That in fact I needed *her* to show me *how* to use it. She wasn't having any of it. I needed a better way to quickly communicate a bunch of information. I pantomimed drawing on my palm with a pencil. She nodded and grabbed a thin pencil from the desk, then a small scrap of paper from beside the stove. I drew a quick outline of an airplane, and she identified it with a word in Chinese. Then I drew two round circles on the wings – the rising sun symbol of the Japanese. She made a quick exclamation and looked at me with obvious confusion. I pointed at the drawing, showed two fingers, then pointed at the sky above the mountain. Then I moved my hand around in the air to show a plane flying. I pointed to the radio with urgency. She apparently understood the situation, and moved quickly to the radio. She connected a power cable from a small hand-cranked generator, then motioned for me to crank it. I stood and walked toward the table, a wave of nausea hitting me in addition to a now throbbing headache. I fell into one of the chairs next to the table and started cranking. She flicked a few switches on the front of the transmitter. I recognized the soft glow of the vacuum tubes as the set warmed up.

I kept cranking, trying to figure out how to explain that I needed to contact Jack in the Goose. I knew the frequency that Jack would be monitoring – it was the standard channel for the Hump pilots. But how to tell her this? She was going to alert the early warning network. Fair enough. But I needed to reach Jack first. Still cranking with my left hand, I grabbed the paper and pencil with my right and drew another airplane, this time with stars on the wings. They were the well-recognized symbol of the American planes being used for the airlift over the Hump and elsewhere in China. She nodded understanding. Then she put two and two together, pointed at me, and pointed at the plane. I nodded yes, I was an American pilot. That really confused her. I realized that she must now think that I crashed my plane. Into an abandoned truck. Then slid down the hill to crash the truck at her shack. As far as I knew, only Sara Hudson had seen me do something that ridiculous.

I sighed and rubbed my forehead.

I motioned for her to crank. She took over for me. Both hands free, I tore the piece of paper in half, holding the Zero in my left hand and the Goose in my right. I flew them in the air, with the Goose chasing the Zero. She had much to say at this point. Probably something like "This is better than a picture show. And free too."

I pointed toward the radio, then toward the Goose. Now it all came together for her. She nodded vigorously, grabbed the headset from the table and placed it on my head, then slid the microphone toward me. I slid my chair toward the table and studied the transmitter. It was simple enough to figure out. I dialed in the proper frequency, adjusted the squelch to minimize the static, and clicked the transmit button. "Jack Campbell," I said. "Jack Campbell! Hank here, over."

No response. I repeated my transmission twice with no success. I adjusted the frequency dial and tried once more.

The receiver crackled in response. *"Hank! Hank! Jack here. Where are you? Over."*

"Jack! I can barely hear you. I'm safe in the hills above Longzhou. You can't pick us up yet. Are you in the air?

Over."

No response.   I tried again.   Nothing but dead air.

Chapter Twenty-Three

Jack was exasperated. His body was running on fumes. The Goose had only forty-five minutes of fuel left. He was in the clouds, somewhere to the north of Longzhou, hopefully heading south on the downhill side of the mountains. He was navigating by compass, by an intermittent direction finder, and by the seat of his pants. He didn't know where the Zeros were. He didn't know where Hank was. He knew that Hank had a radio, which was the one bright spot of a long, dreary, taxing day. He had finally established contact with Hank, when his radio overheated and blew its circuit breaker. Kam had warned him clearly enough, but the radio popped at the worst possible time. He turned off the radio, reset the breaker, and waited as long as he dared to let the radio cool. Five minutes. A lifetime.

He finally turned on the radio and took a deep breath. "Hank, Hank, Hank. Jack here. Over."

I can't tell you how great it was to hear Jack's voice. He was still alive! I responded immediately with a short, practiced message, anticipating radio trouble. "Jack we're safe on the ground. Uphill of Longzhou. Where are you?"

"I'm airborne north of Longzhou. I'm in the soup and I don't mean hot and sour. I've got forty-five minutes. What's the plan?"

"Jack the Japanese Army is west of the city, moving fast. You need to delay them. The Chinese need time to prepare."

"Delay them? With what?" I could hear disbelief in Jack's voice.

"What do you have?"

There was a pause. I actually heard Jack sigh. *"Fireworks,"* he replied.

I didn't understand but I didn't need to. Jack always *got stuff done.* "Good luck. Meet us at the Longzhou air field. Stay safe. Out." With that I leaned back to massage my temples. My head hurt terribly. I turned to my host with a smile, and waved my flattened hand from side to side. "All done." I bowed slightly. "Thank you."

She bowed and smiled.

I was suddenly very tired. But I had to move. I stood slowly and motioned to the door. "I must go now."

The woman motioned toward the stove. She moved her hand to her mouth. She was offering me food. I couldn't accept it. I'd been lucky enough to eat breakfast that day. Or was it yesterday? She needed food more than I did. I wished I had something to give her, but I left my pack uphill with Paul before I jumped in the truck. Then I had an idea. At least it was something. I grabbed the pencil and the piece of paper with the drawing of the Goose, turned the drawing over to the blank side, and drew a cowboy on a horse. I had practiced the same pencil drawing repeatedly during quiet times in the bunkhouse. It was my favorite. Then I simply wrote "Hank" at the bottom. The woman smiled deeply when I gave it to her. She accepted it with both hands, as if it was a priceless gift. She bowed and I returned the gesture. Then I turned and made my way out the door.

The wind was cold.

It was raining.

The *Flor De La Mar* lay at the bottom of the Strait of Malacca, waiting patiently for her rescue. Over the centuries the ships of many countries passed over her on their voyages through the Strait. They evolved from wooden sailing ships, to steamships, to warships, to massive diesel-powered cargo ships laden with goods. The ships grew in multitude and size, yet few, if any, carried a cargo as valuable as the *Flor De La Mar*. Storms came and went, wars began and were finished, countries rose and fell, influence shifted from continent to continent. And still the *Flor De La Mar* waited, in the deep blue abyss of the busy Strait of Malacca. It was quiet there under the water, a quiet, peaceful place for a ship to rest. For a time.

The *Flor De La Mar* was built in Lisbon, Portugal in 1502. She was a carrack, a type of sailing ship built specifically for the annual India Run. At 400 tons, she was also significantly larger than any carrack previously made. The India Run voyage, made by an armada of ships from Portugal every year over the entire sixteenth century and well into the seventeenth, was created to procure valuable spices from India. The most notable of these were the "five glorious spices": pepper, cinnamon, cloves, nutmeg, and mace. The India Run route was pioneered by the famous Portuguese explorer Vasco da Gama. The ships sailed south from Portugal, in a wide counterclockwise circle following the Atlantic currents, often stopping in Brazil for supplies. They then sailed southeast, rounding the southern tip of Africa at the Cape of Good Hope, north along the African coast, then finally northeast across the Indian Ocean to India. On this voyage, timing was everything. The seasonal currents and monsoon winds of the Atlantic and Indian Oceans could either aid or hinder a sailing ship, depending on the time of year. When done correctly, the round trip voyage took a bit over a year. The annual armada would depart Lisbon in the spring, round the Cape in early summer, then hopefully arrive at the mid-African east coast in August in time to catch the monsoon winds across the Indian Ocean to India.

The return trip would begin with a January departure from India, with an arrival in Lisbon in the summer, taking advantage of the seasonal reversal of the currents and winds.

On the outbound voyage, the ships had to reach the mid-African coast by August to catch the monsoon winds. If a ship was delayed (by storm damage, for example), they would be stranded on the Africa coast until springtime. This would add an entire year to the voyage. This wasn't unusual - the Cape of Good Hope was notoriously dangerous and often damaged ships regardless of the time of year.

The *Flor De La Mar* departed Lisbon on her maiden India Run voyage in 1502, under the command of da Gama's cousin Estavao. The ship made it to India uneventfully, but once loaded with spices she proved difficult to handle, especially in the currents in the Mozambique Channel between Madagascar and the African coast. These currents were quite similar to the currents of the Strait of Malacca. She made it back to Lisbon two months late, then departed again the next spring for her second trip. Due to a series of fateful events and decisions, she would never again see her home port of Lisbon.

On the return leg of her second voyage, the ship again had difficulties in the Mozambique Channel, and was forced to stop at Mozambique Island for extended repairs. She languished there for almost a year while her frustrated captain tried repeatedly to depart for home. Another returning carrack armada found her there, and the commander of that armada transferred her cargo to his ships for delivery to Lisbon. She was then drafted into an India-bound armada and soon became a vessel of conquest. The *Flor De La Mar* participated in several Portuguese military campaigns, and eventually became part of the western Arabian Sea patrol of Afonso de Albuquerque. She would meet her demise in the Strait of Malacca under his fateful command. Despite her difficulties, the *Flor De La Mar* sailed for over nine years, at a time when most carracks lasted only three or four, especially if they were making the India Run. It was a considered an accomplishment if a ship survived even one run. By the time of her sinking, the *Flor De La Mar* was worn out. She had earned retirement.

The India Run was difficult, taxing, dangerous, and hard on ship and crew. But the spices! Oh those Five Glorious Spices! The reward was apparently worth the effort. Spices were the lingua franca of the day. The gold and jewels that Albuquerque discovered in Malacca were merely a diversion. But now, in 1940, oh the things that could be bought with the cargo of the *Flor De La Mar*! Spices were a commodity. Gold and jewels were something different entirely. The ship lay there at the bottom of the Strait awaiting her rescue, her value increasing with each passing day. Could this be the year? She could only wait, there in the indigo abyss.

Chapter Twenty-Four

Lieutenant-General Akito Humaki of the Imperial Japanese Army was feeling better. His forces were moving quickly westward toward Longzhou. There had been no resistance so far. He was ahead of his ambitious schedule. He was also experienced. He knew that complacency at this point could be disastrous. Every five minutes he halted his advance to allow his lookouts and sentries to survey their surroundings. He was most wary of an attack from behind or from the sides. The enemy would be smart. A classic flanking maneuver would be strategically advantageous in this terrain. His forces were moving through rolling terrain, which could easily conceal a foe.

He halted his advance once again to reconnoiter. His commanders allowed their men to take a brief rest, while ensuring that they maintained their readiness. Weapons were loaded and at the ready. Engines were running. The rain was still falling from the low clouds, the wind unpredictable and cold. Other than discomfort, the weather was not a factor for Humaki's seasoned fighters.

Suddenly and without warning there was an explosion on their right flank. Followed by rapid gunfire. His men started yelling, "Enemy contact to the north!" More explosions followed in rapid succession. Humaki immediately directed a third of his force to pivot to the north and engage the enemy. They moved quickly, both on foot and in their armored vehicles. Humaki wasn't concerned. He'd half expected resistance at this point in his invasion of Longzhou. But he wasn't prepared for what happened next. Within a minute there was another booming explosion to the southeast, on his left rear flank. Again followed by rapid gunfire. It was a coordinated attack on his two weakest points of defense. He immediately directed a third of this force to pivot to the left and rearward to engage the enemy there. They moved with precision. The remainder of his force dug in and prepared to reinforce the two flanks. The extent of the resistance was unknown at this point, but no matter what, his advance had been halted.

"Paul!" I cupped my hands and yelled uphill again. "Paul!"

Paul appeared at the lip of the hill near the railroad. "I hear you!"

"Jack's overhead. Grab Lhasa and Marco. We need to get to the airfield in Longzhou." I pointed toward the city. "I'm on my way now on this road. Meet me as soon as you can!"

"Got it. We're on the way!"

I half jogged down the dirt road that led away from the shack, dragging my bronco-busted leg with me. I went a mile or so. I crossed a rise and reached a fork in the road. The path to the left appeared to climb the hill. It was the switch-backed road we had seen from above. The path to the right went downhill toward Longzhou. I stopped and scanned the valley below. It was now late afternoon and the light was beginning to fade. There were many lights visible now in the city, and smoke flowed from a thousand chimneys. All looked normal. I figured Longzhou was an hour away on foot. From my vantage point I couldn't see the valley to the east, so it was impossible to determine the position of the Japanese Army. But I had faith in Jack. I sat down on the side of the road and waited for my companions. So tired.

The man walked along the dirt road, his face held low in the rain. He carried a freshly killed rabbit, slung over his shoulder. He and his wife would have rabbit stew tonight. The stew and a few fresh vegetables from their modest garden would make a fine little feast.

He approached his shack at the side of the hill. What was this? Old Man Tso's truck was in a crumpled heap just beyond his shack. Perhaps the rain caused a landslide that brought the truck down? But it had been in the same place on the hill for years. A rusted fixture of the mountain. The man quickened his pace. Was his wife okay? He reached the door and called to her before entering. He didn't want to startle her. She responded as she usually did. He entered their home and was relieved to see that his wife was safe and nothing was amiss. She yelped in glee when she saw the rabbit. She hugged him and took the rabbit and his bag. He removed his jacket and placed in on the worn hook by the door.

"Old Man Tso's wreck is outside. What happened? I thought you might be in danger."

"I wasn't in danger," she replied. "But a strange thing happened this afternoon. A man appeared at the door. He was tall and white. An American I think. He had a bad wound on his head. He arrived on the train. He crashed the truck. He needed to use the radio."

"What? This is a very strange thing. Why did he need the radio?"

She told him the entire story.

He nodded from time to time, a worried look on his face. "So this man was an American pilot, huh? Perhaps one of the cargo pilots flying over Burma?"

"Yes I think so. He called to another pilot for help. To

stop the Japanese attack I think. I offered him food, but he had to leave. He's gone."

"Hmm. Perhaps he will return?"

"I don't think so. But he left this for us." She showed him the pencil drawing of the horse and cowboy.

"Hmm. I cannot read this word. Perhaps his name? But I have seen pictures like this before. From America. This man is a horse rider and cattle keeper." He paused. "There's a word that they call themselves. But I can't remember it."

They returned to their dinner preparations, talking more about the strange afternoon. At last they sat down to enjoy their food and their good fortune. They ate quietly.

"I remember the word now!" the man said suddenly. "It's *cowman*. This American is a cowman!" He chuckled. "The Cowman of Longzhou. You never know what the rain will bring, huh?"

She nodded. "That is true. I hope the cowman stays dry in the rain. And safe."

"I think he will be good. You know what they say. 'He who is drowned is not troubled by the rain.'"

She thought about the proverb for a moment. Then she smiled. She felt blessed to be with her husband, here in this warm shack on the side of the hill.

Chapter Twenty-Five

Jack Campbell had flown in mountain storms, tropical storms, at night, in the snow, in the ice, in the rain, over land, over sea, with Yellow Fever and without. He had never been challenged as much as he was now. He was flying in the clouds, the sky darkening in late afternoon, visibility one eighth of a mile. The storm was unpredictable, the rain falling hard, the wind a jumbled mess. And he was alone. Any right-minded pilot would have a co-pilot with them for a flight like this. But circumstances were most definitely out of his control. Jack was merely reacting as best he could, with what he had. *What he had* was a box of firecrackers, his lighter, a sporadic navigation system, and forty minutes of fuel. But in life, often in the most dire of circumstances, it's the intangible items in our personal inventories that rise to the surface to govern our actions. Whether we admit it or not. Today, here above Longzhou, the circumstances were certainly dire.

Task One. Find the Japanese Army. Jack literally had the upper hand in this endeavor. The challenge was to find them without being found. He had to assume that the Zeros were still providing air cover. It was only the muck and gloom that had spared him their wrath. He didn't dare to descend below the clouds and give himself away. But the very characteristics of this storm, the ones that made it such a bear to fly in, gave Jack the advantage he needed. This storm wasn't one of those calm and steady rains; the kind that caress your house with a light touch and make you want to spend hours reading a good book in front of a nice fire with a hot cup of coffee. This storm was a roiling mess.

It was the type of visitor that would sweep into your flat, drink all your beer, eat your food, toss the leftovers on the floor, kiss your girlfriend, and then leave with your best leather jacket. And your dog. The clouds were confused and jumbled, being pushed every direction by sporadic winds as the two air masses fought for dominance. As a result, the clouds weren't continuous. They had occasional gaps. Jack simply looked for the gaps, then surveyed the ground below as he passed over them. This allowed him sporadic snapshots of the situation below. After dodging, weaving, and observing for ten minutes, he was able to piece the snapshots together into a sort of movie in his mind. It wasn't something he had learned or practiced, it was just one of those skills in his personal inventory that rose to the occasion. It worked surprisingly well. He now knew where the Japanese Army was. Now he was going to *light them up*.

Task Two. No right-minded pilot would light a firecracker in the cockpit of an airplane. A cockpit that was surrounded by fuel, and that contained instruments and controls necessary for one's very survival. But what the hell. He only wished he had a co-pilot to share in the fun. He placed the box close to him on the center console, pulled his lighter from his jacket pocket, and selected two firecrackers. One was a big boomer. The other was a string of smaller firecrackers that sounded like a machine gun when they went off. He twisted the fuses together so he could light them at once. He slid open his side window and readied his lighter. Then he watched the second hand of his watch. He was still in the clouds, but he knew he wanted to fly north, toward the mountains, for three miles. One minute at his speed. While he flew he reveled in the fresh, cold air blowing in through his window. He was dead tired. Yet he felt so *alive*.

Fifteen seconds to go. He flicked his lighter and held the flame to the fuses. He had to do this over the co-pilot's seat, as the slipstream from his open window fanned him with rain and wind. The fuses caught fire and filled the cabin with acrid smoke. He held the firecrackers for a few seconds until he was in position, then he tossed them out the window. He immediately turned to the right in a coordinated 30 degree bank, which he knew would change his compass heading at a rate of 20 degrees per second. He counted off nine seconds, turning 180 degrees. He was now heading back to the south. He flew straight and level for another three miles, readying an impressive assortment of firecrackers as he counted off the seconds. He repeated his light-and-throw process, this time with a wider variety of ammunition. He only wished he could hear the show. For good measure he flew in a tight circle and dropped several more firecrackers on the rear flank of the Japanese.

Task Three. Assess the damage, so to speak. Jack went back to his lazy loops, glancing here and there through the holes in the clouds. From what he could see, the Japanese Army was now moving in three directions. None of them toward Longzhou. The ruse worked. Jack said a quick prayer of thanks for Kam's foresight. Then he checked his fuel. Twenty minutes remaining. He turned quickly to the west toward Longzhou and slowed his speed to 160 knots – the best endurance speed for the Goose. This would enable him to travel the maximum distance with his remaining fuel. He did a quick calculation and figured Longzhou was no more than fifteen minutes away. Probably less. He stayed in the clouds and counted off the minutes, the Goose droning steadily on.

Chapter Twenty-Six

Marco, Lhasa, and Paul caught up with me at the junction in the road. We set a quick walking pace for Longzhou. The three had helped the train passengers settle in to their temporary shelter in the tunnel, and were confident that all would be fine. The passengers would stay in the tunnel overnight under the protection of a small detail of Chinese soldiers, and then journey to Longzhou the next day if it was safe. I didn't know it yet, but due in large part to Jack Campbell it *would* be safe for months. The Chinese were able to use the one day firecracker delay to set a proper defense, and over the ensuing months they drank the Japanese Army's beer, ate their food, stole their jacket, and took their dog. The entire fight became a stalemate, until September 1940 when the French eventually capitulated, allowing the Japanese Army to occupy Indochina and therefore control the Longzhou – Hai Phong railway. Longzhou fell to Japan, but in a controlled, non-violent manner. The city was spared the horrors that Nanking had suffered.

But I digress. We made our way to the Longzhou airfield. It was early evening now and the sky was growing dark. I hoped that Jack was on the way, but I couldn't be sure, which made the walk an anxious one. We reached the airfield at dusk. All was quiet in the city. The wind had calmed and the storm had settled into a steady rain.

Jack felt he was close enough to Longzhou, and far enough from the Japanese, to drop from the clouds and do some proper visual flying. He descended carefully, finally clearing the clouds just below 1,000 feet. The city lights were ahead and to the left. He made a slight course correction toward the airfield at the far end of the city. He turned on his running lights, and wagged his wings from time to time. He wanted everyone to see him. At this point, *no surprise* was the key. No surprise meant the Chinese wouldn't mistake him for an enemy plane. He didn't want to be shot down now. He had saved four firecrackers for himself and it would be a darn shame to waste them in a fireball of cooked Goose.

I saw the Goose long before I could hear it. Jack had wisely turned on his running lights, and his plane was easy to spot against the dark storm clouds. I could eventually hear the drone of its engines. Both engines. Which meant that Jack had two good engines to land with. Where's the challenge in that?

There was a contingent of Chinese soldiers at the airfield cautiously watching us approach. Lhasa spread both his arms out in the universal sign of "not armed, not a threat" and called to them in Chinese. Two of them walked toward us quickly. The remainder stayed at the ready. Lhasa spoke to them and pointed to the Goose. One turned and yelled an order to the others. They immediately jogged to two trucks on the tarmac and turned on the headlights to light the air strip.

Jack could see the air strip ahead. He reached it quickly. He circled above it to survey the layout and the wind, and then entered a downwind leg paralleling the runway, with the runway to his left. He dropped his wing flaps and landing gear, and throttled the engines back. He flew past the end of the runway, until it was forty-five degrees behind him. Then he made a sweeping 180 degree left turn to align himself with the runway. He was on final approach now, with very little wind and a light rain. The noise of the slipstream diminished as his speed dropped, the engines now in a low drone. The world suddenly seemed very quiet. He landed with a slight lurch, came to a stop at the midpoint of the runway, then taxied to the tarmac. He shut down the engines and took several deep breaths.

"What was I thinking," he asked himself, as he cleared his mind and calmed his heart. "I forgot to tell Kam to take the rest of the day off."

Jack jumped down from the Goose and all five of us came together in a huddle. There was much to say, but we didn't need to say it. The silence was filled by five big smiles. There's an old saying back home, "Never slap a cowboy that's chewing tobacco." We had just slapped the cowboy, and we came away clean. *Don't that beat all!*

"Let's get ourselves some hot and sour soup," I said. "Then some sleep."

"Sounds good, cowman," Lhasa replied.

I can't tell you how much those three words meant to me.

We walked toward the city, tired but awake, hungry but fulfilled.

Over dinner in a small inn on the outskirts of the city, I revisited a bowl of hot and sour soup. It was masterful. As we ate, Marco, Lhasa, Jack and I glanced at each other, the same question on our mind. I could see we all reached the same conclusion. Words weren't necessary. Paul had earned the right to join us. "Paul," I asked, "What are you up to the next couple a months? How about tagging along with us?"

Paul took a swallow of some warm Chinese beer. "Well, His Majesty strongly suggests, via my commander, that I stay here in Longzhou and help these chaps with their little skirmish. Seeing that it would be treason to disobey, I think I'll abide."

"How long?" I asked.

"Until it's done, one way or another."

I nodded. "How will you help?"

"Let's just say I have some special skills, earned in another fight. The Japanese have some weaknesses. Not many, but some."

"Like what?" I asked.

"Well, for one, they believe wholeheartedly in their superiority. And that's a huge weakness. It makes them prone to incorrect assumptions about their enemies."

"I don't understand," I said.

"Well, take Jack's little adventure with the Zeros. No offense to you Jack," he raised his beer glass in Jack's direction. "I'm in awe of what you just accomplished. You deserve a medal. You saved some lives this afternoon. But those Japanese pilots were well trained, and in superior aircraft. It was only a matter of time before they caught up with Jack in a bad way. But I would bet that they just couldn't allow themselves to believe that they had been outsmarted by a civilian pilot in a float plane. Their superiority complex likely convinced them that Jack turned and ran, and that's why they broke off their search for him in the clouds. They'll never admit that Jack was the victor. Even if they eventually put two-and-two together. So, you see, that's a chink in their armor. And it happens to be my specialty. That chink is going to make the Japanese lose the war. I'm just hoping I can be of value to the Chinese."

I nodded. "I hope so too."

Paul smiled. "I will say it's been an inspiration traveling with you folks. I wouldn't have missed it for, as they say, all the tea in China. But I'll be on my way in the morning, toward the rising sun. And the Rising Sun." He chuckled at his pun, and took another long drink of beer.

We finished our dinner, paid our bill, then walked into town to gather supplies. We then walked slowly back to the Goose at the airfield, enjoying the quiet night air. We slept in the plane that night. It felt like...home.

Chapter Twenty-Seven

I woke up the next morning just before dawn. All was still and quiet, with the exception of a variety of birds chirping in the trees that bordered the airfield. I was getting used to Southeast Asia, but as I listened to the birds I realized I didn't recognize their songs at all. They were foreign to me; not the birds I would hear at home in Idaho. It's funny how many things we don't notice until they're absent. In all my years in Idaho, I had never realized that I was memorizing bird songs.

I wondered what was happening at the ranch today, which reminded me that I'd never finished reading Grandma's letter. I had been interrupted by all the excitement on the train. I pulled it from my pack, unfolded it carefully, and held it to the light from the airplane window.

... I started reading a good new book called Gone with the Wind. It's about the Civil War, but it seems to apply now. The Civil War was a terrible thing. But when it was over, the slaves were free and our nation was one. Perhaps the outcome was worth the price? I just don't know. We make life so complicated. As I get older, I seem to understand that the simpler things are the most important. Seems to me that if we live for others, and not ourselves, then life is worth living. So that's my idea for today. Enjoy your day and make the most of it. I can't wait to hear from you again. With Love, Grandma

Grandma had a way of cutting through the bull and getting right to the heart of the matter. It was a quality that I hadn't really noticed until I was away from her. Much the same as the birdsongs of home. I wondered how many other things I would begin to notice as my time away grew.

There was a postscript below Grandma's signature, in AJ's handwriting.

P.S. Hank get your cowboy butt back home and get your chores done. Your horse stinks. He needs a bath. The fence line ain't getting any younger either. Love, AJ

Now *that* was something from home that I hadn't forgotten: AJ and her ribbing. All in good fun. I'm sure I owed her a few favors by now. I'd pay up when I got home. Besides, my horse didn't stink. He smelled like…a horse. Nothing wrong with that.

The rest of our team awoke. We all stepped outside the Goose. The Chinese Army patrol had a small fire burning in a pit alongside the tarmac. They beckoned to us to join them. We had rice cakes with hot tea for breakfast. It wasn't ham and eggs, but I'd gotten used to light breakfasts. And lunches. And dinners. I actually enjoyed them. My body just didn't need a lot of food anymore. Possibly because I'd lost about twenty pounds since Hawaii. I now weighed the equivalent of four Lhasas. Down from five. I mentioned this to him.

"There's an old samurai saying," he replied. "'Hara Hachi Bu.' It means 'eighty-percent full and ready to fight.'"

"Lhasa," I laughed, "a little rice ball would make you eighty-percent full. You must be eighty percent full all the time!"

"Then what does that tell you about me, huh?"

"But I've never seen you fight."

"I hope you never do." He left it at that. It made me

curious. I'd seen Lhasa diffuse a fight or two. Especially the one at the Mekong River when the Japanese found us. But what if he *had* needed to fight at the Mekong? It was something I simply couldn't picture. Like a one-hundred percent full Lhasa. Or a horse that didn't smell like a horse.

Lieutenant Paul Keast in His Majesty's Service left us after breakfast, heading to the eastern front to assist the Chinese Army in their defense of Longzhou. He didn't know our plans or our destination, but he wished us luck just the same. Having worked together on such a trying task, we were now birds of a feather. I hoped I'd see him again. He was taking a big risk in the service of the Chinese.

The four of us spent the morning preparing the Goose for a flight to Malaysia. Jack opened up the instrument panel to see if he could fix the sticky compass, then wisely decided to leave it to someone better qualified. I did a full inspection of the Goose, checking the landing gear, the control surfaces, the engine oil, and several other items. I found three new bullet holes in the tail, undoubtedly from Jack's latest adventure. They were small caliber, from a rifle and not an aircraft gun. Jack had been close enough to the ground at some point to take some hits from an infantryman.

We purchased a full load of fuel from the Chinese at the airfield. It would carry us 1,200 miles. It was 1,500 miles from Longzhou to Malaysia as the crow flies. But if we took the direct route, we'd fly over Laos and Thailand. That would be a dicey trip, as Laos was suddenly in the same situation as Indochina. It was a French protectorate, but was about to fall to a Japanese occupation. Thailand, noticing that Laos was on the ropes, would soon align itself with Germany and the Axis powers to attack Laos. This would all happen within a month or two. It was easy enough to see it coming. It's difficult to hide impending conflict on a national scale, one only needed to listen to the gossip around town. I'll admit, the rapid advance of the Japanese caught us by surprise, and concerned us greatly.

As a result of this widespread instability we had two choices. We could fly to the east, taking a semicircular course flown mostly over the South China Sea. We would start by heading east to the sea, turning south and skirting around the eastern shore of Indochina, then finally turning toward the southwest to Malaysia and the Strait of Malacca. In total it would be a crescent-shaped trip of 2,000 miles. Almost all of it over water. We could land in the ocean, but we couldn't refuel there. We would need to land in Indochina somewhere along the coast for fuel. But we had to assume the Japanese Army would be present throughout Indochina. We weren't their enemy, but the Goose certainly was. Option one was exceedingly dangerous.

Option Two was a big backtrack. We could fly to the west, staying over Free China, then turn to the south and fly over Burma all the way to its southern coast. Burma was relatively stable at this point, and our course would skirt, but not enter, the northern borders of Thailand and Laos. At the southern coast of Burma, we would turn to the southeast over the Andaman Sea, and follow it all the way to Malaysia. This also had another benefit. There was a string of islands in the Andaman Sea that belonged to the Dutch East Indies, now Indonesia, which had yet to feel the Japanese presence. We could hopscotch the islands to Malaysia if necessary. This course was a crescent in itself, facing the opposite direction from our first option. It would be a 2,200 mile trip. It also meant that our train ride to Longzhou was completely unnecessary. We could have departed Kunming will full bellies and no bullet holes, and saved a bunch of time and gas. But I didn't consider our trip to Longzhou to be a waste. For me, it was *the faith* and *the fire* in action. It gave me a chance to build *the friendships* that would play a big role in our journey, as we had very little idea of what lay ahead.

We discussed our two options then made our decision. We were heading to the west, over Burma. The Goose was ready to go. We buttoned her up and strapped ourselves in, me in the left pilot's seat, Jack in the co-pilot's, and Marco and Lhasa in the seats to the rear. I fired up the two engines and did my pre-flight checks. The Goose's engines didn't have the power of those on a C-47, but they felt precise. They responded quickly to throttle changes. It was the difference between a big draft horse, meant to pull heavy loads, and a nimble pony. I always preferred the pony. The Goose just felt good.

We taxied to the runway and halted at the threshold, my feet pressing the brakes on the rudder pedals. I ran up the engines to full power and checked the magnetos, switching from primary to secondary to make sure they both worked. The engines ran smoothly, the props' slipstream buffeting the plane's tail, bouncing us in anticipation.

The rain had stopped. The sun broke through the clouds and played across the rice paddies, its reflection bathing the cockpit with rippling waves of light. A flock of white cranes took off from the wetlands. They turned to the south, skimming the water in search of food. The drone of the engines seeped into my flesh and soaked into my bones. It felt as if the entire world was vibrating, buzzing, spinning along in a whirlwind of energy. I released the brakes. We jumped forward, bouncing down the runway as we accelerated. Soon the wind was rushing past the windows, making that familiar sound of airspeed that so reminded me of a waterfall back home. Jack, watching the airspeed indicator, announced "rotate", the indication that we had reached takeoff speed. I pulled back on the wheel. We left the ground, climbing into a silky smooth sky. I wagged the wings from left to right to get a feel for the Goose, and to wave toward the Chinese Army at the field below. I climbed to 1,000 feet, heading for the train tunnel that we had departed the day before. But I wasn't looking for the tunnel. It was merely a landmark. I was looking for the shack on the side of the hill.

I found it easily enough. There was a thin stream of smoke rising high from the shack's chimney in the still morning air. The woman was no doubt warming herself after a chilly night. I flew a tight circle around their home, banking to the left so I could see the shack out my side cockpit window. At last a couple emerged from the shack. I recognized the woman immediately by her tight gray hair bun. She pointed at us, then they both waved. I wagged the wings and waved through the window, then turned toward the west and climbed. We were finally underway to the Strait of Malacca. I looked to Jack with a grin.

"Friends of yours?" he asked.

"Old pals," I answered.

I leveled off at 10,000 feet, marveling at the bright blue sky ahead. It was going to be a hell of a day.

PART TWO. INTO THE WHIRLPOOL

Chapter Twenty-Eight

We flew to the west, cutting across northern Indochina before crossing the border into China. The terrain below was rough and unfinished, consisting mostly of range after range of mountains and jagged hills. There were occasional villages wedged into small valleys between the ranges, but for the most part we were over the vast wilderness of southwest China. It was empty, rugged, forlorn and inspiring.

After a solid hour of the same scenery I began to feel as if we were all alone here in the Goose, suspended in time and place, the only living souls in the world. It reminded me of a Sunday afternoon long ago. I was five, maybe six years old. My dad took me fishing at a small lake an hour's ride from our ranch. We tethered the horses under a canopy of oak trees, and walked a short path down to the lakeshore. He found us a good spot among the willows, then helped me get my lure into the water. He left me there for ten minutes to gather firewood to cook our lunch. That morning everything was calm and quiet. There was no breeze, the lake was mirror smooth, and even the birdsongs were absent. After a few minutes I noticed the silence. After a couple more I felt totally alone. It was a strange mix of power and fear. I held on as long as I could, then gave in and called for my dad. He answered with a quick whistle. Suddenly all was well. I always remembered that day. I'd been alone many times since, sometimes riding the fence line alone for a full two days or more. But there was always something to keep me anchored to the world. The breeze, a blustery wind, a rainstorm, the screech of a hawk, the many and varied sounds of nature. Things you can feel or hear. Things to keep me plugged into God's creation. But that day at the lake helped me understand something fundamentally simple: we're made to be a part of the world. Being disconnected from it, even for a few imagined minutes, is an unnatural thing.

The air was calm, enabling the Goose to cruise along at a good pace. There was a kind of stillness to our speed, as if we were simply hanging in the air as the empty terrain rolled toward us. The drone of the engines, coupled with the rush of the air, merged into an unchanging hum that eventually faded into the background. It became the sound of silence. I was suddenly a six year old on a fishing trip that needed to hear a whistle.

"Lhasa," I said over the drone. "Tell us about the shipwreck."

He leaned forward in his seat, beginning a tale that went on for almost an hour. I'll give you a shortened version of his story. You already know a fair bit about the *Flor De La Mar*. But Lhasa helped us to understand the bigger picture. It started with something called the *Age of Discovery*. The Age of Discovery, along with the Renaissance, could be called the transition between the Middle Ages and the Modern Era. It began in the fifteenth century, and lasted for almost two hundred years. It was driven by the European exploration of the world, primarily the Americas, Africa, Asia, and the Pacific. Many of the explorers were driven by the sheer joy of discovery, but on the whole the European powers were driven by trade. That is to say, they were driven by the acquisition of wealth and influence. Which really meant the acquisition of valuable spices and sometimes, gold and silver.

This rapid overseas expansion drove significant

competition between European countries, creating the colonialism that is only now fading away. It drove the conquests of Africa, Asia, and the Americas. It initiated worldwide trade, created a vast increase in knowledge across many new disciplines, and drove a vast cultural expansion that made the world what it is today. It was innovation at work.

India and the East Indies were spice-rich countries, and the European powers expended a good bit of effort and ingenuity finding efficient ways to reach them. If one happened to live in an island or country along one of these trade routes, your life became mighty interesting. If you were enterprising and lucky, you might find a way to earn a nice living by supporting the European voyages. You might help to resupply them, or to repair their ships, or to guide them in areas that you knew well. But it was a dangerous fence line to walk. If you were too enterprising, and became rich on their dime, then the European powers might cut you out of the deal. And that could mean some nasty things if you were an individual. You might wake up one day and find your pockets empty. Or worse, find yourself missing entirely. If you were a city or small nation, and the Europeans determined that your cut of the action was "unfair", you would simply be conquered. The reward for your success would be the forfeiture of your wealth to your new nation. That nation would then gave you some new laws to abide by, and they would assign a governor or administrator to help you understand all the new benefits you qualified for as a colony of a European power. Your new king would certainly appreciate your contribution to his nation.

Like so many countries or kingdoms of the world, Malacca found itself in this exact situation. Malacca was ideally positioned on the Strait of Malacca, which rapidly became a fast, convenient route for shipping goods. Valuable goods. Ships from many nations would naturally stop at Malacca for supplies. So the little kingdom found itself awash in stuff. Stuff like spices, gold, silver, jewels, and European explorers. This was great for a while. Until the European powers noticed how much stuff Malacca had accumulated. Then the explorers suddenly became conquerors. It was the arrival of Afonso de Albuquerque on the *Flor De La Mar* that finally ruined the party. Because Portugal decided it was time to muscle in on Malacca's success and get a piece of the action. Only they didn't just want a piece. They wanted it all. The Sultan of Malacca didn't think that was fair. Which was unfortunate, because it then it became a bloody and destructive conquest. Malacca lost. Portugal got her strategic port. For a while. And Albuquerque got his treasure. For an even shorter time. That treasure, all of it, the wealth of an entire kingdom, was now lying in the Strait of Malacca right were Albuquerque left it. Well, at least somewhere around there. Hey, I've lost my wallet a few times in my own bunk room. I guess it makes sense that one could lose a ship in a vast ocean strait.

I'll be honest, I forgot I was flying an airplane, forgot I was in China, forgot the Japanese Army, and forgot that I owed Sara Hudson a raft. Lhasa's story came alive in my head, taking me back in time and far away. It was a story about people and places that I never knew existed. It all seemed so exotic compared to my life in Idaho. So much bigger than me. So long ago. The best I can explain it, is that it made me feel as if I was now tethered to the world with a much thicker rope, strong and taut and...humming. The kind of hum you can feel through your fishing rod when you have a strong salmon on the line. Only this wasn't a salmon.

When Lhasa finished his story, I looked at Jack who simply raised his eyebrows. Until now, I thought of Lhasa's shipwreck as a pile of water-logged timber and a few trinkets. Now I had an entirely different perspective. Now that I fully understood the story of Albuquerque and the *Flor de la Mar*, I realized that our journey was another event in the long, unresolved story of the ship. I had a much better perspective, as if I were viewing our journey from a great distance and across a great deal of time. I had a vision that the events were jumbled together in a giant whirlpool that had been spinning for centuries. Until now we'd been orbiting just out of its reach, but when we crossed into Burma and turned to the south, we would be on a crescent-shaped course to its center. We were in its pull. I looked out the window. We were moving again. I felt alive once more. *Dang* I wished I could share all of this with the folks back home. I was about to burst.

But something troubled me. "Lhasa," I asked. "Why now? How has the wreck lasted for so long without anyone touching it? Why is it still there?"

"Because fate smiles on the worthy, my friend. As I said, the ship hit a reef and sank. The survivors knew where it hit the reef because it was the shallow reef that saved them. The survivors reached the nearby Malaccan village and told their story. The villagers paddled out to the reef three days later. The wreck was gone from the point where it hit the reef. There were a few bits and pieces but nothing more. The night of the wreck there was a vicious storm. It lasted for two days. I believe the waves pushed the wreck off the reef and into deeper water, perhaps pushed by the current in the Strait. The villagers had no way to search for the wreck in deep water. But they remembered the location on the reef.

"For centuries the wreck was not seen at all. People have looked for it off and on. There have even been periodic search expeditions. No sign anywhere. Malacca eventually became a British colony under a treaty with the Dutch. The Dutch East Indies to the south then became a Dutch colony. The border between the two is the Strait of Malacca. There's much piracy in the Strait. There always has been. There are many valuable goods moving through the Strait all the time. The British and Dutch have tried for years to stop the piracy, but it has been difficult and costly for them.

"Last year, in the waters off Malacca, the British Navy returned and began testing a new weapon to stop the pirates. Or perhaps to stop the Japanese. A type of torpedo. The villagers say British ships fire torpedoes at targets that they tow behind their ships. The torpedoes don't work very well. They usually miss. Sometimes they hit their target but don't explode. Sometimes they miss and explode underwater. The villagers like when that happens because it causes a big geyser to go into the air. Like a show. For a few days last year, there were some geysers near the reef. Almost half a mile from the old wreck location. Then the British ships left. The villagers went fishing again at the reef, and found many dead fish. Probably killed by torpedo explosions. But they also found something else. The fisherman began finding pieces of pottery in their nets. Every day for weeks. At first they saved them. But there were so many they started throwing them back into the sea.

"One day a young woman in the village was looking through the scraps of pottery. She found a piece that had a design, or symbol, embossed into it. She liked the symbol. The piece also had words on it but she couldn't read. She gave the piece to the village elder as a gift. He agreed that the symbol was artful, and that it was a thoughtful gift. He didn't recognize the symbol, but he could read and write. He definitely recognized the words. He sent me an urgent letter that still took months to arrive. This is part of the letter." Lhasa removed a piece of folded parchment from his bag and passed it ahead to me. "He drew the symbol at the top."

Jack took the controls. I took the parchment and looked at the symbol. It was a shield decorated with a four-square checkerboard pattern, with a Christian cross on two of the squares.

"He also wrote down the words that were stamped into the piece of pottery. Unfold the parchment," Lhasa instructed.

I unfolded it and there were four words written in a shaky hand and underlined. I showed it to Jack.

Flor de la Mar.

The wreck had been uncovered by the torpedo explosions. Jack whistled in surprise. It reminded me of Dad's whistle that day at the lake, when I was a young boy and called for help.

Chapter Twenty-Nine

The Japanese military had a problem. Throughout 1939 and 1940 the Japanese Empire had expanded rapidly, via conquest, to the Philippines, Korea, China, Indochina, Laos, and soon Thailand. Their victims usually resisted, causing Japan to fight simultaneous battles on several fronts. The Japanese war machine grew rapidly, making it thirsty for oil. Japan had no native source of the stuff. The United States supplied over 90 percent of Japan's oil needs. The Japanese military knew that the flow of American oil would come to an abrupt end, and soon.

So the military surveyed its ever-expanding region of influence and realized that the Dutch East Indies, now called Indonesia, had huge supplies of both oil *and* rubber. Rubber was another valuable commodity necessary for Japan's war effort. The Dutch East Indies suddenly looked like that nice, well-stocked market on the outskirts of town. But there was one problem. *That end of town* belonged to the Dutch. The Japanese military couldn't afford to buy it. So they decided to take it. It was time to lock down their existing conquests and hit the road for the Dutch East Indies. The sooner the better. Their thirst was growing by the day.

We crossed the border into Burma. The Dutch East Indies began about 1,200 miles away. Malacca was another 500 miles past that. We had flown almost 500 miles in three hours, so we decided to land in the first sizable town to refuel and stretch our legs. Jack surveyed his charts and decided on Kengtung, a town in the eastern province of Burma. We adjusted our course, heading for the town.

The terrain began to change. The mountains were diminishing in height, if not in quantity. We eventually reached a valley that was covered wall-to-wall with multicolored of crops. The town of Kengtung was in the middle of the valley, surrounded by the fields. There was a river that fed the valley from the north, and a large lake in the middle of the valley, on the west side of the town. We couldn't see an airstrip so we opted for the lake. We circled it at 1,000 feet to survey our landing site. There were docks on the southern end, with a few small fishing boats. The docks would do just fine as a tie-up.

A water landing in a float plane takes some skill. I had never done it. I asked Jack to show me the ropes. He took the controls and explained the process. The key was to hit the water straight on, not crabbed to one side or the other by a crosswind. If you hit the water at an angle, the impact would roll the plane in a big, bad splash. Water was unforgiving in this regard. This meant that, ideally, we wanted to land flat, heading straight into the wind. But that wasn't always possible, if the body of water didn't abide. In that case, you crabbed into the wind during your final approach, and then straightened and leveled the plane at the last moment, just above the water. It required excellent timing and a good understanding of the wind. Any waves or swells added another dimension to the challenge, which often made a water landing impossible.

Jack circled the lake, looking for signs of the wind direction. The best indicators are flags or banners blowing in the wind. If there aren't any, one then looked at the sway of trees, or the movement of ripples in the grass or water. I soon learned that one could almost always find colorful flags or banners in Burma. From the many banners we could see, we agreed that there was a slight but manageable crosswind.

Jack handled it well. The plane landed softly on the lake. The sound of airspeed was momentarily replaced by the sound of rushing water. We slowed quickly and the floats settled in to the lake. "Take us to the docks," Jack told me. "Just remember, we're a boat now, not an airplane." In other words, we had no brakes. It was all finesse at this point.

I cut the right engine, and cautiously floated us toward the docks using only the left. When we were 50 yards out I idled the engine and feathered the prop to let us coast toward the docks. A few fishermen on the docks were watching us carefully. One moved toward the edge of the dock that we were approaching. I cut the left engine so he wouldn't have to deal with a spinning prop, and used the rudder to turn us sideways to the dock. I miscalculated and left us about fifteen feet from the dock.

Marco ribbed me. "Hank you're a better pilot than boat captain. I'll haul us in." He opened the side left side door and squeezed behind my seat to exit the plane. He slid down the wing and landed on the left side float. A fisherman threw him a rope from the dock. Marco caught it, tied it to the float, and pulled us easily toward the dock. I stretched my long legs to each side of the rudder pedals. It would feel good to stand up.

Lhasa replaced the villager's letter and repacked a few belongings in the back of the plane. Jack turned off the instrument switches and the fuel valve. One by one we climbed out the left door, slid down the wing to the float, and then stepped onto the dock. Marco had tied us to one of the dock posts, so the Goose was now secure. Jack grabbed our packs, passed them to us, and then closed the cockpit door. We had arrived in Kengtung.

I took a quick look around. Kengtung was a nice little

town. It reminded me of a small version of Kunming, without all the frantic activity. It was clear the residents didn't feel in danger from the Japanese. It was just business as usual. It was a refreshing feeling. The environment put me at ease.

I had forgotten that there are challenges anywhere, war or not. I would soon be reminded, sure enough.

Chapter Thirty

After getting some quick directions from the fishermen, we walked a few blocks into the heart of the town of Kengtung. Just beyond the small town square was a three-story palace, made of white stone with many arched windows and pointed domes on either side. It was a distinct South Asian style, not the Chinese-style I had become so familiar with. Alongside the square there was a market, consisting mostly of carts with a variety of different foods. Some of the vendors were cooking noodles or various soups over charcoal fires. Others offered skinned ducks, chickens, or fish, and still others had small varieties of vegetables or fruits. We picked up some vegetables, fruits, and rice cakes, walked to a shaded area on the edge of the square, and ate quietly. Not a bad little meal, in a nice little place.

We quickly found there was no aviation fuel to be found in Kengtung, but we didn't need any for several hundred more miles. We took an ambling path back to the lake, wandering around the town to take in the sights. That's when we ran into trouble. The central part of the town was fairly compact, with many one and two-story buildings. The town had been built small and compact, no doubt to maximize the agricultural space of the valley. There were alleyways between the buildings. Some were quite narrow. As we passed one alleyway, we heard a muffled cry, as if someone needed help. We stopped, backtracked, and entered the alley. It was about four or five yards wide. There were four men there, and one woman. They had formed a circle around her, and were pushing her back and forth between them. She was young, maybe in her late teens. They laughed each time she bounced off one of them. Though she covered her face with her hands, I could see that she was sobbing.

Now where I come from, these types of games just aren't neighborly. We don't treat women that way. Nor men for that matter. It's simply not the type of thing you want to do to folks. I had learned that lesson clear enough in my early years. As I child, I had been told, repeatedly, to do unto others as you would have them do unto you. Treat others as you wanted to be treated. I figured the same rule applied here in Kengtung. But here's the thing. As I got older, I realized that there are times when someone really might deserve an old-fashioned ass-kicking, particularly if it was necessary to knock some sense into them. I realized that these guys needed the same tough love. I took a step forward in reflex, and was ready to deliver some loving, when Marco put his arm in my path to stop me. "It's okay," he said. I studied him. He was taut and intent. I looked to Lhasa. He nodded. I stepped back to let Marco step ahead.

"Hey! What's this?" Marco yelled. He continued forward with his open hands outstretched. He had nothing to fight with, if it came to that.

The four knuckleheads stopped and turned to Marco. But they didn't move. The woman was still between them. One of them answered defiantly. I didn't understand his words, but they were clear enough to me. Marco continued his advance, step by step. Eventually the leader pushed the young woman aside and lined up with his buddies, staring Marco down. The woman slid to the ground, pulled her knees to her chest, and covered her head with her hands and arms. I couldn't get to her – Marco and the knuckleheads were in the way. The four sized up the four of us, and seemed to conclude that we were sacks of meat. To be used as punching bags. We were in for a fight, sure enough.

I surveyed our opposition. They were young and strong, probably in their early twenties, lean and mean. They didn't appear to have any weapons, but their fists were gonna hurt. Now here's the thing. I've been in a few fistfights. I'm not afraid to say, I hate getting punched in the face or head. It hurts like hell, but most of all I hate that sound it makes inside your head when you get smacked. Just thinking about it makes my ears ring and my jaw hurt. So in that rare case when good old country manners fail and a fight is necessary, I always prefer to fight with my shoulder. I just lower my shoulder and drive it into my opponent, knocking them backward and hopefully knocking the wind out of them. I learned it easy enough. It's a great way to push a heavy steer into moving the direction you want him to go. Best of all, it doesn't hurt your face. I decided a little cow punching would work here just as well, and again took a step forward toward Marco.

"No," Lhasa said quietly. "He doesn't need any help. You'll only get in his way."

It all happened quickly. The four walked toward Marco with anger in their eyes, obviously irritated that he had interrupted their fun. Marco stood his ground as long as he could, then he stepped to the side and grabbed a broom that was leaning against the wall. He stepped on the broomstick with his right foot, just above the bristles, and snapped it off. He kicked the bristles aside, placed both hands in the middle of the stick, and swung it back so it was horizontal with the ground, against his right shoulder, and pointing toward the four. They tried to circle him, but he whacked the first one in the arm then punched the second one in the foot with the end of the stick. That guy yelped in pain. It only energized his buddies. But they were no match for Marco. I gotta say, what he did with that stick was a work of art. Minimal movements, carefully timed, unpredictable, with power and conviction. He hit those guys five ways from Sunday before they could even begin to react. His hands were hardly moving, there in the center of the stick, but each end was moving in wide, powerful arcs that connected loudly with various body parts. Sometimes the arcs were horizontal at waist level, sometimes vertical toward the top of a head, but most often they were a combination of the two, which allowed Marco to strike almost anywhere he wanted. Even on a moving target. If that wasn't enough, he often reversed the arcs in a split second to keep his opponents on their toes. At any given time, at least two of the four were temporarily stunned by a hard hit. The other two were jockeying for position while trying to block or dodge the arcs. When Marco wasn't swinging he was jabbing, which was just as effective. Especially in the stomach or the foot.

As I watched I realized that Marco was holding back. He wasn't fighting to cause serious injury. I could tell he could hit much harder than he was. He was just trying to get their attention and wear these guys down. He had *my* attention. He wore *them* down. It only took a minute and a half. Marco was tougher than a twenty-cent steak. Two of the guys were on the ground trying to protect their heads, and the other two were leaning against one wall or the other trying to protect their sides. Marco stopped, took a few steps back, and re-chambered his stick. Then he yelled, "Go!" motioning with his head toward the far end of the alley. The two against the wall helped their two buddies on the ground then all four ran off down the alley and disappeared into the far end of town.

Marco put the stick against the wall. He wasn't even breathing hard.

"What was that?" I asked, still stunned by what I'd seen.

"That's what you learn when you grow up in the Philippines. When you get conquered repeatedly over the generations, and your masters take away all your weapons to prevent you from fighting back. You learn to fight with broomsticks, threshing sticks, wheat scythes, and water buckets. You do it with restraint, because you don't want to break your good farm tools." He looked toward the wall of the alley. "Which reminds me," he said, wiping a bead of sweat from his brow, "I owe someone a broom."

Chapter Thirty-One

The young woman hadn't moved. She was still sitting in the alley, her knees to her chest. We approached her slowly. She was shaken and scared. Lhasa knelt down and spoke to her in soft tones. She nodded and started sobbing again. Lhasa sat down next to her. He just sat there quietly, staring at the ground. He was...being present. I figured he would sit there all afternoon or all week long if necessary, until the woman felt safe. Good for him.

"Guys," I said quietly, "She's in good hands. I think we're making her nervous." I called to Lhasa and told him to meet us at the Goose. He nodded. The rest of us turned and walked back out of the alleyway. That's when we met the town constable.

It was easy enough to figure. He was middle aged, medium height, dressed in a white tunic and khaki pants. The dead giveaway was his belt. He wore a brown belt with a loop at the side. It held a well-used nightstick. "Let's see what we have here," he said. "American, American, what...Filipino? And Chinese or Tibetan there in the alley. Am I right?" He spoke remarkably good English.

Jack answered. "Lhasa's from Tibet. Otherwise, you're right."

The constable looked to Marco. "I saw a bit of your action there at the end. Tell me what happened."

"Those guys were mistreating that young lady. Very bad manners. I wanted them to stop. They finally did."

"Um hm. Did you ask them to stop before you did the broom-stick dance?"

"I tried to. But they didn't listen."

"Um hm. Where you fellows from?"

"Kunming in China. We flew in a bit earlier today. Just stopping for some food and rest."

"Um hm. I saw you fly in. Interesting plane. Hard to miss. I always like to greet visitors. Sorry it took me so long." He paused. "How long did you say you're planning on staying?"

"Until Lhasa's done calming the young lady," I answered.

He looked to me. "You're a tall fellow, even for an American."

I wasn't sure if it was a question or a statement. "We grow them tall where I come from."

"I see." His eyes softened. "Wait here please." He walked into the alley and knelt down next to the woman. He spoke with her for a couple of minutes, and then seemed to consider something. After a moment he patted her knee, stood and walked back to us. He ran his hand through his short salt-and-pepper hair. "I'll tell you what," he said to Marco. "You did a nice job there in the alley. All four of you. You took action while your friends showed restraint. Never seen anything quite like that. Why don't I get you some tea while you're waiting for your friend? My house is just that way a bit." He pointed down the block.

"Much appreciated," Jack said. "But not necessary."

"Oh I wasn't asking," he said to Jack, with a slight smile. "I was saying."

"Well then some tea would be fine."

"Can you help me find a new broom?" Marco asked.

He nodded. "I'm glad you mentioned that. I'm sure we can find one somewhere."

"My name is Sandar," the constable said, "but you can

call me Sandy."

We sat cross legged on some pillows on the floor of Sandy's small home. He noticed my look of surprise at his nickname.

"I attended prep school in Britain," he explained. "It was an adventure and a privilege for a villager from these parts. A missionary couple were my benefactors. They sponsored several other orphans as well. My role here is my way of repaying that gift."

"I see," I responded. "This seems like a good town. Looks like you're doing a fine job."

"Depends on the day. We have our problems, same as anywhere else. But here everyone knows each other. The same families have lived here for generations. Doesn't mean they get along, but it does mean they can't hide. Take those fellows in the alley for example. I know all four of them. I know the young lady. She's a sad story. Her mother died six months ago. Her father disappeared a couple of years ago. She lives with her aunt, but they're struggling. Those young men prey upon the needy. I'll leave it at that."

"Will she be okay?" I asked.

"Yes, we'll take good care of her. At the moment, she's embarrassed and shaken. No reason to be embarrassed, but I certainly understand. She told me she feels safe with your friend. I'm grateful for his presence. I'm not good at comforting folks."

"What about the four men?"

"Yes, we'll take care of them too." He took a sip of tea and looked off into the distance. "Very unfortunate. They're all four on a bad path." His face took on a downcast expression. "And one of them is my son."

Sigh.

Chapter Thirty-Two

I had a dream that night. It was vivid and real. In my dream, I was sitting by a campfire on the beach in the East Indies. It was nighttime. The Goose was floating in the water just off the beach, tied to a palm tree on the shore. The moon was out and the calm ocean waves reflected the moonlight in a silvery glow. There was a light tropical breeze that felt refreshing and cool compared to the warmth of the fire. I suddenly realized that I was alone. I was confused as to where Jack, Lhasa, and Marco were. I stood, anxiously looking for my companions. After a minute or two, I noticed a figure moving through the palms, weaving its way carefully among the vegetation. I couldn't quite make it out among the shadows of the trees, but I knew instinctively that it was a man. I couldn't tell who he was, but his gait – his manner – was somehow familiar.

The man arrived at the edge of the palm forest and emerged onto the sand of the beach. He wore a cowboy hat and was whistling a familiar song. He held a fishing pole over his shoulder and a bait bag around his waist. He walked directly toward me and at last looked up. His face was no longer in shadow. I recognized him immediately. The man was my father. But not my father as he looked now. He was my father when he was younger. He was the man who took me fishing that day when I was a boy and who whistled to break the silence when I felt so alone.

"Mighty fine evening, isn't it son?" he asked. He grinned, rushing to embrace me. I could smell leather, tractor oil, and dirt. The smells of home.

"It sure is Dad. How did you get here?"

"Oh I rode Ole Painter as far as the creek. Tied him up and walked the rest of the way. Not easy making my way through those palms. You need to build a proper path."

"I'll get to that tomorrow," I said. Making a path suddenly seemed sensible and urgent.

"I see you got a nice fire going for us. Let's catch us some fish for our supper."

When we got to the edge of the surf, he cast his line into the sea. We sat down on the sand while waiting for a bite.

"Mighty pretty place you got here," he said.

"I'm just passing through. But I do like it here."

"Where you headed?"

"East, to Malacca. Got some urgent business to take care of. Then I'll be heading home." I was about to explain more, but I couldn't remember what was so important about Malacca.

"How long, you figure?"

I tried to do some quick flying distance calculations in my head, but my mind was blank. "Not rightly sure. Three, four months I guess."

"I see." He paused. "Can I give you some advice, son?"

"Always."

"It seems to me, that you could get to where you're going much faster if you wanted to."

"How?"

"Well, it seems to me that this airplane of yours," he motioned to the Goose, "is slowing you down."

"How's that? The Goose is a fast plane. Fastest way to get where I'm going."

"You sure about that? I don't mean are you sure about the Goose being fast. I can tell just by looking at her that she can gallop. What I mean is, maybe the Goose is an easy way to get somewhere fast. But maybe it would be quicker to get there slow."

I gave him a puzzled look. I was rightly confused.

"I guess what I'm trying to say is, I think you're in a hurry to get to a *place*, when you should be trying to get to *something else*. Maybe if you slow down, you'll be there."

"What are you talkin' about Dad?"

He paused to check his line then reeled it in just a bit to keep it taut. "You know how it is at home. If one of our family, or friends, or neighbors needs something, we find a way to get it to them. They do the same for us." "Sure, I know that."

"So why are you here?"

"To help a bunch of people," I responded defensively.

"We'll that's mighty fine. But where are those people?" He looked one way and then the other, up and down the beach, as if searching for a bunch of folks.

I couldn't answer that one easily. "They're all over the place. In West China, and Dutch East Indies , and soon Thailand and Laos. And the Philippines, and..."

"Whoa!" he interrupted. "You've stuffed yourself a might heavy backpack to carry. Does Malacca have something that's gonna set everything right? That's gonna lighten that load? Is that why you're in such a hurry to get there?"

"Well...yes." I remembered now why Malacca was so important. "Yes, it does."

"You sure about that?"

I looked at my father. I realized I wasn't sure.

"Like I said, son, I think you're pretty close to your goal. Don't confuse a place with a destination." He paused for a bit. "I know you want to help a bunch of folks. Seems to me that whether you catch a whole mess of fish at once, or a couple of fish one at a time, you're still gonna eat. One at a time is more fun." His pole jerked. "Well look at that. Dinner's on the way. Feels like a nice rainbow trout. She's got some fight in her too!"

A rainbow trout? In the ocean? Then I woke from my dream with a start. I was sitting on the beach at the lake in Kengtung Burma, my head resting in my folded arms, which were in turn resting on my raised knees. It was nighttime. There was a campfire. Marco was whistling a melody. Lhasa and Jack were cooking fish on the fire. I realized I had dozed off, maybe only for a minute or two.

I looked toward the water, at the Goose, floating there at the dock. She lifted and settled in the small swells of the lake. She was tugging at her bridle, waiting to fly fast to Malacca. Waiting to slow me down.

I could smell freshly cooked rainbow trout. And leather, and tractor oil, and dirt. Plain as day.

Sigh.

Chapter Thirty-Three

A dream is just a dream, right? I mean, it wasn't really my younger father giving me advice in my dream. It was just *me* giving me advice, in a creative way. So it wasn't as if it was sound advice from a wise elder. It was just...well...me. Just medium-wise Hank. Well, maybe medium-rare wise Hank. I'll admit that I'm not done yet. I still have a lot to learn. But just admitting that means I'm still cooking. Right?

And why is this important? See, when we were at Constable Sandy's house, and he told us that his son was one of the knuckleheads that Marco broom-swept, my first reaction was sadness. Sadness for Sandy. I could only imagine how he must feel. All I could say was "I'm sorry."

My second reaction was the usual reflex. What could I do, or what advice could I offer, to make things better? It's the man thing to do. Then I wondered, what would I do anyway? I don't know anything about Kengtung, about what it's like to live in Kengtung, or about what it's like to be a constable in Kengtung. I definitely don't know what it's like to be a knucklehead in Kengtung. Then I realized, I do know what it's like to be a knucklehead in Idaho.

I did some monumentally stupid things when I was seventeen. I was on a good path, but then I decided I wanted to be a famous rodeo star. To earn a bunch of money and get a bunch of attention. See, I saw an image one day in a magazine. It was a painting of a cowboy riding a bucking horse. It was a classic image of the Wild West. It was romantic and heroic. I decided I wanted to be the guy in the painting. I wanted to be a bronco buster. The bronco-busting event in a rodeo was a real crowd pleaser and attention getter. We had plenty of wild horses in the country around our ranch to practice with. So I jumped in headfirst and headstrong. I fell in with some older cowboys to learn their skills. I also absorbed some of their bad habits. I started neglecting my responsibilities at the ranch to pursue fame and fortune. I rode in a few country rodeos, won a little bit of prize money, and felt I was a big star. I treated my family poorly when they needed help. That was bad enough. But what happened next was the worst. The older cowpokes were a bad influence and their behavior began to rub off on me. I'll spare you all the details. But as one example, they regularly stole from their ranch owners, and often bragged about it. They challenged me to prove my mettle, and I stole a good bit of money from my dad. To show that I could be a big man too. To earn respect from the wrong folks. It was hard on my parents. They just didn't raise me that way. It hurt my dad deeply. AJ suffered too, filling in for me when I didn't show up for work. Which happened often. I spiraled into a dive, driven by false pride. I became a headstrong, self important, unreliable, thieving, lying sack of manure.

Then I broke my left leg in a bad fall when a horse rolled over me. It was a bad break and didn't heal right. My rodeo career was over before it started. So then I had to deal with my pride. I wanted to be that cowboy in the painting, and now I was just a cowboy in a leg cast. For a spell it just made things worse. I stopped working the ranch altogether. Became sulky and impatient with the folks that loved me. My dad tried hard to lift me up from the pit I'd dug myself into, but I resented him and didn't trust him. What a piece of work I was. I did mean things. Never as mean as what the gang in the Kengtung alley did to the young woman.

But still hurtful. My family never gave up on me. They held the door open and kept my place at the table. But I didn't listen to them. I thought I knew more than they did. Pretty soon most of the folks that knew me started avoiding me. The ones that didn't were a bad influence.

Then one guy turned me around when nobody else could. I knew him from the close-by town of Stanley. He was a miner. Worked a claim outside the town. It never panned out, so he earned most of his money doing odd jobs here and there. He was gigantic Yugoslavian guy, blue eyes, dark hair, darkly tanned, and stronger than an ox. His upper arms were as thick as tree trunks. He could've been a real bad hombre if he wanted to. But he was as gentle as a puppy. Went out of his way to help people. His name was Stef. Short for Stefan or Stephen? I never knew. But everyone just called him Stef. I had no idea what his last name was. You could know Stef well without knowing his full name. He was just one of those types of people.

Stef was a genuine hero. There was a fire in town one night. It started in the kitchen of the hotel on the first floor. The folks in the saloon on the ground floor got out. But there was a family of four in a room on the second floor. They were trapped. The townsfolk set up a water bucket brigade from the river to fight the fire, but it had already taken hold. A portion of the second floor collapsed, the doorway was blocked, and the building was too dangerous to enter. It was a tragedy in the making.

When all seemed lost, Stef appeared with a wet bandanna around his face, ran through the front door, muscled a five-hundred pound timber and a pile of burning rubble out of the way, then fought his way to the family on the second floor. The stairs were half gone at that point and he still made it. When he reached the family he realized they had no way out. The only window was small and it was a long drop to the downhill slope of a boulder field on the bank of the river. So Stef improvised. He used his big legs as a battering ram, kicking a huge hole through the exterior wall on the second floor. He carried the family through the opening to the roof of an adjoining building. Saved them all. Stef was a cast-iron hero. Then he just went back to his odd jobs and didn't want to hear anything about it. He was the most humble guy I'd ever met.

Stef passed by me on the road one day, driving his old dusty truck. I was riding into town. My cast had been removed but my leg was still weak. He stopped in the middle of the road and waited for me to catch up. "Hank Evans, right?" he asked.

I nodded.

"I need some help at the Anderson ranch. Why don't you follow me there? It'll be a solid day's work."

I just stared at him. Who did he think I was? I didn't work for him. I had important stuff to do. But he just motioned toward the Anderson ranch, said "I'll see you there in thirty minutes," and drove off.

Damn. So I rode to the Anderson ranch to give him a piece of my mind. But when I got there I didn't have the courage. Next thing I knew, I had helped him split firewood all day. It nearly killed me.

"Nice work Hank," he said. "Meet me at the Tanner's place tomorrow mornin'. Need your help there." His blue eyes drilled into me. I couldn't refuse.

I worked a bunch of odd jobs for two weeks. All over town and at a few different ranches. It was always the same thing. Stef just told me where to be. Didn't give me a choice. Didn't pay me neither. I never got up the courage to ask for money. I finally figured out that there wouldn't be any. Stef was making me do work for the folks as a kind of penance. To get the poison out of my system and give me a chance to make amends.

It worked. Took a while, but it worked. When I think of Stef I still get tears in my eyes. He took a stand for me. My parents and family welcomed me back with open arms, and I got back to life on the ranch. AJ still remembers a few irritating things from time to time, but my parents just treat me like the bad stuff never happened.

So it turns out I probably had some experience being a knucklehead, and unless the actions of a knucklehead varied based on the language you spoke or the food you ate, I probably knew exactly what it was like to be a knucklehead in Kengtung. I guessed that Sandy's son was probably about my age, which made it even more likely that we had something in common. A kind of international knucklehead kinship. So I realized, sitting there in Sandy's home, that I knew more than I thought I did. About being a knucklehead...or not.

When Sandy was talking about the gang, and said "and one of them is my son," it took me about two seconds to think all the stuff I just told you. That's when I sighed. Because I realized that I couldn't really convince myself that there was nothing I could do. That was very inconvenient, because the Goose was waiting for us at the lake. We had a flight to catch. Malacca wasn't getting any younger, the treasure wasn't hidden away in a safe lockbox, and the Japanese military wasn't on vacation. Of all the things we had or didn't need, time was not one of them. Yeah, I know that was confusing sentence. I meant to say that we were running out of time. I tried to say it in a medium-wise way, but...well...whatever. Like I said, I'm not done yet.

It was clear to me that Sandy invited us to his house for

two reasons. First, he was being a gracious town constable. He wanted to treat us as guests. Very neighborly of him. But second, he wanted help with his son. Who better to impact a troubled kid than an exotic visitor from a far away land? It was time for me to fill Stef's size fifteen boots. It was time to take a stand for someone like he had for me.

The four of us walked back to the lake, and the Goose, after spending a couple of hours with Sandy. Lhasa apparently did wonders with the young lady. When I last saw her she was laughing at a stupid joke from Marco. It was too late to fly out, so we decided to stay the night there at the lake. Now you understand the question I faced when I dozed off at the campfire. Now you understand the dream I had. You ever notice how we usually know the answer to a personal dilemma? But we often pretend that we don't, when that answer doesn't agree with us. Our dreams are more pure, as if somehow when we're asleep the question gets simpler. Or we stop fighting the obvious, and give in to the right thing to do. Or we stop making noise and start listening. To God. Dreams are smart that way. Smarter than a medium-rare cowboy, at least.

Chapter Thirty-Four

"Hank, what's on your mind?"

I looked up from my dinner plate as Lhasa sat down next to me.

"Bad fish?"

"No," I answered. "The fish tastes great. Bad appetite."

"Hmm. Bad appetite or bad mood?"

"Bad son, is what it is." I tossed a rock into the fire. "Lhasa, I need to stay here. You guys should leave in the morning. I'll catch up when I can. I gotta help Sandy with his son." I glanced to Lhasa. I felt sheepish. But I was sure of what I was saying.

Lhasa exhaled a long breath. It was frosty in the night air. "Did Sandy ask you to help his son?"

"Not in so many words. But you know he needs help. That's why he invited us to his house. He wouldn't ask for that big of a favor from four strangers that are just passing through. Some folks are too proud to ask. Sandy needs help. He cares about his son. I have a bit of experience that might help."

"Hank you're not old enough."

"Old enough? What does my age have to do with the price of tea in China – er - Burma?"

"I meant you're not old enough to have experience with a son that's gone bad."

"Maybe I was the son that was going bad," I said. "Maybe I figured out how to get back on the right trail. So maybe I can help Sandy's son. Doesn't matter anyway. I gotta try."

"How can you be sure?"

"Because my father rode Ole Painter down to the creek in Malaysia. Hiked through a bunch of jungle to reach me. We went fishing at the beach and he caught a rainbow trout. Which is nuts."

"It is nuts, as you say. Your father is not in Malaysia. There aren't rainbow trout in the ocean."

"No, it's not that. It's nuts because my dad is a terrible fisherman. He never catches anything. I'm the fisherman of the family. My dad couldn't catch a goldfish in a jar."

"Hank, you're not making sense."

"Sorry Lhasa. You see, my dad always said that he's not good at catching fish, because he's great at fishing for people. At finding people that are lost, or that are searching for something. He just finds 'em. Even people that we see every day that others overlook. He finds them. He knows what to say, and what to do. They trust him. He gives them a hand up, and points them in the right direction, and off they go. It's hard to explain but it's what my dad does best. The ranch is just a way for him to do it. My mom's the same way. Some folks are good at picking up stray animals and caring for them. My parents are great at picking up stray folks and inspiring them."

"Hank your parents sound like fine people. But I still don't understand."

"I had a dream, see? About my dad at the beach in Malaysia, right? In my dream, my dad caught a fish and I didn't. Don't you see? My dad and I were reversed. In my dream Dad was the good fisherman, because now *I'm* supposed to be the one fishing for people. *I'm* supposed to be my dad. It's my turn now. It's plain as day, at least to me. It's what I gotta do. It's my chance to make things good. To pay back a lot of things that good folks, including my parents, did for me. I gotta fish for Sandy's son."

Lhasa nodded. He placed his hands together as if in prayer, and bowed his head. He said something, too quiet for me to hear. He just stayed that way for half a minute. I knew better than to interrupt him. At last, he spoke. "Hank, I'm well pleased."

"So you agree with me staying here?"

"I'm well pleased because you've become a fisher of men. I'm more sure than ever that you're the one I was looking for. I could tell when I first met you in Dinjan. You were willing to take me on a dangerous flight over The Hump simply because Jack asked you to. Because Jack told you it was important to me. Because Jack told you that it would help people. You risked your life without asking for anything in return. You're skilled, honest, and humble. You're the same as Marco, and I've trusted him with many lives."

I didn't quite know what to say. I'm not good at receiving compliments. Makes me uncomfortable. Makes me want to talk about someone else. "Thanks Lhasa. I like Marco. I trust Marco. Marco's a good fisherman by the way. He caught a net full of fish at Lake Dian that day I met him."

Lhasa laughed his funny little laugh. "Hank you're mistaken. Marco caught a net full of minnows, in a lake that's famous for perch. Big perch. The locals told me that Lake Dian is so full of perch that you can walk across it without getting your ankles wet! Marco is one of the worst fishermen I've ever seen." He chuckled. "And based on your dream, maybe that's why he's one of the best people I know." He paused and studied me. "I don't know if Jack can fish or not, Hank. But it doesn't matter. Jack is on the right path too, believe me."

He stood and put his hand on my shoulder. "Hank, I have a big idea. You stay here and help Sandy's son. Catch up with us when you can. We'll be waiting for you. And Hank?"

"Yes Lhasa?"

"There's an old Chinese saying. 'Make happy those who are near, and those who are far will come.'"

"I see. I think."

"Hank?"

"Yes Lhasa?"

"That fish on your dinner plate isn't getting any younger."

Later that night I spoke to the guys. Explained my plan. They were surprised. They wanted to make sure *I* was sure. I convinced them. Once I did, they agreed with me. They wished me luck. We made a plan on how and where to meet up.

Marco took me aside just before we all fell asleep. "Hank, there's one thing you can do while you're here in Kengtung. Maybe Sandy can help you."

"I'm open to anything at this point, Marco. What do you need?"

"Lhasa brought me along for my diving skills. You know that, right?"

"Sure."

"You know much about pearl diving?"

"There aren't many pearl divers at a cattle ranch."

"I figured that. Well here's my problem. I'm going to need to dive to the wreck. From what Lhasa knows, the wreck is about a hundred feet deep. Not easy to get to. That's why it's still sitting there. I can dive that deep with no problem. But when I get to the wreck, I won't have much time to stay there before I have to come back up. I just can't hold my breath that long. I haven't figured this out yet. I need to either take some air with me, or have air pumped to me. Once I get there, I need to figure out how to uncover and bring up a bunch of stuff with each dive. If the wreck really contains gold, like Lhasa says, it's going to be heavy."

"Sounds like a real challenge. But I don't know a dang thing about diving, or sunken treasure, or shipwrecks."

"I know. But you know about ranch machines. Tractors, engines, pumps, winches and pulleys and such. I heard you talking about the hay baler the other day. And the hoist that you use to lift the bales to the top of the barn. You know how those fancy fishing reels work. They're just a winch, right? Plus I know you can handle ropes. So Hank, you're the guy that needs to solve all those problems. We're all here for a reason. Give it some thought. How do we get me down to the wreck, and back up with stuff? Over and over again? Hank, I really can't do it over and over again. Not in the same day at least. It's a real killer every time. That's why I took up fishing."

Oh Lord.

The next morning I said goodbye to my friends and walked into town. I found Sandy sitting on the half wall in front of his house, keeping a watchful eye on his community.

"Hank! What brings you here? I thought you were all planning to leave today."

"Well Sandy, let's talk about that a bit."

Chapter Thirty-Five

It was now late June of 1940. One after another, the countries of Southeast Asia were falling to the miseries of war. By now, the Japanese Empire occupied most of China. They faced resistance in western China, as the free Chinese dug themselves in and wouldn't let go. They were cut off from eastern China by the Japanese Army, but they were fighting for their lives, and for their children's lives. They were resourceful. Burma was a British colony on southwestern border of China. The country was used by China's allies as a conduit to move weapons and supplies to the free Chinese. The southern coast city of Rangoon – the capital of Burma - became a bustling seaport as the Chinese allies, including the US and Britain, offloaded tons of cargo every week. The cargo was transported north to the Burma-Chinese border via the British-built railroad which ran between Rangoon and the border city of Lashio. From there, the goods were transported by truck via the Burma Road (also British-built) to Kunming in China. To the center of the Chinese resistance.

French Indochina (which eventually become Vietnam) would soon fall to the Japanese Army, despite the best efforts of Brits like Paul Keast and a host of courageous and determined underdogs. They simply didn't have the firepower to stop the Japanese juggernaut. Indochina effectively became a Japanese-controlled puppet government of Germany, as France was now controlled by the German military. Among other things, this new development severely complicated the local restaurant menus.

Japan then moved swiftly to the west, through Thailand toward Burma. They intended to cut the railroad between Rangoon and Lashio, cutting off China's supply line. Burma would also serve as a gateway to India, another country on the Japanese Army's to-do list. The pesky Chinese resistance was a serious irritant that was costing the Japanese Empire time and money. As Japan secured Thailand and prepared to invade Burma, the Japanese government's simultaneous diplomatic gambits finally paid off. Under vigorous threats by Japan, an overwhelmed and panicked Britain agreed to halt the movement of supplies via the Burma Road. The supply line was shut down. The freedom of western China was now hanging by a thread. The Chinese needed The Hump pilots more than ever.

Thailand, on the eastern border of Burma, found itself sandwiched between French Indochina, now occupied by the Japanese but still belonging to German-controlled Vichy France, and Burma, a British colony whose days of freedom were numbered. The Thai government capitalized on the situation. Thailand aligned with Japan (they had no choice) and then took advantage of French Indochina's disarray by attacking the beleaguered country. They intended to settle a long-running argument with France over disputed territory. To help fund the Franco-Thai war, Thailand reached out to Burma, in the form of an invading military force. They wanted a simple, easily transportable but valuable resource. They found it in an abundant opium supply, which the British had effectively nurtured for decades. The Chinese purchased the opium from the Burmese; the British got a cut of the action. The Rangoon – Lashio railway was a cost-effective way to deliver the highly prized, highly addictive opium to the waiting Chinese. But opium can't stop army tanks. At this point, the free Chinese didn't have much use for it. But Thailand did. It was a cash crop. It grew mostly in the Shan State of Burma, which was just next door to Thailand. How convenient. It also happened to be the region that Hank was in. In fact Kengtung was smack in the middle of Shan State. Smack in the middle of a bunch of opium, that was suddenly a strategic resource. For taking, not buying.

Like China, the Japanese had no use for opium. It didn't fuel their machines of war. They needed petroleum. When President Franklin Roosevelt began an embargo of US shipments of petroleum to Japan, the Japanese quickly turned their sights to Dutch East Indies and Malaysia. They needed the region's plentiful oil, and they needed it quickly. Small problem though. The Philippines stood between Japan and Dutch East Indies. The Philippines were a US territory, protected by a crack contingent of well-fortified US Marines.

So many problems, so many miles, so little time.

To keep things in order, the Japanese military drew up a grand plan. Step by step, it went something like this: secure French Indochina, secure Thailand, cut off the Burma Road, weaken then conquer the Chinese resistance, invade and secure Burma, invade India (lots of good resources there, plus the clothes are colorful), while simultaneously invading the Philippines and then moving quickly to invade and secure the Dutch East Indies and Malaysia. Get oil, fill gas tanks, keep going. Oh, one problem. The US presence in the Philippines, blocking the way to The Dutch East Indies. Well, the best offense is…a good offense. So the Japanese military added one item to their to-do list. Attack the US. But where? The continental US is a long haul from mainland Japan. It would take a bunch of oil to get the Japanese Navy all the way to California. Kinda defeats the entire purpose.

But Hawaii's much closer! That's the ticket! Most of the US Navy was based in Pearl Harbor anyway. How convenient. It was settled, then. Mop up a few things here and there, send some scouts to Burma, India, the Dutch East Indies and Malaysia to develop attack strategies, while preparing big attacks on the Philippines and...Pearl Harbor. The Japanese prepared for a long visit to host of countries. It promised to be the tour of a lifetime.

The Japanese military had their plan. They went to work. It was started by waves of spies and scouts, who would pave the way for the Japanese military machine. They fanned out to every country in the region, and beyond. Where they didn't fit in, they bought people who did. Where the people couldn't be bought, they were forced. As soon as the spies learned the landscape, the Japanese Empire focused on the target. They invaded, took control, and then moved on. In the wake of the Japanese Army, opportunistic countries like Thailand took advantage of the turmoil. Often it was simply a case of self-preservation. In the same way, individuals also tried to survive. By any means possible. Some were enterprising, some were desperate, and some failed, to be forgotten in the fog of war.

Thunder rolled across the South Pacific. The thunder of guns.

Ko Than, Constable Sandar's son in the city of Kengtung in the Shan State of Burma, was an enterprising individual. He was a knucklehead, true enough. But to be fair he was only a part-time knucklehead. For his day job, he was a full-time opium exporter. It was a lucrative, if unstable, business. At least for the past five years. The Chinese usually had money, the British took their cut and looked the other way, and he was a big man in Kengtung. On most days everything worked just fine. He made money. More than he needed. He wasn't desperate. Yet. But he was smart enough to see trouble on the horizon. He was smart enough to know that his supply line would soon be interrupted, and that someone powerful would try to muscle in to take advantage of the disruption. An individual is no match for a determined gang. And definitely no match for an entire country. Like Thailand.

Ko Than, therefore, was job hunting. His days were becoming stressful, and he was growing anxious. How does a twenty-four year old opium exporter change careers in the midst of widespread economic upheaval? That was the question on his mind, every day lately. He didn't have the answer yet. He took his frustration out on random residents of Kengtung. They had just about had enough of him, whether his father was beloved Constable Sandar or not.

The ripples of war spread across the land, forcing people from their homes and pushing them to do amazing, resourceful stuff. For all the investment in war and misery, the best things came free: the kindness of strangers as they sought to preserve the goodness of life. It was a tough job. But it was a brand new career that many welcomed with open arms.

Chapter Thirty-Six

The Goose and its three passengers arrived in Rangoon, Burma a few hours after leaving Hank and the town of Kengtung. Jack, Lhasa, and Marco didn't waste much time on the ground. They were eager to get to Malacca. They refueled, bought some fresh food and water, and departed for the Dutch East Indies. They flew directly south over the Andaman Sea, keeping the Burma/Thailand peninsula to their left and the Andaman Islands, with the afternoon sun, to their right. The Andaman Sea was only five hundred miles wide, east to west, but Jack kept the Goose on the westward side, closer to the Andaman Islands. He was a prudent pilot and always had an emergency landing site in mind. The island chain was a convenient series of stepping stones all the way to the western tip of the Dutch East Indies.

The Andaman Islands were a territory of India in 1940. They were therefore, like all of India, a British colony. The islands would soon fall to the Japanese, but they still had a few months of freedom remaining. The Andamans were notorious for two things. First was the brutal British Penal Colony established in the 1850's to house political prisoners from India – those that dared to oppose Britain's colonial rule. It was no resort. In 1940 it was still doing a smashing business. Second, the islands were notorious for their cannibalistic natives. This was no fable. As one example, the Indian cargo ship *Nineveh* wrecked on the reef at North Sentinel Island in 1867. The survivors were promptly attacked by a determined force of cannibals. Only a handful escaped the subsequent neighborhood barbeque. Nothing much had changed over the years. Despite many attempts, the first peaceful encounter with the North Sentinel Islanders would have to wait more than a century– until 1991.

The British essentially confined themselves to the northern-most, and largest, island of the Andaman chain, Smith Island. The only settlement of any size on Smith Island was Port Blair, on the southern tip. It was also the site of the penal colony. The rest of the islands were, as the British would say, uncivilized. And downright dangerous.

An hour into their flight, Jack noticed that the left engine oil pressure was dropping. The needle on the oil pressure gauge was slowing slipping down to zero. The engine would seize long before it reached that point. So Jack had a decision to make. He could land somewhere on the Andaman chain to fix the engine with the tools and parts they had on board, or he could fly on to the better equipped, civilized, western tip of the Dutch East Indies. He chose the latter. It was just one of those decisions you have to make. At the time it seemed that either option was equally as good, and equally as bad. But Jack wasn't one to second-guess himself. His decision made, he flew along the island chain, heading for the Dutch East Indies but keeping his eye out for a flat spot to land in the Andamans. Just in case.

It took two days for Ko Than to show up.

I was eating hot and sour soup from a street vendor at the Kengtung town square. It was different than the Chinese version, but every bit as good. This bowl had a bunch of diced onion floating in the broth, along with a few pieces of lemon grass. First time I'd tasted lemon grass. Made me wonder if we had any at home, growing wild around the ranch. I suddenly had a new respect for weeds.

I'd enjoyed exactly three spoonfuls of the soup. Just

enough to become acquainted. It had the potential to be a great friendship. I had just lifted the fourth spoonful to my mouth when the spoon and my bowl were knocked from my hands from behind. The soup and the bowl fell to the ground, the spoonful of soup splashed on my arm. I stood quickly and turned toward my assailant, my arms up to protect my head, soup dripping from my elbow. It was a reflex action after getting pummeled a couple of times back home in the bunk house. Ko Than stood there with a sneer on his face. He was alone. I planted my feet, my right a bit behind my left, and prepared for a fight. But I didn't want to tangle with the constable's son. It wasn't why I was here. I unclenched my fists and showed open palms to Ko Than, while still protecting my face and head.

"That was my lunch." I nodded toward the puddle of soup on the ground, which was now seeping into the reddish clay.

"You're still here, huh?" he snarled. "Where are your friends?"

"They're busy. Yes, I'm still here. Still hungry, unfortunately." I nodded to my spilled soup. Sadly, I could still smell it. Savory and spicy. Hot and sour. How *do* they do that?

"Your soup is not my problem. *I'm* your problem now. You and your friends interfered with my business the other day. You owe me."

A small crowd had gathered, watching us from a respectable distance.

I studied him for a spell. He was acting tough. Like all bullies do. But I could tell that he was unsure of himself. He was unsettled. He seemed more angry than dangerous. On the other hand, I was calm. I had the upper hand. At least I thought I did. It was time for me to be the bigger man.

Time to defuse the situation. Well, actually, I *was* the bigger man. I'll be honest though. I really wanted to smack the guy for wasting my soup. And for abusing the woman in the alley. In Southeast Asia these days it seemed that entire countries went to war for less. But then I thought of my parents, and what they would do with someone like Ko Than. I'd never seen my dad fight. I knew he was capable. Ranching builds muscle and determination. But he always turned his energy in another direction. So I would too. Lucky for Ko Than. Unless he had some fancy Marco-type fighting skills, I would have whipped his butt right there in the town square. But in the long run, that wouldn't solve anything anyway.

"What do you want from me?" I asked.

He tried to mask his surprise, but I could tell he didn't expect the question. I'm sure he expected anger. He was spoiling for a fight.

"Well…um…my father says you're a fancy cattle farmer from America. Says you know all about running a farm and such. Well I've got some friends who are farmers. They need a piece of equipment fixed. So you're going to fix it." He regained his composure. "Either that, or you're going to be eating nothing *but* soup for the rest of your time in town." He smacked his fist into his open palm for effect.

I have to say, I almost laughed out loud. I felt like I was watching an old western at the movie theater in Boise, Idaho. They only cost a dime and you could watch the same picture two, three times in a row. So me and my buddies would memorize all the really corny lines. I could swear I'd heard a movie cowboy say the same thing that Ko Than had just said.

There was a store next to the theater that sold penny candy. They had these little barrel-shaped hard candies that tasted like root beer. I loved those things. They also sold really cheap cardboard cowboy hats, in either black or white. Each of my buddies and I always bought a handful of candy and a hat. In the movies the bad guys always wore black. Life was simpler back then. The store sold white hats, or black hats. There was no gray. But I digress.

I lowered my hands. "Show me this piece of equipment. I don't want any trouble. But no promises." Step one complete. I had a conversation going with Ko Than. If you could call it that.

"Stop calling me 'Ko Than'. My name is just 'Than'. 'Ko' is a title. Don't you know *anything*?"

We had been walking for thirty minutes, along a dirt track that led to the fields to the east of town. We were walking toward the farm that Ko...er...Than had mentioned. Ten minutes into the walk, I wanted to kick his butt five ways to Sunday. He was impetuous, boastful, and irritating. But I held my tongue.

"What does 'Ko' mean then?"

"It means something like 'older brother'. It just means that I'm not called 'mister' yet, but I'm not 'junior' either."

I get it. No longer a boy, not yet a man. It fit in Than's case.

"So, *Than*, what's the deal with this farm we're going to. Who are your friends?"

"Just some friends."

"I see. So what's broken?"

"Water pump. Their field is above the level of the water in the irrigation ditches. So they need to pump water up to the field. The pump is broken. The crops will die if we don't fix the pump. They need the food from the fields. It's...important to them."

"Well like I said, no promises."

Next thing I knew I was knee deep in a ditch and elbow deep in a water pump. The thing was built like a Wells Fargo safe. Big, made of heavy iron, and rugged. It was driven by two iron bars that a pair of workers, facing each other, would pump up and down. Like those little handcars they use sometimes on railroads. When it worked, it was supposed to suck water from the ditch and lift it about six feet before pumping it onto the farmer's field. But it wasn't working. It was similar to a dozen pumps I'd seen at home. They look different but they all work the same. Not that difficult to figure out. Once I got the cover off, the problem was easy to see. The pump had a loose gear inside, so when you pumped the handles the business end didn't do anything. The gear was missing a locking pin. It spun freely on its shaft. It simply needed a metal pin knocked back into it. I looked around but didn't see the missing pin anywhere. I managed to pull the gear off its shaft. I stood up and showed it to Than.

"This gear needs a new locking pin. To fit in this hole." I pointed to the spot on the gear. "It needs to be hard metal, or it will just bend or break from the force."

He looked at me like I was speaking a foreign language.

"Your friends have any scraps of metal lying around? Maybe a hammer and anvil?"

"I don't know. We can check. Follow me."

We walked to a modest barn on the far side of the fields. There were a few farm tools lying about, but I could see this farm was poor. Probably just scraping by. It was going to get worse if the pump didn't get fixed. Than opened the barn door and we stepped inside. The barn was almost empty. There was a plow and a few pitchforks and harvesting tools. But nothing much. Nothing I could use to fix the pump.

"Hmm. Nothing useful here. You got a blacksmith in town?" I asked.

"Yes. U Shaw."

"Then let's go see U."

"Sheesh. His name isn't U. His name is Shaw. 'U' is a title. Like 'Ko'. But 'U' means something like 'mister.'"

"I see. Thanks for telling me. Come with me and you might learn something. Then one day maybe you'll survive to be U too." If you live that long, and don't get strangled by an irritated cowboy on the road into town.

Chapter Thirty-Seven

Mister U Shaw was a skilled blacksmith. He took one look at the pump gear and knew exactly what to do. An hour later we had a nice hard-steel pin that fit perfectly in the gear. He also fabricated a fancy little locking clip that slid into a hole on the end of the pin, to keep it from falling out of the gear once it was attached to the axle. It was some mighty fine work. When it came time to settle up, Than addressed the fee in a manner that involved a lot of haggling and arguing. I finally couldn't stand it any longer.

"Than!" I said sternly. "Pay this gentleman the fee he's askin' for. He earned it."

Than looked at me like I'd just slapped him. Mister U Shaw looked at me with kind eyes. Than reluctantly paid up with a few coins. Shaw bowed to me in thanks. I figured Shaw wasn't really expecting to get paid, and was either doing the job out of kindness or out of fear. It was time to put a stop to that kind of ambiguity around Than.

We made the walk to the farm for the second time that afternoon. Than was quiet for long while. I figured that was a good sign. I had just disrespected him in front of the blacksmith but Than hadn't fought me. Perhaps he was learning some humility. There's always hope.

"Than, tell me more about your friends and their farm."

"My business, not yours."

Fine. We walked in silence the rest of the way.

It didn't take long to put the pump back together. I buttoned it up and told Than to give it a try. On his own. He took hold of one of the bars and began pumping it up and down. I climbed out of the ditch to see the output.

There wasn't any. "Pump harder, like there's two of you." He was huffing and puffing. Still no output.

I enjoyed Than's hard work for a while. I finally knelt to the output pipe and realized a bit of air was pumping out, as if the pump were exhaling with exhaustion after every stroke. At least it was doing something. Not a drop of water though.

"Okay, take a break. Something's wrong." I jumped back down to the ditch and, with Than's help, found a problem with the input pipe. It was loose and sucking air instead of water. We tried to tighten it but it wouldn't budge. "See if there's something in the barn to help us tighten this pipe. Use your imagination." I figured that would keep him busy for a while.

Than jumped out of the ditch with no argument, and jogged to the barn. I sensed some progress. The 'Ko' was becoming more of a 'U'.

While Than searched for a tool, I reflected on my good fortune. Not with Than, although things were looking better in that regard. I felt fortunate to have met the blacksmith. U Shaw was a craftsman. He was meticulous. He spent more time than necessary to fabricate our little part. He took pride in his work. Because of his diligence, I had just solved a major problem. See, the long wait allowed me to study his technique. I had a revelation. He used a bellows system to feed air to his furnace, to make the fire burn hotter and faster. He needed a hot fire to soften the hard metal we needed for our gear pin. Apparently the bellows made the difference. It was a simple setup, reliable and effective. While I was watching him, I realized that we could use the same type of bellows to pump air to Marco during his dives to the *Flor De La Mar*. And I figured out how to make one myself. Even better, I realized that the double-bar pump at

Than's farm was an easy way to power a pair of bellows, to get a nice continuous flow of air deep into the water. So on the walk back to the farm, while Than was brooding, I was thinking. And that worked just fine for me. I was thinking about how to solve Marco's second challenge – how to set up some type of winch system to get the treasure to the surface, bit by bit. I didn't have an answer for that. Yet.

Than returned with a long leather strap and a garden rake. I looked at them and couldn't figure how they were going to help us tighten a thick pipe. He could see the question in my eyes. He jumped down into the ditch, handed me the rake, and began to wrap the strap around the pipe. He wound it three or four times around the pipe. Then he motioned for me to hold the rake handle against the pipe and perpendicular to it. He then wrapped each end of the strap around the rake handle, and tied them off. The handle was now lashed to the pipe. I realized that we now had a nice long lever which was securely bound to the pipe. We simply swung the lever to tighten the pipe. The leather strap provided the grip we needed. Nicely done, I have to say. Than was resourceful, if nothing else.

When the pipe was tight, I looked to Than with a smile. He smiled back. First time I'd seen him smile since I'd known him. I jumped out of the ditch and Than went to work pumping the handle. It wasn't long before the water began to flow from the outlet onto the field. It was a good size flow too. The Wells-Fargo-vault pump was powerful. "It's working!" I yelled, with the excitement of success. It felt good.

Than stopped pumping and climbed out of the ditch. He just stood there and looked at the water on the ground, at the edge of the field. Then he breathed a huge sigh. He looked to me and said, simply, "thank you." There were tears in his eyes.

Chapter Thirty-Eight

Jack had a definite problem. The left engine was still losing oil. The oil pressure had now dropped into the red zone. He couldn't risk flying any further on an engine with low oil. It would eventually fail and seize, and would be beyond repair at that point. So he had to land somewhere along the Andaman Island chain. They were far past Smith Island and the British settlement of Point Blair. There were a series of islands leading all the way to the Dutch East Indies. None had landing strips, but the Goose could land on the water. But there was a complication. The wind was strong. The resulting ocean swells were visible even from their 10,000 feet altitude. They couldn't land in the open ocean with swells of any significant size. The Goose needed smooth seas. So Jack had to hunt for a lagoon or a protected area where the water was calm. Most of the Andamans were simply round-shaped islands, with no protection from the swells. But they were reaching a number of odd-shaped islands that were grouped closer together. Jack, Lhasa, and Marco started hunting intently for a suitable place to land. Jack figured they had ten to twenty minutes before he had to shut down the left engine. Landing on the water with one engine was a decidedly advanced skill. Even the best pilot would avoid it unless it was an extreme emergency.

At last they found a comma-shaped island with a smaller islet positioned a few miles offshore of the inner curve. Together the two small islands blocked the swells from almost every direction, thus the sea looked calm in the channel between the two masses. Jack throttled back the engines and began a rapid descent. The engine drone was replaced by the rush of the slipstream; it was a welcome sound after hours of flying. He circled the island looking for clues to the wind direction and kept a wary eye for a shallow reef. After a quick survey, he concluded that the wind was blowing from the northwest. The small swells within the channel wouldn't have much bearing on his landing direction. Jack flew a long downwind leg to the southeast, descending to 1,000 feet in the process. He then turned back to the northwest, into the wind, and began his final approach. The winds were light and the seas calm. No challenge for Jack. He descended gradually then landed softly on the surface. The Goose slowed quickly in the sudden drag of the water, eventually settling in to the ocean with a hush. He taxied as close as he dared to the beach of the main island, then cut power to both engines. There was no sound now but the lapping of the waves on the plane's floats. Marco opened the door and threw out a small anchor to keep the Goose from drifting. The cabin filled with the humid air of a tropical island.

Jack unbuckled himself and stepped back to the cabin. "Lhasa, there are some cans of oil in the back. And a tool kit."

Lhasa jumped to the back and sorted through their various supplies. Jack stepped out the door onto the left wing, and crawled carefully to the engine. Lhasa emerged with the tool kit and passed it to Jack.

"You best make yourselves comfortable," Jack advised. "This may take a while."

Marco retrieved a fishing pole from their cargo, attached a small lure, stepped down to the left float, and cast his line into the sea.

Lhasa chuckled. He busied himself by reorganizing their provisions.

Jack removed the access panel to the engine and checked the oil level. It was almost dry, and it was easy to see why. There was a streak of dark oil running out of a seam in the engine cowling, backward to the trailing edge of the wing. It was a sure sign of the oil leak that Jack had suspected. He could add more oil, but it would simply leak out again. He had to find the source of the leak. He unscrewed and removed two more access panels, then settled in for a fairly challenging hunt for the problem. It was hot and muggy. The exertion from holding himself in various positions as he inspected the engine, coupled with the rocking of the plane in the swells, brought back a spell of dizziness from his recent bout with Yellow Fever. He focused on the horizon and held as still as possible until it passed. It was a good reminder that he wasn't fully recovered.

"Jack?" Marco asked. "You saved a few firecrackers, right?"

"Yes."

After a moment, Jack's dizziness passed, and he reflected on Marco's question.

"Marco, why do you ask?"

"Oh, probably nothing to worry about. But I was just looking at the beach."

Jack lifted his head and focused on the beach. It was now occupied by a host of natives. They were either agitated or excited. They were dragging canoes out of the tree line toward the water. They each carried a long spear.

"Lhasa!" Jack yelled. "Firecrackers please!"

While Jack waited for Lhasa, he quickly filled the oil reservoir in the left engine, screwed on the oil cap, and began to replace the access panels. "Marco!"

"I've got it. Just get the engine together." Marco reeled in his line and threw his fishing pole into the plane. He shuffled along the float and pulled in the anchor. "Lhasa! Take the anchor and hand me a big firecracker! Then start the starboard engine. Use the pilot's seat!"

"Hey Lhasa!" Jack yelled. "Remember starboard means right side! Left engine would be bad to start right now. My hands are inside it!"

Lhasa emerged with the firecracker and a lighter, which he promptly handed to Marco. "Left wrong, right right. Got it boss."

Marco took the firecracker and climbed onto the top of the fuselage, using the antenna wires that ran from the top of each of the dual rudders to the cockpit as handholds. "Jack they're on their way. Four canoes, about two dozen men. Paddling hard. Focus on the engine. No need to look up."

Lhasa dropped himself into the left-hand pilot's seat, switched on the master power and the engine fuel valves, yelled "clear!" then cranked up the starboard engine. It coughed once, then twice, then caught after a few revolutions. Lhasa held it at a low idle. "Ready to go boss!"

Jack yelled to Marco. "How close? I need thirty seconds!"

"Too close. Lhasa! Take us away from the beach! Hold on Jack!"

Lhasa couldn't reach the rudder pedals, so he slid forward to the very edge of the seat and stomped hard on the right pedal, to turn the Goose away from the beach and out to sea. He revved the starboard engine and the plane began to move, turning slowly to the right in a gradual turn, spray kicking from the slipstream of the starboard prop.

"Marco!" Jack yelled. "We're going to take off as soon as we're all aboard. But if the canoes are in the channel, they'll block our way."

Marco surveyed the canoes. They were in the channel.

They were determined to pursue the Goose. This was likely the most exciting thing that had happened in these parts in a decade. What did the natives have to lose? They weren't going to give up easily. He studied the softball-sized firecracker. It was printed with Chinese symbols. No clue what this one did, or how to launch it. But he did recognize one symbol – an arrow that pointed away from the end with the fuse. That problem solved, Marco guessed that he needed a tube or a pipe to launch from. He didn't have one. He didn't have time to find one. So in the best tradition of his Filipino ancestors, who converted their simple farm tools into effective weapons, he improvised.

Chapter Thirty-Nine

"I think you owe me some dinner," I said. "You can irrigate this field tomorrow. It'll wait until morning."

Ko Than wiped the tears from his eyes and nodded. "Let's go to town," he said quietly. "For some soup."

He removed the rake handle and strap from the pump's inlet pipe, and ran them back to the barn.

We walked into town for the second time that day. It was late afternoon now. The heat and humidity were finally starting to break. A breeze had begun, blowing in from the west. It felt good against my face. There was a buildup of clouds on the western horizon. I could tell from the breeze that a storm was on the way. The sun peeked through the clouds as it settled toward the western hills. The sunlight played across the hills in dapples of light, and painted the clouds a dozen shades of purple. I figured it was going to be a great sunset here in the valley of Kengtung, in the Shan State of Burma.

Than was quiet, again, for most of the walk. But about a half mile outside of town, he spoke. "I don't think I know your name. I'm very sorry."

"It's Hank. Hank Evans."

"Thank you, Ko Evans, for helping me today." He stopped in his tracks and looked me in the eye. "I called you 'Ko' because of what you did today. You acted like an older brother to me. I have never had anyone do that before. So I apologize for my behavior and I thank you much."

"Apology accepted, Ko Than."

We walked in silence the rest of the way. I could smell rain, far away to the west, blowing in on the cool breeze.

We reached the town square and Than bought us each a bowl of hot and sour soup from one of the street vendors. It was my second bowl in the same day. But this one was a bit different. It had onions, but no lemon grass. Instead it had a nice amount of cabbage. It was magnificent. This time I got to enjoy the entire bowl. We ate quietly for a while, and then I figured it was time for a conversation.

"So Than, what's the story?"

"What story?"

"Your story. What does that farm mean to you?"

Than sighed. "Long story. Hard to explain to someone that hasn't lived here."

"Try."

"I bought that farm a month ago. From a widow. Her husband died and her only son was killed two years ago. She had no way to take care of it herself. So now she'll have a bit of money to live with, and now I have a new job."

"What was your old job?"

"Some bad stuff. That was going to get worse. So I was looking for a way to change. The farm was just good timing, that's all."

Uh huh. "So the farm is yours?"

He nodded.

"The water pump is yours?"

He nodded.

"If the crops fail, you can't sell them. If you can't sell them, you can't afford to pay the widow the money you promised her. Is that right?"

He nodded.

"Who is this widow?"

"That's not important. Her son was a friend of mine, that's all."

"Was his death your fault?"

Than shook his head. "No. Not my fault. But I should have helped. It could have been me just as easy. I was lucky."

"I see. So now you have a second chance."

"Something like that."

"So I don't understand. Why were you harming the young woman in the alley?"

Than looked to the ground and shook his head. "That was a bad night. I met up with some old friends. They were looking for trouble. They accused me of turning soft. I didn't have the backbone to resist. I decided I'd join them to show them I was still tough."

"Why the young lady?"

"One of the other guys was angry with her. Not me. I feel badly about it. It was the old Than. But I'm trying to change."

"Well," I said, "you can fix a lot of past mistakes by taking care of the widow, can't you?"

He nodded.

"So it seems to me, that everything will be made right, once you ask forgiveness."

"Forgiveness? From whom?"

"You tell me."

He was silent for a long while. "That will take another bowl of soup."

"I've got all night."

Marco didn't have much time to explain. He simply yelled "Jack! Cover your ears!" Then he dropped the lit firecracker into the empty oil can sitting on the wing next to Jack. Two seconds later the charge exploded with a wallop. There was a bit of oil left in the can, and the explosion sprayed burning droplets like a fountain. The rocket took off straight into the air, leaving a trail of red sparks. It hit its zenith and exploded a hundred feet high. It was late afternoon but even in the strong sunlight the yellow-orange fireball was impressive. Two heartbeats later the boom hit the water and rolled across the channel to the islands. It wasn't a loud crack. It was a low, powerful rumble that Marco could feel deep in his chest. It reverberated off the islands and bounced back to them in a loud echo. Marco marveled at the sound. Then he realized he could smell something burning. He looked down at Jack.

"Hey Jack! Your shirt's on fire!" It was mottled with dozens of holes from the burning oil. Each one was smoldering.

"I know. I'm okay. Damn I love those things!" Jack slapped his knee in excitement, a huge grin on his face. "I hope we have more!"

Chapter Forty

Ko Than told me his story, over another bowl of soup and a couple pots of tea. I got the picture. The guy got into a bad crowd. Found an easy way to make some money distributing opium, which was a common endeavor in these parts and had been for centuries. But money often attracts locusts. That's what happened to Than. He slid down a long slope, and finally hit rock bottom. Problem was, he couldn't figure out how to climb back up without asking for help. By then he didn't think anyone in Kengtung would throw him a rope. If he would have asked me to help him fix the pump, I would have gladly agreed. But instead he tried to intimidate me into helping him. Anybody else would have told him to pound sand. But he felt he had some leverage over me, being that I was the new guy in town. Yes, I felt like telling him to pound sand. Actually I felt like doing the pounding myself. But I threw him a rope instead, and now he can climb his way out of his hole. I hope. He has a lot of work to do to make things right. Needs to apologize to a lot of town folk. Made a commitment to me to get it done. Then he's got some hard work to do on his farm, and some good incentive to do it. He wants to make good on his agreement with the widow he bought it from. I respect him for that. But I gotta say, that farm needs more than just Than. He's going to have to get some hands to help. That'll be the next big challenge for him. He's gonna need to make some friends.

The next morning I decided it was time to hit the trail. I was prepared to stay a month in Kengtung if I had to. But thanks to the water pump breakdown, we'd had a little breakthrough. It was all in Than's hands now. There was nothing more I could do.

I met up with Constable Sandy. We went for a meandering walk through the town, and then on to the lake. It was a fresh, cool day. The storm had arrived the night before, washing out all the humidity. The sky was partly cloudy and the air smelled like a fresh shirt just off the clothesline. The fields were a vibrant green in the morning dew, the air restless and alive. Let me ask you something. When you step outside in the morning, do you notice the air? Is it still and quiet? Are the leaves fluttering in a light breeze? Or does a gusty wind tease your hair and brush your face? On those mornings when the wind is present, don't you feel a bit more alive? As if the wind has a purpose. A kind of restless energy that rubs off on you and makes you think of faraway places or of big goals. There's adventure in the wind, sure enough. I've often felt it. Especially in the morning. I was feeling it this morning in a big way.

I told Sandy about the events of the past two days. Filled him in on Than's situation and next steps. He was relieved and mighty pleased.

"Hank, I can't tell you how much I appreciate what you've done. I hardly understand why you did it. But you've given me a great deal of hope. When you have a son or daughter of your own, you'll understand. You've given me hope for Than, and hope for Kengtung. We're probably going to need it."

"What's in store for Kengtung?"

"You've been around. You see what's happening. The world is changing around us. For good and for bad."

"How so?"

"Look, you know I studied in Britain. It's a big reason

I'm a constable here, being that Burma is a British Colony. They feel that I march the same way they do. But my studies opened my eyes to a lot of things. I'm living them now here in Southeast Asia, on the opposite side of the coin."

He was losing me. "You mean the impact of the war?"

"It's much more than that. What's happening now would have happened anyway. The war is just speeding things up. Think about it. French Indochina is falling and will no longer be a French colony. The British are already pulling back from India, and it will soon be a country of its own. The same will happen here in Burma. We'll be our own country, assuming we don't become a state of Japan. The Dutch East Indies will fall away from Holland. The Philippines will fall away from the US. All these countries, which were pushed into the twentieth century by their European or American leaders, are about to pull themselves up by their bootstraps and become their own masters. It's quite exciting."

"Before this little trip of mine," I admitted, "I really had no idea of the history of the world. I've learned more in the past two months than I learned in twelve years of school. I had no idea there had been so many masters."

"Oh I'm not complaining," he clarified. "Look what we'll be left with! A great railroad system, harbors and roads, administrative buildings, basically an infrastructure that we would have otherwise had to build ourselves. It would have been a great expense, completed over a long period of time. Or maybe never. But a century of European imperialism built it for us.

"Think about the Roman Empire," he continued. "What was its purpose? You could argue that it was to civilize the barbarians on the fringes of the known world. I agree. But it was much more than that. The purpose of the Roman

Empire was to build the roads, and the aqueducts, and the cities and towns, and the law, which allowed one to travel safely throughout the empire. Before the Romans, there was no possible way to travel safely over any distance more than a few miles. That's no good when one has a profound message that must be shared throughout the world."

I nodded in a sudden bit of clarity, thinking of my Grandma. "The message of the Christian Church."

"Exactly. I believe the purpose of the Roman Empire was simply to build the groundwork for the message of Christ. The timing had to be right. Otherwise that message might have faltered for lack of a road. Or been drowned out by the noise of commerce. But the Romans came along at just the right time. They were just a part of the plan. When the plan was underway, the Romans simply faded away. Their task was complete.

"So Hank, you can look at Asia and see the same thing. The Brits, the Yanks, the Dutch, the Spaniards, the French, they all helped to build the twentieth-century-equivalent Roman roads in Asia. They did a great job. They're all done now. It's the sunset of the great imperial age. We're all set to be on our own. To be reborn as new countries and new people. It's a massive rebirth of half the world. We're sitting right in the middle of all the change. The war is accelerating it, but it was going to happen anyway. It's going to be painfully exciting. I'm glad to see a bit of it.

"So the big question for folks like you, Hank, is 'what's the message going to be this time?' It's an important question for my son too."

I had no answer for my profound friend Constable Sandy. But Lhasa popped into my head. I had a notion that little guy was bigger than I thought.

Chapter Forty-One

The Goose was running on one engine, skipping through the swells heading away from the small armada of determined natives. The firecracker explosion had the desired effect. The natives had stopped paddling. They appeared indecisive. Marco decided to capitalize on their confusion. He remained on the top of the fuselage, stood tall, and raised his right arm to the sky. He yelled something in Filipino. Loudly. That sealed it. The natives turned around and paddled slowly back to the beach. The channel was clear for the Goose to make a fast takeoff.

"Nice work Marco," Jack yelled. "Get inside. I'm done with the engine. We're getting out of here."

Marco slid down to the wing and climbed inside. Jack passed him the tools and the empty oil can, followed him inside, and secured the door.

Lhasa made a move to switch seats to the right-hand copilot's seat.

"You're fine Lhasa. You're the pilot on this leg." Jack slid into the copilot's seat. "Start the left engine while I bring us around."

Lhasa cranked up the engine and Jack used the rudders to spin the Goose in a sharp right-hand turn, bringing them back toward the northwest. The channel ahead was clear and the sea was still calm.

"Hey Marco, can you pass us Lhasa's booster seat?"

Marco passed two of the unopened parachute packs to Jack, who added them to the seat back behind Lhasa. The added padding allowed Lhasa to lean back against the seat and still reach the rudder pedals. He strapped himself in, trying to mask an excited grin.

"Lhasa, get us out of here. Watch the RPM sync between the two engines, don't push the rudder pedals until we're in the air. Hold us straight and level until I tell you to lift off."

"Got it boss." Lhasa pushed the throttle levers forward, the Goose began to move. The plane plowed through the small swells at first, but soon the airspeed built and the plane began to lift itself out of the water.

"Not yet. Hold her down."

Lhasa didn't move a muscle. He looked as if he was carved of marble. Jack wasn't sure he was even breathing. They reached takeoff speed. "All yours Lhasa. Pull back evenly and climb out straight ahead."

Lhasa pulled back on the wheel. The tail dropped and the Goose left the water. They climbed into the afternoon sky.

"Lhasa, take a breath. You're a pilot now. Take us to 10,000 feet and turn to the east."

Lhasa smiled in response.

"We need to get to the tip of the Dutch East Indies before the oil leaks out again. I figure an hour or so in the air. It's going to be close." Jack turned toward the back. "Hey Marco! Nice work with that firecracker. I wouldn't have thought of the oil can. That was some quick thinking."

"Sorry about your shirt. It's all full of holes."

Lhasa glanced at Jack's shirt. "Sheesh! What happened to you? *You're* the holey man now!"

"Funny, Lhasa. Funny. Just fly."

My work done in Kengtung, I had to get myself to Malacca. Without an airplane. Not the easiest thing to do. But Jack and I made a plan before the guys left. First step was to get myself to Rangoon, the big port city in the south of Burma. Sandy helped me with that. The British railroad ran from Rangoon all the way north to Lashio, a city to the northwest of Kengtung. It was a long trip to Lashio, but I didn't need to go that far. If I traveled directly west I would reach the city of Meiktila, which was a stop on the north-south rail line. China and her allies were moving supplies from Rangoon to Lashio then on to Free China via the Burma Road. I didn't know it, but the Burma Road was about to get shut down. By the British, ironically, under diplomatic pressure from Japan. The British knew this was imminent, and they were jamming the train as hard and as fast as they could up and down the Rangoon-Lashio line, pushing to the point of failure to get as much stuff to China as they could. It would be no problem catching the southbound train. I just had to make tracks to Meiktila. It was a 375 mile journey by road from Kengtung. I figured I could walk it in ten days. But ten days was an eternity in the war-seeped world of June 1940. Entire countries were falling in less time, especially to the Nazis in Europe.

I didn't have ten days.

The western-most city in the Dutch East Indies was Kutaraja (now Banda Aceh), on the very western tip of the island of Sumatra. It was currently 250 miles from the Goose. Each of the two engines on the plane held eight quarts of oil. Each engine normally burned at least one quart during every two hours of running time. When they weren't leaking. The left engine had a leak in its crankcase seal. Jack hadn't had time to find it during their quick stop at the comma island. Even if he had found it, he wouldn't have been able to repair it while floating there in the channel.

The leak was only the diameter of a pencil lead, but the oil was under pressure and the leak drained a quart of oil from the left engine every ten minutes. Eighty minutes of flying time would run the engine dry. An hour was the max to be safe. Jack had done the math after tracking the oil pressure gauge for a period of time.

The trio had an hour to fly 250 miles. The max speed of the Goose, slowed by the drag of its floats, was 200 miles per hour. At that speed it would take an hour and fifteen minutes to reach Kutaraja.

They didn't have that long.

Chapter Forty-Two

I had to wait three days for my transportation from Kengtung to Meiktila, in the form of a bus ride. It cost me little, and it was much faster than walking. I said my goodbyes to Sandy and Ko Than. I hoped I would see them again. I worried about what was coming for them. But Sandy assured me that they would adapt to whatever came their way. I had to trust that he was right.

I boarded the bus early in the morning, along with six other passengers. We departed for Meiktila. I could tell two things right away. The bus was faster than walking. Much slower than flying. Still, it was well worth the three day wait.

I gotta say, I really stood out on the bus. The other passengers were all Burmese. I was the tall white American. They spoke Burmese and some Chinese. I couldn't speak either one, except for a few important phrases that Lhasa and Marco had taught me. One, which should have meant "I'm pleased to meet you," turned out to mean "I have huge balls." It didn't take me too long to figure that one out. It gave all the Burmese a good laugh at the expense of the clueless American. Just another item on my payback list for Marco.

The road we traveled was far from straight, and farther from smooth. It was full of ruts, potholes, switchbacks and curves. It traversed an endless kaleidoscope of hills and valleys. Barring a breakdown, it would be at least a twelve hour trip to Meiktila, not counting several stops along the way. I had my backpack, a canteen full of water, some rice cakes and dried fish from Kengtung. It was all I needed.

Once again, I felt as light as a feather. I met all the folks on the bus. Once we got past the size of my nuts we found a way to communicate. It was the first time I'd been immersed in the language by spending a good amount of time with a group of locals. I'll tell you, I had more fun than a fox in a henhouse. Turns out you don't need to speak a common language to have a conversation. We drew pictures, pointed, and mimed. Whenever a new passenger boarded at one of the stops along the way, the others would introduce me as "the American with unusually large testicles." It was the joke that never got old. For the other passengers, at least.

Between conversations, I had some quiet time to just gaze out the window and enjoy the ride. There's a Burmese saying that translates something like "if you take big paces you leave big spaces." I had been taking big paces ever since I'd left Idaho. Now I had a chance to just see the ground for a while. To enjoy the spaces. I highly recommend it. The scenery was fantastic. For the first third of the trip, we wound through green forests filled with pines, saw many waterfalls and streams, traversed fertile lowlands, and crossed several large rivers. It reminded me of Hawaii. The landscape gradually began to dry out the closer we got to Meiktila. The locals told me that Meiktila is in the central "dry" zone of Burma. Which reminded me the landscape of Idaho or Montana. The forests gradually gave way to rolling, rugged grasslands with mountainous outcroppings. It felt just like home.

The weather was sunny and cool all day long; a really comfortable day. The bus benches were definitely not comfortable, but I didn't expect much. I just hunkered down to enjoy the trip. The bus made two long meal stops during the journey, each time at towns placed along major river

212

crossings. The rivers ran from north to south. The largest, the Salwan, reminded me of the Salmon River back home. It ran all the way south to the sea near Rangoon. I imagined floating it in a raft with Sara Hudson. Just us two meandering through Burma, stopping here and there for some sightseeing or a bite to eat. It was a nice little daydream. It prompted me to grab some paper and a pencil from my pack to write a letter to Sara. I summarized my travels, told her where I was going, and told her how much I looked forward to seeing her again. I really had no idea what might happen between us when I got home, but I had my hopes.

In my letter to Sara, I described the Salwan River and its resemblance to the Salmon. I admitted that I owed her a raft after my ill-fated attempt at the necklace delivery. That's when I solved Marco's second problem. How to raise heavy treasure from the *Flor De La Mar* wreck. I had always been amazed how buoyant a rubber raft is. The air inside just makes those things unsinkable. When I was younger, a bunch of us would try to push a partly-inflated raft under water, which was very difficult. So I was instantly reminded of the lifting power of a bag of air in the water. I realized that we simply needed a raft, or a strong balloon, connected to a basket. Once at the wreck, Marco could fill the basket with artifacts, attach his air hose to the deflated balloon, and rise to the surface. Then we could pump air into the balloon, sit back, and wait for the elevator to arrive. It was simple. I had learned many times that *simple* is always the best. Both of Marco's challenges solved, I sat back, finished up my letter, then drew a couple of cowboy and horse drawings for my new friends on the bus. In return, they gave me a few trinkets and a little woven reed basket, about the size of a baseball. It was skillfully made. It fit nicely in my pack.

I saved some paper for letters to my family, which I figured I'd write once I boarded the train in Meiktila. I had so much to tell them that I didn't even know where to start. I gazed out the window for a long time, watching Burma slide past like a movie. It was a beautiful country. It would soon fall under attack from Thailand, and would then be occupied by Japan. But as I watched the picturesque little villages slide past the window, it was hard to imagine the hardship that was to come.

Chapter Forty-Three

"Lhasa, it's time to learn to fly a twin engine plane on one engine."

Lhasa responded to Jack with a mixed expression of surprise and trepidation.

"You have to learn sooner or later. In case you lose an engine. Better to do it when you have some space between you and the ground."

"I never lose anything. I don't plan to lose an engine. Anyway I'm not a pilot."

"You never know when you might need to be a pilot. Besides, it's good job security."

"I have a good job." Lhasa clarified.

"And what is that job again?"

"Saving people. You know that."

"That includes you. Time to learn to fly on one good engine."

"Is this the best time?" Lhasa asked.

"Definitely. It solves two problems. First, if we keep flying like this we're going to wreck our left engine before we get to Kutaraja. The oil will run dry fifteen minutes before we arrive. We need that engine. Landing on one engine is risky. So we'll shut it down now to save some oil, fly on one engine, then restart the left when it's time to descend to Kuta. Second, it gets you some important practice, which you're going to need if you're going to be my relief pilot. I'm enjoying being a passenger for a change."

"Okay, what do I do?"

"Throttle back the left engine very slowly. Compensate with right rudder to keep our heading from drifting to the left. Once you've brought the engine all the way back to idle, the Goose will feel sloppy. Be ready. Our airspeed will drop and the controls will feel mushy. It's easier to feel than to explain. Oh one more thing. The left engine's rotation won't be counteracting the right engine's spin, so the Goose will want to bank. You'll need to correct for that too, using a combination of ailerons and rudder. You'll get the feel for it."

Lhasa took a deep breath. "Okay, I'm ready. Here we go."

The Goose slowed and veered instantly to the left as Lhasa pulled back on the throttle. He overcorrected to the right, and then brought the plane back on track. The next few minutes were a series of mistakes and corrections, but Jack patiently allowed Lhasa to get a feel for the plane. He improved dramatically, although their altitude varied widely during Lhasa's maneuvers. Jack would address that later. Lhasa was already overloaded. He held the wheel with white knuckles.

Jack feathered the prop on the left engine to minimize the drag, then shut the engine down. The engine fell silent, the prop slowed to a stop.

"Nice job, my friend. Take a breath. Then take us on to Kutaraja."

It was now evening. The sky was darkening quickly. Jack would need to land in an unfamiliar place at night. Not the best situation, but he'd done it before.

I finally arrived in Meiktila after a long day on the bus. It was evening. The lights of the city were a welcome sight in the distance. As we pulled into the center of town I immediately noticed the difference between Meiktila and Kengtung. Unlike Kengtung, Meiktila had room to grow. It wasn't surrounded by valuable farmland, so it spread into the countryside. The town radiated outward from the large Meiktila Lake in the center. It was another new town to figure out. Fortunately two of the bus passengers invited me to join them for dinner. We found a little noodle place that served simple but tasty food.

My two friends helped me to negotiate a bed in the loft above the restaurant. It was small but comfortable. I fell asleep to the muted sounds of Burmese conversation and the smells of noodles and fish. It was a fitting end to a day I'll always remember.

The Goose was fifty miles out from Kutaraja, Dutch East Indies. Jack traded places with Lhasa so he would be in the more familiar left-hand pilot's seat for the nighttime landing. They were fifteen minutes from landfall. It was time to start the left engine. Jack carefully adjusted the propeller pitch on the left engine until the prop began to windmill on its own. He watched the oil pressure build to the proper amount, then opened the fuel valve and flipped the ignition switch. Once the engine started, he slowly increased the throttle to match the power of the right engine. He had two good engines now, and presumably had more than fifteen minutes of oil for the left engine. They were flying in broken clouds so Jack descended to 5,000 feet to try to drop them out of the cloud ceiling. The clouds were still present, but visibility was clear between the clumps. As they approached the lights of Kutaraja, it was easy to see the demarcation between land and sea by the reflections of the lights along the coast.

"Hey Marco – can you get Lhasa his booster seat so he can see?"

Marco passed the now familiar parachute packs to

Lhasa, who situated himself in the right hand seat. Lhasa prepared himself for…something. Jack always kept him on his toes. Jack radioed the airfield control tower using the common air traffic frequency. He identified himself, his position, and his intent to land. One had to be careful these days. There were jumpy military personnel everywhere. The Dutch would be no exception. An unidentified airplane was reason for alarm. Permission granted to land, he descended to two thousand feet to survey the position of the landing strip. The tower lit the field lights for him so its location and orientation were easy to determine. Jack set himself in a left-hand pattern, flying a counterclockwise circle as he lined up with the field. He descended to 1,000 feet and set the flaps for final approach.

"Lhasa. Your turn. Land us!"

"Ay! I knew you were going to say that!" Lhasa grabbed the wheel, took control of the throttles, and leaned forward in his seat.

"Easy does it." Jack advised. "Pull the throttles back and keep us at 80 knots airspeed. Dive to speed up, climb to slow down. There you go. Down a bit. Down a bit. You're drifting to the right. Left rudder. Left rudder. Good. Steady. Set another notch of flaps. Good. Hold her there." Lhasa turned to marble once again.

"Crossing the runway threshold now. Hold her steady. A bit more. A bit more. Okay now a gradual flare. Pull back on the wheel. Flare. Flare. Hold it there." The stall warning horn sounded. "Ignore that. You're fine. Keep the nose up."

The main gear touched down on the field, followed quickly by the tail wheel.

"We're down. Use the rudders to keep us straight. Push the brake pedals at the top of the rudders, evenly so we don't spin off the field."

Lhasa brought the Goose to a stop.

"Nicely done, my Tibetan pilot friend. Now taxi us to the tarmac."

Marco wiped a bead of sweat from his brow. "Whew. It must be humid here," he explained.

Jack chuckled. "Lhasa, you're a pilot now. You'll thank me one day."

Lhasa merely nodded, a satisfied yet unsure grin on his face.

The next morning, I awoke before dawn to the crowing of the local roosters. It was still dark, but I wanted to get to the train station to figure out the schedule. The station was easy to find. I just walked toward the center of town until I hit the tracks, looked left and then right, saw the station, then walked toward it. It took me twenty minutes. The eastern sky was now aglow in a pre-sunrise splendor. It was going to be a beautiful June day. I sat on a bench outside the station to enjoy the dawn. The air was drier and thinner here than in Kengtung. As I cooled from my brisk walk I felt the morning chill. I donned my light jacket.

The station operator arrived shortly after sunrise, followed by a host of residents that appeared to work at the station or nearby. I entered the station and attempted to ask about the southbound train, but I couldn't understand the operator's response. Then I heard an English conversation as a pair of British officers entered the building. "Well what do we have here?" the first asked when he saw me. "You're decidedly not Burmese."

I introduced myself and they responded in kind.

"I'm on my way to Rangoon, hoping to catch a ride on the train," I explained.

"You're in luck," the first soldier said. "There is a high probability that the southbound train will pass through here this afternoon. At least we hope it does. It was delayed yesterday by some sort of breakdown. Flummoxed the entire bloody schedule."

"Will there be room for me on board?"

"May I ask about your business in Rangoon?"

"I'm a Hump pilot. I was asked to help ferry some aircraft to Singapore." It was a plausible, and true, story. Jack had heard that the British Royal Air Force needed help rotating aircraft around the rapidly changing Southeast Asia military theatre. The route from Burma to Singapore was starved for pilots. Never mind that it was Jack who did the asking. He felt that his pilot buddies in Rangoon would happily accept my assistance.

The officers nodded. "I'm sure there will be room for you. The southbound trains are rarely full. It's the northbound trains that are jammed to the gills." We chatted for a while about the overall situation in Southeast Asia. I found that British soldiers were always the best source of information. They were trying to hold their crumbling empire together, by juggling pieces across many countries. Not to mention trying to defend their own homeland from the Nazis. The daily challenge required them to be well informed regarding the political situations of many countries. They always knew the lay of the land.

"I'm a bit embarrassed to ask, but could you fellows give me a hand at the ticket counter?"

The first Brit smiled. "Anything for a Hump pilot. Even if you are a Yank."

Five minutes later, and a pile of dollars lighter, I had my ticket. I didn't want to spend hours waiting in the station, but also didn't feel like straying far. I walked through the city, never wandering more than a quarter mile from the station. I figured I could get back to it quickly when I heard the train approaching. I received many polite stares from the locals. They were apparently used to British soldiers, but not to a tall American in civilian clothes. There weren't many of me in these whereabouts. I stood out as usual. No matter. I was getting used to it. It was no liability in Burma. At least not that I knew.

During my walk through town I passed a telegraph office, and immediately remembered that I needed to get a message to Jack. I stepped inside to composed a short message, telling Jack that I was in Meiktila and on my way to Rangoon as planned. The clerk spoke English fairly well. I was able to send a cable to Kutaraja, to be held for Jack Campbell. Just for good measure, I sent the same message to Malacca and to Singapore. I wasn't sure where Jack, Lhasa, and Marco were at this point, so I wanted to cover all my bases. I had no reliable way to contact them via radio, certainly not at their distance. I hoped they were safe. I also sent a cable home to my parents, letting them know that I was safe and on my way to Rangoon then to Malaysia. I promised them that a pile of letters was on the way.

Chapter Forty-Four

The southbound train arrived in Meiktila just before noon. The operators were pressed to get it underway quickly. They didn't waste any time refueling or loading it. We were underway in less than thirty minutes. It was 320 miles from Meiktila to Rangoon, a twelve hour trip on this train. I settled into one of the few passenger cars. The train was mostly cargo cars, returning to Rangoon almost empty after delivering relief supplies to Lashio in the north. This train was larger than the one from Kunming to Hai Phong. It had decent seats, two on each side with an aisle in the middle. My car was almost full. Again, an ethnic variety of Burmese and Chinese. There were no other Westerners on the train. Once again I was in a sea of languages that I didn't understand. If you would have asked me two months ago how I would feel taking a train from Meiktila to Rangoon, by myself, without being able to speak the language, I would have thought you crazy. But here I was, feeling right at home. It's amazing how fast we can adapt to something entirely new.

I used the first hour or two to write letters home. I wrote about my travels, my observations, the people I'd met. I explained where I was headed, and promised to write again from Malaysia. Then I packed the letters carefully away in my bag and just stared out the window for a long while. We were running down a long north-south valley, mostly river land and fields interrupted by an occasional pine forest. We passed several villages, most of them small and neat. The scenery eventually grew monotonous and I dozed off for an hour or so. When I awoke, it hadn't changed much. We moved steadily toward Rangoon, the click-clack of the rails counting off the seconds, then the minutes, mile after mile. I looked around for someone to attempt a conversation with, but most of the passengers were dozing. So I sat back and tried to figure how to build the air bellows we would need for Marco's dives. It kept me busy for a good long while. Until I dozed off again. I dreamt of Malaysia and the sea. The warm, blue sea.

The closer we got to Rangoon, the more passengers we picked up and the livelier our car became. Everyone suddenly wanted to know each other, as if they'd been neighbors all their lives. I joined in the party and fumbled through some conversations about America and cattle and such. Everyone had questions for me. What's America like? Do you grow rice there? Are all Americans tall? Do you raise water buffalo? What's your favorite food? How much does a chicken cost? How much does a buffalo cost? How big are the cities? Who is your President? How rich is he? Where did he come from? And on and on. I should have paid more attention in school. I was unprepared to be an ambassador *and* a teacher. I made a personal vow to learn more American history when I got back home. When I asked the same questions of the locals, they all knew the answers. They took pride in their country. That was clear enough to me. Then the conversation turned to the uncertainty of war. I'll spare you the details. But these folks were confused, and scared, but brave. It was the widespread theme of Southeast Asia.

We finally arrived in Rangoon. Even at ten o'clock at night, it was a wild and frenetic place. In 1940 Rangoon was a city of a half million people, the largest in Burma. Its harbor was bustling twenty-four hours a day, as tons of cargo passed through on its way to China and elsewhere. The British military had an obvious presence, you couldn't take two steps without running into someone of apparent authority. The whole place was a giant beehive. It had the feel of Kunming, where everyone was in constant movement. It was a rude awakening to me. I had become accustomed to the quiet rural towns. This place moved fast and never seemed to stop.

I soon found a place to stay for the night, using the same approach I had learned in Meiktila. I found a simple little restaurant where I got a bite to eat, and then offered a bit more money for a place to sleep. The owner gladly agreed. I ended up in a cot on the back porch, which had been partially enclosed by a bamboo screen. I lay awake for a long time listening to the nighttime sounds of a foreign city. I finally decided to go out for a walk. I ended up in a saloon with a gaggle of boisterous British soldiers. They taught me a number of "colorful" songs and limericks. After a few beers I became quite good at singing them. The soldiers were a welcoming bunch and good company, but eventually the party broke up as they headed back to their barracks. I found my way back to my little cot and hit the hay. I awoke the next morning with a massive headache and absolutely no memory of the songs. But a couple of limericks stuck in my head which still make me laugh. All in good fun.

I ate a quick breakfast before setting off for the British Army Air Base in Rangoon. I intended to walk but it became clear that the primary mode of travel was a rickshaw. They were simple two wheeled carts pulled by a human runner. It seemed strange to me, but I didn't want deprive a runner of a few dollars. So I jumped in a rickshaw, told the runner "British Air Base", and off we went. The runner was much smaller than I. I felt like trading places with him. But I wasn't sure if it would be an insult or not. I had learned that Asian countries often had a bit of a caste system. Confusing the caste just confused everyone. So I bit my tongue and enjoyed the ride. At the very least, it was an efficient way to see Rangoon. As near as I could tell, the outlying areas were mostly colonial. The buildings were clearly of British construction. I recalled Sandy's comments about the imperial building efforts across Southeast Asia. They were certainly on display in Rangoon. It was a reasonable place to enjoy some classic examples of colonial architecture.

Once we reached the base, I paid the runner a nice tip to offset my size and weight. He thankfully took the money then began to look for a return faire. It would be a British soldier on leave, no doubt. I wondered how many limericks the runner had memorized over the past few months.

I found my way to the base air command office, and stepped inside the small colonial bungalow. The desk sergeant gave me a quick glance. "American?"

"Yes. Hank Evans, Hump pilot, looking for the air commander."

"What's he done this time?"

"I'm sure I can think of something. But for now I'm here to offer my services."

"As a pilot?"

"Yep."

"Any recent crashes?"

"Just the one. At the bar last night."

He smirked. "You'll find Major Watson in the hangar. That way." He pointed over his left shoulder.

"Thanks."

"I hope you're better than the last bloke," he remarked as I walked out the door.

At what? I wondered.

I found Major Watson inspecting a C-47 in the hangar. "Problems?" I asked.

He turned to me and gave me a quick appraisal. He was in uniform, but it was faded and a bit disheveled. His sleeves were rolled up and there was grease on his hands. This guy worked for a living. "Yes, problems. We can't figure out how to wind it up. Do you have the key?"

"We just push them. Really fast."

"I hadn't thought of that. You a pilot?"

"Yes. Hank Evans, Hump pilot. Jack Campbell sent me. Said you could use my services."

"Jack Campbell huh? He okay?"

"Fully recovered, as far as I can tell."

"Oh he'll never be fully recovered. But that never stops Jack. Major William Watson." He extended a greasy hand. "You can call me Will."

"Good to meet you, Will." I shook his hand and instantly wished I had a handkerchief. "I'm headed toward Singapore. Jack suggested I check in with you. Need a copilot for a one-way flight?"

"Always. I need to get three aircraft to Sing. Let's go back to my office to take a look your flight papers."

"All I have is my flight log, but every entry is signed by Jack. He taught me everything I know."

"My condolences. Let's go have a look."

Chapter Forty-Five

It was morning in Kutaraja, when Jack finally had time to attempt a proper repair of the Goose's left engine oil leak. The Goose was sitting on solid ground, they weren't being pursued by natives, and they had all day if necessary. Lhasa busied himself gathering provisions in town, while Marco worked on the engine with Jack. They opened the access panels and traced the oil streak to the crankcase seal. This was unfortunate, as they would need a good mechanic to fix it. It was beyond Jack's ability.

"Well, I need to find a mechanic." Jack explained. "Can I ask you to stay with the Goose? I'll bring us some breakfast."

"Sure thing. Anything I can do while you're gone?"

"Sure. Inspect the plane."

"What am I looking for?"

"Anything that Lhasa might have broken while he was flying us around up there." Jack motioned skyward with his head.

"Yes, I'll do that. Lhasa is a wild pilot," Marco said in a serious tone, shaking his head.

Jack studied him and laughed. "Uh huh. So the mighty Marco is a bit afraid of flying, huh? You hide it well. It took me a while to notice."

Marco shook his head and stared at the ground for a long while. "It's embarrassing."

"No need to be embarrassed, my friend. Some of the bravest people I know would never touch an airplane. You would be shocked at what I'm afraid of. I just hope you never find out." With that, Jack wiped his hands on a rag,

227

tossed it in the tool box, and set out for town. "See you soon."

Marco took a walk around the plane, studying its control surfaces, propellers, float struts, wheels, tires, and anything else that Lhasa might have damaged. He broke into a sweat. But the more he studied the aircraft, the more he realized how it all worked. The more he realized how it worked, the less nervous he was. He cautiously tested the strength of the aluminum skin, and found it to be surprisingly robust. The propellers were crafted of the strongest metal he had ever seen, comparable to the steel of a fine sword but much thicker and heavier. The struts that attached the floats, and landing gear, to the plane were solid. He realized they connected to the wing spars and to the bulkhead that he noticed inside the cabin. The overall design began to make sense to him. Even the moving parts, the control surfaces – the twin rudders and the elevator on the tail, were solid and...wait...made of fabric! Flimsy fabric over a sparse frame of what? Wood? Bamboo? The sudden realization made Marco weak in the knees. He sat down in the shade under the nose of the plane and tried to compose himself. He had flown more miles than he could count in an airplane made of fabric. He had many more to go. He said a silent prayer. "Lord, give me strength."

Then he wondered what Jack Campbell could possibly be afraid of.

And that concerned him even more.

Jack took a walk to the nearest eatery, a small grill just off the main road to the airport. It was fairly full of breakfast clientele, half sitting inside and half outside on a bamboo covered patio. He entered the small building and took a seat at the counter. The cook acknowledged him while finishing up a plate of fish and rice. He delivered it to a table on the patio, walked back behind the counter, and slid a glass of water to Jack. He nodded in anticipation.

"English?" Jack asked.

"Small English but okay," the cook answered.

"Two plates of fish and rice, please." Jack motioned to the table the cook had just served.

"Two fish and rice, yes." The cook went back to his small kitchen and went to work.

Jack studied the crowd. He was looking for a local who might know a mechanic. This was going to be a bit of a challenge. How to find a trustworthy mechanic in Kutaraja? Where would a good airplane mechanic keep himself? It was a question Jack pondered for a while. Then he realized he was being too specific. He merely needed an engine mechanic. Anyone that could fix an engine would have the tools to fix the Goose.

The cook returned with two plates of rice and fish.

"Thank you," Jack nodded.

"Sure," the cook answered. He waited in anticipation for Jack to taste the fish.

Jack took a bite. It was fresh and savory. He smiled. "Good. Very good."

The cook was pleased. "Good! Where from?"

"Montana, United States. But I flew here from Burma."

"Oh, Burma. You fight Japanese?"

"No. I help Chinese fight the Japanese."

"Oh, that good too. I hope they stop them from here."

Jack nodded. "Me too."

The cook excused himself to greet a new customer at a patio table. Jack finished his breakfast and placed some money on the counter.

The cook returned. Jack asked for a bag for Marco's breakfast. The cook ducked in the kitchen and returned with a piece of butcher paper.

"Thanks. Good food."

The cook was pleased.

"Say, do you know a mechanic? Engine repair? Motor fix?"

"Oh, motor fix? Yes. How you say...tractor fix! Tractor fix in town. Look for sign. Tractor. Easy find."

"Thank you."

Jack walked back to the Goose with Marco's breakfast. He found Marco sitting under the nose of the plane. He looked a bit green.

"You okay?"

"Why do you ask?"

"I brought you some breakfast."

Marco gladly took it from Jack. "Thanks. Hey, can you tell me about this airplane?"

Jack smiled and sat down next to Marco. "Certainly. Anything you want to know, my friend. Then you can help me with a tractor repairman."

Chapter Forty-Six

"So you have pilot hours in a Beech twin and a C-47. Anything else?" Major William Watson of the British Royal Air Force asked.

"No, that's it. But my hours are significant," I answered.

"I can see that." Will was reviewing my pilot log. "Engine fire in a snowstorm over The Hump, then a single engine landing on a river bank in a fully loaded C-47? That's some tough work."

"It was a learning experience."

"I'll bet." He returned to my log book. "Single engine take off? From a dirt field? You're kidding."

"No, that's true. I studied the flight manual first and saved myself from a deadly mistake."

"Let me guess. You were planning a full-power single engine take off, and then thought otherwise?"

"Exactly. Full power on one engine is too much for the rudder on a C-47 to counteract. It would have been a short and sad trip."

"As others have discovered." He had a faraway stare, then he met my eyes. "Just out of curiosity, how did you get the C-47 from the riverbank to an airstrip?"

"A hundred Chinese peasants showed up, part of the free Chinese resistance. They repelled a Japanese platoon. Then they towed the plane a good quarter mile to the airstrip. By hand."

"Bloody hell. Are you serious?"

I nodded.

"That's one for the books." He stared at me again for a while. "Hank, based on this logbook, you're a very well qualified pilot. You've done some things my own pilots have never tried, and they're quite good." He tapped his pencil on my logbook. "Tell me about your navigation skills. How would you get me from here to Singapore?"

I explained what I knew. Will nodded. "That'll get you there. Here's one for you. Tell me about the crossfeed on the C-47 fuel tanks."

That one was easy. I wished school would have been this simple. I explained the C-47 fuel system to Will.

"You know your aircraft systems, that's for sure. Let's just go for a little check flight. You can fly me around the pattern and do a few touch and goes. Let's see how you handle a Dakota."

'Dakota' was the British name for the C-47. "Fair enough," I said. "Let's give it a shot."

The Dakota we flew handled like any other. They were all built the same, with some minor variations. This one was empty. It was the cargo that brought out the differences between planes. When fully loaded, subtle differences in the controls became noticeable. Some planes felt like they had a heavy tail, while others might have mushy rudders. It was all in the way the control surfaces and control cables were installed. But it only took a few minutes to get used to the peculiarities of each plane, and this Dakota was no different. In fact, it was a joy flying an empty plane. It handled like a newly tamed mustang pony.

We did a few touch and goes on the airfield at the British Air Base. On our third takeoff, Will cut the power to the starboard engine to see what I would do. Jack had done the same thing when he was teaching me; it was no surprise. I compensated, maintained my heading, identified a place to land, and pointed it out to Will. Then I checked the fuel valve, checked the ignition switch, cycled the magnetos, and checked the prop pitch controls. Satisfied, Will ran the starboard throttle back to full power. "Go ahead and land this thing. Nice work."

We landed uneventfully. I taxied back to the hangar and shut down the plane.

Will looked me eye to eye again. "Hank, I must say, you're a skilled pilot. I'd be happy to have you ferry a plane to Singapore, and then fly with my team as long as you want. We need good pilots like you. We're going to need more before this thing is done."

I was touched. I would have never dreamed that I measured up to a fully trained military pilot. Either Will was blowing sunshine up my Idaho cowboy butt, or I was actually a decent pilot. There's nothing like having an impartial expert, whom you don't know, evaluate your skills and tell you you're good. I barely graduated from high school. A skilled pilot? It was not something I had ever planned. But I was good at it just the same. *Well don't that beat all.*

It was only mid morning, but I could already tell that it was going to be a hell of a day here in the city of Rangoon.

Chapter Forty-Seven

Jack found the tractor repairman easy enough. She turned out to be a Dutch woman by the name of Anna Van Roorda. She was now up to her elbows in the left engine of the Goose. She and her husband had owned a farm in Holland, but he had taken a position as a government administrator in the Dutch East Indies. He spent nine months on the island before he got things squared away and sent for her. During that time she kept the farm running, and out of necessity she learned how to fix farm equipment. At first they were minor repairs, but when a blown tractor engine threatened the harvest, she simply found a repair manual, borrowed some tools, and went to work. The tractor was still running back home. She moved to Kutaraja to join her husband, but grew bored in between government functions and decided to do a little repair work on the side. That was five years ago. Now she was the go-to-gal for everyone in Kuta with a broken piece of mechanical equipment. She loved her work and was good at it. She was only challenged on the days that she had to combine roles. Greasy hands and formal gowns didn't go well together.

Marco watched her nervously, until Jack suggested that he help. He hesitantly agreed.

"Anna, this is Marco. He'd like to help if he could."

"Hello Marco," she said over her shoulder. "I could use your help. Can you hand me a spanner wrench?" She pulled her left hand from the engine and held it behind her back, toward Marco.

Marco looked at Jack and shrugged. Jack silently pointed to the adjustable wrench in Anna's toolbox. Marco grabbed it and placed it in Anna's open hand.

She swung it around and inserted it into the engine. "Thank you. That's the one."

"Anna, what do you think so far?" Jack asked.

She paused to look over her shoulder. "You were right about the oil leak. I need to replace the crankcase seal. Easy enough to do, but I don't have a replacement and I'll never find one. I'll need to make a custom gasket, which will add another hour or so. We're looking at, oh, three or four hours of solid work. In about an hour I'll need some muscle to help."

"Sounds good. Marco's your muscle. I need to go into town for a bit but I'll be back shortly. Can you tell me where the telegraph office is?"

"Two blocks past my garage, on the left. Look for the big yellow dog out front. Can't miss him. I can guarantee he won't miss you."

"Thanks Anna. Marco, I'll see you soon."

He gave Jack a sheepish look.

Jack understood Marco's trepidation. He was a fish out of water. But this would be good for him. The more he learned about the Goose, the better.

Jack found the big yellow dog soon enough. He apparently loved a new face, and was more than happy to introduce himself to Jack. Jack tousled with him a bit then stepped into the small telegraph office.

"He likes newcomers," the clerk said. She was a blond haired Dutch woman as well. From what he'd seen so far, Jack figured half the town was Dutch.

"He's a friendly dog. Is he Dutch also?"

"No, he's a local. He adopted us when we arrived. What I can do for you?"

"My name's Jack Campbell. I'm hoping you have a cable waiting for me."

"I believe I do. Let me check." She ruffled through a pile of envelopes on her desk then pulled one out and handed it to Jack.

He was relieved. "Wonderful. I'll be back in ten minutes to send a response. Will you be here?"

"All morning, at least. See you soon."

Jack stepped outside, opened the envelope, and read the message from Hank. Good news. Hank was in Meiktila on his way to Rangoon. He had sent the cable two days earlier, so Jack had to figure he had already arrived in Rangoon. Or was at least close. He was moving faster than Jack expected.

Jack composed a message to Hank, letting him know they had been delayed but were on the way to Malacca via the city of Medan in the Dutch East Indies. Expected arrival in Malacca: two days. He stepped back into the office and asked the clerk to send the cable to Hank in both Meiktila and Rangoon, just in case. "You have a very mobile friend," she said.

"He gets around. Pretty common these days though, don't you think?"

"It's getting that way. I'm not sure what's in store for us. We have one foot out the door on any given day, in case we need to leave here for Holland."

"Holland's in a bad way now too. Hard to say where it's safe."

"I know. I see many cables every day. It's unsettling, to say the least. Give me a minute while I send your message." She sat down at her desk and transmitted the telegram to its two destinations, then waited for confirmation. When she received it from both stations, she turned to Jack. "All done."

Jack paid her and wished her luck. "Stay safe," he said, as he walked out the door. He had learned something new. Telegraph office clerks probably knew more about the overall political situation than anyone else, on a day to day basis. He'd keep that in mind.

"How soon can you fly to Singapore?" Will asked. I'd passed his tests and was now one of his substitute pilots.

"I'm ready to go anytime. What if I worked up a flight plan this afternoon, with your help, then departed tomorrow morning? Do you have a plane ready to go?"

"Yes, it's the Dakota you saw in the hangar. It's good to go. Just had a fuel leak repaired."

"Bad fuel tank?" I asked.

"Bullet holes."

"Sorry I asked. That reminds me. What happened to the last guy?"

"You mean Lieutenant Smith? He crashed and burned."

"Oh, I'm sorry to hear that. In a Dakota?"

"No. Rickshaw. He was pulling one of his buddies. Ran down a hill. Tripped and fell. Got run over. Broken arm. Dumb luck."

"I'll say."

"Alcohol was involved, as you can imagine. He'll heal. And yes, I'll help you with a flight plan this afternoon. Go see Sergeant McElroy at the Air Wing Office. Tell him you're one of my pilots now. He'll have some goods for you. Oh Hank?"

"Yes?"

"Stay away from the rickshaws tonight, will you?"

Chapter Forty-Eight

Jack returned to the Goose and found Anna and Marco hard at work on the engine. They had arrived at the step that required muscles, and Marco was playing the role well. Jack left them to their work and climbed into the Goose. Lhasa was in the back of the cabin, stowing the provisions he had gathered in town.

"Did you find everything you needed?" Jack asked.

"Yes. Food, water, some equipment Marco asked for, oil, and a few other things. Here. Have a banana." Lhasa tossed it to Jack.

"Nice. Thanks. I love these things."

Jack went to work on the instrument panel, hoping to repair the sticky compass. He'd gotten used to flying without it, but only because he'd been able to view obvious landmarks on a regular basis. He couldn't assume that would always be the case, especially at night. So he unscrewed the dashboard and pulled out the compass, hoping to find a way to fix it. Whatever he did, he couldn't make it any worse.

An hour, and much fumbling, later, Jack had the compass back in the dashboard and was confident it would work. It would require an in-flight test, but that would come soon enough. He climbed outside the cabin to check on Anna and Marco, who appeared to be in the end stages of reassembling the engine.

"How's it look?" he asked.

"I think she'll live," Anna responded. "I was able to fashion a nice replacement for the leaking seal. I also checked the others. They're all in good shape. Marco and I are almost done. Give us twenty minutes, then we'll test it."

"Wonderful. Thanks."

Jack took quick walk to the eatery where he had breakfast that morning. He ordered a good-sized meal to go. It was enough food for a hearty late lunch for Anna, Marco, and Lhasa. He paid the cook and added a nice tip, thanking him for the referral to Anna. He carried the warm bags of food back to the Goose, where Anna and Marco had just finished. They were just putting Anna's tools away.

"It's all set. Start it up and let's see how she runs," Anna suggested.

"Sounds good. Stand by." Jack made sure the landing gear chocks were holding the Goose tight, checked the tie-down chain at the tail, then climbed into the cockpit. He switched on the power, yelled "clear!" then cranked the left engine. It caught after a few revolutions and Jack ran it at idle for half a minute, watching the oil pressure gauge. It climbed quickly into the green and stayed there. He looked out the left window to Anna and Marco. They were standing well to the left and just in front of the Goose, so he could see them. Anna gave him a signal to increase the engine power. Jack pushed hard on the brakes then moved the throttle forward to run up the speed. The oil pressure stayed in the green. She and Marco were watching closely, but there were no leaks. Anna gave him a thumbs up. Jack shutdown the engine and feathered the props to slow it quickly. He climbed back outside.

"Looks good from inside. How about here?"

"No leaks," Anna replied. "But let's open the access panels just to be sure." She and Jack deftly removed the screws and opened the panels. The engine was nice and dry. No oil leaks.

"Nicely done, Anna. You do good work. Let's settle up

and have some food."

"I couldn't have done it without Marco. Thanks Marco."

"My pleasure," he responded. Jack noticed that Marco looked a bit more confident, like the Marco in the alley with the broom handle.

They started to unpack the variety of food the cook had prepared for them. "Did you get this at Sulei's place?" Anna asked.

"Yes. He's the one that recommended you this morning. I'm just glad you were available."

"Sure. We've known Sulei for a while. I repair his bicycle at least once a month. He can't afford to pay me, but he always makes me a big plate of nasi-goreng. Have you had it?

"No. What is it?"

"Basically, fried rice. It's the national dish of the Indies. But it's Sulei's specialty. He adds salted dried fish. It's the best. If we're lucky, there's some in this bag."

They were lucky. And it *was* the best. They ate until they were tired.

"Well gentlemen," Anna said, "I best be on my way. It's been a pleasure. I wish you luck. Where you headed next?"

"Medan, then Singapore," Jack answered. At this point he didn't feel like being much more specific. Singapore was close enough to Malacca.

"Safe travels. If you're in Kuta again, stop by and say 'hello'".

"Will do. Have a great evening."

"I'll try. I believe my husband and I have a diplomatic dinner to attend. Believe it or not, in two hours I'll be in an evening gown. Oh the burdens we bear for king and country."

Jack laughed. "Well, try to enjoy it. Thanks again."

Anna Van Roorda departed in her small truck. Jack turned to Marco. "What do you think?"

"Well," he responded, "I think she would look great in an evening gown."

"No…well…yes, I agree. But I meant what do you think about the Goose?"

"Oh! Well, the engine was simple. Not many parts. Easy to take apart and put together. No magic in there. Just metal and bolts. So I'm feeling little bit better."

"Good. Let's take the Goose for a quick flight before the sun goes down, just to give the engine a workout. Then we'll walk into town and see what Kutaraja is all about. Lhasa!" he yelled, "let's take a quick sunset flight!"

"Okay." Lhasa emerged from behind the plane. "But you're flying this time. I'm too full."

"I thought you were always eighty-percent full and ready to fight."

"I broke that rule just now. The nasi-goreng was too good. I am not ready to fight tonight."

"I'll try to remember that."

Hank finished his flight plan for Singapore, and received Will's approval. Will introduced Hank to the Dakota's mechanic, who confirmed that the plane was ready to go.

"Stop by the Sergeant's desk in the morning on your way here," Will advised. "He'll have an updated weather forecast for you."

"Will do."

"Did he arrange for a bunk for you in the barracks?"

"Yes, I'm all set. Can you point me toward the communications shack? I need to send a cable to Jack to let him know my status."

"Certainly. Walk west about fifty yards, then turn right.

Just look for the tall antennas."

"Thanks Will. How about a post office to drop some letters?"

"Same place."

"Will I see you in the morning?"

"I'll be around. Listen. I want you to consider joining my squad. Like I said, you're a good pilot and we could use you. Get this Singapore project wrapped up, whatever it is, and come back here to help. You can contact me from Singapore and we'll figure a way to get you back here."

"Much appreciated Will. I can't make any promises. But I'll keep it in my mind."

"You do that. Give my best to Jack. He's a courageous guy. He won't tell you this, but he saved a platoon of British soldiers along the Burma Road. It was pure guts on his part. They never knew who the pilot was, but I figured it out easy enough. It's why I was willing to spend some time with you today. We're all on the same team and we need to help each other."

"That's my plan," I said. Yes, I had noticed the willingness of so many people to help me along the way. Will summed it up well. When you're under attack, or recovering from it, or even preparing for it, you tend to want to reach out to help others. Strange how that works. Big challenges bring us together. Small ones don't. I never could figure that out.

I found the communications shack and sent a quick cable to Jack. It read "In Rangoon. Flying Dakota to Singapore in morning. Solved Marco's problems with equipment. Will explain. Stay safe." I dropped off the pile of letters I had written to the folks at home. Then I grabbed some chow in the mess hall and settled into my bunk. Long day. Time to sleep.

PART THREE. THE MALACCAN PLAN

Chapter Forty-Nine

My flight from Rangoon to Singapore was uneventful. Will assigned me as pilot. He paired me with a new copilot from his squadron. He was a young chap from Scotland. I could hardly understand him. Didn't matter. We flew fast, flew straight, and laughed hard. Partly due to my mishearing of several things he said, partly due to his misinterpretation of my favorite bunkhouse jokes. Turns out they just don't translate well into Scottish. Which apparently makes them even funnier.

The Dakota had been loaded to the gills with ammunition and weapons for the British soldiers in Singapore, who were preparing for an inevitable battle with the Japanese. The plane was close to being overweight. It handled like a sack of potatoes. It didn't matter. Will had given me a huge boost in confidence and I felt like I could do single-engine barrel rolls if I had to. The distance from Rangoon to Singapore was 1,700 miles. It was an easy route to fly. We simply followed the Burma – Malaysia peninsula all the way to the end, looked down, and there was the city of Singapore. The flight took us nine hours, including a refueling stop along the way. Southeast Asia is vast and large. We touched down at the British air base in Singapore in early evening. Just in time for dinner and a warm beer.

My long journey was almost done. On the flight in I gazed upon the Strait of Malacca, the *Flor De La Mar's* resting place, for the first time. The Strait bordered the southern coast of Malaysia. We actually passed over the town of Malacca as we approached Singapore. As I surveyed the sea from our 5,000 foot altitude I realized that somewhere below was the reef that sank the *Flor De La Mar*. The ship was there somewhere. Only 5,000 feet away. It was a real kick. It was all I could do to focus on our approach to Singapore. I had shared nothing about our endeavor with my copilot. I'm sure he thought I was merely enjoying the scenery.

From Singapore, Malacca was 150 miles to the west along the southern coast of Malaysia. Worst case, I could easily get to Malacca by bus. Best case, I would reach Jack and have him pick me up in the Goose. I did my usual evening routine. I found the telegram office and retrieved the message Jack had left for me. I sent a quick cable to Malacca for Jack in case he arrived there before I contacted him otherwise. Then I found the base communications office and, with a bit of help from the British radio operator, tried to contact Jack in the Goose via shortwave radio. I had a slim chance of reaching him, but it was worth a shot. No luck though. I decided to stay overnight in Singapore and then try again in the morning. If I couldn't connect with Jack, I'd find some other way to get my butt to Malacca. I was so close I just didn't feel like waiting around. I was itching to get to Malacca and felt like I might crawl right out of my skin.

Jack's sunset flight in the Goose confirmed that the oil leak was fixed, and that the compass worked correctly. The Goose was almost whole for the first time in a long while. It still had an intermittent radio problem but Jack could live with it until he could find a replacement. He had developed a process with the radio. He switched it on as often as he could, for five or ten minutes at a time. Then turned it off to let it cool before it blew its circuit breaker. It was an annoyance but it was the best he could do for now.

The trio slept in the Goose that night on the tarmac in

Kutaraja, then departed early the next morning for Medan. Medan was a city on the northern coast of the Dutch East Indies' island of Sumatra, 450 miles from Kutaraja, almost exactly halfway between Kutaraja and Malacca. It was a two and a half hour flight. The trio arrived in Medan in time for lunch. As they approached the city they caught their first glimpse of the Strait of Malacca, which bordered Medan to the north. They were near their destination and the excitement inside the Goose was contagious.

Medan was surrounded by Dutch tobacco plantations, and Dutch architecture was evident everywhere. Most of the newer buildings in town were of Dutch design, while the older buildings had an Asian or Islamic influence. It was the usual confluence of Asia and Europe. At this point it was entirely familiar to Jack.

Lhasa had provisioned the Goose with a large variety of food that would perish quickly in the tropical heat. While Jack sought a source for fuel, Lhasa prepared a quick lunch of bananas, rice cakes, dried fish, and dates. They ate in the shade of a nearby tree, then packed up. They used a tow bar to pull the Goose to the nearby fuel pump, where Jack topped off the tanks.

While Jack was filling the tanks, an Asian man arrived at the boundary of the airfield on a bicycle. He was winded and sweating profusely after pedaling a good distance at the fastest speed he could manage. He immediately took notice of the Goose and its three passengers. He stood under the shade of large banyan tree and studied them for a few minutes. Satisfied, he pulled a small diary and pencil from his pocket and filled a page with notes. He then sat unnoticed in the shade and merely observed. He could see that the trio was preparing to depart. He needed to see which direction they went. It was critical to know. He had all day to find out.

The next morning I tried Jack on the shortwave again. No luck. I decided to hop on a bus to Malacca. They ran once a day, and I was able to grab a seat on that day's bus. It whined along the road at a glacial thirty miles an hour. It would be a five hour trip. An eternity. My seven-month journey had taken me from Idaho to San Francisco, to Hawaii, to Manila, to Dinjan, to Kunming, to Kengtung, to Rangoon, to Singapore. It was a huge semicircular rotation over the entire western hemisphere and it wound me up like a watch spring. I was coiled and ready to snap.

They departed to the east, flying out over the Strait of Malacca. He watched them as long as he could. They flew toward Malaysia. To Kuala Lumpur? Or Singapore perhaps? It didn't matter. Their plane was distinctive and easy to spot. He would make his report. Someone else would find them on the other end. All in all a good day's work. He knew from experience that rewards come to the vigilant.

Chapter Fifty

The Goose touched down in the harbor at Malacca after dark. The Strait was calm that day so Jack was confident he could land after sunset. It didn't take long to cross the Strait, so the trio decided to do a bit of aerial reconnaissance. They spent the afternoon flying over the Strait to study the geography, the reefs, the currents, and the boat traffic. By the time they made it back to Malacca it was after sunset. The city lights lit the entire bay. Jack used the reflections to guide his landing in the smooth harbor. They taxied to a berth at one of the numerous docks, tied up, locked the plane, and set off on foot toward the town center. It was a quiet evening. A layer of clouds that had been building all day, now lowered itself like blanket above the city. The shops were closed for the night, but from time to time the trio could hear conversations, laughter, and muted music from an eatery somewhere close by. Otherwise they didn't see a soul.

Malacca was a small city, dominated by St. Paul's Hill which contained the ruins of the old Portuguese fortress, built by Afonso De Albuquerque when the Portuguese conquered Malacca in 1511. The city was bisected by the Malacca River; the eastern side was predominantly Dutch architecture, the western side primarily Chinese. It was the usual mix of Asian and European influence. The trio hiked to the top of St. Paul's hill, finding themselves at the gate of the old fortress. Its thick walls were built of reddish-brown stone blocks that were still partially covered with layers of whitewashed plaster. The gate was dominated by a massive arch with a bell tower on top. There was an elaborate bas relief chiseled into a frieze at the top of the arch – the symbol of the Dutch East India Company.

"Why the Dutch East India Company?" Jack asked.

"The Dutch drove the Portuguese out of Malacca in the 1600's," Lhasa answered. "Looks like they wanted to leave their mark."

Marco touched the wall of the arch. "This makes it seem quite real, doesn't it? We're finally here."

"This fortress was built a few months before the *Flor De La Mar* sank," Lhasa responded.

"It's old," Jack said, "Centuries old." He surveyed the ruins. Lhasa and Marco both understood his meaning. The wreck was just as old. It was difficult to imagine that any of it had survived. But the ruins had, and that gave them a tangible connection to the ship.

"It's quiet here," Marco said. "I expected a busy place."

"After the Dutch, the British took over in the 1800's," Lhasa explained. "They moved the commerce, and most of the population, away from Malacca to Penang and Singapore, which they had better control of."

Jack turned and viewed the town below. It had once been the center of the Malaccan kingdom. Now it was a sleepy coastal town on the Strait of Malacca, watching the world pass by through the busiest waterway in the western hemisphere.

"Alright Lhasa," Jack said. "We're here. Where do we go? Who do we meet?"

"Follow me." Lhasa led them down the path back into town, toward the *Custodian*, who would take them to the wreck of the *Flor De La Mar*.

The town was now dead quiet. It started to rain.

"So you're sure it was a twin-engine, twin-tailed

Beechcraft airplane with floats?" the Japanese major asked excitedly. He released the transmit button on his shortwave radio.

"Yes," the response crackled through the radio headset. "It had an American flag on the tail, and the floats that you described. There was an American and two Asians on the plane. Civilians. They departed Medan and flew to the southeast. Toward Kuala or Singapore. They filled the tanks before they left."

"Excellent work. You'll be rewarded as usual. Out."

The major grabbed his codebook and sought the frequency and station names for Kuala Lumpur and Singapore. He commanded a broad network of spies and informants throughout the Dutch East Indies and Malaysia. Among the many items on his to-do list, he had been tasked with watching for the Goose. His superiors were well aware of its actions in Longzhou, where it had effectively stalled what would have been a rapid Japanese Army advance on the defiant Chinese city. They wanted the plane and the crew. They would deal with them harshly, as the civilian fighters – spies – that they were. The major radioed his stations and told them to watch for the Goose between Kuala Lumpur and Singapore. It would land somewhere along that line, he was sure of it. The word was out. The major smiled. How hard could it be to hide an airplane like that?

Our bus arrived in Malacca that night, after a long delay caused by a breakdown on the road between Singapore and Malacca. I was jumping to get on with my journey. I tempered my impatience by helping with the bus repairs. It was messy, requiring some significant improvisation. I greatly enjoyed it. We finally got rolling again in the early evening and reached Malacca after 10pm that night. I was so tired I slept on a bench outside the bus station. The next morning I awoke early, found a quick bite to eat and downed a cup of hot tea, then walked south toward the sea. The telegraph office wasn't open yet so I figured I'd take a close look at the Strait of Malacca firsthand.

The town was just waking up and a few residents were out and about. I received the usual polite stares from the folks I passed. Once again, I stood out. Although I did notice that the residents of Malacca were more diverse compared to Burma and China. I saw a few Europeans, probably Dutch or British, along with the usual mix of Southeast Asians. Many smiled at me. I walked straight to the harbor, intending to turn to the east and walk to the beach. But I stopped momentarily to gaze at the docks and as I did, I immediately saw the Goose. It was tied up at the end of a dock on the edge of the harbor. I grinned. I would shortly be reunited with my friends. I realized I had missed them the day before – I arrived so late I didn't bother to check, as I assumed they were still en route.

I walked quickly to the harbor's edge and then onto the dock. I crept quietly to the Goose, figuring I could surprise my buddies and have a little fun. As I peered through the cockpit window I realized the plane was empty. Disappointed, I tried the door to see if they'd left a note inside for me. The door handle was locked. Jack was always prudent in that regard. I peered in the windows to see if they had left any clue as to their location, but couldn't see much. Not much at all. Which told me that they'd already departed with their packs and supplies. But where to? Jack would have left something, or someone, to let me know. I turned to walk back along the dock, and that's when I saw them. The first guy was innocent enough. Just another Asian guy appraising me. But the menacing look on the second guy's face was all I needed to see. Because it was such a rare thing in Southeast Asia. It stood out as much as I did. I was in trouble, sure enough.

Chapter Fifty-One

As the two approached me there on the dock, I realized I didn't have many options. I was at the end of the dock. I had nowhere to turn. It looked like they meant business. I decided I didn't want to find out what it was. A couple of things went through my head in a split second. I didn't even have to think the words. That would have taken too long. I just had to think the thoughts. The first was a bit of advice my Grandpa gave me long ago. He said "Never ask a barber if you need a haircut." I wasn't going to ask these guys what they wanted, or what their problem was. I knew from their demeanor that I wouldn't like the answer.

A word popped into my head. Roll. Well actually it was two: drop and roll. But it was the roll that was important. So in a split second I knew what to do. Whatever I did, I wasn't going anywhere with these guys. That was the second thought. No matter what, don't let them take you. However unpleasant it would be here, it was likely to be much worse wherever they wanted me to be.

My decision made, I decided to give them some good old fashioned ranch courtesy. I tightened my pack on my back, held up both hands with open palms, just like I had done with Ko Than, and gave them a big smile. I walked toward them so I could meet them at the dock away from the Goose, where there was water on both sides, and kept a silly grin on my face. The menacing guy was about three steps behind the lead guy, just to his right. When I was three steps from the lead man, I quickly dropped my weight and lunged hard with my legs. I hit him with my left shoulder and pushed through him. He coughed as I knocked the wind out of him. I caught him completely unprepared. He hadn't braced himself at all. It was the old bunkhouse shove I'd practiced many times, borne from the shoulder shove I used to make obstinate cattle move the direction I wanted them to go. A large steer weighs a thousand pounds or more. This guy weighed one-twenty at the most. I pushed him right off the dock and into the water. I landed face down on the dock, and then used my arms to push me into a left-hand roll. The second guy was now scrambling toward me. I simply rolled right into his legs. He fell over me and planted his face hard into the dock. I heard a crack and assumed it was his nose. He screamed. I rolled onto my right knee, then sprang upright and ran. I ran as fast as I could down the dock and back to the town of Malacca. I wasn't sure where I would run to. I hadn't quite figured that out yet. Didn't matter. I just put as much distance between me and the two thugs as I could. Didn't even look back. I figured the guy with the broken nose would have to fish his buddy out of the water, which bought me a half a minute or so.

I ran straight into the town, then started looking for a good place to turn. I planned to turn down one of the left-right streets to find a place to hide. But I didn't need to figure it out. A dark-haired man, probably Malay, stepped around the corner from the street to my right, smiled, and motioned me to follow. I made a split second decision and turned after him. He jogged about twenty yards then turned right into the open door of a shop. I hesitated, then followed him inside. It was a shoe repair shop that had large windows facing the street. I couldn't imagine a threat inside such a public shop. The Malay motioned me behind his workbench, and I dropped to the floor in a crouch.

"You must be Hank," he said, in almost perfect English.

"You must know Lhasa," I answered, breathing hard.

"Long time. My name is Alex. Just Alex."

"Happy to meet you, Alex. Believe me."

"Likewise. Nice job there on the dock. You can run fast, that's for sure."

"When I need to. Who were those guys?"

"We've been keeping an eye on your plane, and noticed them taking an interest. They're no good. They arrived here a month ago. It's a small town so we noticed them. We figure they're Japanese scouts. We've kept our distance. But I'm puzzled as to why they'd take an interest in you. They usually stay quiet. Now they'll have to leave town. Now everyone knows they're trouble. So why would they risk that for you?"

"I think I have an idea. You can blame my friend Jack. We never should have let him play with those fireworks over Longzhou."

An hour later I was sitting on the floor behind Alex's shoe repair workbench, cutting leather for the uppers of some fishing boots. It was better than doing nothing. We figured I had to hide here at least until dark. At that time, if it was safe, Alex would take me to Jack, Lhasa, and Marco. "They left late last night for the reef," he told me. "They were anxious to get there and didn't want to wait until morning. They asked me to watch for you. You're easy to find. Lhasa told me to watch for a tall white guy. Hank, you stand out. That's going to be a problem."

"I know. Can't change that. Hey it sounds like there's more than one of you. Who are you guys?"

"The *Custodians*. Of the location of the *Flor De La Mar*."

I spent a lifetime in Alex's shop that day. Evening

couldn't come soon enough. In the late afternoon, Alex left to confer with his friends. He locked the shop, leaving me hidden away behind the workbench. There was nowhere else to go. His shop was one small room. The workbench was the only cover. He gave me some cushions to sit on. I just sat there cooling my heels, working on leather blanks for Alex. The leather smelled like the tack room back on the ranch. Like home.

Alex returned at dusk. "We have a plan. The two Japanese haven't been seen all day, but we can't assume they've left. We got a message to Lhasa, so they know you're here. They're a safe distance from here, at the reef. Nobody's noticed them, so we got lucky. We're going to get you there tonight in one of the fishing canoes. I should say, in the bottom of a fishing canoe. The fleet goes out around midnight to go lantern fishing, so we'll be a part of a crowd. We'll slip away from the others and take you to the reef."

And that's what they did. They had me carry a heaping pile of netting to cover my head and face. It was heavy so I stooped as I walked, which helped to minimize my height. We walked toward the harbor, then eventually merged in with several fisherman making the same trek. Alex walked close beside me, carrying two oars and an unlit lantern. He was a bit under my six foot height. He seemed strong and nimble. He wore sandals, shorts, and one of those white cotton shirts with buttons down the front and an embroidered design across the top. Marco called them "wedding shirts". Alex reminded me of Marco. Like Marco, he didn't waste any motion. He walked quietly and carefully, as if every footstep was worth money. I could also tell that he was vigilant. He was clearly observing everything around us.

"How many of you are there?" I asked quietly.

"Oh, more than you would think. We've been waiting a long time. Thanks for coming."

"Well I hope it all works out. But it seems like the hard part hasn't even started yet."

It was an unusual ride, there in the bottom of the canoe. I lay on my back, just watching the stars drift by as we paddled out of the harbor with the lantern fishing fleet. The lanterns were attached to a vertical pole at the bow of each canoe. As they swayed with the waves the shadows played across the water. The waving lantern and the rocking canoe made me dizzy, so I focused on the stars while taking deep breaths. After a while I got used to the motion and began to enjoy the ride. Alex paddled consistently for a good ten minutes, took a break for a couple of minutes, blew out the lantern, then slowly moved us away from the other canoes. We half drifted, half paddled for five minutes. Suddenly Alex started paddling hard. "Stay quiet," he whispered. "We're on our own now. We crossed the point at the south end of Malacca. Now we can move fast toward the reef. If the two Japanese are still watching us, we'll know. Our friends are watching *them*. It's going to take a while to get to the reef. In a few minutes I'm going to ask you to help paddle while I watch for the rocks."

Five minutes later I was paddling my guts out. The canoe was heavier than I thought and it took some muscles to keep it moving through the swells. I had instant respect for Alex's strength. He had the stamina of a bumblebee during wildflower season. It wasn't so much my arms that got tired. It was my upper legs and lower back, as I tensed to keep myself anchored to the canoe. I had paddled a river raft many times, but it was the river current that did most of the work. This was something different entirely.

It took us a good thirty minutes to reach the tip of the reef. Alex kept the lantern dark. He used the various lights along the coast as waypoints to help him navigate. He had clearly been here many times.

"This reef is fairly remote," he explained. "It's offshore between towns. There's nothing on shore close to the reef. There's little reason to come here. There's a small village about five miles to the southeast. Once in a great while the fishermen from that village come to this reef to fish. They found the pottery from the shipwreck a few months ago, and told us. We've handed down the location of the wreck – I should say the spot the ship hit the reef – for generations. Four hundred years. We hoped that one day it could be found, to redeem the treasure from the Malaccan kingdom. We just never believed it would actually happen.

"We're at the spot now where the ship hit the reef and sank."

I looked into the water, as if I could see the *Flor De La Mar*.

"The pottery was found two miles from here, along the reef but in deeper water. We figured the ship drifted off the reef during the storm that sank it. So we finally know where it's been all these years."

We paddled along for another ten minutes then stopped. Alex whistled quietly. There was response from fifty yards away, just to our left. I looked that direction and could sense a form floating on the water. Then I saw the flare of a match then the sudden glow of a newly lit lantern. "Paddle that way," Alex said.

And I did, with renewed energy. We reached a large fishing boat that was apparently anchored to the reef. I looked up to the gunwale and saw Jack, Lhasa, and Marco looking down into the canoe, with big grins on their faces.

"What took you so long?" Marco asked.

We tied the canoe to the boat and climbed aboard. The three greeted me with hearty handshakes. It was great to be back with them. It felt like I'd been on my own for half a lifetime. "I assume you guys know Alex?" I asked.

"Yes," Lhasa answered. "And from what I hear, you're lucky that Alex knows you."

"Alex, thanks for what you did today," I said. "I was in a bad pickle."

"My pleasure Hank. Glad to be of service."

We stayed awake long into the night, filling each other in on the events of the past two weeks. Collectively we'd covered a lot of ground. But we were finally here.

"So is it really here? Below us?" I looked over the gunwale down into the black water.

"This is the place we found the bits of pottery," Alex explained, "after the British ships detonated their torpedoes. If it's not here, I don't know where it is."

I had lost track of how many miles I'd traveled, just since Kunming. But we were quite possibly only one hundred feet away from the *Flor De La Mar*. Even though we'd traveled thousands of miles, the last one hundred feet was going to be the hardest by far.

Alex stayed on board. We finally got some shut eye. I had to get used to sleeping on a rocking boat. Not the easiest thing to do at first, but once I got used to it I slept deeply. We woke at dawn and ate a quick breakfast. I was anxious. We cleared the remnants of breakfast from the table and I pulled out my drawings of the bellows. "This is what we need to give Marco more time on the bottom." I explained my ideas about the bellows and about using a raft, or some type of airbag, as a lift for whatever artifacts Marco gathered on the sea floor.

"I like it," Marco said. "But we need a long rubber hose. It will need to be thick to get enough air to me. The airbag will also need to be rubber or something like that."

"Leave that to me," Alex said. "You're in the middle of Malaysia and the Dutch East Indies. We're known for two major exports. Oil. And rubber. Give me two days. I'll either find something for you, or have something made. One of my colleagues will get a message to you tonight with a status."

We gave Alex a short list of additional supplies. He dropped into the canoe and paddled to the south, toward the coast, with powerful strokes. He was a brave guy. And he clearly *got stuff done*.

"Interesting guy," I said. "I hope we can make him happy."

"Oh he already is," Lhasa answered. "He already is."

Chapter Fifty-Two

Humans have been free diving for centuries. Koreans dove for shells and highly prized sponges as early as the 4th or 5th century BCE, and are the first known deep free divers. Japanese pearl divers are the most famous; they sought pearls for trade and for income. The island of Kalymnos in Greece was a center for sponge diving. Free divers there would venture as deep as one hundred feet to gather prized sponges.

At a one hundred foot depth, a skilled free diver can hold their breath for about five minutes, at the sea floor, before ascending. To maximize their time at depth, the diver uses weights to speed their descent. They then drop the weights when ready to ascend. Free diving is dangerous and has significant impact on the body. Water pressure increases rapidly with depth. For every thirty-three feet of depth, the pressure increases by one atmosphere. So a diver at one hundred feet experiences a body-squeezing pressure of three atmospheres. This pressure squeezes the diver's lungs, organs, and tissues, with the potential to cause serious injury. For example, at pressures at or beyond three atmospheres, the lungs are squeezed so hard that they can shrink and wrap into themselves, causing permanent damage or even death.

Aquatic mammals have developed the *mammalian diving reflex* to combat the effects of high pressure at depth. Seals, whales, otters, and dolphins, for example, have a strongly developed reflex. It has several effects during a dive: it drops the heart rate, sometimes significantly (reflex bradycardia). It shrinks the blood vessels (vasoconstriction) to direct blood away from the extremities to the heart, lungs, and brain. It also contracts the spleen, flooding the bloodstream with red blood cells to move oxygen more efficiently. During very deep dives, the reflex also triggers a blood shift. This allows blood plasma and water to pass freely into the thoracic cavity around the lungs. This increased fluid allows the lungs to offset the external water pressure, by filling the air sacks of the lungs with liquid themselves. As the mammal ascends, this liquid is reabsorbed into the bloodstream. Together, these effects have a measureable impact and allow an aquatic mammal to stay underwater, at depth, for an extended period of time.

All land mammals, including humans, have the diving reflex in a weaker form. It's triggered when the face, and only the face, hits cold or cool water. Free divers exploit the mammalian diving reflex to extend their diving ability. Marco, a Filipino pearl diver, had unconsciously learned to use the reflex quite well. But despite his skill, *if* the *Flor De La Mar* was indeed below, at a depth of one hundred feet, and *if* he found it, he would only be able to stay at the wreck for five minutes at a time. Unless Hank's air pump worked. So there were many things on Marco's mind this morning. He knew that, ultimately, their success was now on his shoulders. It was a burden he welcomed. But he simply wanted to get to work. So he donned his mask and fins for the first time since leaving Lake Dian at Kunming in China, stepped to the gunwale of the boat, took a deep breath, and jumped into the deep blue sea.

I watched Marco descend deeper into the water until he simply merged with the darkness of the sea. Then I waited. It was morning, there was a constant breeze blowing from the south. The swells were about a foot or two high.

Nothing to write home about. The sky was aqua blue, dappled with bright white cumulus clouds that were slowly drifting in the breeze. The water below the boat was a deep blue. Further out it shifted to a steel blue color. There was a bright ocean haze on the horizon. In between there were a hundred shades of bluish green.

The swells lapped at the sides of the gently rocking boat. It was a lazy day. I just sat on deck enjoying the sunshine, gazing out upon the Strait of Malacca, trying to envision what happened that day in 1511 when the *Flor De La Mar* hit the reef and sank. It was difficult to imagine a ship in distress on a day like this. But who knows what happened to the *Flor De La Mar*. Was she overloaded? Unlucky? Was it fate? Stupidity? Hubris? Probably all of the above. For whatever reason, the ship never made it home, thus the treasure stayed close to *its* home. There had to be a bit of karma involved, but it was a mystery to me why karma was so random. Why does fate smile on some and punish others? I'd seen firsthand the vagaries of fate. I'd seen unfortunate things happen to good people, and vice versa. Why did the Japanese military find it so easy to conquer country after country, and inflict so much pain and turmoil, when so many good people were resisting them? Why didn't fate intervene? Why did God allow the imbalance? I decided to talk with Lhasa. But he was below deck working on a cargo basket for Marco, and I was on watch in case Marco needed help. So my question would go unanswered for now. But not forgotten.

Five minutes after Marco dove in, he reappeared at the surface. I could hear him coming as he blew his air out just under the surface. Then he popped out of the water and took a deep breath. He looked to me with a smile. "Felt good. I can still dive." He swam to the ladder on the stern, tossed his flippers onto the deck, and climbed aboard. I handed him a towel and he sat on a bench to remove his mask.

"What's it like down there?"

"Deep. Water's pretty clear though. The reef is solid on the inland side, but thins out right beneath us. Then there are patches of reef scattered across a sandy bottom. I didn't see anything unusual, but I didn't take much of a look. I only dove halfway."

"Can you make it to the bottom?"

"Yes, I'm sure I can. The question is, how long can I stay there? We'll see. Here's what we need to do though. Each time I dive, we'll drop a weighted line in the water. I'll follow it down to the sea floor. I'll then search an area in a circle around the line. As big of a circle as I can. Then I'll follow the line to ascend. We'll pull up the line, move it the appropriate distance in the right direction, and then drop it again. I'll use the new line location for my next dive. That way I can cover the largest amount of ground without diving to the same spot twice. If I find anything, I'll anchor the line at that spot so we don't lose it. Make sense?"

"Perfect sense."

"So I'll need you to manage the lines. Try to keep a drawing or a map of the various line locations and my corresponding dives. We'll see how much area I can search each time. I'll be looking mostly for large bits of pottery like the ones the villagers found after the torpedo testing. But if there are many of them, and if they're scattered all over the reef, then I'll look for something different. That's the best plan I can think of at this point."

"Sounds good to me. I'll prepare some lines with weights. We have plenty of both. Lhasa's working on a basket for you. Alex is gathering the supplies for the air bellows and lift bags. Jack is trying to figure out how to pilot the boat. In case we need to move it without Alex's help."

"Sounds good. I need one more thing. Some kind of hand rake that I can use to comb through the sand. I realized that parts of the wreck might be buried in the sand. I need a fast way to check. Can you make me something like a small pitchfork that would fit in one hand?"

"Consider it done."

I went below deck to Lhasa's impromptu workshop. There were pots and pans, baskets, and pieces of bamboo sitting on the table. Lhasa was sitting in the corner weaving a basket of reeds around the bottom of a double A-frame of bamboo that was three feet high. The two frames connected at the apex.

"A basket for Marco," Lhasa explained. "We can fill it with ballast to help him descend. He holds on here, at the top of the frame. This ring," he pointed out a brass ring at the side, "goes around the guideline so the basket doesn't drift or get lost. At the bottom he removes the ballast and fills the basket with stuff. Then he ascends with the basket if he can. Otherwise, if it's too heavy, we use your lift bag and pump it full of air. The bag will connect to the top of the frame. The air hose will connect here, where the air will rise into the bag when we pump it."

"Looks perfect. I'm going to build a small rake for Marco. What on this table of stuff do you still need?"

"Take anything you want. I'm almost done."

We worked diligently for at least an hour, but I was beginning to lose track of time. It was just "day" or "night", sleep or not. That was all I really needed to know at this point.

Chapter Fifty-Three

Marco made two more exploratory dives using the line system we discussed. He was able to effectively search a radius of ten yards, a bit more than the length of our twenty-foot boat, on each dive. We raised anchor and carefully repositioned the boat; Jack had figured out by now how to pilot her. She had a small but decent inboard engine, and moved with ease despite her apparent bulk. Jack explained that the boat belonged to Alex's village. They were happy to loan it to Alex for our efforts. But we also understood the implications. As long as we were using it, it wasn't providing fish for the village. That created almost as much urgency as the approaching Japanese.

I realized I didn't know the name of the boat. I leaned over the rail at the stern and read the hand painted letters on the back. *Pango*.

"What does *Pango* mean?" I asked Jack.

"I asked Alex the same thing. He wouldn't say. Just smiled and said we'd find out sooner or later, depending on the weather."

Well that didn't sound promising.

Alex returned later that afternoon via canoe. We unloaded a good bunch of materials and supplies onto the boat, including a long, coiled rubber hose that was at least an inch and a half thick. He also brought some sheets of rubber that had apparently been cut from an old raft.

"This is all I could find at short notice," he explained. "Is it enough?"

"Definitely," I said. "Let's get it below and Lhasa and I will put it all together."

Alex also brought some round, stacked wooden containers full of rice and cooked chicken. It was a welcome surprise and a nice change from our usual diet of fish, rice, and fruit. The chicken tasted like...well...chicken. I can't tell you how novel that was. He also brought a bag of fruit and four large canteens of fresh water. We had ourselves a nice little feast, then went back to work.

"Some good news," Alex said. "I don't think we were followed here. But they're keeping watch on your plane. They're subtle but noticeable. They're waiting for one of you to show up. Be careful if you go back to Malacca. It seems that they're focused on the plane, which means they're not aware of the treasure. If they knew of the treasure, they'd be looking for you out here. Not back at the harbor."

"Good point," Jack responded. "But if we need the Goose, we'll have to figure out how to lose them."

"Just be careful."

It was now July of 1940. The Japanese had secured French Indochina, cut the railroad from Hai Phong to Kunming, invaded Thailand, and were now expanding rapidly into Burma, the Andaman Islands, and the northwest tip of Malaysia. The British dug themselves in at Rangoon, but they knew their days were numbered. The British in Singapore were preparing for a walloping fight with the Japanese. They expected an invasion "at any time, with little warning." In an extraordinary operation of unmatched magnitude, the British completed the evacuation of Dunkirk, France, rescuing 340,000 British and allied troops from imminent capture by the German Army. It would become known as the Miracle at Dunkirk. From the deck of the *Pango* I watched regular flights of British Dakotas overhead, as they flew supplies to Singapore to prepare a defense. In Europe, Norway, Holland, and France had surrendered to the Nazis. Italy has declared war on Britain. Canada has declared war on Italy. Hitler ordered the invasion of Britain, and the Nazis were attacking British ships in the English Channel. In the US, President Roosevelt listened to Winston Churchill's pleas for help, but had no firm answer for the British Prime Minister. Tommy Dorsey was number one on the Billboard Music Singles chart, with his hit *"I'll Never Smile Again."*

The mists of war rolled in from every direction as we sat there in the *Pango*, suspended between sea and sky.

Chapter Fifty-Four

Marco did two more exploratory dives while Lhasa and I finished building his diving accessories. We built the lift bag and air bellows with the flat rubber sheets, and connected the rubber hose to the output. We dropped a new weighted line into the water, let it run all the way to the bottom, then tied the loose end to the gunwale cleat. We connected the clip ring from the combined basket/lift bag to the line and let the whole thing slide into the water. It held about fifteen pounds of ballast in the form of rocks Alex had brought from shore. I held the basket with a small leash while Marco prepared. He spent a good five minutes deep breathing, then he slid off the gunwale into the water. He grabbed onto the top of the basket and I let go of the leash. He turned head-down, kicked his legs up straight, and dove rapidly into the sea. He was out of sight within five seconds.

I started pumping the bellows to feed the hose with air. At first it was easy, but the force required to compress the bellows rapidly increased. As I thought about it, I realized that the deeper Marco went with the end of the hose, the higher the water pressure at the hose end. Therefore the higher the air pressure necessary to counteract the water pressure. Within twenty seconds I could no longer compress the bellows on my own. Lhasa added some manpower - the two of us were able to keep the bellows pumping. But it was a definite struggle. I could tell that Marco was going deeper. We needed to keep pumping for several minutes. I had opted not to build the dual-bar hand pump like I'd seen at Ko Than's farm, thinking we wouldn't need it. But now I realized it would be a necessity. We'd need more materials to build it. My previous decision would cause an unnecessary delay. Suddenly I felt an urgency that I can't fully explain. It started gnawing at my stomach like a dog chewing on a bone. It got magnified every time I saw a Singapore-bound British Dakota fly over us. This entire region would soon be at war. There was no escaping that fact. The British knew it. The Dutch knew it. We were in danger. The Goose was, well, a sitting duck. We were out of place and far from home. The treasure was most likely exposed now, after centuries of safekeeping by the Strait of Malacca. We had to *get stuff done*.

For some reason, the random thought of childhood chores popped into my head. I mentioned at the beginning of my story that my sister AJ and I had many ranch chores from the time we were five years old. Some of them were difficult. But we simply worked hard and got stuff done. It was just what we did. What everyone did. So we didn't think of them as chores, and we often had a bit of fun doing them. What else would we do anyway? It was the way of the ranch. When we got them done, we kept busy with other things, like catching fish for dinner. Which was really just another chore when you think about it. What I'm saying is, it's all in the attitude. So I decided to reset my attitude and embrace the fact that I was on a once-in-a-lifetime adventure, floating in the exotic South Pacific searching for a long-lost treasure, with three – now four – friends that meant the world to me. In this adventure, the bad guys were easy to spot. They all wore black hats and they were just over the hill. There was no cavalry to rescue us. I was riding shotgun behind a team of galloping horses, holding on with both hands and trying to keep my hat from flyin' off my head in the wind. I was a character in a ten cent movie. Only the movie wasn't going to end in an hour. Or two, or ten. There was no root beer candy at the five and dime next door. But I was doing what I'd wanted to do from the time I viewed my first picture show years ago at the movie theater in Boise. Back when I was six years old and saw nothing but adventure in the world. I was *in* the adventure now, sure enough. I had the *faith*, the *fire*, and the *friends*. I decided that it couldn't get any better. I was exactly where I wanted to be. I felt a surge of strength. I remembered one of Grandma Evans' favorite sayings: "Stop asking for God's blessing, and start doing something He's already blessed." In other words, stop whining. I got myself all fired up once again. Then I couldn't help myself. I whooped like a cowboy on a bucking bronco.

I startled Lhasa and he jumped.

"Sorry Lhasa!"

"What was that?"

"Just a little celebration."

"But we haven't found anything yet," he replied, a curious look on his face.

"Oh we have, kemosabe. We surely have."

I felt the bellows' resistance diminish. I hoped it meant that Marco was now ascending.

Jack was keeping watch while we pumped. "I see him! Here he comes!"

Hank, it was so good to hear from you. I'm glad you're safe. Seems that every day when I read the newspaper there's nothing but bad news. Seems the world's just falling deeper into conflict. First Europe and now Asia. You're out there somewhere in the middle of it. I hope you're being careful Hank. I want you to come home quickly. I want you to know that I miss you. There. I said it. I miss you. I keep thinking about the campfire we shared. About the good times we had even if we didn't have much time. I wear your necklace every day. I'm keeping myself busy, river guiding and working at Doc's office whenever he needs me. My nursing skills are getting better but I have a bunch of things to learn. I enjoy it. Makes me feel like I'm doing something to help the town. Helps me to understand a bit why you're out there trying to help folks. It's a good feeling and I know you're experiencing it too. Just helps me to understand why you're there. Your folks are doing great, and your Grandma is doing just fine. She sure enjoys your letters. AJ ran the river with me last week and it was a hoot. She can pull some oars, that's for sure. It's springtime now and you know I love this time of year. The snow's gone, but the mud's back. Trees look great and there's fresh new grass everywhere. A bunch of new calves on your ranch too. They're keeping the hands mighty busy. Hey Rosco Hanson qualified for the State Rodeo! His wife's a bit worried but Rosco's hoping to win some prize money so he can fix the engine in his truck. I sure hope he does. It gives us all something to cheer for. And Hank, we're all cheering for you. Everybody. The whole dang town. You stay safe Cowboy. Write me when you can. Stay focused and get it done, whatever that might be. Then come home and tell me about it. Love, Sara

Well, don't that beat all.

Chapter Fifty-Five

Marco broke the surface and took several deep breaths. The now-inflated lift bag popped up right beside him. It worked! We pulled Marco aboard and he removed his fins and mask. "Didn't see anything," he said, in between deep breaths. "But I did learn something about the air hose. Let me catch my breath first."

Jack handed him a canteen of fresh water and Marco downed a few gulps. I reached over the gunwale, grabbed the lift bag, and pulled it enough to grasp the handle of the basket. Then I unsnapped the line ring and pulled the basket aboard. It was now empty, the ballast rocks left on the sea floor.

While Marco recovered, I told him about my discovery with the air bellows. That it became almost impossible to pump the deeper he dove. He nodded. "I think I realized the same thing, in reverse. I didn't need to take a breath from the hose on this dive. But I did use it to inflate the bag. As I rose, the bubbles from the hose rose with me. They started out small close to the bottom, but expanded in size as I rose. Near the surface they were huge. They expanded as they rose. Because the water pressure decreased. If I would have filled my lungs with air on the bottom, it would have expanded in my lungs as I ascended. I don't think I like that idea. Seems very dangerous. So I think I'll only use the hose air to fill the lift bag."

Made sense to me. It was a relief. We didn't need to build the dual-handled pump after all. Turns out Marco had stumbled upon a critical issue, and had averted disaster with his observation. Had he used our pressurized air on the seafloor, he very likely would have burst his lungs on the way back up. It gave us all a healthy respect for the work Marco was doing. We realized there was a lot more to deep diving than, well, diving.

We developed a new plan. Marco would ride the weighted basket down as usual. It worked well because it saved him time, energy, and oxygen. He'd do his search for as long as he could. If he found something he'd put it in the basket. When he was ready to ascend, he'd tug on the line a couple of times then start his ascent. We'd then start pumping, filling the lift bag so it could ascend on its own at about the same time and rate as Marco. That way we didn't have to pump during his dive, only at the end. We'd still get the basket back to prepare for his next descent.

After a recovery break for Marco, we repositioned the weighted line to center a new search area, readied our now-proven equipment, then launched him on another dive. We waited with realism-tempered expectation. After several minutes, we felt the tug on the rope and started pumping air. Marco popped to the surface with the inflated lift bag close behind. No luck on this dive, but our system worked so we had a repeatable process. We were on a roll.

Our stealthy host Alex left in the early evening to paddle back to his village. He wanted to check on the Goose and see what the Japanese scouts were up to. Marco was done for the day. But it was a productive day and we felt like we'd accomplished something. We learned some good lessons. We developed a working process. But the same question was on all of our minds. How many dives would it take? Because we could all see that even one day of diving was hard on Marco. He looked like he'd been rolled by a hay baler. We only had one Marco. We wanted to keep him. Alive, that is.

The next day Marco made three dives. On the first and second, he found pieces of pottery. Nothing on the third, but he felt like he was getting a much better feel for the seafloor. Alex returned with no news about the Goose and scouts, and with a bag of fresh fruit. We were grateful for both. At this point, with all the turmoil, we figured no news was good news.

Alex spent the evening with us and told us more about himself. His family had lived in or near Malacca for too many generations to count. In his lifetime he'd traveled as far to the east as Singapore and as far to the west as Penang. He visited the Dutch East Indies, across the Strait, once. He had a genuine love for his country and its people. He had no desire to travel far, but he loved hearing about the places we'd been and asked many questions. Especially about the ranch in the wintertime. He couldn't picture a landscape covered with snow. With each revelation about how we dealt with subzero temperatures and snow and ice, he just shook his head.

After a long day, everyone turned in for some rest. I wasn't tired yet so I decided to sit on the deck and enjoy the stars. Lhasa soon appeared and sat quietly beside me for a long while. I enjoyed Lhasa's company. He didn't feel the need to talk. Just to be. It was something new to me and I realized how much one can communicate by not saying anything. By just being present.

I finally broke the silence. "Lhasa," I asked, "I don't understand something."

"What's that?"

"I don't understand why life isn't fair."

"Hank that's a big question. I thought you would say you didn't understand something like the mosquito. Which

I don't understand myself. What do you mean?"

I explained my thoughts about fate. About how it seemed so random and unrelated to a person's actions.

"Hank, that's almost as complicated as a mosquito. It's because fate *is* random. Any more questions?"

That wasn't the answer I expected. "Well, yes. Why?"

"Because it seemed like you had more questions."

"What? No. I mean *why* is fate random?"

"It's random from our perspective. We can't see the big picture."

"So you're saying if we could, it would make sense?"

"It would make *more* sense. But not perfect sense."

"But why? I mean, look at what's going on around us? Are you saying that it's part of God's plan?"

"Of course not. God's plan is simple. Love God, and love others. That would be perfection. We're the ones, all of us, that make it complicated."

"But why can't God fix that? Why can't God stop bad things from happening?"

"He could. But he doesn't. Because long ago, we chose free will. He could force us to love Him, and love others. But where's the joy in that? That's not love. So with free will, when we choose to love, we have joy. When we chose not to, we have pain. I'm sure God feels that with us. But we're free to choose and that makes love all the better."

I thought on it for a while.

"Hank, here's the thing. The world is imperfect. We're imperfect. No matter what we do, we make mistakes. Sometimes terrible mistakes. Sometimes people chose conscious action that has terrible consequences. It's the world of free will. And of imperfection. We can try to fix it. Each step we take has an impact. Over time, even the little impacts add up. In the long run, the good far outweighs the bad. The challenges nurture the good, like exercise strengthens muscles. But in the end, it's free will. So what you and I decide to do every day is more important than we'll ever know.

I nodded.

"Just remember this," he continued. "The smallest of things – a quick smile at a passing stranger – can have a profound impact across the ages. And *that*, my friend, is why life is worth living."

Chapter Fifty-Six

The new day dawned calm and humid. I had made a morning ritual of jumping into the water. It was so warm compared to Idaho river water that I couldn't get enough of it. I jumped in, as usual, to cool off a bit before we started our day. Marco, Lhasa, and Alex joined me. We swam around for a while. I eventually noticed that Jack wasn't with us. As I thought about it, I realized that Jack never joined us in the water. I thought maybe he didn't want to leave the boat unattended, but then I realized I'd never seen him in the water at all. Not even when someone else was watching the boat. So I quietly climbed aboard the *Pango*, dried off, and sat down on a bench by Jack.

"Jack, go ahead and take a dip. I'll man the *Pango*."

"No thanks. I'm fine."

"No, seriously. Feel free. The water feels great."

"No, really. I don't need to get in the water."

"Why not?"

"Oh, no reason. I just don't feel like it."

"Uh huh."

"What?" Jack asked, with growing exasperation.

"You tell me. What?"

He sighed. "I'm afraid to."

That was a new concept for me. Jack Campbell was afraid of something. "Afraid of the water?"

"No," he said sheepishly. "Afraid of what might be *in* the water."

"And what would that be?"

"Sharks," he said quietly, looking around as if someone might hear.

"You're afraid of sharks? You're from Montana. Where have you seen a shark?"

"Books. Plus I've seen shark jaws. For sale. In Rangoon. Just thinking about it makes me cold." He folded his arms tightly to his chest and shivered.

I could see clear enough that he wasn't kidding around. "Fair enough," I said. "It's safe with me."

"Doesn't matter. It's just not something I would go around telling people."

"Jack," I said, "Will Watson told me what you did."

"He told you about the rickshaw race?"

"What? No. Wait – you were involved in that?"

"Not as far as you know."

"Okay, whatever. No, Will told me about what you did on the Burma Road. To save the platoon. You denied it, but Will says he knows it was you. Said if you were in the military, you would have been nominated for the Silver Star for bravery."

"Yeah, well, the rickshaw race was far more dangerous. Ask the two guys that lost."

Marco made four dives that day. We had now moved the reference line, and the *Pango*, a good distance from Marco's first dive. He was zeroing in on something. The first three dives all yielded pieces of pottery. But it was the fourth dive that made it all worthwhile. Marco's basket held the unmistakable metal cleat from the gunwale of a large ship. A large *old* ship. The cleat was encrusted with centuries of coral.

"There are more," he explained. "In the sand. And there's pottery. I saw two that have the symbols that we saw in that letter in the Goose. The checkerboard coat of arms. I just didn't have time to pull them out of the sand. I think we found it!"

We whooped and hollered for a good long while. Then we went to work. We drew up a detailed chart of Marco's findings. It began to paint a picture that made sense. A picture of the last few miles of the final voyage of the *Flor De La Mar*. The ship hit the reef a good distance from where we were now. Then it must have been pushed along the reef by the storm as it broke apart and sank. Our map showed a spray of dots, representing the location of pottery pieces that Marco had found. The sinking ship had deposited them in a long broad line, ending at the location Marco had just searched. But Marco was done for the day. We hauled out all the equipment and secured it on deck. We then settled down for a bit of dinner.

We'd been floating over the reef in the *Pango* for three days and three nights now. We grew concerned that someone would notice and would become curious as to our activities. So we debated whether to move somewhere else for a day, return to the village marina for a day, or stay put. We felt we were close to a big discovery. The thought of leaving was gut wrenching. We could leave a buoy on an anchored line so we could return to the same spot. But what if we lost the buoy? Could we find our way back? Ultimately we decided to stay for one more day. Or possibly two. But it was a tough thing. It started a much bigger discussion, one that had been nipping at our heels for a while but that we really needed to get out in the open and finalize under the light of day. We'd discussed it several times, but it was now time to wrap it up. We all agreed that none of us wanted to benefit from the treasure's recovery. We'd gotten to know each other well enough by now to know this for sure. I can't really explain it in words. But when you've spent a bunch of time traveling in a region at war, being pursued by men in black hats, finding time to help people and, well, smile at strangers, you get a pretty good sense of each other's character. I'm sure there are many ways to verify the character of a man or a woman. But I'll tell you what. I think the raft of experiences we'd shared in the past couple of months was one of the best.

Here's the thing. A bunch of guys in Rangoon knew that Jack was a hero. But he just brushed it off and refused the attention. I'd seen Marco at work in Kengtung, when he took on Ko Than and his gang in the alleyway. When it was all done he made sure to replace the broom he'd broken. His actions that day were apparently the *least* remarkable thing that Lhasa had seen him do over the two years he'd known him. Lhasa stood in front of a platoon of armed men at the Mekong River, willing to die rather than let them have the food that was meant for the free Chinese. And to protect me. Alex risked himself in Malacca when he hid me in his shop, and then again when he smuggled me out to the *Pango* at the reef. We trusted each other because we'd seen each other in action. When no action was expected. So we had a bond that was worth more than a kingdom's treasure. Hard to explain but it was as tangible as an old metal cleat from an ancient ship.

We talked well into the night. We'd discussed our plan many times during our travels. Now it was finalized. It was a plan that *was* worthy of, well, a kingdom's treasure.

I realized that Alex had been fairly quiet throughout our discussion. I asked him what he thought of our plan.

He smiled, and simply said "It seems to fit."

Chapter Fifty-Seven

The law that governs the recovery of a shipwreck is known as salvage law. It defines a salvor as a seaman that carries out the recovery of a sunken vessel or cargo that originally belonged to another owner. It defines the rights that a salvor has to that property. Salvage law recognizes that a salvor should have some reward for risking life and property to recover the property of another, especially if that property has been abandoned as a derelict or as a sunken wreck. *The 1910 Brussels Convention for the Unification of Certain Rules with Respect to Assistance and Salvage at Sea* defined an international standard for salvage law. It governed the recovery of the *Flor De La Mar*, assuming there would be one. It's a long a complicated legal document. But what it meant was that *if* our team of five recovered the treasure, or even a part of it, we had a legal claim, under international law, to a portion of its value.

We all agreed that we felt an urgent need to secure the treasure before it fell into the wrong hands. And to put it to good use to by getting it into the right hands. On this there was no wavering. But there was a much broader issue. What would we do once we found the treasure? Where would we find "the right hands?" Who would they belong to? They were weighty questions that we had to work out that night. We burned the midnight oil and got it done.

While we were hammering things out, a storm rolled in from the south. It rained hard all night and the wind grew strong. We were safe and dry below decks. The *Pango* was anchored strongly to the reef. The wind and rain weren't a serious concern, but it was the ocean swells that worried us.

They began to toss the boat and we had to steady ourselves continuously. Then Alex decided to tell us what *Pango* meant.

"It's short for *pangolin*, which means 'one who rolls.' This boat is great when the seas are calm, but when there are strong swells, like there are tonight, it rolls back and forth like a pendulum."

"Well you could have told us that before," I said.

"Why ruin the surprise? A little mystery is good for the soul."

We tightened everything up, lashed down our equipment, and settled in for a rough ride. It lasted all night and into the morning, with no sign of weakening. We then spent a miserable day sitting in the storm, with nothing much to do but tell stories and a few jokes.

In late afternoon the storm finally faded. The swells stayed strong, but the rain stopped and the wind slowed. We went up on deck and looked to the southern horizon. There was a band of blue sky in the distance, beyond the trailing edge of the storm. It held promise for a better day tomorrow. The setting sun was behind a dark, towering bank of clouds to the west. They were a thousand hues of gray and purple. Their dark, menacing shadow fell across the water. But the sunlight illuminated the fringes around the tops of the clouds, like a bright border of shimmering silver. The contrast between the dark and light was a glorious sight. We stood there for a long while, just watching. It was one of the most spectacular sights I had ever seen in nature, and I'd seen my share over the years. It was as if we were on the dark side of something, and the light was just beyond, giving us a glimpse of what could be. Of what *might* be. The silver turned to pink, then orange, and then faded away as the setting sun slid below the horizon. We simply looked at each other. There were no words.

The next morning the rising sun lit the *Pango* like a bright yellow fishing lantern above the dark blue sea. We readied our gear quickly and sent Marco on his first dive of the day. He came back with a clay amphora, shaped like a round vase, wide on the bottom with a narrow neck, about ten inches tall. It was nearly intact but missing a bit of its neck. There was something inside, embedded in the muck of four centuries. We drained the water out. It was still heavy. It had the now familiar coat of arms embossed into it, faded but still recognizable. We used a spoon and fork to carefully dig through the muck inside. We didn't want to break the pottery. It just seemed wrong. After a good bit of work we realized it was going to take some time and patience. Lhasa took it below to continue.

Marco rested for a spell then made another dive. This time he surfaced with two more amphorae and a porcelain tea cup, still white and smooth. These amphorae were the same as the first. They had something inside. Lhasa placed them at his feet. He was making slow progress on the first, and we decided to let Marco rest while Lhasa continued. We wanted to know if the amphorae contained anything of value.

The first contained nothing but dense muck. Perhaps it was originally food or some other common contents. The second contained the same. But the third was the jackpot. It contained a jumbled, encrusted pile of gold coins. They were crudely embossed with a design that was difficult to make out. But they were gold. We had found the treasure of the *Flor De La Mar*. I can't possibly explain to you how we felt, but I can tell you it was a good portion of the range of emotion that a human is capable of, all mixed together. We were speechless. There was really nothing to say at that point. Our emotions did the talking. Now, more than anything, we had to focus and stay on the plan. So that's what we did.

Marco made three more dives that day, and eventually figured out how to identify those amphorae which likely contained gold. There were a number of them buried in the sand, still arranged in patterns as if they had been in arranged in crates that had long ago faded away. Marco determined that the amphorae in one pile held something other than treasure, while the containers just next to them held gold. By the end of the day we had five amphorae of gold coins, each yielding about ten ounces of gold. Fifty ounces of gold altogether. Worth a significant amount of money. Marco was spent for the day, but it didn't matter. If this would have been the entire extent of the treasure, we would have been pleased beyond belief. But the Custodians knew what the ship contained when it left Malacca four centuries ago, because the Sultan of Malacca knew exactly what the Portuguese plundered from his kingdom. Alex told me that the Sultan kept a detailed list, perhaps for some intended future grievance that would never be resolved in his lifetime. But the list was safe with the Custodians. Just in case.

The Custodians believed that, one day, justice would be done. That the world would return to the order that the Sultan knew before the Portuguese arrived, before the Europeans took hold across Southeast Asia. They believed that one day, Malaysia would be its own kingdom again, as would the Dutch East Indies, French Indochina, British Burma and India, and the Spanish Philippines and beyond.

They were patient, because they knew that the kingdom treasure was safely locked away by the sea. Ironically, it was the British torpedoes that broke open that vault, at perhaps the worst possible time. Or perhaps the best possible time. Had the treasure stayed intact, the storm of war may have passed over without threatening the long mission of the Custodians. But perhaps the treasure was meant to diminish the impact of war. They had learned to not read too much meaning into the events of the ages. But they knew that they needed help. And they knew of one outsider they could trust. A Christian missionary they had met years ago, who made an impact on them because he was humble yet strong. Because he was small in stature but large in spirit. But most of all, they remembered that when he smiled, the world felt whole. He was also one who seemed to travel freely across the arbitrary borders of man. So after conferring for two weeks, they sent him an urgent letter requesting his help. They had trusted him with a bit of their story those years ago, so they didn't need to explain much in the letter in case it fell into the wrong hands. Then they waited. Would the letter reach him? Would he return to their village? If he did, would he know what to do? All in good time. They waited with a patience honed over four hundred years.

And then Lhasa returned. He brought three men with him that they didn't know. But he told them, "I have seen the acts of these men. I know what's in their hearts. They are here to help."

And they believed him.

Chapter Fifty-Eight

The symptoms appeared that evening. Marco complained of a backache. It was unusual for him to gripe about anything, so he got our attention. He tried lying down, stretching, sitting and then standing, but the pain didn't go away. "I probably just pulled a muscle," he rationalized. "I just need to rest for a while." He was clearly worn out. He went below and stretched out in his bunk. Jack and I agreed to keep a close watch on him. I checked on him twenty minutes later. He was sleeping peacefully. So we figured he'd just worked himself too hard doing four dives a day.

Eventually we all hit the sack. It had been a long, adrenalin-charged day, tense but exciting. We were suddenly very tired. I fell asleep about two minutes after my head hit my bedroll. Then I awoke sometime after midnight. I had been dreaming of the air bellows we had built. In my dream Lhasa and I were pumping it and it was making its usual artificial breathing sound. Pull in, puff out. Pull in, puff out. But as I was dreaming, I became more aware of the sound. And it was the sound that eventually woke me. I lay there in the darkness for a moment getting my bearings. Then I realized the sound was coming from Marco. He was breathing hard, grunting slightly with every exhale as if he was in pain. As if it hurt to breathe.

I rolled to my feet and knelt by Marco's bunk. "Marco!" I whispered. "You okay?"

He was not. I could tell even in the half darkness that he wasn't right. He was taking shallow, rapid breaths and each one appeared painful. But of most concern, despite his rapid breathing, he was obviously short of breath.

"I can't catch my breath," he said. "And my back is killing me."

"How long?" I asked.

"It started about an hour ago."

By now everyone was awake and hovering at Marco's side. I felt his forehead. It was cold and clammy. Lhasa lit a lantern. We could see that Marco was pale. His lips had a bluish tint.

"Jack," I said.

Jack nodded. "Marco, we need to get you to a doctor. Have you had this problem before?"

"No." He spoke in broken sentences, in between breaths. "But I know…what this is. I've seen it happen…with other divers. Bad lung. Maybe burst. Won't heal by itself. Need help."

"Okay, I understand," Jack said. He took Alex aside. "Is there a good doctor in the nearby village?" he asked in a quiet tone. "One that can do surgery?"

Alex shook his head. "No. Not in this region. Not even in Malacca. We need to go to Singapore or Kuala Lumpur. Malacca's in between the two. Kuala's 90 miles to the west of Malacca. Singapore's 150 to the east. We can get to Singapore by boat, especially from here. Kuala's inland. Can't get there by boat."

"We need to fly. We need the Goose. This thing only does ten knots tops. Singapore is, what, fifteen hours from here by boat? Too long." He lowered his voice. "We can't wait that long."

"I know."

Jack gathered everyone around Marco, so he could hear and participate in the discussion. "We need to get Marco to a doctor. The nearest good one is fifteen hours away by boat, in Singapore. We need the Goose to get him there faster. So I propose that we hedge our bets and do both."

"How?" I asked.

"Hank, neither you nor I can get safely to the Goose. We'll be spotted too easily. But Lhasa can, with Alex's help."

Lhasa's eyes grew wide.

"Alex and Lhasa can leave here by canoe and head for Malacca and the Goose. If you leave now," he nodded to Alex, "you'll be there before dawn. Lhasa, they won't be looking for you. You blend in everywhere. You'll need to get yourself to the Goose, takeoff, and fly to us. The minute you and Alex leave here, we're going to pull up anchor and head for Singapore as fast as we can. You'll be able to find us. Just follow the Strait and look for this boat. It will be daylight by then."

"How do we know the Goose is still safe?" Lhasa asked.

"We don't. But the last update Alex got was good news. The Goose was still there and apparently untouched. I suspect the Japanese agents are using the Goose as bait, just waiting for me or Hank to show up. The last thing they'll expect is for Lhasa to appear in the dark and take off in the Goose. But if the Goose isn't available, we'll still get Marco to Singapore by boat."

"It makes sense," I said, looking at Lhasa. Then I noticed we were all looking at Lhasa. Including Marco. We all understood the potential impact if Lhasa didn't succeed. It was on his shoulders. We didn't want it to be.

"I've never landed in the water," Lhasa reminded us.

"I never had either," Jack answered, "until I did it the first time."

Lhasa smiled nervously, and then looked to Alex. "Let's go. No time to waste."

"Lhasa," Marco interrupted. "You don't need to do this for me."

"I know Marco. I want to."

Jack and I went topside and helped Lhasa and Alex to load their packs and some supplies into the canoe.

I took Alex aside. "Be careful. You know the danger. If the Goose isn't safe, just leave it be. We'll still get ourselves to Singapore."

Alex nodded. "We'll be careful."

"Listen Lhasa," Jack said. "You're a good pilot. You know what to do. When you land on the water, just take it nice and easy. Straight ahead. No crabbing to either side. If it doesn't feel right, go around and try again. Got it?"

"Got it boss." Then with a quick goodbye Alex and Lhasa cast off. They slipped away into the night and were soon gone. I went below deck to check on Marco. No change.

"Hank," Jack yelled to me from the deck, "pull the anchor while I warm up the engine. Let's get underway."

"On my way."

"Wait!" Marco said. "Don't pull up the anchor. Leave it on the sea floor. Untie the anchor line from the boat and tie a buoy to the loose end. So we can mark the spot. The anchor will keep it in place. Otherwise we'll need to start the search all over again. We might not be so lucky."

"Got it. Good idea."

I did as Marco suggested, using a string of three buoys instead of just one. Then we were underway, speeding as fast as we could to the southeast. To Singapore.

"Keep your eyes open," Jack told me over the drone of the engine. "There are shallow reefs everywhere. I have some charts but I'll only be guessing as to where we are. I need your help to track the lights of villages onshore. Mark them off on the charts as we pass them. That will help me know our position. You can see from the chart that the channels get pretty hairy the closer we get to Singapore. Fortunately it will be daylight before we hit the worst of it."

Ten miles per hour. Slower than the train from Kunming to Longzhou. Through the same Strait that had sunk the *Flor De La Mar*.

There was no moon. The sky was clear, but despite a multitude of stars, it was a dark, dark night.

Alex and Lhasa paddled hard for Malacca. They didn't dare to light their lantern but Alex knew the Strait and simply navigated by the seat of his pants, using the intermittent lights on the coast to guide them. Lhasa put in some muscle and the pair moved quickly for the harbor. After a good while they could see the Malaccan lantern fishing fleet, at least a dozen canoes floating in a widely dispersed group. Alex paddled to the fringe of the group then lit his lantern, the reverse of his process to smuggle Hank out of the harbor.

It was still dark. They were early. Lhasa wanted to wait until first light to depart. They used the time to rest, catching their breath and trying to calm their anxiety. When the time was right they paddled cautiously for the harbor, toward the dock where they left the Goose. They rounded the point and were relieved to see that it was still there.

"Do you need help with the Goose?" Alex asked.

"Once I'm inside, when I give you the signal, untie the plane from the dock and give me a push," Lhasa answered nervously. "But I don't need help flying it. If something goes wrong I don't want to risk you too."

"Lhasa I would happily join you. I trust you and I'm not afraid. But if you don't need me, I have an important errand. Either I or one of the Custodians will find you in Singapore. I pray that Marco will be well." He turned out the lantern. They paddled quietly in the dark to the dock on the opposite side of the Goose. The plane was between them and the town and would provide a good screen, at least until Lhasa fired up the engines. Alex reached to the dock, tied off the canoe, then climbed out and onto the dock. Lhasa crept onto the dock. He walked furtively to the Goose. He stepped onto the left float, climbed onto the wing, then quickly unlocked the door. Before he opened it he turned to Alex and whispered. "My friend, it's been a great adventure. You have what you needed. Whatever happens, use it well."

"We have good plans for it."

"I know."

"I'll take care of the rest," Alex said. "I'll see you on the other side."

"Okay. I look forward to it. Give me ten minutes to prepare. When I'm ready I'll give you the signal. Then push the plane away from the dock and paddle away. I'll wait a minute or two before I start the engines. The moment I do, everyone will focus on this harbor. I don't want them to see you when they do."

"Got it."

Lhasa climbed into the Goose. He quietly closed and latched the door. He found his parachute packs, placing them in the pilot's seat to enable him to reach the rudder pedals. He slid into the seat and buckled himself in. Dawn was just breaking to the east, the sky turning from black to gray. He had a couple of minutes before he started the engines. He turned on the master power and tried the dashboard lights to make sure they worked. They did, which meant the battery was still charged. He needed a strong battery to crank the left engine. Once it was running, its generator could power the starter for the right engine. But without a battery, he wouldn't get that far. Lhasa then took a deep breath, concentrating on what he needed to do. He reviewed the takeoff and landing procedures, trying to make sure he wasn't missing anything. Jack had schooled him well. He knew the takeoff speed, landing speed, flap settings, engine settings, and how to use the instruments. He had everything he needed. But now, more than ever before in his life, he doubted himself. He closed his eyes and said a quick prayer. "Lord, help me use the strength you've given me. Take my doubt away." Then he opened his eyes, glanced to Alex, and waved. Alex untied the Goose from the dock then used the wing to push the Goose out and away. He waved, then moved quickly back to his canoe. He untied it, pushed off, and jumped inside. He paddled hard toward the town.

Lhasa watched Alex until he was a good distance away. Then he cranked the left engine. The propeller turned slowly for a few revolutions and then spun faster as the engine fired and started up. Using the left engine alone, Lhasa immediately taxied the Goose away from the dock and toward the open water beyond the harbor. The sky had brightened considerably since they had arrived at the dock. Lhasa aimed the Goose toward a spot away from the returning fishing canoes. Once he was safely underway he started the right engine and ran it up to half power. Good morning, Malacca! The townspeople - and the Japanese - surely knew by now that the Goose was back in business.

Chapter Fifty-Nine

We were pushing the *Pango* as hard as we could toward Singapore, but she had nothing more to offer. She was giving us her top speed. It was going to be a long ride. As we burned fuel she'd become a bit lighter, and perhaps gained a knot or two in speed. But that wouldn't buy us much, and Marco was in a bad way. I wanted to help him but there was nothing I could think of do. How do you treat a damaged lung? I had no clue. I needed Sara. She was a nurse. What would she do? I wished she were here now. In desperation I tried to recall if I'd seen anything similar happen to the livestock on the ranch, but it just wasn't an illness or injury that I was familiar with.

I kept my eyes open for high spots in the reef, trying to keep track of the various villages. I crossed each of them off our charts, using them, and different coastal features, to track our position. We were approaching a series of shoals and small islands and the navigation was really taxing me. Jack piloted the *Pango* and also kept an eye out for Lhasa. If Lhasa and Alex made it safely to the Goose, if it was still flyable, if Lhasa was able to take off, then he should be reaching us soon. I had faith in Lhasa, but there were many things outside of his control. But of all the people I knew, I felt that fate often smiled upon Lhasa. *Lord, please keep him safe.*

Lhasa evened the throttles on the Goose's engines and taxied as quickly as possible out of the harbor toward open water. He made a broad semicircle around the now-returning lantern canoes, setting up for a takeoff run toward the south. Before he left the harbor he had the presence of mind to check a banner that was fluttering in the slight morning breeze. The wind was blowing from the south. The foot-high ocean swells were coming in from the southwest, quartering the wind. It was best if the swell direction and wind direction matched each other, as a float plane could then take off or land without a sideways force to compensate for. In Lhasa's case, he would need to contend with less than ideal conditions. But the variance wasn't extreme. He decided to press on.

Lhasa checked his instruments, confirmed the fuel settings, set his flaps for takeoff, took a deep breath, then pushed the throttles forward. The Goose's nose immediately rose in the water over its bow wave and accelerated to the south. Lhasa pulled back on the wheel to lower the tail and raise the nose, allowing the floats to negotiate the swells as the plane plowed forward. The Goose rapidly built speed, knocking spray from the tops of the swells, then eventually hopping over all but the crests. Just below takeoff speed Lhasa pulled back on the wheel to get the Goose out of the water. He held the plane level just above the water for a hundred yards, allowing it to accelerate before he climbed. The plane finally reached the proper speed. He pulled back on the wheel and climbed into the dawn sky. He had successfully escaped from Malacca, after traveling so far to get there. The irony wasn't lost on him, and he smiled for a bit before he started to worry about landing. The most difficult, most dangerous part of his flight was still ahead.

We set a banner onto a pole on the stern of the *Pango*, so Lhasa could use it to gauge the wind. Then we pushed on toward Singapore. I went below. Marco was fading. He was lapsing in and out of a troubled sleep, still having severe difficulty breathing. His lips and chin were blue. He wasn't getting enough air. I didn't have any hope that he would improve on his own. I couldn't imagine a burst lung healing itself. I gave him a sip of water, then went back on deck to help Jack navigate. I checked my watch. Lhasa had been gone a long time. Longer than I thought it would take. We weren't that far by air from Malacca. We should have seen him by now.

Then Jack yelled, "The Goose!" He was pointing behind and to the left. I looked that direction and immediately saw the plane, about 500 feet above the water, heading toward Singapore on a parallel course to ours. It was about a quarter mile away.

Jack grabbed the wheel and began to swerve the Pango back and forth, creating a serpentine wake, trying to get Lhasa's attention.

"Mirror!" I yelled. I ran below, grabbed a signal mirror from the emergency kit, returned to the deck, and tried to use the mirror, in concert with the sun, to get Lhasa's attention. Then I heard a small rocket whoosh skyward from the deck of the *Pango*, followed by the crack of a firework as it burst overhead.

"Firecracker!" yelled Jack. "Beat that!"

The firecracker worked. The Goose turned toward us. Lhasa had found the Pango. Now came the hard part. I went below and brought the entire emergency kit to the deck. It contained two life jackets, a rope, a rescue ring, and several other items. I hoped we didn't need any of them, but I wanted to be ready.

Jack pulled back on the throttles. The *Pango* immediately slowed and settled into the water.

"We need to sit still so Lhasa can see the wind banner. Our speed was pushing it behind us," Jack explained.

I nodded. We sat and watched the Goose circle. The *Pango* was idling. We were ready to speed to Lhasa's landing site, whatever happened. At ten knots.

Chapter Sixty

Lhasa was overwhelmed. He was focusing on too many things at once. He belatedly realized that he should have donned a life jacket, just in case something went terribly wrong. Too late now. He was watching the instruments to maintain a safe altitude and proper airspeed, and was so focused on flying that he forgot to maintain a continuous lookout for the *Pango*. Too many things to do. Then he saw the firework burst, spied the *Pango*, and realized that he needed to calm down. To simplify. So he decided to stop checking the instruments and just fly the plane. He banked to the left, toward the *Pango*. He did a survey of the water below and saw that it was empty. There were no other craft in the vicinity, which made it easier for him to establish a landing zone. He made a big counterclockwise circle around the *Pango*, in a left bank the entire time. This enabled him to look out the left pilot's window down to the sea. The *Pango* had stopped. He saw the banner on the stern and realized Jack had fashioned a wind gauge for him. He could see that wind direction hadn't changed. Based upon the banner's behavior the wind looked stronger. The trade winds were building. In addition, the swells were larger in this section of the Strait, as it was wider and Lhasa was farther from shore. The reef was high here and Lhasa wanted to stay in the deeper water at a safe distance.

He flew to the north until he was a mile from the *Pango*. Then he turned around to the south to begin his descent. He wanted to touch down as close as possible to the *Pango*. He straightened out and pulled the throttles back halfway. As he slowed he could feel the wind gusts. They weren't terrible, but they were a definite concern for a novice pilot. He set the landing flaps while holding the wheel tight. He rotated it to the left and right to compensate for the rolling motion of the gusts.

Lhasa descended toward the sea, his heart in his throat, his mouth as dry as a grain of sand in the Sahara Desert.

Jack and I watched Lhasa from the deck. So far, so good. He was on the correct heading. The wing flaps were down for landing. It was difficult to hear the Goose's engine, but from the plane's attitude and descent rate we could see he was managing the engine power well. We held our breath while watching.

Lhasa realized that he was having difficulty gauging his distance from the sea surface. He could watch the altimeter as it wound down to zero - to sea level. But he had decided the instruments were taking too much of his attention, so he was trying to gauge his height by looking at the water. But he had no set reference. There were no trees, nor trucks, nor dwellings to study. Only ocean swells. They're a terrible reference because it's too difficult to determine their size from the air. Lhasa was making a classic mistake. He had abandoned his instruments to rely on his eyeballs, but Lhasa was a land animal and his eyeballs weren't calibrated to the ocean. The proper procedure was to use the altimeter, keeping the airspeed in the right zone using the throttles and the plane's pitch. Then, when just above the landing surface, one should focus on the horizon. This allows your brain to determine your descent rate and height. At the proper moment, the pilot then pulls back on the wheel to flare the plane, which slows it and allows it to drop to the ground. Or the water. Lhasa understood most of this from the landings he'd made with Jack. On land. But it was much more critical for a water landing, and Lhasa was struggling.

He pulled the throttles all the way back. The engines were merely idling. He could hear the rush of the wind over the wings. He settled toward the water, then flared when he thought he was a few feet above it. He had miscalculated, and was still fifty feet high. The stall alarm horn sounded, indicated that the airflow over the wings had stalled. This meant that they were no longer creating lift, and that the plane was falling. This would be fine if the Goose was a few feet from the water. But the plane was falling from fifty feet, and would hit the water in a crash. He needed to increase his airspeed immediately. There are two ways to increase airspeed to recover from a stall. Dive, or add engine power. There was no room to dive, so Lhasa jammed the throttles to full power then pulled back from the water into a climb. The Goose struggled, the stall alarm blaring, until the airspeed increase enough to provide lift again. Lhasa climbed back to two hundred feet leveled off, and banked to the left to go around and do it all again. He was sweating. And shaking.

We watched Lhasa and realized he was about to crash. I felt so useless. So helpless. I was watching a good friend, a lifelong friend, fall to a potential death. We were going to have to pull a broken Lhasa out of the Goose, assuming that the wreckage stayed afloat long enough. Damn I hoped he would survive. Jack jammed the engine throttle to full power and turned the *Pango* toward Lhasa's imminent crash site. Then Lhasa did the right thing. He pulled out of his high flare then climbed for a go-around. I thanked God. I choked up. Lhasa was okay. For now. Jack stopped the *Pango*, and we waited.

Lhasa learned quickly. He knew it was one of his strengths. He often applied it to people. He had the ability to relate to almost anyone. He had learned to observe them, to read them, to listen to them, in order to determine what was important to them. Then he simply talked with them in a conversation that resonated with them as an individual. Using as few words as possible. It was effective and it put people at ease. Lhasa had honed this ability over many years. But the underlying skill was his ability to learn quickly from observations. He innately applied this skill to his immediate problem - how to land safely in the Strait of Malacca, in order to save the Goose. But most importantly, to save Marco. He didn't care about himself as much as he cared about the Goose and Marco. Actually, he didn't care that much about the Goose. It was simply a thing. But if he crashed the Goose, Marco might die. Lhasa would gladly give his life for Marco. But in this situation, Lhasa had to live so Marco could live. Otherwise, Marco likely wouldn't survive the boat trip to Singapore in his condition. So as Lhasa circled for his next landing attempt, he reviewed what went wrong with the first one. And he figured it out. It was just a matter of geometry. Although that was a word Lhasa seldom used. Unless conversation called for it. He didn't understand geometry in a classic sense. But his brain certainly did, as did all human brains. It was all in the angles.

"I can do this," he told himself.

And he did. He descended again, watched his altitude, used the horizon, flared at ten feet, and kissed the surface of the sea. He held the nose up until the Goose slowed. The plane settled into the water, slowing to a stop. He looked to the left to see the *Pango* speeding toward him. Lhasa shut down the engines, unbuckled himself, said a prayer of thanks, then wiped tears from his eyes.

Chapter Sixty-One

We were at the Goose within two minutes. Jack brought us to a stop as close as he could. But we realized we couldn't actually tie the two craft side by side, as the wing and tail of the Goose prevented us from moving the *Pango* alongside the fuselage. Lhasa opened the door and threw me a long rope, which I tied to the gunwale of the *Pango*. We could at least float in a loose formation.

We would need to move Marco carefully to the Goose without aggravating his injury. I wasn't quite sure how to do this without walking him to the deck, lowering him into the water, floating him to the Goose, then helping him to climb aboard. It seemed like too much for Marco to endure. But Marco put that notion to rest. He appeared on deck, looking pale and drawn, but at least walking. I crouched to put his arm around my shoulder, then helped him to the stern where we had a small ladder. He could walk but was breathing hard. He was in obvious pain. He had to stop several times along the way to catch his breath. We needed a raft to paddle him to the Goose, but we didn't have one. We had relied on Alex's canoe for that type of thing, and it was an oversight on our part. But we dealt with it. We helped Marco settle into the water. I got in with him and pulled him carefully to the Goose, making sure to keep his head above water. Jack jumped into the water, swam to the Goose, then climbed onto the wing. He had a wild look in his eyes. I couldn't figure out why until I remembered his fear of sharks. Jack and I helped Marco climb onto the wing. Jack helped him into the plane. Jack and Lhasa got Marco settled into the cabin, helping him to recline across a row of seats. Lhasa covered him with a thick blanket.

Lhasa jumped into the water and he and I swam back to the *Pango*. We untied the line from the Goose and Jack reeled it in.

Jack yelled to us from the door of the Goose, "I'll see you in Singapore. I'll leave word for you at the airport. You'll be able to find us."

"Okay," I replied. "Watch for Alex. He'll find you there too."

Jack closed the door, strapped himself in, then fired up the Goose. He didn't waste any time. He took off immediately to the southeast, toward Singapore and a doctor. He wagged the wings and then disappeared into the distance. Lhasa and I started the engine on the *Pango* and made for Singapore as fast as she could go.

Lhasa sat cross-legged on the deck and recovered from his landing.

"My friend," I said, "that was a fancy bit of flying. The go-around, I mean. You saved yourself. I thought we were going to lose you. And I suddenly realized how much I value you. Thanks for everything."

"Hank you're welcome. I was scared. But I had to land the Goose to save Marco, and that knowledge gave me strength. I've got stuff to do. I'm not done yet."

"I understand. Well I'm sure glad you're here." I paused. "Marco will be okay."

"I pray that you're correct."

"Me too," I said. "You steer. I'll navigate."

"You got it."

The Goose was over Singapore forty minutes after takeoff. Jack radioed the British air field, explaining his intent to land.

"We're almost there my friend," he said to Marco.

"Thanks," Marco answered weakly.

Jack landed, taxied to the tarmac, then parked and shut down the Goose. He stepped back to the cabin. "Just rest here for a bit. I'll be back with help."

Marco nodded.

Jack left the Goose and walked quickly toward the nearest hangar. He ran into a British Army sergeant just inside the door. "Where's you infirmary?" he asked. "I have an injured man in my plane."

"Two buildings that way," he pointed to Jack's left. "What's the nature of the injury?"

"Diving accident."

"Need help?"

"I'll grab a wheelchair. He'll have a hard time walking that far. Thanks though."

Jack jogged to the infirmary, found a nurse, and explained the situation. She retrieved a wheelchair for him then left to summon the doctor. Jack pushed the chair quickly back to the Goose. Then he helped Marco down from the plane and into the chair.

"Welcome to Singapore," Jack said. "Ever been here?"

"Never have."

"I'll give you the quick tour. On your right, you'll find an aircraft hangar. Straight ahead, a doctor. That's all I know about Singapore so far. Has your tour been satisfactory?"

"Quite."

"Glad to hear it."

"Jack, thank you," he said, in between breaths. "I didn't...really have a chance...to thank Lhasa. And Hank...and Alex. You all did...a lot for me."

"Marco, save your breath. It's what friends are for."

"Still afraid...of sharks?"

Jack stayed silent.

"I figured it out," Marco explained.

"Well keep it to yourself. I'm more afraid now than ever. If this was your way of having me confront my fear, it didn't work. By the way, when you're better, we're gonna have a wheelchair race. I hear these things are almost as much fun as a rickshaw."

That night, Alex met with the Custodians in Malacca. He opened his pack and removed the five amphorae filled with gold coins. Lhasa had successfully loosened the encrusted coins before he and Alex left the *Pango*. The Custodians checked the symbol on the coins, confirming that it was the well-known imprint of the Sultanate of Malacca. The coins were indeed from the plundered treasure of the kingdom of Malacca. The amphorae, in contrast, were stamped with Afonso de Albuquerque's coat of arms. He was the recognized envoy of Portugal when the Portuguese conquered Malacca, but only during the year 1511. After the *Flor De La Mar* sank, Albuquerque was called back to Portugal, and another envoy took his place. The new envoy used a different coat of arms. So the Malaccan coins were packed in Portuguese amphorae that had been stamped with Albuquerque's mark in 1511. Therefore the Custodians concluded that the coins were from the wreck of the *Flor De La Mar*. The provenance of the treasure was confirmed. The wreck had been found.

The Custodians retrieved their list of the plundered treasure. Years ago it had been matched to the well-documented Portuguese manifest and bill of lading for the *Flor De La Mar's* final voyage. It was the opposite of that document. It was an inventory of a treasure stolen, while the Portuguese manifest was an inventory of a treasure plundered. But they both listed the same items. The only significant difference between the two could be found in the accounting of the women and children that Albuquerque took as slaves and imprisoned on the ship. The Malaccan version listed them by name. It also identified their families. The Portuguese list, however, simply listed them by *quantity*. It might seem a simple thing. But it summarized the fundamental difference between the conqueror and the conquered. Between the victors and the vanquished. If not for the Malaccan list, the slaves would have been forgotten to the mists of history.

The Custodians had vowed, among other things, to do their best to prevent a similar situation from ever happening again. To never let an innocent victim of war go unnamed. It was a vow they took seriously and willingly.

They had another vow, and it was time to revisit it. Tonight. But first they awaited one more member. The Twelfth. He was on his way. In the mean time, they crossed fifty gold coins off their list. Fifty ounces. Out a total of sixty *tons* of gold. But they knew where the remainder was. It wasn't going anywhere. For now, it was in the safest bank they could find in a time of widespread war, with a Japanese invasion of Malaysia imminent. The sea. Alex had carefully noted the location of the wreck. He could find it again using landmarks from shore and simple geometry. The location had been properly recorded and was in the safekeeping of the Custodians. Now that they knew its precise location, they could keep a watch over it. If necessary, on occasion, they could plant rumors about the wreck, identifying a false location to misdirect anyone who might otherwise be close.

They had finally reached the second task of their multi-generational commission. The first, *find the treasure*, was complete. The second, *use the treasure*, was about to begin. Like any bank deposit, the treasure could now be used as collateral. If done correctly. The Twelfth Man was the key.

"Your friend was very lucky. You got him here in time," the British doctor told Jack, in the hallway outside the infirmary.

"Will he be okay?"

"Yes. He'll be fine. He had a collapsed lung. You said he was a deep diver? It happens to divers, I hear. It's a similar injury to being stabbed or shot in the chest. His lung apparently burst, perhaps from holding his breath too long during an ascent from a deep dive. When there's a hole in the lung, the air leaks into the chest cavity. This prevents the lung from filling with air when the chest expands, when you inhale. The lung eventually collapses. It stops providing any oxygen to the body. Just stops functioning altogether. The body's oxygen supply gets cut in half. It's a serious situation. In your friend's case his chest cavity was also filling with fluid, which was impeding his good lung. He wouldn't have made it if you hadn't have gotten him here. As it was, it's relatively easy to repair a collapsed lung if the hole isn't too large. We just suck the air and fluid out of the chest cavity, and the lung reinflates. We'll need to watch him for two, three days to make sure the hole doesn't redevelop. But he's breathing fine now. He'd like to say 'hello'."

Jack sighed in relief. "Thanks Doc. Much appreciated."

"One thing. I haven't told your friend yet. But I strongly recommend that he not dive again. Since we don't know exactly what caused his injury, it may happen again without warning. I hope his income didn't depend on diving."

Jack smiled. "Only a bit of income," Jack responded. "Just a bit."

Jack entered the infirmary. There were a dozen or more patients in as many beds. Marco was in a bed at the far end. He was easy to spot. He was the only one with tattoos. Jack approached him quietly. Marco was dozing, but he was breathing normally. His color had returned. Jack wrote a quick note telling Marco that he was leaving briefly but would be back. He slipped the note into Marco's hand. Then he walked back to the airfield. He left a message for Hank, Lhasa, and Alex at the base office. Then, on a recommendation from the office clerk, he went to a nearby eatery to see a man about a beer and some food. He felt like he hadn't eaten for four hundred years.

Chapter Sixty-Two

The Japanese major was highly irritated. Irritated that his agents in Malacca had let the distinctive twin civilian engine float plane escape the harbor without capturing the pilot and crew. How could they be so easily fooled? The plane and its crew had attacked the Japanese invasion force outside Longzhou. As civilians. They must be punished. But they had escaped. Perhaps to prepare another attack? This type of thing was bad for an invasion. It gave the people hope. His orders went out via coded radio message to all his spies and agents in Malaysia, Dutch East Indies, and Singapore: *FIND THE FLOAT PLANE IMMEDIATELY. Continue preparations for invasion. Determine enemy positions and strength. Identify potential civilian resistance. NO MISTAKES.*

Lhasa and I arrived in Singapore in the early evening after a day long voyage in the *Pango*. We had a difficult time navigating the islands surrounding the city, but we finally tied up at the main harbor and got directions to the airfield which was on the far eastern end of the city. Marco had been on my mind continually. I had a knot in my stomach. Neither Lhasa nor I were hungry. We needed to find Marco and Jack. It was a good walk to the airfield. We paid a truck driver a bit of cash to drive us across the city. He dropped us close to the airfield. We walked the rest of the way. We soon found the airfield office. When we identified ourselves, the clerk recognized our names. He dug through the message pile, finally finding the note Jack had left for us. It was short and sweet. *Marco will be okay. He's resting at the infirmary. Meet us there.* Lhasa and I got some quick directions to the infirmary. We headed there in a hurry to see our wounded friend.

In 1940, Singapore was a colony of the British Empire, located at the southeastern tip of the Malaysian peninsula. It's now a small country of 63 tightly grouped islands, including the large main island called Singapore Island. Singapore is separated from Malaysia by the narrow Johor Strait to the north, and separated from Indonesia by the Singapore Strait to the south. The Singapore Strait lay at the eastern edge of the Strait of Malacca, where it became choked by a multitude of islands.

A British settlement since 1824, the prospering Singapore became the capital of the British Straits Settlements in 1836. The Straits Settlements consisted of four individual settlements: Malacca, Singapore, Penang, and Dinding. Singapore was the largest by far. It was the commercial and administrative hub of British activity in Southeast Asia, administered by British India. The Settlements grew in importance; however, and in 1867 they became a British Crown Colony. They were now administered by London and not by India. Their keepers were even farther away. So if you lived in one of the Settlements like Malacca, and had a legal issue with the British Empire, your request would likely be addressed in Singapore. A policy which was convenient for the Custodians.

The Twelfth Man finally arrived at the meeting of the Custodians. He was the final key to their overall plan. He apologized for delaying them. He sat with them at a long rectangular wooden table. It was simple and rustic, like the men that sat around it. He opened the meeting in prayer, thanking God for the opportunity to be there and for the opportunity to serve. Then they ate a simple meal, enjoying each other's company, buoyed by the knowledge that the treasure was no longer lost. When the meal was complete, the Man started the official discussion.

"God has smiled upon us," he said. "He sent us the four men, and he gave them the hearts, the wisdom, and the strength to succeed. They have helped us to accomplish the first task of our commission. As we all know, the treasure has been found."

They took a moment to celebrate once again.

"Now our second task begins," he continued. "Now we must *use* the treasure. We have all committed, on our very lives, to put the treasure to good use, based upon the wishes of our forefathers. We know what this means. We must not benefit from the treasure ourselves. We must ensure that the treasure is used to alleviate the suffering which we find around us. To be clear, our forefathers placed no geographic border on the distribution of the treasure toward this goal. Do we all agree?"

There was unanimous agreement.

"Good. I therefore propose that we appoint the four men as emissaries of Malacca. We have seen their actions. They are true in heart. The one named Lhasa brought them to us. We knew we could trust Lhasa. We now know we can trust his friends. Do we all agree that the four are worthy of this appointment?"

Again, there was unanimous agreement.

Alex made a motion to speak. The Man acknowledged him.

"If I may," Alex began, "the one named Marco is very ill. I pray that he's in Singapore by now to be healed. We will know soon of his condition. But Marco is the diver, and I don't believe he'll be able to continue in his efforts to recover the treasure."

"This is unfortunate," the Man responded. "Our prayers are with Marco. My friends, it is not necessary that we recover the remainder of the treasure. Our brother Alex has developed a plan, and I'm here to help execute it. Alex, please explain your plan to our brothers."

Alex explained his plan. It had taken him weeks to develop it. It took ten minutes to explain. It hinged on one major point. It required that the Custodians be the legal trustees of the treasure. This was no small issue. The treasure had been plundered - stolen - from the kingdom of Malacca. There was no doubt of this. But Malacca was no longer a sovereign kingdom. It was now a Settlement of the British Empire. It was one of the British Crown Colonies. It appeared that the sovereign entity of the kingdom of Malacca had ceased to exist. So technically, the treasure now belonged to the country of Britain, as successor to Malacca. If Malacca were to be reestablished as a sovereign entity, then one could make the argument that the treasure belonged to Malacca again.

When Alex was finished, one of the men spoke.

"This is a complicated issue. This plan seems quite difficult."

"Actually, it's not as difficult as we might think," the Man responded. "My brothers, I am a part of this group for a specific reason. My predecessors made sure of this. The British may think that Malacca belongs to them. But the sovereignty of Malacca still exists, through the uninterrupted lineage of the Sultanate of Malacca, going back to 1511 and even before. British law recognizes the transference of sovereignty by lineage. As you know, after the Portuguese conquest my predecessor was forced into exile. But he had two sons, both of which became Sultans. Their lines of succession are unbroken even now. As you know, the Sultan of Johor is one of them. I am the other. As the Sultan of Malacca I still represent the sovereignty of Malacca. And therefore I, along with this assembly, am the legal guardian of the treasure, based upon the very laws of the British who govern us."

"But how will we prove this in Singapore?" one of the Custodians asked.

"It will need to be proven in a court of law. But with the help of the Sultan of Johor, who is based in Singapore, I believe justice will be done. It may take years. But realize this. We know war is coming. The Japanese are strong. The British will resist. They will fight the war for us. No matter what happens, when the war is over, Malacca will be a different place. It is quite likely that Malacca, and perhaps all of Malaysia, may become independent someday as the result of the war. I believe the Japanese will fight the British and Dutch, and I believe that of those three, there will be no winner. They will wear each other out, then they will go back to their homes and lick their wounds. Hardship is coming. But after that, I see rebirth. We just need to hold on for a few more years. We just need to guard the treasure a bit longer, keeping it hidden from all but the most trustworthy."

They all nodded in agreement.

"In the mean time," he continued, "I propose that we reward Lhasa and his team. It simply fulfills the second task of our commission, to *use* the treasure. With the four, the impact of that use can extend far beyond Malacca. I believe my predecessors could not have foreseen this opportunity, but would have supported it wholeheartedly. Do we all agree?"

Again, full agreement.

"Then let it be so. Alex will travel to Singapore with two of you. You will deliver my request to the Sultan of Johor, who will make the proper financial arrangements. Then see to the well being of the four. Make sure they are compensated for the investment they've made on our behalf. Invite them to be emissaries of this assembly, assuming they're willing to take an oath to use their reward in the proper way. Please thank them on my behalf, and explain that it would be unusual for me to journey to another Sultan's region without extensive preparation. But I would very much enjoy hosting them here in Malacca, if they would be so kind as to return."

One of the Custodians raised his hand. "If I may, what of the wreckage of the ship that is not associated with the treasure? Who does it belong to?"

"Ah. It belongs to the Portuguese invaders who plundered our kingdom, as do these Portuguese amphorae." He motioned to the now empty amphorae on the floor. "We should begin a pile of ship wreckage, which the Portuguese may wish to collect someday. I propose we place the wreckage in a rubbish pile. Perhaps one day that pile can be retrieved by Portugal."

The Custodians wholeheartedly agreed.

The amphorae disappeared under the refuse of Malacca.

Alex and his partners departed the next morning for Singapore via bus, carrying a bundle of documents for the Sultan of Johor. They arrived that afternoon. Their request for funds was quickly approved, as the Sultan had been expecting them. He gave them a portion of the money in cash, pending the legal arrangements of the remainder.

Alex and his colleagues then left for the airfield. They greatly looked forward to their next meeting.

Lhasa, Jack, and I sat with Marco in the infirmary. He was almost fully recovered and the doctor recommended he be discharged the next morning. I had discovered, by accident, that if I made Marco laugh, his ribs tickled. It made him double over in a funny way. Then they tickled even more. So I was getting some payback for when he taught me the wrong Chinese phrases. Ironically, when I explained the confusion about the size of my testicles during my train ride, it made Marco laugh the hardest. Then it became a contest to see who could use the fewest words make him laugh. Of course, Marco wasn't aware there was a contest. Which made it even more fun. It kept us busy for a good hour. Lhasa was the best at it. No surprise there.

Alex and his two colleagues found us in the infirmary. It was good to see them.

Marco stood to embrace Alex. "Alex, thank you for what you did that night, to get Lhasa safely to the Goose."

"It was my pleasure Marco. Thank *you* for what you did. How do you feel?"

"I'll be just fine. I feel great. But the doctor says I can't dive anymore. Good thing I can fish."

Oh Lord.

Marco continued. "I'm sorry we couldn't finish the job, Alex."

"Well," Alex said, "I think we can consider it finished. Why don't we discuss that a bit. All four of you, in private. When can you leave the infirmary Marco?"

"The doctor told me to stay for one more night. So I can leave in the morning."

"Then I suggest we all meet for breakfast. We'll return after sunrise to get you. I know a good spot. It's the Sultan of Johor's favorite place to eat."

That night we slept in cots in the infirmary, in return for doing some clean-up work around the place. We fell asleep early.

We awoke in the middle of the night to a big commotion. I heard men yelling 'fire' somewhere in the direction of the aircraft tarmac. Jack and I ran outside. Lhasa stayed with Marco.

We immediately saw what was burning. It was the Goose, still sitting there on the tarmac. It was fully involved in fire, some parts already melting from the heat. There was a large black column of smoke rising far into the sky. The scene around the Goose was lit in a bright orange glow. The flames were furiously consuming the plane. Fuel was dripping from the wing tanks and burning in puddles on the ground. Fortunately the tanks were only partially full. Jack hadn't refilled them after his flight.

We ran to help the half dozen British soldiers that were now trying to fight the fire. It was pointless to try to save the Goose. But they wanted to minimize any collateral damage. A fire truck soon arrived to spray water on the inferno. The water wouldn't kill the fuel-fed fire, but it would at least keep the tarmac cool to prevent damage to the airfield. We spent an hour working in the heat and smoke. The fire slowed dramatically, finally burning itself out. The smoking, melted hulk of the Goose lay on the tarmac like an old pile of bones.

"This your aircraft?" a British major, the officer of the watch, asked.

"It was," Jack answered. His face was covered with soot and I assumed mine was too. "Any idea what happened?"

Let's find out. "Sergeant!" the Major yelled.

The sergeant jogged to us and saluted the Major. "Sir, I checked with the two guards on night watch. There were at least two unknowns milling around the tarmac just before the fire started. Asian civilians. That's all guards could see. The two faded away into the shadows before the guards could engage them. I'm sorry sir. We've checked the premises. It's secure. No sign of anyone unusual. They're gone."

"Keep looking. Dismissed."

"Yes sir." The sergeant turned and left.

"Well," the Major said, "someone didn't like your aircraft. Any ideas?"

Jack told him about the skirmish at Longzhou.

"Well, there are Japanese agents about. I'd bet my boots on that. They'll be reconnoitering for the pending invasion. This was just another item on their list of orders, I'm sure. Sorry about your plane. It looked like a useful sort of craft."

"It was. Believe me, it was."

Jack and I walked toward the infirmary to clean up.

"Seems a bit dangerous around here," I said.

"Yep." Jack sighed. "Looks like the Japanese Army has a long reach. We're going to need to be careful."

"No, I think we're okay. I think they just played their hand. Payback is done." I put my hand on his shoulder. Then realized I should have cleaned the soot off first. "Sorry about the Goose, though."

"Thanks. I'm just glad I didn't spend money to get the dang radio fixed." He took a deep breath. "That plane saw a lot of miles though, didn't she? Got us out of some serious pickles too."

"Yeah, she saw some miles. But Jack, it was *us* that got us out of the pickles. Not the Goose. And we're all still here."

"Amen to that."

"You WHAT?" the Japanese Major yelled into the radio. "You burned the float plane? At the British field? You're a colossal failure! They know that we're present in Singapore now! You may have been identified! Get out of there and back to Indochina. You're finished!"

Alex met us a few hours later, just after sunrise. He had seen the still smoldering remains of the Goose on his way to the infirmary.

"Was that the Goose?" he asked.

We nodded.

He turned to one of his colleagues. "We're going to need a bit more expense money."

His colleague nodded and excused himself.

"What was that about?" I asked.

"I'll explain. Let's go have that talk."

Alex took the four of us to the courtyard garden of a small but beautiful private residence on the hillside above the city. There was a table arranged with fresh fruits, breads, and fish, with a carafe of fresh mango juice.

"This is the residence of the Sultan of Johor. He'll be here shortly. He wants to say hello!"

"Well thank you Alex." I said. "This is quite a spread."

"Eat, please. We have much to discuss." He gazed out to the horizon. "It's looks to be an agreeable day, don't you think?"

We then had the most unusual conversation of my twenty year life.

A few weeks later, it was time to say goodbye. I'll spare you the details, but I'll tell you it was one of the saddest days of my life. But good things sometimes come to an end, and the time had come to move on. It was bittersweet. We were all brothers now. I felt like I'd known Jack, Lhasa, Marco, and Alex all my life. We hoped to see each other again and we made some tentative plans to reunite sometime, and somewhere, in the future.

Marco decided to travel with Lhasa to his next destination, as yet undefined, but surely impactful. Alex stayed in Malacca, keeping his vigilance as a Custodian. Jack and I traveled home together. It took us almost a month. We didn't have a plane anymore. We used haphazard modes of transportation. When we finally got to San Francisco I sent a message home to let everyone know I was in the US and on my way to Idaho. Jack heard about a little float plane for sale in Marin County, just across the bay to the north of the city. He took me with him to check it out. She was a beauty. Single engine, four seater, just the right size to fly home with. The owner was selling it for a song, and after a bit of wrangling, Jack was the new owner.

We departed for Idaho the next day. We took turns flying her. She flew slow and calm. We enjoyed the scenery below. It was a great trip. Took two days.

The afternoon of the second day we landed in Boise, Idaho to refuel. I used a phone at a drugstore to call home. My parents didn't have a phone at the ranch so I called the telephone operator in Stanley. She answered on the third ring.

"Hank?" she asked. "Oh it's good to hear from you. The whole town's been following your travels. Where are you?" It was Marge Lewis. I recognized her voice. She was a fixture of the town and a good friend of my mom.

"I'm in Boise," I answered. "I'll be flying home in a little float plane. Long story. I'm leaving in an hour or so. Be there by early evening."

"Oh Hank, that's wonderful. I'll get word to your folks. We're gonna have to plan a big town party real soon."

"Thanks Marge. It's good to be back. See you soon." I hung up the phone.

"Say Hank," Jack said, "why don't you take the plane and fly home to your ranch. I wouldn't mind staying here in Boise for a couple of days before I head home to the ranch in Montana. I think I'll catch a picture show or two. Maybe have myself a couple of nice big steak dinners. Can you come back and get me in two or three days?"

"You sure?" I asked.

"Sure am. Get home and find Sara. I want to enjoy this nice western town a bit, and I don't want to delay you."

"Well, sounds good. See you soon." I was itching to get back home. I said goodbye and took off in Jack's plane for the ranch. For home.

The Japanese did invade Singapore and Malaysia. They would take 130,000 prisoners of war, mostly British troops. For all their preparation, the British forces in Singapore fell in seven days. Winston Churchill would call it the "largest capitulation" in British history. The Japanese would also conquer the Dutch East Indies, the Philippines, the Andamans, Burma, and most of the island nations in the Pacific. But that was as far as they got. As a result of the attack on Pearl Harbor, America finally entered the war to push the Japanese back across the Pacific, island by island, atoll by atoll. It was a tumultuous, deadly, costly effort.

Lieutenant Paul Keast was correct about the chink in the Japanese armor. They believed in their superiority, and this belief contributed, in part, to their downfall. Shortly after the attack on Pearl Harbor, the U.S. Navy broke the codes that the Japanese used to encrypt their radio transmissions.

This enabled the Americans to determine that the Japanese Navy planned a significant attack on Midway Island, strategically located in the middle of the Pacific Ocean. The U.S. ambushed the Japanese attack force and won the battle, sinking four Japanese aircraft carriers that had launched the attack on Pearl Harbor only six months earlier. The Battle of Midway was the turning point of the war in the Pacific. It halted Japan's expansion and began their long island-by-island retreat back to their homeland. The Japanese refused to believe that the ambush was anything but luck. They never changed their codes.

The Allies used this fact to inflict repeated damage on the Japanese military. One of the most famous occurred in April of 1943. The U.S. Navy code breakers determined that Admiral Yamamoto, the commander of the Imperial Japanese Navy and the architect of the attack on Pearl Harbor, would be visiting his troops in the Solomon Islands on a South Pacific morale tour. The U.S. Navy had his full and detailed itinerary. They dispatched long-range fighters from Guadalcanal Island, which had just been liberated by the U.S. The fighters shot down Yamamoto's air transport over Bougainville Island in the Solomons, killing the Admiral and inflicting lasting damage on Japanese morale. The round trip distance for the U.S. attack aircraft was at the very maximum of their operating range, even with extended fuel tanks. They only had a short time to loiter over Bougainville Island waiting for Yamamoto's flight, and were there at just the right time. Yet the Japanese again refused to believe that that attack was anything but luck. The codes didn't change. The chink remained. The Allies would win the war.

When the flames of war were finally extinguished, and Japan lay defeated, the European powers would, for the most part, withdraw from Southeast Asia. It was a new beginning for the region. The rebirth that Constable Sandar and the Sultan of Malacca foresaw would come to pass.

The Custodians would soon be citizens of the sovereign country of Malaysia. For the first time in generations, they had their country back. It was cause for quite a celebration. The fireworks were many, and loud.

When the celebrations were done, the Custodians met again in Malacca. They developed a new plan. A grand plan. It was long-range in both time and location. Once it was finalized, they launched it without hesitation. They had much work to do.

Chapter Sixty-Three

It was a beautiful summer evening in the Salmon River valley of Idaho. A family of thunderstorms had rolled along the foothills of the mountains earlier in the day, wandering now and then over the valley to wash it with a cool drink of fresh rain. The storms had since moved away to the north in a stampede of thunder and lightning. In their place the landscape glistened in the sun. The air was thick with the fresh fragrance of a summer mountain rain.

In the storm's wake, the air had a restless feel – one of anticipation and energy. The wind rustled the cottonwoods along the river, bending them in a swaying, rhythmic dance. The gusts washed over the grass and wildflowers, creating rippling waves that fanned across the fields. The sun dappled the valley as it blinked in and out between the tumbling, silk-white clouds that now filled the sky. The air was losing its daytime heat. Now and again a cool breeze would swirl about, knocking the raindrops from the cattails along the river. As the drops fell they glinted in the sun in sharp star-points of light – a thousand tiny diamonds sprinkling themselves along the riverbank. The birds surveyed the landscape for an after-rain meal, their varied song blending with the sounds of frogs and crickets to form a casual melody. The drone of an approaching plane added to the mix, echoing off the mountains to bounce across the valley.

A horse galloped along a path paralleling the river, its rider standing tall in the stirrups and leaning ahead in anticipation. Her shiny brunette hair streamed behind her, teased by the rush of air as her horse gained speed over the ground. The woman's giddy laughter filled the summer evening air, riding the wind along across the fluttering fields as her horse wheeled and swung through the cottonwoods, speeding toward a bend in the river.

The valley opened below me and the sight took my breath away. A line of thunderclouds was moving out at the far end of the valley, their steeples towering over the landscape. As they left, a raft of cumulus clouds moved in to fill the void. They glistened as white as the gardenia flowers of Hawaii, highlighted with the hues of a setting sun. They covered most of the sky, but I easily found a glory hole with a good view of the ground. I banked the little float plane hard to the right and dove through the hole in the clouds. The windshield filled with the land I had dreamed of for months. I pulled back to level off and surveyed the sight before me. The wet ground gleamed in the sun. The wild grasses took on a rich hue from the earlier rain. The river was a ribbon of silver colored by the dynamic sky. The air was turbulent in a playful way, bouncing me about as I settled toward the river. The sky was thick with moisture and the sun streamed though the breaks in the clouds, forming three distinct rays that shone from above as if from the clerestory of a cathedral. They lit broad ovals on the ground below, shuffling around each other at the whims of the clouds and the wind.

I descended slowly as I looked for a place to land. A field of grass would normally serve well, but this was a float plane and she needed the water. I surveyed the river and found a promising spot a couple of miles ahead, where the river had wandered a bit and carved out a large bend, just like the one at the Mekong River in China. It would do just fine. I focused on this site as if it were the only thing in the universe. I dropped the wing flaps to slow the plane, and watched the trees to get a feel for the wind. They showed a gentle breeze blowing in from the west, from the setting evening sun, from lands far away. I could feel a bit of a crosswind for my landing, but I was an old hand at flying now.

The woman drew closer to the bend of the river. Her horse's rhythmic breaths and the thump of his hooves merged with the beat of her heart to form a drumbeat of anticipation. She rode tall in the saddle and whooped as the cool river air filled her lungs. Her light denim jacket fluttered behind her like a veil. She slowed and finally reined in the horse at the river's bend. She watched the plane drop through the hole in the clouds further down the valley. It leveled off and turned toward her, and as soon as she saw the floats, she knew it would land right where she guessed. Her smile was as bright as the sunlit clouds.

I pulled back on the throttle and added another notch of flaps. The engine fell to a low drone and I could hear the wind brushing over the wings. I floated along just above the river, heading for a nice touchdown at the river's bend. I glanced to the left as I approached, and then I saw her. *Don't that beat all.* All at once I saw her beautiful face, her deep blue eyes, her bright smile, her shoulder length brunette hair, the delicate silver raindrop necklace around her smooth neck, her white cotton shirt, her blue denim jacket, the red bandanna in her pocket, her warm heart, her sense of humor, her deep convictions, her soul. I saw her wave to me from the saddle of her horse. Over the quiet drone of the engine and the rush of the wind, I swore I could hear her voice, her laugh, her whisper. I swore I could hear her say "Amen" and "Welcome Home!" I could hear her say "I love you!" I could hear her say "Take my hand." I could hear her whisper *"Take my heart"*.

I saw and heard all of this in an instant, from a quarter mile away. I seemed suspended there, in this church of the valley. Suspended between the towering spires ahead and the sun rays that lit the ground below. Suspended in time and place, hovering there, gazing upon her face. Feeling God in the fresh, fragrant air. Feeling God in my heart, and in my soul. Feeling at peace, feeling eager, all at once. Feeling an irresistible pull to the ground, to my home, and to my love. Then I started moving again. I turned my gaze ahead and used all my strength of will to focus on the turn in the course of the river. On the turn in the course of my life.

I saw a dragonfly flitting about on the surface of the river. I saw ripples gleaming in the golden setting sun. The plane floated down to kiss the water. I slowed to a drift and ran up against the bank. I cut the engine, popped the release on my shoulder straps, pushed open the door, stepped down onto the left float, and jumped down to the river bank. I looked up and into Sara's eyes. I stepped up and into her arms. Our lives became one, there beneath the face of God.

327

Chapter Sixty-Four

"The first twenty years of my life were just a prelude of what I would become." Hank explained.

The young man of twenty-five years listened intently.

"They forged me in ways that I still can't fully understand. The day I returned home – the day I landed on the river to find Sara waiting for me – was the starting point of a new Hank Evans. Don't get the wrong idea. The new Hank Evans was built upon the firm foundation of the young Hank Evans. That foundation was laid brick by brick during my youth, and finished off during my travels with Jack, Lhasa, and Marco. The day Jack asked me to leave my home and begin a journey with him was the second most important day of my life. The first was the day I married Sara. We married three months after I returned home. We pledged our love and commitment to each other beneath the face of God, and rejoiced in our good fortune. We've lived a life full of promise, celebration, laughter and love. It's also had its fair share of trials and tribulations. But that's just the way life is, and it makes the good times even better.

"If you look at a stand of lodge pole pines, you'll see what I mean. The tallest, strongest trees are the ones at the crest of the hill. Some folks think they get more sunshine there and just naturally grow faster. But that's not the case. They're strong because the wind blows there. They get pushed and shoved and tested throughout their lives. They answer the test with strength. They must in order to survive. The pines on the valley floor don't do as well. They're comfortable. They grow fast and tall but not strong. Whenever there's a bad storm, many of them fall. When you chop them for firewood, they yield easily to the axe. The rare fallen tree from the crest of the hill is different. It fights back against the axe. Its fiber is tougher. Make sense?"

The young man nodded.

"Over the years the valley floor clears itself, and eventually becomes a meadow. You can see it right here in the Salmon River valley. The pines there disappear, their legacy a fading memory. The pines at the crest of the hill live on, sentinels to the rigors and rewards of life. Those pines at the Galena Summit to the south are as tough as nails. People are no different. God tests us repeatedly. Never more than we can handle, although sometimes it feels overwhelming. But it makes us strong. Often stronger than we know. I know for a fact that Jack, Marco, Lhasa and I learned that lesson firsthand during our travels together.

"I realize that the story of the Malaccan treasure is a bit difficult to believe," Hank admitted. "But here's the part that's really gonna exercise your skepticism. Before we left Malacca, the four of us made a pledge to the Custodians of the kingdom treasure. As part of that pledge we made some lifelong commitments to each other and to Alex and the Custodians. We've all kept in touch over the years. I know that we've honored those commitments.

"At first, they seemed cumbersome. Seemed like a real burden. But with Sara's help I soon realized that they were a true joy. Now, Sara and I are reaching the end of our years. It's been a great life. We've been married almost seventy years. Can you believe that? We've had a wonderful time. We raised your father and your aunt Anna. They kept us busy, I'll tell you that. But it was rewarding beyond explanation. If there had been no kingdom treasure, Sara and I still would have had a beautiful life. But the commitment I made to the Custodians made it even better.

I'm telling you all of this because it's time to pass that commitment along to you. Are you ready, Alex?" Hank Evans asked.

The young man shrugged. "I'm not sure, Grandpa Hank. Tell me about the commitment." He'd spent hours with Hank that night listening to his tale. It was the most captivating story he'd heard in years. He knew his Grandpa had traveled a bit in his youth. But he'd always thought of him as a kindly retired rancher. He had no idea he was an adventurer and former treasure hunter.

"Well I'll tell you. See, before we left Malacca the Custodians had a little surprise for us. They were mighty thankful that we'd found the *Flor De La Mar*. We hadn't done it for a reward, nor for fame, nor recognition. We agreed to do it because Lhasa asked us to, because it was important to him. At that point we'd each learned to trust him. When we understood why the treasure was so important; when we experienced firsthand the turmoil that war creates, when we realized that the treasure might help to cure a bit of it, we were even more committed to get it done. We didn't expect anything in return. We just wanted to help a few folks. It was an opportunity to be a part of something bigger than ourselves.

"The Custodians knew that. But they kinda turned it around on us. First, they reimbursed us for all of our expenses. They even paid for the Goose. Up until then I'd been paying my own way with the money I'd earned at the Parker Ranch in Hawaii. A little money went a long way in Southeast Asia. But by the time we found the treasure, my wallet was getting pretty thin. There wasn't much money left. With the reimbursement I was able to return home with a bit of savings, which was mighty helpful. I used part of it to buy a nice little ring for Sara.

"Then the Custodians gave us one more task. They made each of us commit to take a sizable sum of money from them, as a reward. They said that it was on account of 'salvage law'. We were entitled to a reward for salvaging the treasure. Now, the thing is, we only salvaged a small bit of it. But that didn't matter. We found the wreck and it was safe in the sea. The Custodians, with the help of the Sultanate of Malacca, arranged for a loan, using the treasure as collateral. They had apparently planned this for a while. They knew the exact inventory of the treasure. Thanks to us, they knew the location. So the Sultanate funded the loan as an advance on the recovery of the treasure, which would be completed when the time was right. The Custodians used that loan to give each of us a sum of money. But it came with a condition.

"We had to commit that we would give the money away over the years, to folks in need, or to charities, anonymously. Don't that beat all! We had to commit to never use it for our own benefit. That was easy for all of us. We'd found value in friendship and service. Not in wealth. The Custodians knew that. I guess they could see it in us. We each agreed. We each made the commitment. So they had a banker in Singapore set it all up. He was a friend of the Sultan there. He put the money in four trust accounts, one for each of us. Then he made each of us the trustee of our account. So I could give the money to anybody, as long as they were in need, or served someone in need. Can you believe that?"

Alex nodded dubiously.

"Like I said, it was a burden at first. I wasn't sure how to determine who deserved the money. I was afraid I would give it to someone that didn't really need it. I made it too difficult. The money began to burn a hole in me. Then one night, just before we were married, I finally told Sara about it. She loved it. 'Hank,' she told me, 'we can do so much good. We just need to keep our eyes open for folks in need.'

"Then she gave me an idea. I mentioned earlier this evening that our friend Rosco Hanson qualified for the state rodeo while I was gone to Asia. You never met him. Good guy. He was hopeful about the rodeo because he needed the prize money to fix the engine in his truck. He worked for the farm co-op transporting hay and alfalfa, and he needed a working truck to earn his income. Well Rosco broke some ribs in the rodeo, didn't win the prize, then owed the doc in Stanley some money. The rodeo wasn't the smartest plan, I'll give you that. But it was kinda familiar to me, from my troubles when I was seventeen. Anyway, Sara was the nurse for the doctor, so she knew how embarrassed Rosco was. He was doing odd jobs and paying the doc a bit each month, trying to make good on his debt. Honorable guy. He was also trying to save some money for a new engine. So we paid Rosco's doctor bill. Anonymously. Then we went to Boise for a weekend and mailed him a money order to pay for a new truck engine. We sent that anonymously too, and since the postmark was from Boise, Rosco had no idea who sent it. He was mystified. But he cried when he told me about it. Dang, that made me feel great. I wanted to tell him the story so much that I almost burst open right then and there." Hank chuckled for a moment.

"So Alex," he continued, "Sara and I have been making donations here and there over the years. Jack's been doing the same in Montana, and Lhasa and Marco in Asia. Lhasa passed away about fifteen years ago, God bless his soul. He and Marco did some truly amazing things. But that's a different story. Marco took over the remainder of Lhasa's share. But here's the deal. Sara and I were careful with the money and it's lasted longer than we thought. Even a little bit of interest adds up over the years. So now we need someone to take over for us. You're as old now as I was back then. So it's your turn. You're the new custodian of the fund, if you want to be. But you have to make the same commitment I did."

Alex, a twenty-five year old high school physics teacher, gazed at his Grandpa Hank for a long time, a puzzled look on his face. Then he finally spoke. "Am I named after Alex the Custodian?"

"Ha! You'll have to ask your father about that."

"Dad!" Alex yelled into the adjoining room of Hank and Sara's home. "You still awake?"

"I am now," he said, walking into the study. He knelt to the fireplace to stoke the fire. It had been burning all evening, through Hank's entire story. "What's up?"

"Am I named after Grandpa Hank's old friend Alex in Malaysia?"

His father smiled. "Yes son, you are."

"Grandpa Hank's been telling tall tales," Alex said with a smile, nodding toward Hank. "Says he and Grandma Sara have been giving money away for years. Anonymously. To folks in need. I've never heard about any of it before."

"I see," his father answered. "So it seems they were successful. With the anonymous part."

"Well..." Alex responded dubiously.

"Remember that contribution for the robotics workshop at the high school?" his dad asked.

"Of course. My students use the lab every day. They love it."

"Where did that money come from?"

Alex looked to Hank. Hank just smiled and shrugged.

Sara ambled into the room. She walked with a cane now, but she could still get around well. "What's all the commotion in here?" she asked.

"Grandma," Alex asked, "I've never heard of anyone finding a wreck of a Portuguese ship called the *Flor De La Mar*. Grandpa says it was carrying a kingdom's treasure. But I've never heard a thing about its discovery. Don't you think someone would have said something? Don't you think it would have been in the news?"

She walked behind the chair Hank was sitting in. It was his favorite old chair, positioned close to the fireplace, facing toward the window with a view of the hill beyond. She bent down to hug him from behind. He wrapped his arms across hers.

She looked to Alex. "Grandson," she said with a teasing grin. "don't believe everything you haven't heard!"

EPILOGUE

Darfur region, Sudan, Africa. Present Day

The doctor was weary. He was nearing the end of a six hour drive along a dusty, washboard-surfaced, sun-baked dirt road. He was returning from a three day trip to a number of small villages and refugee camps in the back country. It wasn't the road that made him weary. The road was simply the road. He was weary of the strife that infected his country. Weary of the civil war. Weary of seeing so much sickness and death. Weary to the bone. He was a good man trying to help, but against such overwhelming odds! He felt as small as a grain of sand in the hot, dry desert. He felt alone and insignificant. So small. So tired.

He had driven this road countless times. At the conclusion of each trip, he knew he would simply depart again in less than a week's time. He couldn't stay in the back country long, because he needed to return to his base camp for fresh medicine for the patients he treated. It was so frustrating. There were so many patients. So much illness. They were often easily treated. He had plenty of the medicine he needed. The foundations and charities made sure of that. He could treat the cholera, the fevers, the infections. But he couldn't store the medicine in the back country. For the most part it had to be refrigerated. In the back country there was no refrigeration, as there was simply no electricity. Most of the best medicine only lasted for a few days if not kept cold. So it often expired unused. He could stay in the back country until the medicine went bad, then he had to return for more. It was a never-ending back-and-forth trip of strife, sickness, mercy and medicine. Fresh medicine. Cold medicine.

So small. So tired.

He reached his base camp, parking under the mottled shade of an acacia tree. He opened the door of his jeep and stepped out to the dusty ground. He stretched his tired legs, feeling the stiffness in his knees. He took a deep breath, then walked to the back of his jeep to unload.

"Doc," his assistant yelled as he ran from the hut, "let me get your things."

"Thanks Nez," the doctor replied.

"Doc, something strange happened yesterday. Come to the hut and I will show you. You look so tired. Go rest and I will bring your things."

The doctor walked to the hut, bending to fit through the short doorway. He immediately noticed four sturdy equipment cases sitting on the floor, each the size of a medium suitcase. They were obviously rugged, apparently made for rough country. The doctor sat at his small desk and pondered the cases, sipping warm water from his canteen.

Nez entered the hut with the doctor's bags. "You see what I mean, Doc?"

The doctor nodded, too tired to speak.

"A man brought these yesterday."

"What man?" the doctor asked with surprise.

"I never saw him before yesterday. He drove here from town, left these for you, then drove away." Nez motioned to the west with a nod of his head.

"What did he say?"

"He said you needed these. He knew your name. Said they were for you. Said you would know how to use them.

Said they get power from the sun. Said instructions are inside."

The doctor jumped from his chair. He stepped to the first case, kneeling beside it. He twisted the heavy-duty latches on both ends, released them, then lifted the lid from the case. "Oh my," he whispered. "Oh my."

"What is it Doc? Is it okay?"

"Yes Nez, it's most definitely okay. It's a portable drug refrigerator. I've seen these before. But they need electricity. They won't work in the field."

"Are you sure?" Nez asked. "The man said they use the sun."

The doctor studied the refrigerator, then his eyes lit up. "Oh my. Look at this." He turned the lid over. It was covered in solar panels. "These make power from the sun. They will power the refrigerator without needing electricity, or a generator. These will work in the field. For a long time. They will keep the drugs from going bad!"

"Doc, that is very good news. This is a very good day."

"It's a wonderful day. Tell me again about the man that brought these."

"He would not give me his name. But he was an African man. He spoke Sudanese."

"Did he say where he was from?"

"No. But he told me some things. He said that he and his friends made a vow. A promise to help victims of war. Then he told me one thing which didn't make much sense to me. He told me his job."

"Nez, what was his job?"

"He said he was a *custodian*. But if I know that word correctly, it doesn't seem that a custodian would be driving to the back country and delivering equipment like this."

"No, it doesn't. What a strange but wonderful day. I

hope I see this custodian myself sometime."

"He said one last thing when he left. He had a message for you. He made me memorize it. He said to tell you to 'keep the faith.'"

The doctor was quiet for a long time. At last he took a deep breath, then wiped his eyes. "Nez, we have work to do."

THE END

ABOUT THE AUTHOR

Greg Treseder writes contemporary fiction based upon historical fact. He loves a good adventure story, full of heroes, conflicts, sacrifice, and the sheer joy of being alive. Treseder and his family live in Northern California, where they find plenty of opportunity for adventure. And joy.

You can reach Greg at treseder@earthlink.net.